BOOKS BY STEPHEN BECKER

NOVELS

The Season of the Stranger
Shanghai Incident
Juice
A Covenant with Death
The Outcasts
When the War Is Over
Dog Tags
The Chinese Bandit

BIOGRAPHY

Marshall Field III

HISTORY

Comic Art in America

TRANSLATIONS

The Colors of the Day
Mountains in the Desert
The Sacred Forest
Faraway
Someone Will Die Tonight in the Caribbean
The Last of the Just
The Town Beyond the Wall

THE

CHINESE

BANDIT

THE
CHINESE
BANDIT

STEPHEN BECKER

Random House   *New York*

Library of Congress Cataloging in Publication Data
Becker, Stephen D. 1927-
The Chinese bandit.
I. Title.
PZ4.B396Ch   [PS3552.E26]   813'.5'4   75-10255
ISBN 0-394-48561-0

Manufactured in the United States of America

24689753

First Edition

FOR PAUL AND HELEN EDWARDS

CONTENTS

1 / PEKING

1/   That summer they hanged a fat man at the Western Gate as a warning and example to all. In those days the penalty for most crimes was death. They swung him from a fresh gallows on the city wall, where twelve horsemen in silks could ride abreast, and once had. For sure he deserved it. Every man shall be put to death for his own sin.

From within Peking, Jake could not see the face, but when he marched out the gate beside his camel he stopped to look one look, as the Chinese say, and the hair of his flesh stood up. The fat man was a traitor, a thief, a pimp, a merchant and Jake's partner.

The caravan master came worrying back on his shaggy pony. "I saw," he said. "Let's move." And then bitterly, "Dogs defile the old whore, anyway!"

Jake was a big golden man and this was a sunny summer morning, yet he shivered and prickled. He said in English, "God damn them!"

Ch'ing frowned at the foreign words, and tugged his pony's ear for luck. "Foreigners are a jinx and a blight," he said.

Small black birds strutted on the hanged man. A black blindfold covered his eyes; still, it was old Kao, no doubt at all. Now Jake was not shivering but trembling in rage. "I must go back," he said in Chinese. "I must kill someone for this."

"Fool!" Ch'ing said. "Where will you go? What can you do?"

"The left hand must avenge the right," Jake said, and turned toward the gate.

Ch'ing danced his pony into Jake's path, and dug a hand into Jake's shoulder. "Think! Think! What would he have done in your place?"

Jake did think. "Curse his thief's heart," he said, "he'd have cut his losses."

"Yes. And fled nimbly. Remember: you are tall and yellow-haired, and will draw lightning."

"It is like cowardice," Jake muttered.

"Think why he sent you to me," Ch'ing said. "Think what he left you: camels and trade goods. Will you throw those away?"

Jake stood silent.

Ch'ing released him, and said, "Stand to your camel. Come back in a year, rich and strong, and do then what must be done."

"Rich and strong," Jake repeated.

"Hurry," Ch'ing urged. "Hurry. When the hounds are loose the hare must speed."

"Hounds and sons of hounds," Jake said. "But there's no hurry. There's no link to us."

"Who knows what he told them?"

"He told them nothing."

Ch'ing shrugged. "A villain. He traded with the Japanese."

"He never lied to me."

"How do you know that?"

Jake said nothing, only glowered.

"This is no way to begin a journey," Ch'ing said sourly. "I was wrong to deal with you, and we will all suffer for it."

"You took the money," Jake said. "Cheer up."

"I should have charged you more. Hurry now." Ch'ing was a wiry old bastard, part Mongol, Jake thought, a lightweight who rode bareback, hissed softly now at the bad luck, wheeled his pony and trotted after the line of fresh camels and tired men. Some of the men were saddlesore from women and some were hung over. Jake was neither, but had been both, and did not mind so much in China. It was a world away from the beery bars and sluts he had been raised on.

He bided angrily and stared up at old Kao. Under the fat jowls the rope was invisible. Old Kao was smiling a pure, sweet, childlike smile. He dangled and twirled in his usual black gown, black cloth shoes and silky black skullcap—miraculously in place—topped by a red button. Travelers passed through the gateway; some glanced at old Kao, some did not. A small boy entered the city driving swine before him, and grinned up at the corpse. Skinny vendors toted their wares on yokes: cups and plates, cakes and candies, live birds blinded to sing louder, cigarettes of all nations. Bicycle rickshas steered clear of rickety buses, and the citizens wore white masks against disease, and men held hands as they strolled, they were friends, why not, though Jake found it difficult.

Well, he had seen plenty of dead men. This was the summer of 1947 and in his own lifetime many millions had been slaughtered for no particular reason, all of them equal in the eyes of God. Jake had killed several himself, mostly Japanese. But this, this today, this was not good. Jake was not accustomed to fear and did not like it pricking at him; he had not known it since Saipan. He mastered it quickly. He had a way to go and money to make.

"You make a little here, you lose a little there," he said softly to the round, peaceful face; then, "See you again," the Chinese farewell, and he hunched into his shirt and tugged the coolie hat down and trotted back to his place. The holstered .45 bounced at his hip, a comfort. Folks stopped to stare. Only crazy men ran, or criminals, and Jake was a conspicuously large foreign devil, and if anyone came asking questions there would be plenty of the wrong answers. Damn!

He dodged bicycles and leapfrogged children relieving themselves in the road—the young ones had slit pants, and could just squat and do—and came up with his first camel, a gelding seven years old named Bad Smell. The camel seemed small and goaty under a hill of trade goods: bricks of tea, silk brocades, fresh American cigarettes, sets of wrenches, kegs of nails, coils of electric wire, maybe three hundred assorted pounds. A few cameras. His second camel was called Sweetwater and was likewise laden. The camels would last to Gurchen, and if they did not Jake supposed the camel-pullers would eat them.

Soon he could not make out old Kao. A bad omen and no way to begin a journey. He that is hanged is accursed of God. And what loose ends left behind? Police. Soldiers. Damn!

Still, the hot morning was all a man could ask, and the city behind him was spectacular, the city he loved best of all, the dun wall and the low towers, flags and banners here and there, and bright tile roofs, so the golden sun slanted and dazzled off a thousand flecks and splashes of red and blue and green. And ahead of him, to the west, fields and farms and the sharp sunny green line of the first hills.

As he walked, Jake laid a light hand on Bad Smell's freight, and bowed his head. He was not one to pray. He had not prayed in war, nor in peace. But he remembered Our Father, and now he spoke it aloud, softly but clearly, and did not feel ashamed or foolish. Deliver us from evil.

Still, we cannot go through life carrying the dead on our backs. He let his hand swing free, and raised his head, and rubbernecked with pleasure and interest.

Jake was thirty years old and a bull. He was also an exile, probably, and he was on his way to the heart of Central Asia, to Turkestan, where peaches, plums and melons grew, and men had four wives, and a foreigner could grow rich in gold and silver and mountain furs. He would cross half of Asia with the caravan, mountains and deserts, on his way to a new life, and he owed it all to poor old Kao. Old Kao! An elder brother to Jake. Or a good father even, wise and generous and funny.

It all began in a whorehouse.

2/ The Palace of the Night Chickens lay in the southern part of Peking, handy to the Temple of Heaven, the foreigners' hotels, the legation quarter and the railroad station. It was not the brawling whorehouse of legend, where the lips of a strange woman drop as an honeycomb, and her mouth is smoother than oil: the premises were tacky, with two-bit scrolls of standard calligraphy on the walls, or black-and-red paintings of squirrels and tigers. But the girls were not tacky. They were young and liked their work, and a busy night was a carnival, the night chickens wearing anything or nothing, short tunics or a sailor hat or a bathrobe from a fancy shop in London or Paris or Hong Kong.

Often Jake and old Kao had ridden there together, tossing wisdom from one ricksha to another. Bicycle rickshas were most common but old Kao preferred the man-powered two-wheeler. "We live in a seedy time," he said. "The former ways are dying. No more style." In winter the ricksha men were muffled, and cursed softly. In spring they wore cotton pants, and sweated. Kao haggled fiercely over the fare, just for practice and to maintain style, and then tipped heavily. At the house he ushered Jake in with bustle and good cheer.

One night they were the first to arrive, only them and the girls, and everybody half asleep. Kao was indignant. "In the first place, more lanterns," he ordered. "Whiskey also, and glasses. And who are these dead women? Is this a buggering hospital?" He clapped his hands and hopped like a fat lion tamer. "That's better. And music. Soft music. The p'i-p'a, and no singing." He urged Jake forward, hustling him along like some grand vizier with an ambassador of importance.

Jake winked at Mei-li, who was his girl. They were all his girl at one time or another, but mainly Mei-li. There were many rooms in the house, and not cribs either, small but comfortable rooms, and thanks to Kao, who owned the place, Jake lived in one of them when he was in Peking: an old wooden bunk stenciled here and there in Japanese, a mattress of feathers, a small chest and his the only key, a low rosewood table and two armchairs.

The large parlor was everybody's room, with couches and carpets, three leather chairs, a few tables for four, boxes of cigarettes and old-fashioned siphons of soda water, hall trees and even a low bookcase for the elegant pornography. Jake thought of it as his living room, and after Kao had brought the place to life the two men retired to Jake's bedroom. Kao squeezed himself into an armchair while Jake changed; "at home" Jake shed his uniform and wore blue cotton trousers and cloth shoes. The girls liked the curly golden hair on his chest, and made bright paper birds to nest in it.

Jake paid rent for the room, over and above the customary fees: he brought whiskey and cigarettes, shampoo, toothbrushes and toothpaste, and even sanitary napkins, at which Kao raised an eyebrow. "The Americans," Jake explained, "like to be ready for any crisis."

"An astonishing people," Kao murmured.

"Tomorrow the world," Jake said.

Kao smiled politely. "A very generous and skillful people." He remained fully dressed, as always, even to the black skullcap and red button.

Jake drew on the cotton trousers—about forty-four inches around, they were—and doubled them over in front. He was knotting the red silk sash when Mei-li walked in with the whiskey. She was wearing Jake's old sergeant's shirt, and nothing else. "I like you in stripes," he said. She giggled. She was rangy and golden, with large eyes, and she was proud of her bosom. She had not boasted much bosom, as she told Jake, until she entered the trade, and then it had blossomed. She said that: blossomed. Jake thought they were lovely flowers, or fruits, warm and friendly, not perched like apples on the collarbone but soft, full and giving, low, with rich rosy nipples.

He wanted to unbutton the shirt now but his first business was with Kao; he settled for a reassuring glance at the furry mischief below, and Mei-li mouthed a kiss. Kao busied himself inspecting the bottle. "Ballantine's," he said. "Splendid. In my early days I once bought a bottle of Red Label, and some scoundrel of a forger had resealed it to perfection. I never found out what it was, but it dissolved a porcelain cup. Poison. Blindness, paralysis. Unscrupulous traders, giving the world of commerce and industry a bad name. Never trust a foreign seal in Peking."

Jake waved Mei-li out; she flirted the shirttail. Kao was pouring. Over the first cups they contemplated each other with the warm approval of true tycoons. "Dry cup," Kao said, and they tossed one off. He poured again, and meditated. Jake relaxed on the bunk, back to the wall, and scratched his belly. He liked Peking, and whorehouses, and whiskey, and decided that he was feeling mighty fine.

"We're doing very well," Kao said with his sunny fat smile. "Amazing that there is a use for any item. Though we have enough spark plugs for a century. You people are enthusiastic about spark plugs. Last week a sailor offered me a dozen machines for making toast. That would be lovely if we used bread here."

"So you bought them for a few coppers," Jake said, "and sold them to the Wagon-Lits Hotel for a small fortune." In Chinese it was the Six Nations Hotel—much nicer, Jake thought, and showed you who owned the country.

Kao chortled. "You become brilliant," he said. "Did you know about it?"

"No. I just guessed."

"You Americans," Kao said cheerfully, "with your instinct for business. I think of myself as an American at heart, you know, set down by a malign fate in a land of small change. Fortunately, I have a genius for choosing partners."

Jake raised his cup.

"You will be a great merchant," Kao predicted. "They will invent proverbs about you. Your Chinese is extraordinary. Your accent is almost pure. Barring a touch of Tientsin." Kao spoke no English, beyond a couple of dozen words like t'ao-san and ta-la. Or t'u ma-ch'u. "T'ao-san ta-la t'u ma-ch'u," he would say. "Fai ha-na ta-la okay."

"It's not bad," Jake said. "Probably every man can do one thing well. That's mine."

"And you shoot well," Kao said. "A master of arms."

"Anybody can do that," Jake said. There was a considerable component of bullshit in Kao's compliments, but Jake enjoyed them.

"And you do business well. In the blood. You Americans."

"Not yet," Jake said. "I am the meanest of students. It is my pleasure to perform small favors, but in your presence I cannot call myself a true merchant."

"How well you speak!" Kao said. "Nevertheless, these gifts from your fellow sailors are invaluable."

Jake was a Marine and not a sailor, but the distinction was difficult to explain to foreigners. "Until they clap me in the brig," he said gloomily.

"Now, now," Kao said. "Listen to me. All these things, these miracles of American production, will be given to my government eventually, which is a tragic injustice to the common man, not to mention the business community, except that half the stuff—half, believe me—will find its way to the open market—I am a firm believer in the open market—or directly to the Communists at an exorbitant price, and a number of our distinguished public servants will open bank accounts abroad. And along the way there will be some buying and selling for little fish like you and me. Your government is insane, you know. Also the British. Also the French. Also the Russians. Insane. But not you. Not my Ta-tze."

Jake laughed. Ta-tze was his name in Chinese, conferred by Kao; it was not a true name but a nickname. He had no use for a true name. It meant Tartar and he was happy with it.

"Of course," Kao said primly, "I am a wholehearted supporter of President Chiang Kai-shek and a firm believer in the law. Without a government of laws the man of imagination, the, ah, innovative man, drowns in a sea of anarchy."

Jake raised his cup again. "To President Chiang Kai-shek."

"Indeed," Kao said. "In the present favorable business climate—"

"Favorable? The country's one big crisis."

Kao smacked his lips. "Do you know the character for crisis? It consists of two characters taken together. One means danger. The other means opportunity."

"Ah," Jake said. "I can't read much. Can't write at all."

"Nothing," Kao waved airily. "My department. I might have been a poet in other times. My literary style is considered superb. 'In winter the ruddy children skate, poppies on a silver meadow.' "

"Beautiful," Jake murmured.

"What matters is our experience, our sources, and our courage. And the variety of goods and services we can offer." He mused. "Yes. Pistols and ammunition, those cigarette lighters, Zippo, you see I speak English, Zippo, the batteries and tires. The watches were an inspiration." He sighed. "A whole jeep would be impossible, I suppose."

"Couldn't drive it up from Tientsin anyway," Jake said. "The Reds have the roads cut. Still," he added solemnly, "in a crisis nothing is impossible."

"What a good man you are!" Kao said. "Your friendship honors me. Your determination is an example to us all. But I am too poor and insignificant," he grieved, "to thank you properly."

"We'll find a way," Jake said. "But there need be no talk of thanks, Master Kao. You have been my priceless guide through this greatest of kingdoms."

"The kingdom is made richer by your presence," Kao said. "Condoms would be good. And drugs. Penicillin."

"Don't be too specific," Jake said. "Depends on the time and place."

"Of course, of course!" Kao agreed. "I leave such decisions in your hands entirely. But it has to be the twenty-seventh, as we agreed. The men have been hired and instructed. One hundred beggars! Twenty rickshas!"

"The convoy's scheduled," Jake said.

"I'll go down by train on the twenty-sixth," Kao said. "But of course you won't see me."

"No rough stuff."

"Rough stuff," Kao said firmly, "is bad for trade. I am a businessman with interests in Tientsin, not a bandit roaming the continent."

"I'll think about a jeep," Jake said.

"Imagination," Kao said. "Initiative. Perseverance." He raised his cup. "To free enterprise. To the great tradition of your Herbert Hoover."

"To Herbert Hoover," Jake said.

"He was here," Kao said mistily. "He was actually in China."

"More whiskey," Jake said.

"Allow me," Kao said briskly, and poured. "Now let's go through it again. Timing is everything. Minute by minute." He hunched forward, and his eager eyes glistened. From mysterious recesses of his black jacket a pad emerged like a magician's dove, and an American ball-point pen.

Later, with Kao gone to superintend other enterprises, Jake sprawled in the parlor and observed his fellow man. A slow night. The Prince greeted him, a stocky emigré Russian in the leather business, with a huge head and bushy hair; he stood like a giant champagne cork, and sometimes he brought a gift of champagne, sweet stuff made by the fathers. A new gent, older and slightly nervous, greeted him uncertainly in a British voice.

Usually the clientele were Marines, or a few ferry pilots up from Tientsin or Tsingtao, a visit to Peking was so educational; now and then a European, or a local businessman of European origin; for a few months some trainees for an American oil company; attachés of all nations. These last were full of manners and polish, and shamed poor gunners like Jake: his honor the commercial attaché, in a pin-stripe suit with a vest, and his shoes shined, and old Kao leading him by the hand and assuring him that the ladies were clean, absolutely, inspected, grade A and prime. The towel boy hovered and interpreted. "You bet, mister." Whereupon the attaché—husband, doubtless the father of four darling daughters—would risk a glance at the other patrons, wipe his spectacles and treat the girls like movie stars.

Rarely a Chinese gentleman would join them, excessively courteous and faintly contemptuous. But few Chinese could afford it, and those who could had no taste for public display. Once they entertained a Chinese general, or vice versa. He told them how many Japanese he had killed. Thousands. Once in a while a couple of horny bastards would roll in for a fast fuck, usually Marines, and Jake and the others would tone them down.

Jake was hungry, and sent the towel boy next-door for the meat dumplings called chiao-tze. Jake was a noted fancier of chiao-tze and had once devoured thirty-three at a sitting. Mei-li brought him green tea. The house was well located: to one side was a restaurant called the Nagging Wife Wine Place, to the other a drugstore that sold powdered tigers' teeth, ginseng root and ointment, antler fuzz and other such necessities, specializing in aphrodisiacs like dried milt. Behind the house ran a wide canal; in winter the ruddy children skated, and in summer the stench was fierce. Small boats and barges, including honey barges, plowed through the syrup. Jake spent happy hours guzzling on the rear balcony, observing this navigation, often with Mei-li teasing and tickling.

The girls drifted musically through the parlor. Jake offered greetings and dumplings. The girls were easy to be with; he liked them all. They were no trouble. One named Shu-ling, called Sue, was very tall and painted her toenails gold. She played the p'i-p'a, a stringed instrument, and it was pleasant to hear the plucks and quavers, like centuries before, like some ancient civilization with banners, stone bridges and small boats on the lotus pond. Often in the warm parlor they all sipped tea together, and in the other rooms the girls gave men manicures and pedicures and haircuts, and kneaded Jake's shoulders, in the middle where the muscles were tight and sometimes painful.

One of the girls Jake had not trafficked with. She was called Ping-chi-ling, which being translated was Ice Cream, and she had been pregnant for some time; she pranced and joked with her great belly bare over silk pants, patting herself and chortling, shocking an occasional transient. She naturally specialized in horse-upon-horse. Then one day she was not pregnant. Nothing was ever said about the baby.

Still later he stood outside in the open gateway, with the spirit wall behind him. Just inside many gateways loomed a spirit wall; evil spirits traveled in straight lines, and the wall baffled them, while shrewd mortals stepped left or right around it. Often a character was engraved on the wall, or a brief poem: good luck, prosperity, fertility. Jake was exposed to evil spirits, lounging there without a shirt, but took his chances. In daylight the streets were full of brawling life, salesmen of fish and fowl, carters cursing bony ponies, mangy mongrels yapping, public loudspeakers bawling records of Chinese popular music. At night the street was still, only the tires of a distant ricksha swishing and whispering, or the faint chant of a singing drunk; and then from the dark center of a silent block, the aching song of a flute. All over the city people were dying and being born. Spitting blood and making love. Stuffing themselves with greasy duck or groaning in hunger. Jake was laying money by, and glad of it. Life was not merciful.

He caught a murmur within, and thought he knew the voice. He wandered back and surveyed the parlor: only Sue half asleep on a couch, and the Englishman leafing through the Spring and Autumn book. A man would check in and with three or four delectable slaves sprawled here and there he would choose a book, and sit popeyed at the monks, courtesans, princes and serving maids in fine detail, always the grasshoppers or the coupling sparrows in the margin.

Sue smiled drowsily and showed him the tip of her tongue. "Where's Mei-li?" he asked her.

"Ironing your shirt."

He nodded and passed through to the pantry. Among canisters of tea and stacked bottles of liquor, among K rations and cases of soap, Mei-li stood at a stone-topped table folding his shirt. She turned, and he kissed her, raising her by her bottom while her feet crossed behind his hips; their tongues played. He set her down. "Dushok here?"

She showed him with a toss of her head, and led him down a dark hall. The flesh of her legs gleamed gold and silver in the half-light. She tapped at a door, was answered, and opened; they stepped into a room like Jake's, with a comfortable bed, a small coal stove and a scroll of a leopard striking at a butterfly. Sitting on the bed was Wei-hua, a tiny woman and a bit older, and lying naked on it was Sergeant Dushok.

He was a small man and graying, a middleweight with almost no lips and a blocky jaw, light brown eyes and broad eyelashes that you could almost count. All over Asia, in the Corps, there was scuttlebutt about him. He read Chinese and wrote with a brush. He might be queer. He talked perfect slant and smoked opium, but he was a tough old ramrod and ate no shit. Before the war he had put in a hitch at Tsingtao, and had disappeared for weeks at a time and come back in tattered Chinese clothes and carrying scrolls. Officers asked his advice. He had seen the Siberian tiger. In the markets and bazaars he talked with aged men who wore long silky white beards and little-fingernails four inches long.

Two years earlier he had caught Jake palavering with a coolie in the Tientsin barracks, and had introduced himself. "It is a great shock," he had said, "to find a line sergeant speaking Mandarin. Where have you been?"

"Oh Christ," Jake had said. "Pendleton, Cuba before the war, the First on Guadalcanal, then the Third Amphibs and the whole damn Pacific. Okinawa and Japan. Then the railroad here."

"Where you from?"

"Colorado."

"Just plain folks."

"Jesus, yes." Jake sniggered. "Daddy a little old Baptist preacher, Two-Seed-in-the-Spirit. Never said one god damn thing to me that wasn't out of the Bible. You?"

"Pittsburgh. The usual hunky shit. How do you like this place?"

"Peking? I love it," Jake said with no hesitation, and was not sure why he went on, or why he shifted to Chinese: "I have a room there, to sleep in when I want to, with a stove, and I have a gown and a winter gown and cloth shoes."

"Good God," Dushok said. "A Communist."

"And a hat of river-otter fur."

"Tell you what," Dushok said in English, "on that fourth tone, start as high as you can and bring it down sharply. Don't be afraid of it."

"What's the fourth tone?"

"By God," Dushok said. "You picked it up in the street?"

Jake nodded.

"Can you read and write at all?"

"In English," Jake said stupidly.

"Even that's something," Dushok said. "We have captains and majors who can't do that. But I meant Chinese."

"No."

"Just as well," Dushok said. "That's for later. Where's your place in Peking?"

"Pan-chiu hu-t'ung," Jake told him, which being translated was Wild Pigeon Alley.

"Don't know it."

"Near the Western Gate."

"In the native quarter."

"That's how I like it." Dushok might have been making fun of him. Jake did not enjoy the notion and cooled.

Dushok thought that over. "Like the girls?"

"The high-class stuff," Jake said stiffly. "Lying down."

"I know a couple of good houses," Dushok said, "and a fine old pimp named Kao. Last of the great traders. Find you anything. A fat man, a genuine villain."

"Sounds good," Jake said.

"You may be worth saving," Dushok said, and turned to the coolie and called him by name. The coolie was standing there with his mouth open, leaning on his swab in the middle of the barracks like an exhibit in a museum, CHINESE JANITOR, 1947. Dushok told him, "Teach him all you can, elder brother. He'll give you cigarettes and canned milk," and the coolie made teeth and ducked, and that was how Jake had met Dushok, and later Kao.

Now Dushok lay on the bed while Wei-hua massaged his thighs, and the oil glistened in the rosy lamplight.

"In the days of Duke Ch'ang," Dushok muttered, "privacy was respected by men of good bones. You want to watch me take a leak, maybe? A real kick."

"Oh, go to hell," Jake said. "Glad to see you, y'old faggot."

"You on a forty-eight?"

"Yep. Back tomorrow."

"I got a seventy-two. Back Monday."

"I'd like not to go back at all." Jake flopped into an armchair and sighed strenuously. "Son of a bitching Corps." To Mei-li he said, "You go on back. I'll see you in a while."

Mei-li nodded and bowed; she skipped out.

"That's a beautiful girl," Dushok said. "She likes you, too."

Jake shrugged. "Whores."

"Whores," Dushok said sharply, "are people who do well for money what other people do badly for love."

The oil lamp flickered. Its shade was of varnished red cloth, and the room was washed in a warm red glow. Jake's fingernails gleamed pink.

Dushok said to Wei-hua, "Your fingers are flowers," and her eyes glowed. "Some yen now." She nodded, and went to the lacquered cabinet. To Jake he said, "Chrissake, man, in eight years you could quit on half pay."

"I had a little more than that in mind," Jake said.

"Sergeant's half pay keep you like a prince, in Asia."

"You're talking retirement, old man. I'm only thirty."

Dushok grunted. "Anyway, we're all through here," he said. "China's falling apart. We'll all be out by the end of summer."

Jake was silent.

"There's other fine places," Dushok said. "I'm putting in for Kabul."

"Easy duty," Jake said. "Got an extra pipe?"

"It's all easy," Dushok said. "Wei-hua. Another pipe. For Ta-tze." And to Jake again: "All you have to do is get up when they blow the bugle, and refrain from disgracing the Corps. And every once in a while let an officer shit on you."

"These new ones," Jake said glumly. "College boys."

"They're scared to death of sergeants," Dushok said. "You rather be an officer yourself?"

"God no," Jake said. "Paper work. Born to be a corporal, I was. Even three stripes is too much for me."

"You and Napoleon and Hitler," Dushok said. "You were a gunnery sergeant once."

"Twice."

"Well, you ought to climb back up and finish out your time. The Corps's a good home."

Wei-hua had warmed the yen and kneaded two small balls; she pressed them into the pipes and served the men. "I suppose it is," Jake said. "Politicians got to wipe somebody out, they send for the everlovin corps of shitbirds. I can't see the world much different because of this war we just fought. Same kind of jack-offs in charge everywhere." To Wei-hua he said, "Thank you."

Dushok said, "You want to lie down for that? Not here, I hope."

"I'll take it with me," Jake said.

"Take it all in one long draw," Dushok said.

"Bullshit," Jake said. "I'm not an old hand like you."

Dushok sniffed. "First-class stuff."

"I can make a living here," Jake said thoughtfully. "I can clean up."

"Until the Communists fling your ass in the brig. For life." In the rosy light Dushok sniffed again; he was delaying the moment, extending his enjoyment. Gently he touched Wei-hua's cheek.

Jake was envious, and irritated, and could not understand why; Mei-li was far prettier than Wei-hua. "All the same," he said with annoyance, "I could amount to something."

"I hear you've already begun."

Jake sat up. "What'd you hear?"

Dushok's face and voice were harder. "I heard you kindly disposed of some old K rations to save the Corps storage space."

"People tell you any damn thing around here," Jake said coldly. "Forget it."

"No, sir," Dushok said. "I've got twenty-nine years in this outfit, boy. I'm talking World War *One,* now. And I don't plan to stand by while you walk off with the petty cash. The Corps means a lot more to me than you do. I catch you with your hand in the pickle jar, I turn you in so fast your ass smokes."

"Hell with that," Jake said, suddenly glum. "I'd like to stay here, I would."

"God help you."

"I could stay forever, I think."

"You've already stayed forever," Dushok said. "Will you take your pipe and get the hell out of here?"

Jake lay heavily on his own bunk. He was on his side, curled up some, and his head on a small cushion. Carefully he lit his lump of yen, and in the yellow half-light of his own lamp he tried for one long draw. Before the sweet smoke hit his lungs he was cheery. He would not make one long draw; maybe two, maybe three, but it was, yes, ah yes, he knew that much, it was fine stuff all right. He held it down, and let his eyes close; only a faint yellow shimmer came to him.

He drifted off. Most times, drifting off, he tried to capture some particular warmth, a boat on a Japanese lake, or a woman's nest, or a perfumed bath, but pretty soon all that just skittered right out of his mind. No time for it. Too busy feeling all right. Feeling just fine. Heaps of gold glittered gently, and a dim, friendly sunset glowed against his lids. Fine. Just fine.

After some seasons the pipe fell dead. He rolled onto his back, and memory surged slowly. In the dim yellow light. His lamp low. He saw princesses, milky breasts and fat haunches. Great red nipples like strawberries. It always came to that. But then what else was there?

A thought struck him; that was a novelty, and he chuckled. Through the yellow pools he glided to the doorway, and called out, "Mei-li. Mei-li." He floated carefully to the bunk and lay back.

In a moment Mei-li entered, and let the door close, and he saw that she was good. Sergeant Mei-li was all beauty. She was all of China, yellow plains and yellow-green meadows, pagodas and temples, mountains of jade and rivers of gold, silks and spices, and Jake was lord of all under heaven.

Her hand went to the buttons, and he said, "No." She came to the bunk, and slowly he raised the shirt, and gently he took the baby chick in his mouth, and for many days and nights he sat very still, inhaling, his hands warm on her warm, smooth buttocks.

Perhaps he slept. After many whiles he raised his head and his hands went to a button, and very delicately, surely, thinking ahead, thinking out every motion, every pressure of every finger, he freed the button. With equal care he freed another. With devotion he kissed her navel. In time he freed a third and last button; her breasts sprang forth, these two breasts that he loved; he kissed them again and again, and her sharp breath was music. She pressed him back onto the bed, and kissed his nipples. He had told her once that she was the first to do that. It was a half-lie but also a half-truth, because no one had ever done it before without being asked. There were some men, he knew dreamily, to whom that did not happen ever, and he wondered if he had smoked, or was still about to smoke. It was not clear, but he stroked her hair. She untied his sash and tugged gently at his trousers. "Pants," he said. "Why am I wearing pants?" And he laughed happily as the sun rose between his thighs.

There was no hurry, and he said, "There is no hurry," as she caressed him, for some hours he thought, and kissed him, for some hours he thought, and happiness swelled in him like the god of spring breezes; he buried his face between her warm breasts, and soon his risen sun between her thighs, and they were floating on the warm yellow light, and always would be, he knew, from everlasting to everlasting, because if two lie together, then they have heat, but how can one be warm alone?

3/   "**O**n the double," Lieutenant Conn snapped on the morning of the twenty-seventh. For Conn it was convoy day; for Jake it was hijack day. The lieutenant was twenty-two or so, a light-heavyweight who would last maybe half a round with Jake, and Jake said, "Aye aye, sir," deadpan. Tientsin was drowning in a heat wave. Ripples and mirages rose from the parade ground, and sweat hung in heavy drops —lumps, more like—on Jake's brows. His skivvy shirt was soaked through. "If you'll excuse me," he went on, "nobody gonna do nothin on the double, a day like this."

The lieutenant was tall and rangy, black hair and blue eyes, very light skin, fine features, and Jake felt like a water buffalo beside him. Jake had just demolished a second breakfast, four eggs and a slab of pink ham, with hot coffee from his private stock. Thanks to old Kao he owned ten pounds of Brazilian beans. Nobody knew what Marine Corps coffee was. They called it joe or mocha or java and speculated that it was a glandular secretion from some low form of animal life.

Jake was full, and suppressing a belch of considerable proportions. His belly hissed and boiled happily.

"Khakis," Conn said. "Now."

Conn's father had probably been an honest bricklayer who worked his ass off and died young so his boys could go to Notre Dame and learn what their wee-wee was for. Jake was growing tired of these educated pricks. Hurdlers and swimmers and fraternity boys. ("The frat house," they said. It was a foreign language. "The frat house.")

Jake was also nervous. He reminded himself that he was a shrewd merchant and an experienced thief and that nothing whatsoever could go wrong. "Okay," he said.

"*Sir,*" Conn said. "The war's over."

"Yes, sir. I'll round up the others."

"I suppose the bloody trucks'll boil over."

That was another thing. Bloody. These postwar college boys all thought they were limeys. Be carrying a swagger stick before you knew it, and putting in for an elephant to ride. Lady-killers and doubtless fine waltzers. Jake had known Australians who said bladdy-fackin every third word, but it was their language and they fought like hell. They could say any god damn thing they wanted and it was all right with Jake.

Conn was nervous too, Jake saw. Colonel Leonhardt was nervous and his officers naturally followed suit. The Colonel fretted and bitched. All he wanted now was to pull the unit out by the numbers, nobody in a Chinese brig and nobody dead or maimed. It would not be long, China was disintegrating, no question. The exchange rate was sixty thousand to one and rising daily. One of these mornings the Reds would just walk in. The Colonel wanted out. He hated to see a truck leave the compound.

Nobody liked the job: herding a dozen trucks through Tientsin to the docks, and loading them up from the godowns—the warehouse sheds—before thieves or politicians made off with everything, and blaring their way back to the compound. Jake preferred rickshas. Driving in China, a car or a truck, you just leaned on the horn and prayed.

"You ever notice," Conn asked, "that parade grounds and barracks all smell the same?"

"Yep," Jake said. "Depending on the season. Hot wood and hot dust."

"And somebody yelling 'Hut, toop, reep, paw.'"

Almost fondly Jake said, "That's like the old school song to me."

"The old school song," Conn mused, and a distant look came to his eye. Jake figured he was remembering some party with pink champagne. Or the time he maneuvered one hand onto a society tit. "Half an hour," Conn said. "Garreau, his M.P.'s, and your drivers. All in khakis. Better move."

Jake said, "Aye aye, sir," and turned away. Crossing the dusty yellow parade ground he decided not to march. He ambled. He released the belch tenderly—"Don't yank on that trigger, shitbird, *squeeze* it off"—with healthy satisfaction and a hammy aftertaste. Nothing would go wrong. He knew he was safe, and started a cocky smile, but his heart was not in it.

"All right, now." Conn scowled. "We'll stay together and use the horn. Anybody gets lost, you've got the dock in Chinese on those cards, and your home address on the back."

No place like home, Jake thought. The compound had been home to a Japanese regiment. Marines still found an occasional pencil or bottle cap with Japanese on it. The new men hoarded them, and swapped.

"Sergeant Dodds takes the point," Conn said. "Move out."

Garreau scrambled into the cab with Jake. "The point," he said. "How do you like that. Chinese snipers gonna get us, rat-a-tat-tat." Garreau was not blond and not dark, not tall and not short, not fat and not skinny. His nose was normal and his eyes were the color of soup. Jake thought of him as the perfect I.D. photo; he looked like everybody.

Jake had showered and changed and was sweating through his skivvies again. The truck roared. "It works," he said.

"Go ahead," Garreau said. "Lieutenant wavin at us, go ahead."

Khakis. The Colonel had explained that they would lose face if they did manual labor in front of the Chinese. The Colonel was an expert on the Chinese mind. He could say "Thank you" in Mandarin. So dungarees were verboten off the compound. Garreau wore a .45 and carried a carbine. Jake too wore a .45. He had not fired a weapon for some time and doubted that he would today. "Khakis," the Colonel had said. "You can always send them out to the Chinese laundry." The officers and noncoms had laughed heartily. Except Jake; but nobody had noticed. On the whole Jake preferred Chinamen. There was a lot more complicated politeness but a lot less simple bullshit.

He drove through busy Tientsin now, in traffic and pounding the horn. The stream of rickshas, carts and pedestrians parted miraculously; nobody even looked up, but a way was made.

A ricksha man spat as they passed, and called cheerfully, "Dogs defile you all."

Jake slowed and leaned outboard to shout, "Foreign devils defile your mother upside down in a ricksha."

The ricksha man hollered in amazement, and his brows shot up, vanishing under his coolie hat; Jake laughed wildly and slapped the steering wheel.

"Chrissake," Garreau said. "Watch the road."

From the curb beggars waved and wailed. Mothers hustled children off the street. Good smells floated to Jake, spicy hot meats and hot oil and sunshine and honey-carts. The honey-carts gathered all manner of shit, including the small pellets of goat- and sheepshit that in a richer country might be ignored. Jake had heard that honey-cart men cauterized their infant sons' nostrils with hot irons, and the trade was hereditary. They kept the streets clean, and when enough honey-carts had poured enough honey into enough honey-trucks and honey-barges, the poor damn starving country managed to fertilize some of its exhausted fields. Waste not, want not. Jake approved. He enjoyed many smells that others thought putrid.

He noted a sign in English and bore left, and soon he saw the river and turned east, and there were the docks and more signs—BRIBERY, one of them read, IS PUNISHABLE BY DEATH, this because there were customs officials here—and the godowns cooking in the summer sun. He was glad that he was not a coolie today. He was always glad that he was not a coolie, but more so on a day like this. They would curse and sweat, and their loads would slip.

He pulled up, set the brake, and cut the engine. "Report to the lieutenant," he told Garreau. "And try not to kill anybody. They hate us as it is."

The lighter was still fast to the dock, and a burly gray-haired chief presented the lieutenant with a long manifest. He explained one thing and another. The lieutenant made important noises and clacked into an office.

"Sir," Jake explained.

"What's that?" The chief looked him up and down.

"You got to say *sir,*" Jake said. "The war's over."

"That's right," the chief said. "I forgot." A blue bandanna was knotted around his neck; he pulled another from his pocket and swabbed his face. "How long you been puttn up with it?"

"Almost twelve years," Jake said.

"Y'oughta be bettern a sergeant," the chief said. "You look like a god damn ox."

"I was," Jake said. He was tired of this conversation but it was repeated often. "Twice."

The chief grunted. "Gunny?"

Jake nodded.

"And you fucked up."

"My heart just ain't in it," Jake said.

The chief said, "Wish that boy'd sign that paper. Like to get back down the river and out of this god damn heat."

"A scorcher," Jake agreed. "What'd you bring?"

"The usual. Cigarettes and whiskey. Tools. What do they want with all those tools? Sets of wrenches. Tool kits. Hundreds of 'em. For Chrissake. They're gonna be outta here soon."

"It's a way to give the stuff to the Chinese army," Jake said, "without calling it military aid. We'll just leave it all."

"Shit," the chief said. "What they do with my taxes."

"The arsenal of democracy," Jake said. "Beats losing men, anyway. Almost got my ass shot off last year, taking supply trucks up to Peking."

"When they killed that lieutenant."

"You heard," Jake said. "And three other guys. A four-hour firefight."

"Rough," the chief said. "We have to stick our dick in everybody's wars."

"Makes no sense," Jake said. "Another time we took a lot of stuff up to Peking for UNRRA. Chinese all bowing and sucking. Later some brass from the states fly in to check, who's getting what, and the Chinamen take them out and show them a pretty little temple they just built, in honor of UNRRA."

"Chrissake, a whole temple?"

"Well, no, more like a little shelter in a garden where you can drink a cup of tea and jack off while admiring the sunset. Cost them maybe a thousand bags of rice. So the Americans say, 'That's very beautiful.' " Jake spat.

The chief too spat. "Ours not to reason why. Anyway, I got some Zippos. Hope the Chinese army goes for that. Binoculars and compasses, lots of flashlights, I guess that's for night combat, a hundred god damn kegs of nails left over from the Seabees, about a mile and a half of electric wire, a lot of batteries and about a thousand hatchet heads. What the hell they want with hatchet heads? Also some drafting sets, some scope sights and plenty canteens. That's for desert warfare. And then food. Sides of beef, canned goods, coffee. It's all yours. There's tea in there, too," he added. "For Chrissake, tea."

"Beef'll be flyblown, too long in this heat."

"Hell, it was flyblown when we got it," the chief said. "I got eighteen years in. I just wanna go manage a PX in Newport News for the next twelve. After that I live on a sailboat and eat only fresh fish."

"You been out here too long," Jake said.

"I was out here too long about the third day," the chief said. "Where the hell is that dancing teacher of yours?"

The coolies sweated and cursed. An endless snake of them trudged out of the godown heavy-laden, stowed cargo and trudged off. The twelve trucks were backed up to a loading platform. "Bugger all big noses," a coolie muttered. The drivers and M.P.'s supervised, using sign language and grunts.

Jake drifted to the godown. Lieutenant Conn stood at one end of the platform, no detail escaping his eagle eye. Two of the coolies ran dollies and handled the heavier crates. Promoted to stevedore. Quietly Jake said, "Last truck on the left for that. And no food. No meat for that truck."

"Hu-hu," the stevedore said in some surprise, hearing Chinese from this barbarian.

They would load his truck with large amounts of potluck, but a few crates of precision instruments would please old Kao. Jake murmured to the other stevedore. The godown was dark but no less hot than outdoors. Jake murmured to a coolie.

The old chief was long gone; the lighter had cast off and growled its way downstream.

Flashlights were useless without proper batteries.

The insulated wire would do, and the drafting sets. Tool kits and sets of wrenches. Small pumps and compressors. A garbage heap for Yankee know-how. Kegs of nails for ballast: horseshoe nails, ten-penny, twenty-penny, spikes. U.S. Navy Construction Battalion.

Jake murmured again. "No whiskey in the last truck." The officers would miss whiskey, and bitch, and investigate.

"You lead the way, Lieutenant," he said. "We'll bring up the rear." He was soaked. The coolies had flopped against the bulkhead, in the shade of the godown, and were smoking cigarettes. One of them showed off the pack: Lucky Strike. They laughed. They babbled. "Plenty cigarettes, thanks a lot." "Keep it coming, foreigners."

"What are they saying?" Conn asked.

"I don't know," Jake said. "I only understand a few words."

"Cut our throats in a second," Conn said.

"Right," Jake said. "I guess one foreigner's pretty much like another to them."

"Well, we got it all," Conn said easily. "I checked the manifest."

"Some of these guys weigh about one twenty," Jake said, "and they handle a side of beef."

"It's like judo," Conn said. "Tough little bastards. Great balance. Christ, it's hot."

"Let's move out," Jake said. "Close on to four o'clock. Sir."

"All right." The lieutenant raised his voice and issued orders. Jake and Garreau hopped aboard. "Beer," Garreau said. "I am going to drown myself in beer. The only thing the slants make as good as home."

"Won't be long now." Jake's blood zinged, and his eyes gleamed. He let in the clutch and eased away.

They retraced their route. Here and there Jake fell a bit behind, and Garreau squirmed: "Catch up, old buddy." Jake let rickshas cut them off, used the horn less, slowed for pedestrians. The truck passed between rows of open stalls. On the boulevard they swept by large office buildings, and expressionless policemen waved them ahead. Consulates. British American Tobacco. The Coal Board. Then a turn, and they were back in China, the black signboards and gold characters, the shops that sold white vegetables and one hundred teas and small gods. Coal balls and horse-jackets and hats of river-otter fur. It was also possible to buy a boy or a girl, as Jake knew. Not for a night but for good.

There were precious-metal shops, leather shops and luck shops, where you could buy tables of numbers, systems for various games, jade charms, money-drawing oil or ancient coins that concentrated the good fortune of many centuries. No skyscrapers. There were second-story balconies, and on some of them old men drank tea and played cards. Pigeons fluttered.

So did Jake's stomach, as they drew near the Street of the Three Unhappy Brides. Half the column would be past it by now, and Conn a long way off. Jake slowed. The truck in front of them slowed, then pushed forward gently like a boat in weedy waters. Jake too pushed forward but the crowd pressed in, and the other truck drew away.

"What's that music?" Garreau asked. "A parade?"

The mob swirled about them. Jake was short of the intersection and barely moving. This was not the first time he had been cut off; it produced a hollow sensation, always, and then excitement, in the jungle or the city or a back alley.

Beyond the intersection the other truck halted. Its driver semaphored.

Along the Street of the Three Unhappy Brides a sad procession blocked the crossing.

"It's a funeral," Jake said. "Sit tight." Garreau crossed himself.

Jake cut the engine and swung himself half out of the cab, clinging to the open door and standing tall. He waved ahead: Go on. He leaned into the joint of the door and waved with both arms: Go on. The other driver sketched a salute and disappeared into his cab.

"All I want is a brew," Garreau said.

The funeral jammed the intersection now: many well-dressed mourners marching beside a kind of palanquin, half sedan chair and half bier. Jake wondered if a deceased was really in there. Drummers drummed huge hollow banging notes; horns wailed. To either side of the palanquin and stretching back a way were lines of enclosed rickshas.

"A big shot," Garreau said. "A fancy funeral. Twenty limousines."

Beggars hung at the edges of the procession like flies, and more joined them; they limped and stumped among the rickshas, wailing and pleading. They eddied toward the truck. The horns and drums shrieked and thumped; mourners keened. Around the truck the mob thickened; the beggars buzzed and circled.

"Jesus Christ," Garreau said. "Where'd they come from? Roll up your window. Holy Christ, there goes the radiator cap."

"I'm going out there," Jake said. "Show 'em the uniform. You sit tight and hold that weapon where we can all see it. Don't use it."

"Out!" Garreau said. "Jesus Christ, there's hundreds of 'em." But Jake was swinging to the roadway. Beggars pressed at him. He spat; it was traditional to make a disgusted face and spit. Garreau shouted something indecipherable. Beyond the beggars, up at the intersection, Jake could see the first rickshas peeling off.

Ordinarily that would have been good for a satisfied laugh, but the beggars whined and chattered and pressed closer, with their matted hair and their eye sockets full of pus. "Make room," he snarled. "Make room!"

The first ricksha approached Jake and passed him; he watched it circle behind the truck and turned back to the beggars. He raised both arms for quiet and shouted, "Have you eaten, gentlemen?" which was a fancy way to say hello.

The beggars laughed and cheered. One with no hands waved the stumps. Jake checked Garreau, who was pale and trying to appear stern and official.

A ricksha raced back to the intersection. A second and a third had passed behind Jake. The beggars stank. He pressed his hands together and bowed, and they laughed again. The band boomed and blared.

He called in to Garreau, "Only thing to do is stand fast. They'll quit soon. Or the cops'll come."

"Thass a crock. I could fire in the air."

"Colonel have your ass for that. Keep cool, buddy. Ain't but one riot."

Too slow, too slow! Jake felt anger stirring. A second ricksha popped out, a third. There were three or four men on the truck now, unloading. Jake sweated. The beggars clamored. There was a man with no nose. Jake figured there was not much more to see in life, but was queasy anyway. You saw dead men and spilled guts, and a stream in the hills running blood-red, he had seen that, but there was always a surprise to come.

The truck quivered and jolted; Garreau called out. "I'll check it out," Jake shouted.

Thirty seconds a ricksha, they had calculated. Maybe it was just that time seemed to pass slowly. The loop of rickshas was endless, down the street, around the truck, up the street.

He fought his way back, cursing the beggars. Out of Garreau's sight he mopped his sweat. The beggars jeered and danced. "Misbegotten turtles," he said. Rags and boils and simple snot. His belly rippled. Were they with him or not? There were syphilitics and madmen.

The near hind wheel was gone. Jake laughed aloud. The beggars echoed him. The truck lurched slightly. He had no need to investigate: the off hind wheel would be gone. He had not foreseen that and enjoyed the joke.

He lingered at the rear, but did not interrupt the work or complicate matters for the coolies. Beside him rickshas lined up, three, four. Amiably he nodded to one of the ricksha men. The man nodded back, a fierce, abrupt, puzzled nod, and then seemed to look around for police or soldiers. A touch of nerves was understandable.

After a respectable delay, Jake headed for the cab, ramming his way again through a platoon of beggars. They were like packs of dogs in the street. There were millions of them in China and they annoyed the decent foreigners. Jake knew that many were organized, an elaborate union with territories laid out like wards and districts, with apprentices and journeymen and masters, and for all Jake knew a training academy. Seeing one with rotten stumps for teeth, he grew queasy again, but he reminded himself that all serious money was hard-earned, so pushed on. Their foul breath sickened him; it was the stench of a bad latrine, and inhuman.

He rapped on the door of the cab and waved cheerfully to Garreau. "China!" he bawled, over the music.

Garreau called, "The lieutenant won't like this."

"Stand by the truck."

"Couldn't move if I wanted to," Garreau said.

"Stand fast and show the colors," Jake said. And they stood fast, with the music for entertainment and the beggars for company; and finally no more rickshas came, and the crowd of beggars thinned.

The funeral seemed to have moved along.

"You know," Garreau said, "this vehicle is on a slant."

"We lost the rear wheels," Jake said.

"And a radiator cap and a pair of windshield wipers," Garreau said.

In doorways, at the mouths of alleys, a few loiterers still watched. Jake heard one of them say, "It is a foreign engine for uphill travel."

Jake said to Garreau, "It'll be a story for your kids."

Garreau strangled on a hysterical laugh.

Jake squinted at him: "You about to *cry?*"

"I'm a Christian," Garreau said. "I never saw a place like this."

"Hell," Jake said, "we're lucky we still got our jock."

"Okay. We're lucky. Now what?"

"Back to the compound."

"On two wheels?"

"We'll take a ricksha," Jake said. "Must be some around."

"You got no brains, Sergeant. What about the cargo?"

"Shucks," Jake said, "you're right. Well, you're the M.P. You stand guard. I'll go report and bring some help."

"That's it," Garreau said. "See if you can get the United States Marines. I hear they're tough."

Jake hailed a bicycle ricksha, and settled back in great contentment.

4/   Jake was announced; he marched in, halted briskly and froze at attention. He looked at Harry Truman's bow tie. The photograph was tilted. Not Jake.

Behind him the door swung shut. Jake swallowed hard, up to his ass in it now.

Colonel Leonhardt said, "At ease, Dodds."

Jake stood easy, but not at rest; he shifted briskly into the new position, and once there he was motionless, staring at the polka-dotted bow tie. He figured they would break him to private and brig him for five years, and then a dishonorable discharge. His blood ran bitter.

"Oh hell," the Colonel said. "Sit down there."

Warily, Jake looked him in the eye.

"Come on, come on," the Colonel said, waving a fat hand. "You've got twelve years, I've got twenty-five. We don't need to bow and scrape."

"Aye aye, sir," Jake said. His muscles eased and his mind leapt: could he hope? Maybe. He sat and waited with that look of respectful interest the brass always appreciated. He saw his service record on the

Colonel's desk. Warm air flowed through the screened windows. The Colonel was a thickset man, and could not be enjoying the heat. His hair was crew-cut, black with a sprinkle of silver over the ears; his brown eyes were hard as bullets, and his nose was a wrestler's snout. A good man in a waterfront bar, once.

"Dodds," he said, "I hear things about you that I don't like. That I don't understand."

"Yessir," Jake said, and heard the beat of his own heart.

"You've got twelve years. You've got a Navy god damn Cross, a Silver Star and a Purple Heart. You're an expert rifleman. The only thing you ain't got is a Good Conduct ribbon, and I guess you never will."

"Yessir," Jake said.

"You know more about small arms than any man in Tientsin. Maybe more'n anybody west of Pearl."

"Yessir," Jake said.

"And now I hear this strange story."

"Yessir," Jake said, "what's that, sir?" His skivvy shirt lay sticky. He was too big, and short of breath.

"I hear you want to quit," the Colonel said. "Now I ask you, Sergeant, what kind of talk is that?"

"Well, I've just been thinking about it, sir," Jake said. My God. "Just thinking it over. From all angles." Was that all!

"That's what I figured," the Colonel said. "That's why I sent for you. I said to myself, the man is too good to lose. I have a duty to the Corps, and part of that duty is to hang on to sailors like you."

Jake smiled briefly in acknowledgment. "Sailor" was an insult at first, or from your equals, but after some years, and from your superiors, it was an endearment. Behind his polite smile Jake was laughing insanely.

"Now, tell me what's on your mind," the Colonel said.

"Well," Jake said, "it's a big world out there. And no more war. Thought I might go into business. Be my own man. I mean, what's America for."

"No particular beefs about the Corps."

"No, sir. Corps been mother and father to me."

"Ah," the Colonel said warmly. "But are you sure. I see you've been up and down a couple of times. Might bear a grudge."

Jake shook his head and looked shocked. "No grudge, sir. First time it was my own temper. I, ah, struck an officer." A flash of anger brightened him even now, years later; son of a bitch of a Navy lieutenant with a million-dollar doll on his arm, and Jake half bombed with the usual scrawny whore, and this sailor saying, "Oh, Marines. We have Marines aboard the carrier, you know. Officers. To wash the admiral's skivvies, and keep the head clean." And Jake the only jarhead in the place, surly, stumping up like a dinosaur and flattening the prick, and turning to smile sweetly at Tits there and say, "You know, a broad with an ass like yours," and then somebody hit him with something and he woke up behind bars. "I don't seem to be a gentleman," Jake went on.

The Colonel chuckled in a fatherly manner.

"Probably officers and enlisted men should never drink in the same spots," Jake said.

"Second time seems to have been just bad habits."

Jake nodded firmly. "That's it, sir. Sorry to say it was the best week of my life."

The Colonel cocked his head. "What'd you do? Record doesn't say."

"No, sir, I guess it doesn't. I spent it in a kind of hotel a few miles from Kobe. Bathhouse, whorehouse, restaurant and so on. It was pure pleasure from start to finish. Only thing was, I, ah, extended a forty-eight by about five days."

"Dumb damn thing," the Colonel said. "Could've been back there every weekend forever."

"Well, that's it." Through his shirt front, Jake scratched his chest. His fingers came away moist. "If I was my own man I could do as I pleased."

"You know," the Colonel said, "it's little enough the Corps asks." He opened a desk drawer and set one foot on it; he leaned back in his swivel chair and broke wind absently. "Just show up on time, and don't bitch when you're asked to kill somebody. Once we settle in anywhere, like here, discipline's not too rough. Plenty of time off, and we stand up for each other. Hell, you know all that." He brooded. "Look. The war's over. They've cut us way down. That means whoever we keep ought to be the best. You understand? We'll have some little wars, skirmishes. But mostly it'll be good times and free beer, and afterward a pretty fair pension. Chrissake, Sergeant, if the Corps runs to seed what's the country got?"

"Well, I don't know what they got anyway," Jake said. "They got a lot of folks made money out of the war. They got a lot of politicians came in for half a year to pick up a record and a cheap medal. They got the same fraternity boys in the same leather chairs playing high-low with their stocks and bonds."

"That's unimportant," the Colonel said. "The main thing is we won a rough war. We did save the world, you know."

"We did, huh? You don't mind my saying so, Colonel, it looks like just about the same kind of shitbirds in charge of the world as before. They just call themselves other names."

"Not true," the Colonel said. "Although I wouldn't give you one Chinese dollar for the average civilian. I'll agree with you that far. There's another thing: why would you want to leave the Corps and go out into a world full of shitbirds?"

"Tell you," Jake said, "in a world of shitbirds even a half-wit can go places."

"That's so," Leonhardt said grudgingly. He extracted a kerchief from his hip pocket and swabbed his wrinkled brow. Jake took the act for permission to do the same. "No question that you're better than average all around. What would you do outside?"

Cautiously Jake said, "Thought I might stay here awhile, and see what export-import was all about."

"Here?" Leonhardt flung up his hands, rocking forward to scrabble for the edge of his desk as his chair rolled. "This place is *finished*. The State Department's pulling out. *We're* pulling out. The Reds come in, there is *no* export-import. You're crazy, Sergeant. How you even going to get a passport? Not to mention that we don't have to discharge you here. We can send you out home first."

"Then I might try Japan," Jake said.

"Ah." The Colonel nodded, canny and sympathetic. "You really like Asia."

"Yes," Jake said.

"You'll go crazy," the Colonel said flatly. "These people haven't even got an alphabet. You ask for the men's room and get directed to the train station. Chrissake, even *I* got in trouble last year."

"Heard about that," Jake said, "but no details. What was it, anyway? If, ah, if I may ask, sir."

"It was my driver, not me," the Colonel said, "but when they embarrass a colonel they get more apologies, and gifts, and formal acknowledgments and all that. We were tooling along the boulevard in my jeep and a little old lady pigeon-toed out of the mob, dashed right across, and we hit her. Broke her leg. Turned out it was an evil spirit."

"Evil spirit," Jake said.

"That's it," the Colonel said. "That is, there was one following her. I had it all explained to me. Evil spirits only travel in straight lines. So if you've got one on your tail and you want to shake him, you cut in front of a vehicle, and cut it close. Vehicle detaches evil spirit. So this old dame cut it too close. We paid the bills. Listen, these people are very different. Different enough so you could really hate them. You understand?"

"Well, I know they're different," Jake said comfortably, but the Colonel was not listening.

"Or you'll die of it," the Colonel said. "Sooner or later. Cholera. Typhoid. Dysentery. All that night soil on the lettuce. Or you go Asiatic, and start creeping around in women's clothes. Chrissake, boy. Not," he added quickly, "that I have anything against these people. You take your average educated Chinaman, he's all right, quite a fellow, good businessmen and some of them very artistic and all that. But hell, boy, you're no businessman anyway." He slapped Jake's records. "You're a fighter and a wild man. You're a big, strong dumb fucker with a bad temper. Exactly what we need. An *outlet.* The Corps is an outlet for all that. You use it *constructively.* You try this other thing and you'll be sorry as hell ten years from now, when it's too late."

"Nothing ventured, nothing gained," Jake said.

"You're important, Dodds," the Colonel said. "You know the Takarev Model Forty?"

"Seven point six two millimeters," Jake recited. "I could break it down blindfolded."

"And reassemble it. Well, that's the sort of thing we need. I hate to see you throw away a good career. Listen: I'll get you a transfer anywhere you want if you take another hitch. That's a promise."

"I appreciate it," Jake said.

"Washington," the Colonel said. "The embassy in Paris. I just don't want you to make a mistake." He considered, and glowered. "Business! They *hijacked* you. That's what they call business around here. Clean you out in a minute. Can't trust a Chinaman." With real curiosity he asked, "How'd that all happen, anyway? Were you scared?"

Jake said, "No," and eased off: "I was scared on Saipan."

"That was the Purple Heart."

"Right," Jake said in a lively voice. "A Jap grenade went off right between my feet. I was all blood inside the legs and I figured the family jewels were blown right off me, and I was going to put a bullet through my own head if that was true. I was lying there in the tropical jungle and I was never so cold in my whole life. *That* was scared. The other day, that was nothing. At the worst, in a jam like that, you shoot two or three and the others run for home. Sorry, sir. Didn't mean to talk so much."

"No, no. Interesting, interesting," the Colonel said. "You think about this. You do right by the Corps and the Corps'll do right by you. Hell," he said, "I know how you feel. After Niggeragua there wasn't a god damn thing to do until Pearl Harbor. We just drank and whored. But then they needed us, and we were ready. Always happens. You're something like me, you know. No reason you shouldn't be an officer. You wouldn't believe," he said gloomily, "the lieutenants they send me now. Anyway, my advice is to forget about China. You really don't want to spend your life with these people."

Don't want to spend my life with *these* people, Jake thought. To the Colonel he said, "I'll think hard about it. I won't do anything until I've talked to you again."

"That's the spirit. Maybe you'd like further training, some specialist school. Surveyor. A pilot, maybe. You think about it."

"I will, sir." Jake rose. So did the Colonel, and extended a hand. Jake shook it. He had ten pounds on the Colonel and maybe four inches of reach. Plus fifteen years, maybe more. He imagined the Colonel puffing hard, and folding from a shot to the gut. Then a chop to the side of the head. A big round man. He would bounce twice.

"Have a good time meanwhile," the Colonel said. "Watch out for clap. Use the pro kits. You wear your decorations?"

"Oh, yessir," Jake lied.

"Good. We like to impress these people. I suppose there's still a chance we can save this country, but the odds are against us."

Jake made sympathetic noises.

"You come and see me a week from today," the Colonel said.

Jake promised, and the Colonel shoved his records to one side and fussed with desk drawers. Jake was halfway out the door when the Colonel's voice, crisp and cold, halted him.

Jake turned. "Yessir."

"It is customary," the Colonel said, "to stand at attention until dismissed. It's the Corps' polite way," and he smiled thinly, "of demonstrating respect."

"Aye aye, sir," Jake said, and waited, rigid.

Dushok had loitered, waiting for him in a corner of the parade ground. They walked together in the shade of B barracks.

"What was that all about?" Dushok asked.

"Reenlistment."

"I thought it might be the truck you lost."

Jake said nothing, and they walked along for some way.

"In the old days," Dushok said, "if a village had two stonemasons and one butcher, and the butcher committed murder, they would hang one of the stonemasons for it. That way justice was done and society was not discommoded."

"Now what's that all about?" Jake asked.

"The Chinese police have shot four beggars for that hijack," Dushok said. "Tomorrow morning the Colonel will receive a long, flowery letter from the Chinese government. Just for the record."

Again Jake said nothing.

"I may have to nail you to the wall," Dushok said.

"Ah, blow it out your ass," Jake said, and walked another way.

5/   "A festive evening," Kao said. "Like a national holiday."
It was so: the Palace of the Night Chickens seemed noisy and crowded.

"Carrying things too far," Jake said. "Two lieutenants and a captain." He drank, openly annoyed, and huffed aloud. "And those civilians look like politicians. The one with the eagle's nose, the little guy, he waves his hands when he talks."

"There is plenty of talking," Kao said, raising his voice slightly.

The Marine officers laughed in gusts. "Shee-it," one of them said, "I never did learn Morse code," and they rollicked some.

"More wine," Kao suggested.

"Yes indeed," Jake said. Kao poured the hot, clear grain spirit. With his supper Jake had drunk the hot yellow wine, but this clear by-gar, as the Chinese called it, was sterner stuff, to match his mood.

Mei-li had said helplessly, "I didn't expect you tonight."

"Dry cup," he said to Kao.

"I am older and less ferocious," Kao said. "Forgive me if I don't keep up with you."

"Got to celebrate," Jake said.

Sue was beating the p'i-p'a like a banjo, and the Prince was browsing at the library.

"All right," Jake said, and set down the cup unlipped. "Maybe I ought to smoke."

Across the room the two new civilians argued. The taller of them, the one with a goat's nose, spoke in booms and blasts. "A hundred years," he claimed. "Until then they've got to have foreign management."

The little one said, "Ze question is," and was drowned out by the captain, at a table much too close to Jake: "In San Francisco. You couldn't tell if it was a house or not. I mean, a *sorority* house maybe."

"That's what they are," Jake muttered. "A god damn sorority."

"Forgive me," Kao said. "My stupid way with foreign languages."

"No, no, no, I'm sorry," Jake said. The p'i-p'a whinnied and twanged. The little fellow was a Frenchman, maybe. Jake drank up. "Tell me something cheerful."

"Well, I've told you plenty," Kao said. "About four thousand dollars' worth."

"Look at the medals," Jake said.

The captain and the two lieutenants were properly bemedaled. The lieutenants wore theater ribbons, American and Asian.

"You never wear yours," Kao said.

"That's why." Jake gestured.

"Like children with bits of colored glass."

"Well, sure," Jake said. "But some of those little rainbows, a man puts it on the line for them. There's nobody and nothing in the world worth walking up to a machine gun for. But once in a turtle's age you do it."

" 'To bear arms, and to meet death with no regrets, that is the energy of northern men,' " Kao quoted respectfully.

"You old poet, you," Jake said. "Dushok wears his because he's all gung-ho, by the numbers. They think he's an odd one but he lives by the rules when he's wearing the uniform. I just feel like a show-off when I wear them."

"You have a natural delicacy of style." Kao had to raise his voice again. "The Master said, 'Things that are done, it is needless to speak about; things that have run their course, it is needless to complain about; things that are past, it is needless to blame.' "

"Right," Jake said. " 'Riches and honors depend upon heaven.' "

Kao clapped in delight. "You remember!"

"How not?" Jake began a compliment, but one of the lieutenants was shouting, "So he says, 'Twenty bucks! For twenty bucks I screw the turkey and eat *you*,' " and the others roared laughter.

"Bugger," Jake said. "I *am* going to smoke. I need a pipe."

The Prince looked up in puzzlement, inspected the guffawing officers, put the book away and wandered out to the hall.

Mei-li and Ping-chi-ling came in together, wearing their public smiles and not much else, and the captain cried, "Aha! Hey, girlies, bring us some more of that chow, will you? That chicken stuff, and the pancakes."

Mei-li was confused until the darker lieutenant, slim and dapper, said in Chinese, "We'll eat more, please."

"God damn," the captain said. "A Harvard man."

"Amherst," the lieutenant said.

The lighter, louder lieutenant sang out, "The University of Ioway. Only two years," with a gleeful grimace, "because I could not get by the ladies. I mean I spent hardly *any* time in class."

"And whiskey," the captain called.

Jake caught Sue's eye and gestured. She set down the p'i-p'a and came to him. Helplessly she said, "Mei-li did not know you would come tonight."

"Just don't play music," Jake said.

She bowed, and went away.

"Four thousand," Jake said. "Well, that's fine." And not UNRRA supplies either. He had never spoken to Kao of UNRRA supplies. He wondered if Kao knew of the thousand-dollar temple.

"It's a decent wage," Kao said.

The Frenchman was saying, "Your politicians have never understood. What is right for you may not be right for ozzers."

"I agree absolutely," the older man said, an American, bluff and gruff and gray. "Roosevelt damn near gave Indochina back to the Indians."

The little man blinked and peered. "Ze Indians?"

"More wine," Jake said to Kao. "That was a dinner to remember. I'm just too full to give thanks, that's my problem."

"Allow me," Kao said. "You ate like an ancient warrior."

The officers laughed at a joke of their own. "Goosey goosey," one said.

"You eat well yourself," Jake told Kao.

"The comfortably fleshed man," Kao said, "inspires confidence. I have a look of probity. The angular man has a tendency to wrangle and cut corners, and appears famished at all hours."

Mei-li and Ping-chi-ling served the officers, who chattered and chuckled, said, "Yo-ho," and slapped fannies. "No grab-assing till after chow, gents," the captain said.

Jake's face complained to Kao.

"I have no idea who they are or where they come from," Kao said.

"Delicacy of style, you mentioned."

Kao beamed. "You have it."

"You may be right. I am becoming a professor and a man of virtue. I don't like Mei-li running around with no pants on and all these strangers in the place."

"She's working."

"I know. Ah, Master Kao. I'm thirty. I feel about sixty."

"With business success, maturity." Kao did what he had never done before: patted Jake's hand. He poured wine.

"Four thousand," Jake said. "What should I do with my share? What's good these days? What moves?"

"You, girl," the Frenchman called to Sue; and then in Chinese, "Little sister. Come over here and sit with us."

"That's a big beautiful girl," the American said. "What would that cost me for the night?"

"No, no," the Frenchman cried, both hands up in protest. "It is to my expenses. Say no more."

"That fellow from Amherst," Jake said. "I wish he wouldn't do that to Mei-li."

"What is Amherst?" Kao asked politely.

Jake sat there with a full belly and a little sweat on him. He wore his blue cotton trousers. Because it was a festive night and he was Kao's guest and their dinner had been formal and boozy, he also wore a light blue silk shirt, with a rounded Prussian collar and knotted silk buttons down the front. It was a size too small for him but he bulged nicely in it. Mei-li liked his neck. "Like a bull's neck," she said. "Like an elephant's neck."

"Why do they have to be so loud?" he asked.

Kao made no answer.

"Is it just because I know English? So I hear it clearer?"

Kao drew a small, lacquered black box from his pocket and offered Jake a cigarette. "No thanks," Jake said.

"By golly," the gray American bellowed. He had Sue on his lap and a hand up her skirt. Jake simmered; maybe this fellow was some kind of corporation president, used to diddling people in public. Jake rubbed his hands together and said, "Ha."

The room rang with loud voices, and yellow lamplight fought sinister shadow, and the faces were like slabs of meat. Jake understood: Americans were thick people. Not elegant fat like Kao, but layer on layer of rich red beef. The pasty ones, pork. Some well marbled. Even the soft light shimmered off them lush and veined.

He was fairly lush and veined himself by now, and swallowed off another cup of hot by-gar with a peculiar heat of his own, restless, a night-before-the-landing warmth: time to be up and doing. "I've been here four hours."

"So you have," Kao said. "But what is time? It is what we trade for pleasure and pain."

The captain's voice was thicker. Also his words were nastier.

"I've traded more time than I thought," Jake said. "These fellows are no poets and furthermore permit themselves a disarray of the clothing."

"They lack style altogether," Kao said sadly.

"They will shortly lack more than that," Jake said. "I feel like a unicorn in rut."

"That too you remember!" Kao cried. " 'The unicorn passes over the mountains scattering fire.' "

Ioway called out, "Hey, how bout a liddl music?" He flapped a jolly hand as the others fell silent. "Music. Play on that peapod."

The captain, an officer and a gentleman, was sniffing his own fingers in a blaze of imbecile pleasure. "Whoo," he called. "Got somethin for ya, girlie."

"What about that music?" Ioway tugged at Mei-li; she plumped into his lap. He yelled in glee, dived, and smacked his lips on a nipple. He surfaced and said, "Ah. Now where's that god damn music."

Kao said to Jake, "Your face is red. Has the superior man his hatreds also?"

"I feel old-fashioned," Jake scowled. "Listen, I'm not jealous, you know that, I know it's business and business is what we're all here for; it's just these big-noses are such piles of birdshit."

"Then perhaps you should smoke," Kao said like a doctor. "It is calming."

The officers were clearing their table, whooping and cackling: "This girl," the captain announced, and he meant Mei-li, "is gonna *dance.*"

"Stronger wine and madder music!" Amherst shouted.

"Where *is* that music girl?" Ioway complained.

The gray American called to him: "She's over here, lieutenant. And here she stays." His hand took a moment to wave triumphantly.

"Maybe they'll kill each other off," Jake said.

"We hoped Japan and Russia would do that," Kao said. "They didn't. They'll kill us twice instead."

The captain grasped Mei-li by her long silky hair and yanked her toward the table.

"Ah," Jake said.

"You go easy, Captain," the gray American called. The Frenchman frowned and puffed several times, like a child blowing out a candle.

"I'll do what I fucking please," the captain said.

"Old Barney," Amherst said with affection. "Nobody tells old Barney what to do."

Old Barney grinned, and tugged again at Mei-li; he forced her head to his lap. "Now we going to have a little dessert," he announced.

The Frenchman said, "Ah merde." The lanterns seemed to flicker, and the gray American said, "Good God," and released Sue.

Kao poured a cup of wine and blinked fatly, meditating, blind. Even the lieutenants paused in their day's occupation; Amherst swallowed hard.

"Chrissake, Barney," Jake drawled happily, "you got no manners? Only Americans with manners," he told the others, "come from orphan asylums." He stood up and padded to the officers' table, slouching and shaking his head.

"Now who is this," Barney said, "with fag pants and a girl's shirt."

The gray American spoke sharply: "See here. Let's have no trouble, now."

"That's it," Jake said. "See here. You heard him. See here." Quickly in Chinese he added, "You girls move aside, and evade things that fly." Small Change, the towel boy, peeped through the curtained doorway; Jake waved, amiable and fatherly.

The lieutenants waited. Jake noticed that with pleasure. Barney remained seated, which was also good news. "I don't know who you are, boy," Barney said, "but you look like a cutie to me. Gone Asiatic, you have."

"Your fly is open," Jake said, and as the captain looked down— they always will—Jake set both hands on the edge of the table and bulled forward. He rushed them all some six feet while cups and bowls flew, and the gray American, from his corner, called out, "See here!" The captain slid backward, still in his chair, and through the curtained doorway; Jake hoped that Small Change would deck him there, but doubted it. Amherst leapt and staggered; Jake overtook him with one step and walloped him; the boy almost left his feet, arching through the room like the man shot from the circus cannon, except that Amherst dragged his heels, and fetched up hard against the bookcase. After that he just lay there asleep under several layers of colored pictures: fleetingly Jake recognized the courtesan, the two archers, and the woman-with-old-face-but-young-body.

Meanwhile Ioway had staggered back to the wall and made a recovery. He pushed himself off the ropes like an old-timer, with his chin tucked behind his shoulder. That way Jake could not hurt him. Jake waited for him. Jake shook a finger like the school librarian and said, "Young man, it's supposed to be quiet in here. Also I have thirty pounds on you, you dumb son of a bitch." Then Jake busted him. By that time the captain was climbing through the curtains again. His fly was still open but Jake never made the same joke twice in one evening, so took him on the rise instead—old Barney had to climb over the table, and Jake never let him: Barney hit the top of the barricade and jumped, and Jake buried a satisfying right hand about three feet into the solar plexus, feeling the good cheer of it all the way up to his shoulder.

Barney took time out to gag several times, and Jake explained, "Trouble with you is, Barney, you're no fucking gentleman." Barney retched his way forward squatting, a blind heavy step at a time like a large, infirm frog; Jake walked along with him and waited for a sporting shot. Pretty soon they bumped into old folks there, little Frenchy and the gray American. There was not a girl in sight, which

Jake thought proper. Behind the gray American was the balcony, and Jake wondered if he might maneuver Barney through the curtained archway and over the railing.

Jake realized that he was middling drunk and quite happy. The unicorn passes over the mountains scattering fire. Yo-ho!

Barney surprised him, and shot up out of the crouch like some South American boxer, throwing a short, hard left into the sweetbreads. Jake closed; nine times out of ten it was better to close, and he did it now by habit if not by instinct. He chopped at the ribs and muscled Barney backward. Those other two fellows seemed to be talking a lot. Jake thought maybe the Frenchman was saying "Horrors." He backed Barney against their table and caught him on the side of the neck; Barney sprawled backward among the porcelain and chopsticks. "Ass over teakettle," Jake said, and poured some hot oolong on Barney's crotch.

"See here," the gray American said.

"Who the hell are you, now?" Jake snarled, rubbing his hands.

The Frenchman said, "My friend, zis is—"

"Wrong," Jake said. "I am not your friend." He stepped toward this tourist. "I do not like the French because they eat frogs."

"No no," the Frenchman said quickly. "I am a commercial attaché. No no. I am French. *I am French,* I tell you!"

Jake's face fell solemn. He clapped one hand to each of the man's padded shoulders, kissed him once on each cheek, and fired him through the archway to the balcony.

"All right, mister," the other's voice growled. "I don't know who you are but you're in bad trouble."

Jake looked him over. All beef, this one. Not so old after all, and plenty of muscle. "Trouble with you is," Jake said, "you're a fucking gentleman." He took the old boy by the shirt and tried to ram him toward the archway, but this gent fought back, and Jake had to do some work. Jake breathed, "Aha. Aha."

The voice growled again: "You better disengage, mister."

Jake had him in position now. He heard a commotion behind him.

In steely tones the man said, "I am an officer in the United States Army Air Corps."

"What rank?" Jake asked.

"Brigadier general," the man said.

Jake nodded happily, said "That beats the old record," and knocked him through the curtains. He heard a cheer behind him, the girls were back, and then Mei-li called "Watch out!" and he turned fast. When he saw the black uniforms his stomach churned. There were four of them and they carried clubs and pistols but he made a last try, scooting and dodging, and damn near made it over Barney's table to the front hall.

He ran smack into a large cop, as large as a sumo wrestler, almost as large as a tank. Jake had just time to wonder where his old friend Master Kao might be in this time of crisis, and then the large cop hit him with the wall, and Jake saw no more that night.

6/ He awoke many moons later, and with no strong desire to open his eyes. Or for that matter his nose. He floated on the surface of sleep; trod water; sank. Some weeks more and he groaned. Chickens pecked at his skull; their droppings filled his mouth, and their feathers. A p'i-p'a quavered. He lay flat on his back and lashed down, and in his dream a gross villain, with tiny eyes and one black curl of hair spiraling straight up, cut his throat.

Jake yowled, and burst out of the dream. He sprang to a crouch and hung on his hands and knees, throbbing. Thunder rolled; forks of lightning split his skull. A hairy green centipede scurried across his shoulder and down his arm. Jake slid forward, the side of his face on slippery straw, and understood: he had been beaten almost to death by Dr. Fu Manchu's men, and imprisoned for life in a verminous dungeon.

He freed his eyelids a slit, or one of them anyway, and saw, three feet from him, the back of a human head. He was not alone, then. He watched a small, tidy, industrious gray louse march up the back of the head and burrow into the black hair.

What he had heard was not a p'i-p'a but a singing voice; there was a third guest. Squinting, Jake made him out: an emaciated elder with blank eyes, squeezed comfortably into a corner and humming on one note. A running ulcer on his forehead oozed pus.

Jake rose to a sitting position and panted. He hawked, and with bone-cracking effort spat. His captors, fiendishly cunning, had sealed his eyes with cow-pie. They came unstuck enough to see a barred window and a shaft of blinding sunlight.

The centipede, he decided, had scampered playfully across his throat, and awakened him. Jake was a trained fighting man with a Navy Cross and a Purple Heart, one hundred ninety-five pounds, standing over six feet and free of hernia, with an I.Q., according to the horse marines, of one hundred and eighteen: he concluded that if he went about it with care and intelligence he could open his eyes like a bird, stand erect like an ape, and relieve himself like a man. Survival manuals rarely mentioned the matter, but a man could hardly rise to gunnery sergeant—twice—without learning how to pee.

Cautiously he freed both eyes. His left eye gave him great pain; he felt it, and found it whole but swollen. He was in a concrete cubicle. The exit, or entrance, was a wooden door that looked massive and menacing. His colleagues were in rags.

Another brig. Life was just one calaboose after another. In Cuba, he remembered, scorpions. "Buck up, boy," he said aloud. He rolled heavily to his knees, and levered himself upright. He swayed and bucked against waves of dizziness. After half a minute he managed a deep breath. He stepped to the wall and leaned. He saw no bucket, but after a time—time passed slowly here—he found a round hole in the floor, and went to fill it. Range was off a bit but direction good, no windage necessary. In Jake's condition every shot was a deflection shot. Chinese trousers have no flies, and after hoisting his he was obliged to fold the waist double and knot the sash, while not falling down.

All that he did. He lurched to the door, and pounded upon it. Without result. "Water," he screeched. No man answered. He stumped to the wall, sat back, and massaged his temples. He discovered a large bump on his head, named it Mount Kao, and remembered Constable Sumo. The evening fell vividly into place. He was thinking in two languages. I suppose this is home for a while, was one of his thoughts. Well, I always have my memories. They can't take my memories away from me.

"Aw, darn," he said aloud.

When the key sang in the lock, later that morning, Jake's musical companion blinked without real interest. The other one had not moved and might be dead. For a time Jake had not been sure that the head was fastened to the body. The door swung open, and a bony, cold-eyed little warden looked in. A carbine stabbed at Jake: "You. Foreign prisoner. Come out."

Jake obeyed, weaving slightly. To the others he said, "Adios, compañeros."

In a concrete corridor Jake breathed deeply many times. "Water," he said. "Is there water? Is there tea?"

"Move along."

Jake moved. They passed through another doorway and Jake stepped into a police station. Anywhere in the world this was a police station. The same desk sergeant. The same plainclothesman. The same guards and off-duty coppers. Race, creed or color. The same. Flat, cold eyes and they had not smiled for a decade.

His guide gestured toward another door. Jake entered a small office. He saw a desk, a chair, a cot, old Kao, six hot dumplings, a pot of tea, chopsticks and teacups.

"Good day to you," Kao said heartily. "Sorry to be late. Inexcusable. But nothing could be done before the banks opened. That is an absolutely classic black eye."

"The trouble you make me!" Kao cried. "And your mother and I have tried so hard."

"You could have brought aspirin," Jake said bitterly.

"For a dying man you did very well with the dumplings."

"Rats," Jake said, "spiders, lice and centipedes." By now they were in the public bath and extinguish-aches parlor. Jake lay back in a sunken stone tub; steam condensed on his forehead and ran merrily to the end of his nose. Kao sat naked in an alcove, an open window beside him, and contemplated his bungling assistant. Jake wondered what he looked like to Kao. A pink whale. A polar bear. "That fat one really clobbered me."

Kao shuddered. "Rough stuff. Barbarous."

"Who sent for them?"

"Small Change. It is one of his responsibilities." A tiny paper sack appeared magically in Kao's hand; he nibbled at a pickled turnip.

"And where were you?"

"Looking out for your interests," Kao said. "It occurred to me that dressed as you were, you had no identity at all. A desirable state of affairs should you survive the evening. So I removed myself discreetly from the battlefield and absconded with your uniform, wallet and dog tags."

"Brilliant," Jake said. "I wish you'd absconded with me instead."

"You were preoccupied," Kao said, "and very likely would have ignored my earnest solicitations."

Jake waved a friendly fist. "My head's clearing. I never thought of the identification. Still, if they'd known who I was they would have sent me home, no?"

"Ah," Kao said. "Indeed. The notion crossed my mind. Upon reflection I questioned the wisdom of such a course."

Jake said, "Uh-oh."

Kao cocked his head. "An interesting sound. What does it mean?"

"It is the noise made by those who are about to hear bad news."

"Exactly so," Kao said. "An expressive language, English. But my manners! A piece of turnip?"

"Not right now," Jake said. "I suppose you'd better tell me the worst." He lay back, resigned. The stone ceiling was beaded with moisture; a cold drop fell on his sore eye. "Bugger," he said. "Bugger, bugger, bugger! The world is full of evil. Those buggering Americans! Buggering cops, buggering lice, buggering centipedes, buggering hangover!"

"Modern poetry," Kao said appreciatively. "It has a more virile ring than the lacy verses of Tu Fu."

"Bugger Tu Fu too," Jake said.

Kao munched.

"Well, go on," Jake said.

"The three young officers," Kao said, "will doubtless recover. Contusions, inner bruises, injured pride. They were nevertheless officers in your own branch of service, and are surely in a position to, ah, alter the course of your career."

Jake winced, and said, "Oy."

Kao cocked his head again. "Another interesting sound. The meaning?"

"It is the noise made by those who acknowledge bad news."

"Exactly so," Kao said.

Jake grinned, and could not hold back a crowing laugh. "I really wiped them out. Did I not!"

"You wiped them out indeed. The small Frenchman was offended to a high degree. He fetched up in a corner of the balcony. No bones broken, but he was unconscious for an hour. He has several loose teeth and the side of his face looks like a skinned rabbit. He is preparing representations to your diplomatic and military authorities." Kao paused, and nibbled.

"An error," Jake said. "A little fellow like that. I take no pride in it."

After an uncomfortable silence he went on warily: "All right. Let's have it. It was that general, wasn't it?"

"I'm afraid so," Kao told him. "Your well-placed blow—in self-defense, I agree—knocked him not only through the archway, and not only to the railing, but off the balcony altogether."

"Shit," Jake said. "Into the canal."

"I'm afraid not," Kao said. "He landed in a honey-barge, breaking his left hip, and recovered consciousness at dawn, some twenty miles downstream, while being spread on a field of lettuce."

Jake could think of nothing to say.

"You see," Kao went on, "why I thought it well to remove your belongings."

"I thank you," Jake said. "I surely do."

"My knowledge of your laws is limited, but I imagine there would be punishment."

"There would be punishment," Jake said.

"Certainly loss of rank and salary."

"Certainly loss of rank and salary."

"Probably a term of imprisonment."

"Certainly a term of imprisonment."

"Perhaps as much as ten years or so."

"Certainly as much as ten years or so."

"And I further imagine," Kao said diffidently, "that in the course of the investigations, certain details of your—our—business career would come to light."

Stunned, Jake lay silent in the steaming, scented waters.

"It occurred to me," Kao went on, "that such a series of events would be undignified."

"Undignified," Jake said. Suddenly his belly ached. "Hsüü," he said. "This worsens fast."

Kao nodded sadly. "It is very bad. Hiding would be difficult. You are so *noticeable*. To smuggle you out by boat is impossible, with the ports so closely supervised. And we are surrounded by police, soldiers, informers."

Jake felt a wee cold ripple of fear. He was only an hour out of a Chinese jail; and a Marine Corps brig would be worse. They would release him an old man, battered, gap-toothed, flat nose, cauliflower ear, hunched and shambling.

"It has occurred to me, however," Kao said, "that you have demonstrated an aptitude for business. For languages. For travel. A man of the world, we might say."

Jake blinked, and sagged. He drew in a deep breath; his eyes closed; he sighed a long, sad sigh.

Kao was silent. Jake waited. He raised the sponge and squeezed; warm water cascaded over his face. He shook his eyes clear and glared at Kao, who was rummaging in his little bag of pickled turnips.

"All right, spit it out," Jake said finally. "What are you offering me?"

Kao beamed gently upon him. "Escape. Fortune. Life itself."

Jake sponged his face, and sat up straighter in the stone tub. "Tell me more."

Kao asked, "Do you think you could learn to drive a camel?"

7/   Caravan Master Ch'ing was also a master of the pumpkin seed. He propped one on the tip of his tongue, cracked it, tucked away the meat and spat the hull to the floor, over and over. Jake and Kao and Ch'ing were taking their ease on the second floor of a Mongolian restaurant in the Tung An Shih-ch'ang, which being translated was the Market of Eastern Peace. Pumpkin seeds were a traditional appetizer in Peking, and they were waiting for the main course.

Ch'ing was cranky, and Jake suspected he would always be cranky. He was a small dark man who smelled of animal fats or maybe camels, and he was from Tientsin, and was part Mongol. He was cranky because it was well known that foreigners could not pull camels. He had been a camel-puller but was now a caravan master, and he had once before carried a passenger, he announced, a man of learning with eyeglasses who knew everything that had happened two thousand years ago and was not worth sheepshit on the trail.

Kao spoke of a leasing arrangement. If necessary Jake would buy a camel but leasing was more logical. Above all if two should be necessary.

"It is not unheard of," Ch'ing said grudgingly. The waiter bustled. He built up the fire and set out platters of finely sliced meat. The fire burned in a small chimney that rose through the center of the brass pot. Around the chimney water boiled.

"I'll work too," Jake said.

"Work," Ch'ing said. "Have you ever pulled a camel?"

"No. But I once broke a general's leg."

Ch'ing cackled suddenly and his eyes warmed. "It's a start. What else can you do?"

"Look at me," Jake said. "I can throw a small man ten feet."

"We have very little occasion to throw small men."

"He has the strength of a bull," Kao said calmly. "That is not to be despised."

"Do you need guards?" Jake asked.

"Guards? We are all guards. Can you fight?"

Jake shrugged.

"He is a master of arms. Please," and Kao gestured with his chopsticks at the strips of meat. Ch'ing plucked one from the stack and dropped it into the boiling water; the others did likewise. "He was a sailor," Kao said. "A sergeant. He is a famous marksman."

Ch'ing nodded. "You have your own weapons?"

"None," Jake said. "I suppose they can be bought."

"You are a foreigner," Ch'ing said. "What weapons can you know? Foreign weapons."

"What weapons have you?"

"Li-en-fi-la. Eh-ma ti-i. A-li-sha-k'a and chiu-shih-chiu."

Jake grinned around a mouthful of meat. Lee-Enfields, M-1's, and the Japanese Arisaka and Model 99. "I know them all," he said, "with my eyes shut."

Ch'ing fished in the boiling water and landed a strip of beef. He slapped it into a bowl of sauces, stirred, and popped the meat into his mouth. "Mmmm," he hummed. Jake and Kao also ate. They dropped several strips into the boiling water. It was not obligatory to retrieve your own strips. Ch'ing extracted another, sauced it, and stuffed it into a sesame bun. "What is a Nambu fourteen?"

"A common Japanese pistol," Jake said. "Eight millimeter. There is also a baby Nambu but they are rare."

Ch'ing refrained from eating and examined Jake. He was seeing Jake for the first time, and he did not rush the inspection. He chewed slowly and said, through his mouthful, "That is so."

Jake and Kao ate, and waited. The food was new to Jake and he was enjoying his meal. He was not sure that he was enjoying Ch'ing, but had become hopeful.

"You have the proper papers, of course," Ch'ing said.

Jake glanced at Kao and continued chewing.

Kao said, "Of course. He has his military identification."

"Passport?"

"No passport," Kao said. "Have you a passport?"

"Of course not," Ch'ing said. "If we meet Communists?"

"Then he has no papers, like all your men. He is stateless, if you like, and he works for you."

"If there is trouble, the camel is mine and so are the goods."

"Well now," Kao said easily, "he is my agent, after all. If there is trouble the camel is yours and the goods are on consignment from the House of Kao."

Ch'ing considered. Jake ate with noisy pleasure. "What is all this?" he asked. "Beef and pork?"

"Pork!" Ch'ing was disgusted. "No pork."

Jake looked to Kao.

"Hui-hui-ti," Kao said, meaning Mohammedan.

"Right," Jake said. "My apologies."

"Two hundred," Ch'ing said.

"Two hundred what?"

"Two hundred American dollars. Bring your own weapon. That is to Hsinkiang." Hsinkiang was the great western province. Turkestan was the old name, and Jake liked the ring of it. "To Ku-ch'eng-tze. After Ku-ch'eng-tze you go alone."

"That is Gurchen," Kao said, "the great western terminus. It has another name too but we call it Ku-ch'eng-tze."

The waiter set cruets of hot wine before them and Ch'ing said, approximately, "God be praised."

Jake was amused. "Wine? The hui-hui-ti?"

Ch'ing cackled again. "Listen, foreign devil," he said, "three Mohammedans are one Mohammedan, two Mohammedans are half a Mohammedan, and one Mohammedan is no Mohammedan at all."

They all laughed together; Kao said, "It sings like poetry."

Jake asked, "Do I ride a horse?"

"A horse!" Ch'ing fell crusty again. "We have no horses for passengers. Maybe after Pao-t'ou, a pony. To Pao-t'ou, you walk."

"Walk!"

"Camels carry," Kao said reasonably. "They carry goods. Goods mean money." He poured yellow wine for them, into small light blue porcelain cups. "Kan pei."

"Dry cup."

"Dry cup."

They quaffed, and Kao poured again.

"If there is a camel with a light load, you ride," Ch'ing conceded.

"But it would be better," Kao offered smoothly, "to do as the others do. A trader is not a passenger. And how many camels," he asked Ch'ing, "have you?"

"From Peking only one lien. The rest are in Pao-t'ou."

Kao said, "A lien is a file of eighteen."

"How many altogether?" Jake asked.

"Three pa and a few."

"A pa is two lien," Kao said.

"That's a lot of camels."

"We are an old house," Ch'ing said, "older than the dynasty that bore my name." He shrugged. "Besides, it's safer."

Kao sighed. "It is a high price, but doing business is difficult these days."

"And I'll have to buy my own weapons," Jake said glumly.

"A pistol," Ch'ing protested. "A pistol merely. We have rifles aplenty. And buy goggles."

Jake did not know the word.

Kao explained.

"Oh. Sunglasses."

"Not sunglasses," Ch'ing said. "Heavy goggles. For sandstorms."

"Good."

"You eat what we eat."

"Good."

"Not good," Ch'ing said. "*This* is good. More wine, please."

"And what sort of camel will he have?" Kao asked.

Ch'ing considered. "A good camel. A gelding. Seven years old."

"It will carry how much?"

"Three hundred fifty pounds," Ch'ing said. "Four hundred in a pinch. What are your goods?"

"Miscellaneous," Kao said. "Some binoculars, some cameras, electric cable, fine brocade, kegs of nails and spikes, hatchetheads of the best steel, several tool kits and a few minor items."

"Kegs," Ch'ing grumped. "They split. They break open."

"Not these," Kao assured him. "These are American surplus and are banded securely with steel ribbon. They are sealed, and they bear the mark of—who are those people?"

"Seabees," Jake said.

"Never heard of them," Ch'ing said.

"They are the carpenters of the American Navy," Kao explained. "They build all manner of things. Stoves. Battleships."

Ch'ing grunted. "All right. Remember, I permit no overloading."

"Naturally not. I think we must have two camels."

Jake also thought so. The goods came to six hundred pounds at least.

"Four hundred," Ch'ing said.

Kao scoffed. "And will Ta-tze eat twice as much because he has two camels?"

Ch'ing blinked. "The Tartar?"

"My nickname," Jake said.

"Three hundred," Kao said firmly.

"Nonsense," Ch'ing said. "Two camels eat twice as much. Their hoofs blister twice as much. They shed twice as much in summer and freeze twice as much in winter."

They settled on three hundred and fifty American dollars. Ch'ing glowered. "I'll regret this."

"You will not," Kao said amiably. "He is a famous fighter and a famous enemy of generals, even as you are."

"That much is true," Ch'ing said. "I hate dogs, bandits and generals."

"Why dogs?"

"They make the camels nervous."

"No watchdogs?"

"Some caravans use them. I use men. Dogs bark at every little thing: at a desert mouse, at the wind."

"Are there still bandits?"

"There are still bandits," Ch'ing said darkly, "and it is bad luck to speak of them. It is double bad luck when a foreigner speaks of them."

"Now that we are working together," Jake said carefully, "I think it would be better for the caravan if we did not make so much of my foreignness. It is probably a good topic to drop."

Ch'ing surprised him with a true grin. "Good thinking for a Tartar! Let us gobble meat."

They gobbled meat and drank wine for half an hour more. Now and then they wiped their mouths with hot cloths and gossiped: the Hollywood Beauty Saloon on Morrison Street was a part-time whorehouse, and Jelly-Belly the Tailor had internal troubles, evil winds. But mainly they ate, swabbing sauces from their chins in that perfect community, as Kao murmured, of good feeders thanking an inscrutable universe for a meal far above the just deserts of lowly man. When the meat had vanished the waiter brought white vegetables; they shoveled them into the simmering broth and ate a splendid soup. "If it's like this on the road," Jake said, "I'll never reach Gurchen."

Ch'ing laughed outright, and fought hiccups. He held his nose and sipped soup, laughed more, belched and finally wiped his face again. "You will eat," he said, "what the camels have already eaten." Then he giggled for a time.

Jake drank up, tingling, in the grip of a rare excitement. Deserts. The wilderness and the solitary place!

They allowed him to pay the bill. As usual he tipped well, and in a moment was glad of it; as they bumbled heavily down the wooden stairs, their waiter leaned after them and shouted the amount of the bill and the amount of the tip, and a chorus of hao-hao's approved. Jake was tipsy and full and beamed upon the street-floor customers, who nudged one another and pointed: look, look, a foreign village idiot.

In the street Ch'ing set a rendezvous. If there was any change he would notify Kao. "God help me," he grumbled, and then said fiercely, "Listen, no foreign wines. No foreign bottles."

"I eat what you eat," Jake said. "I drink what you drink."

"Then God help you too," Ch'ing said, and walked off, bowlegged and shaking his head.

Kao said, "You did well."

"That was a meal," Jake said. "I want to come here again."

"I think not," Kao said. They ambled up the busy street. "From now on you will never go to any place a second time."

8/ The room was handy to the Western Gate and only half a mile from the Field of Camels. "But don't hang about the Field," Kao told him. "Don't even go there. Don't hang about *anywhere*."

"Nobody knows me," Jake said.

Kao sat plumply on the stone bed; the straw mattress crackled. He touched his flaming lighter to the wick of a small oil lamp, and reset the grimy glass chimney. The room was suddenly bright as day. Kao loomed, fat. "Draw the curtains, please," he said.

"You make a great fuss."

"Well, you see," Kao said almost apologetically, "we are such a poor country."

Jake looked his puzzlement.

"To turn you in would earn anyone praise, also a cash reward. And even the smallest cash reward—you see. Think," Kao said gently, "how grateful your own authorities would be. Think what a hero they would make of some local cop on the beat."

Jake said, "I can't sit here doing nothing for ten days."

"No no no," Kao said. "We must prepare. We have shopping to do, and I must tell you of the west, and of my friends there. But certain elementary precautions I insist upon. As you see, for example, I had your wooden chest brought here; but I suggest that you wear the long gown and the low hat, and save the khakis for Mongolia. We shall use, for another example, enclosed rickshas, though the season be warm."

"Why can't I stay at the Palace?" Jake knew the answer and knew how sullen he must sound, like a kid in trouble, with his lower lip stuck out.

"Now now," Kao said. "Of course not. This is not bad, here. A good mattress, your chest, a table and a stool and a lamp, and the conveniences just out back. Now. Are you ready?"

"Whatever you say," Jake answered. "This landlord here, what about him?"

"Absolutely safe."

"He looks a villain."

"He is a villain," Kao said. "You will like him. He is a quiet, easy-going fellow. His hobby was knifing Japanese at night. All in this alley fear him, so you will be comfortable."

"All right then," Jake said. "Let's go shopping."

With Kao he prowled remote bazaars, vast sheds like hangars with naked steel beams high above and only screens or partitions separating the flower merchant from the costume jeweler, or the foreign toilet bowls from the crickets in cages. Customers, wholesalers, police and sweepers swarmed and chattered. Cries echoed, and low arguments.

"Yes, goggles, here we are," Kao said. "Look at that: a diver's helmet." He carried a cloth bag heavy with bank notes. The dealer was obsequious. Jake sampled goggles and bought a pair used but intact, much like the foolish goggles that adorned aviators' helmets in the five-and-ten when he was a boy.

"Would you like some sweet corn? Hot off the grill, about a block from here. Later, perhaps," Kao said. "Here we are. You'll want maps, I think. Linen maps. Expense no object. You know how to read maps?"

"You bet I do. But in western letters."

"Those we have. Good day, master."

They stood at a booth near one end of the great bazaar. Kao's roving eye checked the entrances, and the street beyond. The young map-seller made them welcome.

"This inspection of exits and entrances is rather vexatious," Kao complained. "I am accustomed to order and serenity."

"You worry too much," Jake said. "If we have trouble, you don't know me."

"Ta-tze!" Kao's features sagged in pained reproach. "Business is built on trust. Never would I sell you out."

Jake said solemnly, "I am unworthy."

And Kao said sternly, "You are a troublemaker, and incurably frivolous. One does not cross the Gobi smiling."

Nights he took a humble meal at a place called Cheap Restaurant: boiled rice with plenty of sand and gravel, fatty lumps of pork and pale vegetables like boiled celery. He sent out for sweet corn; the boy returned with half a dozen three-inch ears, the kernels tiny and white. This was real life, Jake decided. You ate dirt and corncobs.

After supper he stood in the street, or in his own alleyway, observing and overhearing, learning. Girls passed by who spoke of working in factories. A repairman of bicycles lived next-door. In this alleyway were hovels, houses of earth and stone, and none of the frilly lattices or spacious courtyards he had known. Sometimes his landlord joined him, a gnarled man of middle age, and they gossiped. They agreed that peace was better than war, and that all government was bad. Nights were balmy now, and the mutter and tinkle of the city were soothing. "Well enough in summer," the landlord said. "But in winter there is nothing to eat and coal is expensive, and they make stacks of the dead on corners."

Another night the landlord said, "The body contains barrels of blood. It is astonishing how much. If you use a long blade, and go in here," he touched Jake between the left ribs and the right, "striking upward, there is less mess. If you use a pistol, use a heavy caliber unless you are sure of a perfect shot. I've seen men who were killed and took a long, long time to die. Unpleasant. Unworthy. Undignified."

One night at a light knock Jake prickled; he padded to the door and asked, "Who is it?" and was given, as he should have known he would be, the Chinese answer: "It is I." He then did the Chinese thing, and opened the door, and it was Mei-li, who rushed into his room, and his arms.

*   *   *

They did not sleep, but caused spring showers and made the beast with two backs, as well as snake-eats-snake. Waves of desire shook Jake, and strange aches, and not only between the legs. He was on his way to somewhere he had never seen; and certain familiar places, like Mei-li's bub and thatch, were all he knew of hearth and home. He clung, and his heart contracted like a schoolboy's, and afterward he felt sheepish, almost cowardly. He touched all of her with all of him, as if some magic might rub off, and protect him.

In the middle watch they lit the lamp and smoked a pipe. "First the Chinese flatfeet swarmed like bees," she said. "Then the officers came, your officers, and asked questions."

"And had no answers."

"No answers. No one knew who you were. You had not come there before."

"Dushok," he said.

"He did not speak of you."

Jake forgot what they were talking about. With his cheek on her belly he dreamed dreams and saw visions. Later she lay with her cheek on his belly, and his tired little private first class warm between her breasts; at ease, at rest.

At dawn she left. They dressed quickly, and Jake hesitated. He made an effort to think, to think like Kao, like a fine gentleman. He nodded. He did not offer money, but went into the street with her, and found a bicycle ricksha for her, and paid the man. When she was comfortably settled he placed his palms together and bowed slightly, and she inclined her head like a great lady and dazzled him with a devilish look and a bright smile, and he was cheerful all the morning.

The binoculars were Kao's gift; Jake recognized them, and why not? He had hijacked them. "With a good stout leather case," Kao said. "Thus you will see with your eyes and with mine."

"If I could only think with your mind."

"Your own is good, your own is good," Kao insisted.

"I jump into things," Jake said unhappily. "I move before I think."

Kao's eyes narrowed as he recollected. " 'Chi Wan thought thrice, and then acted,' " he quoted. " 'When the Master was informed of it, he said, "Twice may do." ' "

"Ah," Jake said. "What a fine people you are."

"We are like all people," Kao said. "Now. You have cloth shoes for lounging. A compass, goggles, linen maps, binoculars."

"Pistol and ammunition."

"A good knife."

"Both kinds," Jake said. "A killing-knife and a six-small-tools knife."

"That reminds me," Kao said. "You must mention Ch'ing to no one."

"No one," Jake said. "Not a word."

"Good." They were in the heart of another market. "It may be a near thing," Kao went on. "We may squeeze through by no more than a gnat's tooth. Hints of unwanted attention have come my way."

"Not good."

"Not good. You see, we must look ahead. Next trip I think we shall move west altogether, in partnership. I am laying serious plans, even now. Myself the practical man, a professor, if I may say so, of the marketplace; you a famous traveler and linguist, a man of action, and also a representative of, well, other lands and cultures."

"A foreign devil."

"Ah, that phrase. Not worthy of us, I fear."

"Or a Big-nose."

"Now that," Kao said, "is mere vulgarity. Never have you heard the words on my lips."

"Never."

"These are troubled times and we are groping," Kao said, "but the longest journey begins with one step. In a year or two this part of the world will surely be unpleasant for the creative businessman. But Turkestan! The border areas! A trader's paradise."

"A new life," Jake said. "I owe you much."

"Nothing," Kao said. "We are sincere partners."

And together they acquired a first-aid kit, a few bricks of cocoa butter for sunburn oil, two bandannas, a packet of buttons for the strange foreign fly, and a dozen K rations. They considered a quilt, against cold nights on the desert, but decided not: too bulky, and there would be sheepskins and robes, and Jake was to be as much like the others as possible. Drugs they had. Pills, magical. An untimely clap was ruinous to trade; who could negotiate shrewdly, oozing and burning? Kao would supply the flashlight and cigar lighter from his own stock. "What's the best kind of money to carry?" Jake asked him.

Kao said, "That's for tomorrow."

"All right. And where's all my goods?"

"They will be delivered to the Field of Camels in plenty of time. They are important," Kao said, suddenly sober. "Every bundle. This is, when you think of it, a daring venture."

"You're a great executive," Jake said.

"Indeed," Kao said modestly. "And do you know where I would be if I had lent my talents to the government?"

"Where?"

"Behind a desk," Kao said sourly, "waiting in vain for my salary to catch up with the inflation."

"It's an awful thing," Jake said.

"It is. The only safety is in gold. Do you know that the ricksha men make more than the professors? They raise their fares every day. The professors wait six months for their cost-of-living augmentation, by which time it is worthless. The best of the country is dying. I tell you, in bad times the true patriot must turn anarchist, and salvage what he can from the ruins."

"Well, I guess that's me," Jake said.

Later the thought came to him that he might spend the rest of his life in exile. Others had done so. He would make a home and a business and raise a family, perhaps a few families; it was done here. It would not be painful. In many ways it would be more pleasant. Interesting and busy and not so cheap and grubby. He would amount to something, be a man of importance. And the women were superior. Not just prettier but nicer people. They were not loud, painted or vicious, and their husbands did not die young.

He studied his maps. The Gobi was a large space with few dots, few names. Caravan trails. A few dry streams, broken lines. To the west, a long river running north. And the names changed. They became Mongolian names, and from the look of them they were spoken the way they were spelled. Dengin Hudag. Was that Den-jin or Den-ggin? He would like to see Dengin Hudag.

He would like to see rivers of gold, and mountains of jade, and women of ivory.

They would call him Ta-tze, and speak of him in the marketplace, and he would wear fur-trimmed boots.

9/   Jake and Kao rode to Gold Street in a two-man bicycle
ricksha, Jake wearing the long blue gown and the coolie hat, and
sitting well back under the black cloth roof. "My friend is a foreigner,
and very sensitive to the sun," Kao had explained, and the bustling
young biker had manipulated his convertible top. Gold Street was in
the outer city, south of Ch'ien Men, and so were Precious Stone Street,
Furniture Street, Hardware Street, and others. No shuttling all over
town. You came to a street here and found ten, twelve shops all selling
the same sort of merchandise. True competition, Kao said with approval.

At the True Weight Precious Metal Shop the driver announced that
he would wait. Kao rebuked him and began to pay him off, but
beggars gathered from nowhere. Kao said hastily, "Wait then," and
tugged Jake quickly into the shop.

Jake was curious: "Why shouldn't he wait?"

"The beggars see the ricksha. They too wait. They are ferocious
here."

The two were received by a withered, bright-eyed old man who looked as if he might burn away in a warm wind. Shining from an infinity of wrinkles, his eyes were like restless mice in dry grass. His hands were pale, smooth and graceful; he pressed them together and bowed.

Kao made oily introductions, and they all exchanged honorifics and best wishes. They then discussed the sad state of the gold and silver business. Trade in all but ornaments was, the ancient explained, punishable by death. Anything over fourteen karats was dangerously illegal. He was only jacking up prices before the serious talk began but Jake and Kao expressed sympathy. It was indeed sad. Honest tradesmen were being squeezed. Forced into undignified procedures. It was barely possible to stay alive. Some months one actually lost money. Above all if one gave honest weight, which was the age-old boast of this shop.

A false balance, Jake remembered suddenly, and said it aloud, translating as he went, awkwardly but gravely, "is abomination to the Lord: but a just weight is his delight."

The old man sighed his own delight. "It is not every day that we hear such elevated sentiments." He cast a shrewder eye on Jake.

There followed some jokes. The phrase for "weigh out" was p'ing tui; the p'ing was the p'ing of Peiping and another tui, on the same tone, meant correct, or in agreement. The jokes were elegant for a country boy and Jake was pleased with himself.

Also surprised. He was not so well-spoken in his own language. It did not seem normal to make good jokes in another.

Kao was pleased with him too, and it bothered Jake that Kao looked pale again, with a light sweat starting so that he mopped his face and asked for a chair. The old man had a boy set one out immediately. Jake wondered if Kao had a weak heart: a fat man.

The goldsmith liked Jake. He was gladdened by the jokes. It was not every customer these days who could joke. Most came with dry mouths and a smile writhing, and a bracelet or ring in a secret pocket.

He reminded them again that the penalty was death, and added that after all, the penalty for living was death.

Jake exhaled admiration. This fellow was a thinker. Eight half-ounce pieces at seventy dollars U.S. the ounce. Seventy! Ah, but the penalty was death. And after all, honest weight. The pieces were round and unmarked, and not milled. There were also ounce pieces but those were harder to change. One of the ounce pieces was a farmer's earnings for a whole year.

By this time the boy had served tea.

Should Jake perhaps take rings? a bracelet? an armlet? He was in some doubt. These last were more conspicuous. Earrings would be torn off by evil persons. Ornaments, perhaps, in the shape of animals: with a small foundry in the shed out back, anything could be cast—

"Such tea!" Kao cried. "Tea for the gods!"

The goldsmith subsided, blinked, bowed.

"And that pot," Jake said.

Ah, the inestimably precious gentleman had noticed! There was no lid to the teapot! The old man was charmed. He demonstrated, turning it over: it was filled through a hole in the bottom, into which, when the pot was righted, a valve settled. Most ingenious. Appropriate for a worker in fine designs, a goldsmith.

"Indeed," Kao said. "I think coins are the only answer."

They settled on two hundred and fifty dollars. "Because Master Kao and I are old friends," the ancient said.

"And have done much business together."

"Have we not!" the old man said. "And will again."

Politely, with care, he counted the pieces into a small cloth bag. Politely but with a magician's skill he counted the notes Kao had peeled off, and carelessly he tossed them to the counter where they lay ignored while the three men drank another cup of tea. They performed a few bows, and wished one another good health and long life. By its drawstring Jake hung the bag around his neck beneath the gown. The old man approved, and bowed. Jake bowed. Kao was outside when the old man touched Jake's hand and nodding gently, with a faint, dreamy, affectionate smile, said, "I wish you a safe journey."

Jake paused. Now what did this wispy old gent know about Jake or Jake's plans? Well, maybe he had meant the journey through life. Jake was grateful to him, and thanked him, and for a moment reversed their hands, so that Jake's lay on the old man's. They nodded. Jake left.

The street was bright and noisy, and Jake blinked a bit, believing at first that there had been an accident or a brawl. Forty beggars thronged the ricksha. Jake cursed to himself, drew a deep breath, and waded in. They were deformed and mutilated. Some were children. All were in rags and most barefoot. They gave off a bad air, a stink of sickness, coming death, and the clamor was fierce.

Jake was suddenly wild with anger, and not sure why. He shoved at them, that mob of Oriental bodies, Oriental faces, Oriental smells, and his breath came shorter, and Kao shouted, and the driver shouted, and the beggars shouted back, the air rancid with menace, and Jake shoved harder and roared at them, fought through with his fists and his elbows, and laid a hand on the ricksha, and was about to step into it, when one of them jostled him hard from behind, and Jake turned furiously, ready to slug.

The beggar was a young man with blond hair and shining blue eyes, and was cursing Jake savagely in Chinese.

Jake went cold and could not move or speak, only stare. He was looking at himself. Sweat started on him, and the blood pounded in his head, but he could not move or speak. He could not look away. Chinese scum, okay. But blue eyes! Blond hair!

The beggar fell silent, and gleams of hate, gleams of greed, shot from his shining eyes. He drew closer and whined, and stabbed a hand at Jake, a claw.

Jake yelped like an animal and ripped himself away from it. He vaulted into the ricksha and prodded the driver. With the driver pedaling and hollering, and Jake slashing to one side and Kao to the other, they cut their way clear.

Jake was shaking. His stomach heaved. He had never trembled or been sick in combat and now he wanted to spew.

"Dogs defile them all," Kao gasped. "They should be shot."

"One of them—" But Jake could not say it. Say what? That it was wrong for white men to be beggars? That he had not until now thought of beggars as human? That he had not until now thought of Chinamen as human?

"All of them," Kao snarled. "How can honest merchants prosper in a jungle like this?"

And then it was Jake's next-to-last night in Peking, and Kao swept him off to a dark doorway in a dark alley, and a meal to remember, and there was no talk of beggars: roast honeyed duck and sliced leeks, black sauce and papery, savory pancakes to roll them in; and hot yellow wine; and the open fires and fat crackling, and Jake the only white man in the place and glad of it, eavesdropping on the talk of money and war.

"I once ate a whole duck," Kao said. "In my youth."

Later Kao said, " 'In youth beware lust; in maturity beware belligerence; in age beware greed.' "

And later Kao said, "Those gold pieces. What have you done with them?"

Jake patted his own chest and said, "I bought a little leather bag and strung it with braided wire."

Kao said, "You have spoken to no one?"

And Jake said, "No one."

"Good. Do not. From now on you have no name, even. Ta-tze. No one knows who you are or where you're going."

"What did you do with my dog tags?"

"They're safe," Kao said. "I'll try to plant them on a dead foreigner."

Jake nodded easily, but the words left him cold and empty. He did not believe in good luck or bad, but did not like that fate for his dog tags.

"You may want to dispose of that I.D. later," Kao said.

Jake nodded again but felt no better.

Kao said, "Now. About the goods. Do not trade on the way. Do you understand? I am instructing you now. You cannot know the relative value of what you carry. What is insignificant to you may be of importance in Gurchen. Every last leaf of tea, every last nail. Trade nothing on the way. Lose nothing on the way. Sleep with your goods. Do your own loading and off-loading. The goods are your link and mine between here and there, between today and tomorrow. In Gurchen you will be met." And then, "Self-control. Do not brawl. You are a trader now and you must bear a responsibility beyond your experience. You are not of the Navy now, with a battleship to come if things go wrong, and comrades to roister with. You will be alone and there is much at stake. You must remember always how much is at stake. The course of our lives.

"Do not trust Ch'ing either, by the way, not altogether. He is an honest man but you and you alone are responsible for those goods. Ch'ing does not know precisely what they are or what they are worth, or whither they are destined. Is that clear?"

"It is clear."

"Ah, well. Enough advice from a nervous old man."

They paid the bill and made a quiet farewell inside the front door; they would leave separately. "I'll try to be there," Kao said, "but it may be better not. There is no one in the world to connect you and me. Only Ch'ing. No outsider to connect the three of us. The goods are there now and your camels are sound. If I'm not there I'll see you in a year or so."

"A year or so," Jake repeated. This ancient, far-flung, slow-moving world, where you made appointments for next year, and journeys of many months, and old men were respected.

"It's in your hands," Kao said.

"I'll do right," Jake said.

"You will," Kao said. "I believe the gods brought us together." He joined his hands and bowed, smiled sadly at Jake, and thrust a hand forward awkwardly, palm almost up; Jake grasped it, and pumped it, and clapped the old boy on the shoulder.

"I owe you a life," he said. "I'll do right."

In his room the next night he surveyed his small passel of belongings, his worldly goods, and a prickle of excitement overtook him. This was Jake Dodds, these few items, this body and brain, and there was no telling where Jake Dodds would be this day twelvemonth. Hell, not even Jake Dodds. Ta-tze.

He leaned forward to study the map of Hsinkiang. He saw himself with horses and women and fur cloaks for winter.

At the knock he started up, hoping it was Mei-li, but in the same moment he knew that it was not her knock. He plucked the .45 from the small table and stepped softly to the door. "Who is it?"

"Dushok. I'm alone."

At the sound of English Jake was stunned. But if Dushok was not alone then Jake was doomed anyway. He opened the door.

In a long black gown, almost invisible at night with the alleyway black around him, the old sergeant stood.

Jake said, "The landlord?"

"I told him Kao sent me." Dushok stepped into the room, and Jake shut the door.

"Hah," Jake said. "Security."

"Put the weapon away," Dushok ordered. "Or point it somewhere else."

Jake hesitated, then set it on the small table. "How'd you find me?"

"Wei-hua. No woman can keep a secret."

"Can a man?"

"Some men."

Jake wondered.

"Maps," Dushok noticed.

"Thought I might travel, once I get on my feet."

"You ought to have a sizable stake by now."

Jake met his eye for a few seconds, then quailed.

"They'd sure love to have you back," Dushok said comfortably. "Even the locals are in an uproar."

"The locals? What do they care?"

"Sucking up to the Americans as usual. Cash reward, too."

"God damn," Jake said sadly. "I was just trying to keep the brass in order. They deserved what they got, you know."

Dushok nodded. "Maybe so."

Jake said nothing.

"There's a lot of scuttlebutt in both languages," Dushok said. "There's a lot of people know a lot of stuff about you. Way I figure it, you're about even with the Corps. And there's a good deal to be said for decking a general every so often. But I was wrong. You're not worth saving. You're just another nickel-and-dime punk. You sure fooled me."

"Don't wave the flag. You've gone your own way more than once."

"I don't break my word," Dushok said. "I'm a lifer, remember. Choosy about the company I keep."

"Well, I was a lifer too, maybe," Jake said.

"No more. You're out, and good riddance."

"You about to nail my ass to the wall?"

"Maybe. Maybe I don't have to. Maybe China would do it for me. You're a babe in arms out here. Milk on your chin. I see you in ten years down to a hundred pounds and up to four pipes a day, or pulling a wagon with a chain around your middle and your nuts in somebody's ditty bag."

Silence thickened between them; the street too was still.

"That's if you even made it through the next month or so," Dushok went on. "We're all clearing out, you know. More shoving off for Guam, and the rest to Tsingtao pretty soon."

After another silence Jake spoke: "Well, good luck. Not much more to say."

"I suppose not." But then Dushok said angrily, "For Chrissake, I'm here for your own good! You're a man without a country."

"Thass a crock," Jake said. "Or maybe I always was. I was a kid and then I was a Marine. I was an exile before I could even vote. I killed a man before I was even old enough to make a bank loan."

"You're a fool," Dushok said. "Don't blame it on the rest of the world. You had it made."

"Made!" Jake said. "Thass a crock too! You kiss their ass all your life and if you don't get a bullet in the belly or beat to death in the brig, they give you a pension and let you sit on a rocking chair in San Diego for the rest of your life. I got places to go. I got things to do. God's sake, man! I never even lived alone!"

"You were a good professional," Dushok said. "Now you're nothing. Less than nothing."

"God damn you," Jake said hotly.

"You're on the run," Dushok pressed him. "But you can't make it. They'll crucify you. They talk here, word goes around, a poor country like this there's always ten men to do any dirty job. And you trust Kao!"

"Leave him out of it," Jake snarled.

Dushok said, "I don't know what's up, but I guarantee you one thing—there's more to it than you know about. They've got your balls in a vise and you're too dumb to shake loose."

"Ah, go to hell," Jake said. "Go on. Go home."

"You moron," Dushok said, suddenly waggling a .45. "Up against the bulkhead. I'm taking you in. For your own good."

"You bastard," Jake said. "You bastard."

Dushok crowded him back to the wall and took the other .45 from the night table. "Grab your socks," he said with a joyless grimace. "Move slow. Someday you'll bless me for this."

Jake hoisted his pack, half blinded by his own rage.

"Move out." Dushok prodded him. "I got a hand on this pack and don't fool around. Just move out, and turn left, and let's us walk down the alley like real gents. There's a jeep waiting, and the Shore Patrol."

Jake stepped into the warm night. "Christ, I never get one break."

"Just turn left."

They padded down the dark alley, between the high walls. No place to run. S.P.'s with handcuffs, and billies. Jake cursed aloud. He cursed with bitter ferocity. They had him now, after all this they had him, because that god damn Mei-li could not keep her mouth shut and neither could that hag Wei-hua, they had him in chains, and someday I will beat the shit out of this little hunky fag emperor. "This is what you call not breaking your word," he snarled. "This is what you call honor and all that shit," and he cursed Dushok slowly and savagely.

He made so much noise cursing that he barely heard the slither, up on the roof tiles, but he heard the crunch of one body battering down on another, and the whack and thud when Dushok dropped. The landlord! Thank God for the landlord! "Don't hurt him," Jake whispered. "Don't kill him!" He stooped quickly then, saying, "Wait one wait," and slipped his .45 from Dushok's inner pocket. He grinned at this sport, even as he heard voices far down the alley.

"Follow quickly," the Chinese said. It was not his landlord. Jake did not care who it was; he paced swiftly after. Behind him the S.P.'s cursed, stumbling over Dushok. Jake ran. He skidded, threw a hand behind him and came to rest with his palm in a large patch of slime. "What have you found?" the Chinese asked.

"A mound of dogshit," Jake said unhappily.

"Over this wall."

Now Jake heard his landlord's voice, behind him, arguing with the S.P.'s, outraged, shouting like a lunatic. This new fellow was on the wall and reaching down: "Give me the other hand." Jake clasped, set, sprang. He scrabbled for the top of the wall, lay on his belly for a breath, and dropped hard on the other side, the pack slewing. "Through here."

Jake panted, "Did you knife him?" They were racing through a courtyard, around a spirit wall. Their footsteps echoed off a dozen walls. They slipped like shadows into the street, a thoroughfare, rick-shas, shops, knots of men, lanterns.

Jake wiped his hand on a rough wall, and inspected his new friend. "What are you? Who sent you?"

The man was young, and round of face, with eyes that sparkled like a funning child's. "Why, I am a camel-puller," he said, "and the gods sent me. In the person of Master Ch'ing, who has been urged to watch over you. I have drunk much hot wine with the landlord and kept a wide eye on you. That is a beautiful woman you have, and one day you will introduce me. Just in here, now. A safe restaurant, and a couch, and a pipe if you desire. Then go to the Field of Camels at dawn."

"Did you knife him?"

A swift pass, and the blade gleamed. "You see: clean. The hilt, however, is of brass, and was in my fist when I bashed him. He will sleep."

Jake was sweating, and now he quivered. Obstacle course with full field pack. Who else lurked on dark roofs. "I left a pair of leather boots."

"Then they are gone. You will never go back, now." Old Kao had said something like that.

They entered a moon-gate, and crossed a courtyard to a dim restaurant. Jake said, "I am called Ta-tze, and I thank you."

"My own unworthy name is Chin Tan-te," and the young man bowed. It sounded like "Jim Dandy" and that was good enough for Jake. Jim Dandy's nose wrinkled: "A bowl of hot water, to wash those hands."

"And the cloth shoes," Jake grumbled.

"Wash the shoes too," Jim said. "Such an omen! With all the elements, arts and precious things that might bless our meeting, you choose dog's-donation."

Jake washed, and cleaned off his shoes. This was a Mongolian restaurant. On a table in the center of the room stood a grill like a giant mushroom; within it a coal fire burned, and on its charred outer surface patties of beef and lamb lay plastered, cooking slowly. They were doused with spicy sauces and laid between halves of bun.

On his last night in Peking he was eating hamburgers.

The few other diners, evil and swarthy in the low light, checked him once and then ignored him. The proprietor saw to his wants and made no conversation.

Soon Jake was murderously sad, two-o'clock-in-the-morning sad. He ached for Mei-li but she did not appear.

He remembered much that night: how it was to be a boy, and how it was to be a gunnery sergeant. He raged at Mei-li, and burned for her. After eating he called for a pipe. A griping at the heart. A night of evil portent.

At first light he took up his pack and left, walking cautiously through empty streets that filled as he moved along. The Field of Camels was all noise and motion, and the sun was rising. The camels looked huge. He reported to Ch'ing, who told him to stand by, and introduced him to two camel-pullers. One of them was Chin Tan-te, who bowed gravely and made a solemn face, and then sniffed fastidiously, with a wink.

By then Jake was wide awake. He was expected to help load, and that was new work, and warmed his heart, and soon they were shouting back and forth and prodding the surly camels, and the sun was up. His own sweat cheered him, and sight and smell of the animals, and the action and the racket.

He did not see Kao, and was disappointed.

Then he led his camels into place, and Ch'ing trotted up and down the line and called out, yipping like a Mongol, and they were on their way. Shoving off. Moving out. While children scampered and hollered at the roadside, Jacob Alvin Dodds plodded toward the Western Gate of Peking, the greatest of all cities. Old Ta-tze plodded toward the Western Gate and the camel in front of him broke wind copiously. Toward the Western Gate, toward Mongolia, toward the middle of Asia.

Toward his last sight of Master Kao, friend and partner.

Some hours later, when the sun was westering, when the caravan was well past the Six-Bullock Shortcut, when Peking had begun to cool after the midday doldrums, one of the black birds pecking at Kao dislodged the blindfold, and a young farmer, strong and cheerful, who had just become engaged and was driving some thirty white geese into Peking, hissed in horror at the burnt-out eye sockets.

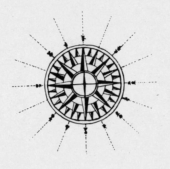

11 / MONGOLIA

10/   "Dogs defile your great-grandmothers, all four of the chicken-defiling bags of dung!"

"What's that for?" Jake asked. Master Ch'ing had a way of talking. Kao had said to trust him somewhat, but any one of these people might turn out light-fingered, or a cutthroat. Jake was sleeping with his pack for a pillow and the automatic to hand beneath it. He was trying to develop the habit, to remember to reach for it as his eyes opened. Mornings he woke light-hearted, blinking and yawning into the pearly dawn, and most days only saw the belt and holster when he had loaded, eaten and swung his pack aboard Bad Smell. The first few days he looked back often, riding tail-end to be the first to spot pursuit; but there was no pursuit, so he felt pretty perky on the whole.

"A camel is down," Ch'ing hollered, and trotted to the rear.

"Bugger it," Jake called after him, "that's not my fault," and he barely heard Ch'ing's answer, floating on the dusty air above the sound of hoofbeats: "Ya! Foreigner!"

Jim Dandy said, "Let's go see."

The lien had halted. They were through the Great Wall and headed for the Yellow River.

Jim was Jake's partner, and there was a third partner for the lien of eighteen camels, because Jake could not be trusted to do a camel-puller's work; this third partner was Chu-chu, a stocky dark man of about forty, bald as the moon and full of lore. He was a Mohammedan and the only honest way to translate his name was Pig-pig.

Jim called, "They're all yours, Chu-chu," and waved Jake into a trot. Jake was finding that he had marched for too many years to run well now. Jim was twenty-five or so but had the manner of an old hand, cursing the meals, the road, the sun, the soldiers, women or the lack of them, the lice. He had pulled camels for nine years and was mischievous, a round-faced prankster. He and Jake puffed back to Ch'ing and Hsü-to and the injured camel. Hsü-to was another Mohammedan, bald and skinny, a famous camel-racer in his youth.

The camel was a cow about eight years old that had wandered off the trail and broken her near foreleg; she had wedged the hoof into a crevice between black rocks. "Bugger," Ch'ing snarled at Jake, and sat there on his lean pony for half a minute, orange-eyed and with a mouth full of rage. He cursed, and cursed some more.

"One thing after another," Jim said pleasantly. "It is the way of the caravan. No need to blow the mustache."

Ch'ing said approximately, "Bullshit," and glowered for some time while the others awaited his wisdom. Finally he told them, "All right. Split the load. Can't be helped. Foreigner's luck."

Jim took up for Jake in swift Tientsin slang, and when Ch'ing said something else that Jake could not catch Jim spat and told him to shut up. Ch'ing said, "Defile you all. Next time mules."

"What does that mean," Jake asked, " 'blowing the mustache?' "

"To talk wildly," Jim said, and to Ch'ing, "Five mules carry what four camels carry."

"They're faster."

"But do not last."

This was singing more than talking; an old conversation.

"Nor do they spit."

"But they bite."

Hsü-to and Jim were off-loading, swiftly, old hands, wasting no motion in the scorching sunlight.

"Nor do they reproduce, and take time off like women."

"But they are as stubborn as women, and argue as loudly; and when a cow camel drops a calf, she is back on the trail that same day."

Ch'ing surrendered sourly. "Camels it is. But no more foreigners. Hurry now."

Jim's look reined Jake in, but when Ch'ing had trotted off Jake defiled all caravan masters, in particular one Ch'ing, who was better fitted by ancestry, looks and talent to be master of a honey-cart.

"That's not bad," Jim said, "but remember he's the boss. The sole and absolute boss, and he can have you shot. On the trail even the owner obeys him."

That was a jolt.

"It is the way," Jim said.

Hsü-to pouted heavily. "Times have changed. In the old days a man did not show sorrow or anger when he threw away a camel. In the old days he said, 'It is nothing. One camel.'"

That Chinaman could have Jake shot. And take his goods because they belonged to no one else now.

Chu-chu shambled back to them leading two camels.

"Those are my camels," Jake said.

"Master Ch'ing orders the load split," Chu-chu said, and yawned.

"I pay for the use of these camels and they will carry my goods and no one else's. Besides, this would overload them according to the precepts and ordinances of the aforementioned Master Shit-merchant Ch'ing himself." Jake was pale with anger. "Ch'ing is a turtle. More-over a grasshopper. Moreover a cow pie. Moreover diseased. Call him back and I will tell him this."

The cook, who was called Head of Pot, shuffled up with two more beasts. "Split four ways," he announced.

"Split Ch'ing four ways," Jake said.

Jim said, "Let it be, now. A fourth part will not hurt your camels. In Pao-t'ou it can be discussed, and arrangements made."

The four Chinese waited without expression. Jake paced and snorted, for show. "All right," he said. "Four ways."

They worked quickly: in ten minutes four hundred pounds of cargo had been divided, reloaded and secured. Every man but Hsü-to took a rein, and they led the camels back. As far as Jake's eyes could see the plain lay yellow, shimmering in the heat. He was still furious, and the sun was a fierce burden, and he could see for miles, and it was exhilarating. At certain moments he felt a true emotion, and could not help it. China. Soon Mongolia.

After a few steps he remembered, and called to Jim. "That cow."

"What about her?"

"You just leave her?"

They had all halted now, and the camels nattered softly. The Chinese were bewildered but hoped to be helpful. "Why does that matter?"

"It's cruel. Barbarous. She'll suffer."

Hsü-to was astonished. "*You* call *us* barbarous?"

Jim asked, "What do you want to do?"

"Shoot her."

The four exchanged glances.

"You waste a bullet," Hsü-to said, "but go ahead."

Jake jogged back the few steps, hearing Hsü-to go on to the others, "It is not for sport, surely?" The cow's eye was dull and vacant. She was chewing her cud. Her snob's nose was dry. Her foreleg angled weirdly but she seemed not to notice. Jake drew the .45 and shot her at the intersection of a cross between her ears and eyes. She sagged, rolled over, quivered once, stretched mightily and died.

Ch'ing came galloping back. "May you be defiled," he screamed, "by the elf that eats the brains of the dead!" He shouted it to the winds, to the plain, he wanted all to know in Karakorum and Peking and Kashgar what a pack of maggot-ridden goat droppings he was cursed with. "Now what?"

Jim explained.

Ch'ing slumped and blew a despondent breath. "All right. This I know about. Foreigners love animals and beat children. They have secret societies for the protection and advancement of animals. But I never in my life saw so many bad signs on one trip." He jabbed a finger at Jake and said, "I cannot risk the luck of the whole caravan."

"You did that when you took my money," Jake said.

"And the lord of all under heaven will punish me for it." Ch'ing brooded. Jake brooded, too, and the others were hot and tired in the midday sun, and tension rose like sweat. Ch'ing broke it. "At least you kill what you shoot at."

After a moment the camel-pullers snickered, and then laughed, and after another moment Jake joined them. Ch'ing was his sole and absolute boss.

11/   Dushok sat in his room at the Palace of the Night Chickens. He was comfortable in a black cotton robe and black cloth shoes. His oil lamp burned brightly, and on the table before him was stationery of coarse texture, also rich ink that he had mixed himself and a pair of fine writing brushes.

Wei-hua glowed, and Dushok knew deep melancholy. Wei-hua was unaware that he must soon leave, a week, two. She was a nice old girl, close to forty but not the least crease, not even behind the knee, and she was less trouble, more comfort, and more wisdom than any woman he had ever known.

He wetted a brush, and wrote. It was his eighth letter, and they were the same except that some began "Elder Brother" and some "Younger Brother." They described a large, yellow-colored American, former partner of the late merchant Kao Hu-tsuan, and stated that he was a villain. No man knew where he was now or might be later, but his return, to any set of authorities, would be a favor to Dushok, Tu Hsia-k'u, who hopes that you will feel yourself bound, as he does, by ties of ancient friendship and dangers shared.

He paused, and rubbed his sore head. Wei-hua came closer, a question in her eyes.

"No no," he said. "It is well and will heal." He gazed into her round, loving, untroubled face. "My friend," he said. She blushed for joy.

Dushok wrote on. *Should he suffer damage, or noxious influences, no man will grieve. It is not that he has done worse than you, my friend, or I; it is that he lies to those close to him, and takes from them and does violence to them. He is a man of talents but poor bones, who will never look upon the face of the lord of all under heaven.*

"A pipe, Wei-hua." The Palace was to be owned now by an assistant to General Liu; Dushok had spoken to the man. For a year at least Wei-hua would be safe. After that . . . after that, Communists, and the poor old girl would be out of a job. He would leave her money.

One of the letters was addressed to a certain Pei Ti-wen, a scholar and gambler in Lanchow, a city in Kansu, a western province; and in a corner of the envelope, writ small, was the character *hu,* meaning tiger. Pei, whose surname meant Cowrie Shell, or Treasure, and whose given name meant Guide to Literature, was also the head of an extensive family society in northwest China, and friend, as Dushok was, to more than one wandering outlaw. Dushok could not know which of the eight letters was the best bet; but he did know that the word would go forth, by crooked ways, all over China, and someday, in a wineshop or on a barge, at a customs post or a beggars' clubhouse, the connection would be made.

Dushok had heard of Kao's death with sorrow. Old Kao had lived a natural life in iniquitous times; while Jake Dodds had betrayed two centuries of courage and honor.

I must now depart from you, and from this middle kingdom that I love, and only the lord of all under heaven can know when I shall see my friends again.

Long life and prosperity.

12/   The caravan had run across no Communists but plenty of Nationalist soldiers, a small detachment quartered on most villages of any size, surly riffraff in half-uniforms and an officer in shiny boots. All these Genghis Khans had the authority to stop them, to check papers, to inspect goods, not to mention hanging everybody or lining them up before a firing squad, so every day or two out came the documents, and the arguments, and a handful of squeeze, and men stood sweating and camels stood farting while Ch'ing palavered. There seemed to be an established tariff. Ch'ing objected not to graft but to greed.

"There are honest men too in the army," Jim said. "Think how they must feel."

Jake shut up and kept out of sight. Foreigners inspired pushy officers with superfluous zeal. They came prowling and sniffing with their three words of English, and told you how they had killed Japanese, or maintained order among these villagers. They would confide in Chinese, "Peasants, of course," and Jake, who was also a peasant, stood with a face of stone pretending little skill in language.

The people were skinny. Jake saw few dogs and no cats. Once he saw the fuselage of an American pursuit plane housing two families; once the wreck of a Japanese Zero; more than once a dead tank or jeep. Villagers lined the road and stared. "The Communists are an hour from here," one lieutenant told Jake. "These people are not thinkers. They are peasants. The Communists deceive them." Jake stood by his camels. In some villages the walls were plastered with posters and announcements. Jake could not read. If the posters were important, Jim would tell him so.

Often after a day's march they would file through a village while music blared, or political speeches, from scratchy phonographs or a loudspeaker outside the police station. Jake saw no power plants or generators, and decided all this noise was transmitted by battery-operated relics of another age.

Most places the police station was the only government building. Being a deep one, Jake figured this meant the police were the only government.

Once he saw a man beaten by the authorities: a flexible bamboo slat snapping across the soles of his feet like a lash.

Once a joker in the crowd asked if he was Russian. "American," Jake said.

The man cried, "Hu! Pei erh-shih chiu! Pei erh-shih chiu!"

Jake turned to Jim. "Bay twenty-nine?"

"B-29."

"They bombed here?"

Jim shrugged. "He heard about Hiroshima."

Under the sun they shambled, Jake looking back less and less but still uneasy, still a fugitive. Mile after mile. Day after day. Jim Dandy said, "You exaggerate. New men always exaggerate. They march and march, and fall asleep marching, and after a hundred days they say, 'Five thousand miles.' " Depending on the terrain, and on the number and quality of the military grafters encountered, they covered twenty to thirty miles each day. Jake slogged along, with plenty of time to think, and to listen to Jim, whose mouth ran on.

His worries slowly dropped away, and he hoped he was turning Chinese. The memory of Kao grew warm and less bitter: a good fat man, and a bad break, a sad end, but maybe it had nothing to do with Jake. Jake was not Kao's only enterprise. He remembered Kao's cautions, and was puzzled. The goods were ordinary. He wondered if there could be jewels hidden among them, or opium.

Not opium, he learned. Jim rode down—the caravans "walked up" west and "rode down" east—with a stash of opium in cold weather. "But in hot weather it smells. They sniff it out and confiscate it, and show you the smile of a weasel."

Jake kept seeing equipment, a young woman wearing a Japanese fatigue cap, or a man in Japanese boots ditching. In one village the community was building a wall, everybody out slaving away, singing and shouting, skinny and short-tempered, hauling buckets of mud, buckets of water from the ditch; hauling sacks of dirt; half a dozen hauling a cart full of broken stone, and the cart was a Japanese caisson. He saw khaki.

One day he saw a dozen farmers, men and women both, he supposed, making hay about a mile off, like a mural on a schoolhouse wall, the vast yellow-green blotch of the grassy hillside, and the tiny figures hardly seeming to move, the dark clothes and light hats, beyond them the crest of the long slope, and then the endless sky and a single round white cloud; and no sound, only the figures, as if they had stood so for a thousand years and would never alter. One scythe would be forever uplifted, another forever cutting; one figure upright, another bent; night would never come, or winter.

He was a long way from home. About a thousand years.

No one came after him. No one touched his goods. No one here knew who he was; no one there knew where he was.

They joined the great river east of Pao-t'ou, and Jake took some time for a long by-golly look at the flow of it: broad it was, and majestic, and yellowish, sure enough, the great Huang Ho, the Yellow River, born far off, high in the snowy mountains. This was the big one, that swelled with the rains and runoff, that drowned land and people, flooded crops and left famine, killed its millions; and it was also a great road, one of the greatest and oldest, older even than the Old Silk Road. There were boats on it now, making their slow way through the glassy afternoon, fishing boats and small junks and one decrepit motor launch trailing soot, and above them a flight of cranes beating west.

Too bad he could not send a card to Dushok: having a wonderful time, you bastard.

Pao-t'ou was a big city, pigs, dogs, chickens and children, smells and racket; the streets were jammed. The caravan filed through the center of town. Jake felt fenced in. The camel-pullers bowed their heads and spat.

After an hour the slums fell behind and the road opened out. They passed between walled compounds, and once more there was plenty of sky. In midafternoon, well out of town and muttering thanks, heads high again, they filed through a broad gateway into a vast dusty field of scrawny grasses, where four hundred camels lay groaning and blowing. A few grazed on dirt.

Now Jake saw why the city was called Pao-t'ou, or Head of Packages.

Four hundred camels! Men sat among them in twos and threes; others circulated, examining hoofs or eczema. Jake saw half a dozen wells, and huge troughs. On the city side of the field stood low godowns with groups of men lounging in doorways, or hunkered in circles.

Jim Dandy sniffed out the field like a bull in a fresh meadow. Over them hung the dusty golden smell of summer air, a hint of desert, much corrupted by the stench of dung. Small, brightly colored birds scavenged in the manure. Men squinted, identified the lien, and called out. The camels wove their way among heaps of trade goods, and soon the camel-pullers were welcomed by a scurvy platoon of shirtless pirates in baggy pants and cloth shoes. Most sported charms hung around their necks on rawhide. Some had shaved heads. When they saw Jake they grimaced and said ai-ya and hu-hu.

They led the camels into place and tapped or tugged them down, Ch'ing shouting orders and the men shouting back. Across the field trooped a delegation, bosses, Jake could tell, in light gowns, some in a kind of Panama hat, a couple with parasols. They came to Ch'ing, and he reported, and the bosses examined the camels and made professional noises. Jake squatted between Bad Smell and Sweetwater and waited for instructions. A boss turned to stare at him, and then they all did, like a court-martial. One wore glasses that glittered. A fat one was chewing—gum? tobacco? a virility-root? They were like cartoons in the westering sun, with the hats and the glasses, a wrist watch winking silver, the faded pink of a parasol, one wispy white goatee.

Ch'ing cried out, and the men set about off-loading.

13/   "We have one night," Jim said.

"We leave tomorrow?"

"Day after. But tomorrow night we eat and sleep here. We leave before sunrise next day."

"What do you want to do?"

"Fuck," Jim said.

Jake grunted.

"There will be many dry weeks between rains," Jim said.

Jake grunted again, in alien territory.

Jim sighed. "I suppose you are incapable, like all foreigners."

"Bugger yourself. Then how come there are still foreigners?" By now this was routine chitchat.

Jim grinned a round grin. "Snakes."

"Bastard yourself," Jake grumbled. "This is my first time here. How can I guide you?"

"Guide me! I am Chin Tan-te, and all of Pao-t'ou knows that I am here, and ready. All of Pao-t'ou expects thunderstorms tonight."

"Dogs defile your unborn children," Jake said. "Then go spend yourself with thousands. What do you want from me?"

"Ehhh," Jim said, and fussed with an ancient, nicked pipe; he struck a wooden match and puffed intently. Jake had not before seen him embarrassed, so waited innocently for Jim's eyes to meet his own. "Ehhh," Jim said. "Listen. There are cribs. Five to a room and hags, in and out, three minutes and a sour taste for a week. Also the willow disease." Syphilis. Jake winced. "And then there are two or three places worth a man's time. Flowery willow lanes."

Jake took pity on him. "You poor sad prick. You mean money."

Jim cleared his throat.

"And you have none of your own."

Jim shrugged. "I threw it away in Peking." With an impish grin.*

"Thunderstorms."

Jim laughed aloud. "Spring and summer showers."

"You are a filthy hot weasel and no Christian," Jake said. "I owe you for one timely rescue. How much do we need, and what can we buy with it?"

"Ah," Jim said, "now that is what I call elegance of speech," and his eyes lit up, and he leaned closer.

Round-faced, raffish and jaunty, Jim led the crooked way. Jake had left his little bag of gold pieces with Ch'ing, his sole and absolute boss, but had exchanged one: his pockets bulged with bank notes. He and Jim sauntered through the summer dusk toward the city's darker center, Jim rolling like a sailor or a cowboy, singing bawdy snatches, shouting a path for the foreign devil; both in loose trousers, shirt, silk sash, cloth shoes. Citizens shied in alarm and Jim laughed them away, his black eyes bright, excited, glittering in the occasional lamplight; a beggar whined, and Jim called him a capon and shoved him off contemptuously. To pretty girls he bowed, palms together, fingertips at his lips.

They paused to watch a barber work by the flickering glow of an oil lamp, an old man, servile, shaving a policeman's head. The cop glared; they moseyed along.

Late shoppers loomed out of the purple evening, and a road gang squatted gossiping around a crusted brazier. A truck or two clanked by, and an old square-fronted automobile. Outside a wineshop music twanged and jangled, and nearby, behind a small table, sat a scholarly young man in a long gown and metal-rimmed spectacles. On the table was a tiny lamp, and in its feeble shimmer Jake saw paper, a bowl of ink, brushes. "The letter-writer," Jim sang out. "Send a poem to your within-woman."

"And why not," Jake said. "How much for a short letter to Peking?"

"Good evening," the young man said formally and quietly. He named his price, a handful of the play money, and Jim said, "A fair price. With scribes we do not bargain."

"Very good," Jake said, and to the young man, "Yes. I will send a letter."

"I am at your service." He dipped a brush in the ink and tuned up on a sheet of scratch paper. A tired donkey clopped past, towing a cartload of stovepipes, and a flight of gossiping city birds hedge-hopped along the broken pavement; the darkness deepened and a tranquil, dreamlike air settled over the street, as if they had caused an eclipse of the sun, or the past was returning and they were characters in a bearded Chinese painter's evening landscape. For many moments no one spoke; the spell lay heavy on Jake. His heart thudded, as if he had crossed a threshold and silken curtains had closed behind him forever.

"You may proceed," the young man announced.

"To the woman Mei-li," Jake began, "at the Palace of the Night Chickens, next-door to the Nagging Wife Wine Place on the Street of the Eight Virtues, south of the Ch'ien Men in Peking."

"More slowly," the letter-writer said.

Jake waited. When the brush was still, he went on: "In all Pao-t'ou there is no woman of your beauty and—" He wanted to say charm but did not know the term.

"And—?"

"Skill," he said. "The day after tomorrow, at dawn, we start west." He saw her face, the loving eyes, and drowned for an instant in the memory of her golden breasts, felt her warm hip beneath his hand; the heat of her tingled painfully in his flesh, and her woman's odor choked him. "All day on the road I remember you with—"

"With—?"

Jim came to his rescue, goggle-eyed: "With a painful discharge from the cock."

A tiny flash of anger turned to melancholy, and again the night deepened. Somewhere a hawker shouted, and the air was cool on Jake's face. "With pleasure," he said morosely. "I will ride down in spring with rings and bracelets and fine furs. And sign it Ta-tze."

"Ta-tze as the tribe?"

"Yes."

"A noble name," he said. "And that is all?"

"That is all."

"There is none other to write to?"

"None other."

"It will arrive," the scribe said. He fluttered the sheet of paper, folded it, addressed an envelope, inserted the letter, showed Jake the stamps. He pulled the lamp closer and melted the tip of a small bar of wax; removed a heavy ring from a slim finger, and pressed it carefully to the seal. He handed Jake the envelope for inspection, and counted the money. "That is correct," he said. "Thank you," and held forth a hand for the letter.

"It is I who thank you," Jake said, "but I will keep the letter for now."

The scribe was indifferent.

"A waste of money," Jim said.

Jake glared. It was not for Jim to speak of money.

"I take it back," Jim said, and in English, "Okay, okay," laughing, and Jake had to laugh with him. A waste of money it was, yes, this letter that could not be sent because Mei-li had gossiped once, and might again; but there were many things to be done in life, even love letters, and it was sinful not to do them. There would always be money. There would be a jade mountain, or a plantation of melons, or herds of fat cattle on the slopes of the western hills.

The house was not walled, not a compound; it was a two-story wooden house smack on the alley, with an overhanging balcony. Jim pushed the door open without knocking and Jake followed him into a parlor, and saw benches and small rosewood tables, cloth screens and latticework and half a dozen hurricane lamps.

A round gent, slightly gray, in a blue gown pattered to them, spoke in a singsong, bowed, gestured. He led them to benches and called out; a girl, maybe twelve, an apprentice, Jake supposed, glided in to serve them tea.

Jim and the round man haggled. Jim was specific. He ordered like a rich and corrupt businessman. Thus the rice, and the beef with white vegetables, and lotus-root, and thus the tea, and the women of such and such a height, and of this age and that disposition, and clean and not fat. In the west would be fat women aplenty; now they desired slim and musical women, as an emperor might keep.

The round man nodded and approved. He appreciated clients who were knowing and sensitive to quality.

"First we will be bathed and groomed, and will rest a bit," Jim said. Then supper, and then more rest. Were there foreign cigarettes? Good. Of what name?

"Fool," Jake said. "I have thousands."

"Those are goods," Jim said. "Besides, these will be Russian, long and with gold tips."

The round man left them, and Jim winked. He rubbed his hands in pure lechery, and patted his crotch. Jake showed disgust and Jim chuckled. At the sound of footsteps they fell silent. An old woman with bound feet hobbled into the room, and four girls followed, all in silk.

They knelt in a row, and bowed, and rose to be judged.

They look so clean, Jake thought; his blood surged.

Jim went to them, and surprised Jake: he stood before each in turn, and did not laugh, and gazed into their eyes. With the tip of a finger he stroked their bodies. He selected the one in red, and they bowed a brief greeting. Jim urged Jake forward, and Jake did as Jim had done. The old lady watched closely. Jake chose the one in saffron; the other two bowed and retired. The old lady clucked and muttered. "Prepare the bath," Jim ordered, "and set out good cigarettes." The old lady hobbled out. "Tea," Jim said, and the girl in red poured. The two girls stood patiently as the men sipped. "No hurry," Jim said. "It is wrong to hurry. A man must make the most of each time. There are poisoned wells in life, and sandstorms."

Jake said, "Yes," and ogled his saffron beauty.

They climbed a flight of wooden stairs, still courtly, no grab-assing on the stairway, and entered a dim and steamy room. Jake saw two k'angs, and two huge stone tubs, and a warm mist rising from the tubs and along their edges flasks and jars and lacquered boxes. Saffron led him to a k'ang and plucked at the cloth buttons of his striped shirt; she slipped his shoes off, and untied his red sash, and soon he stood naked and breathless in the yellow lamplight. Saffron made happy moan at the golden hair on his dark chest.

They went to the tubs, and Jake inhaled oily fragrances. He was groaning within, but the others were calm and ceremonious, as if performing rituals in a temple, and then Jim looked close and shouted, "Look at him! Trimmed! A Turk, a Turk!" The girls giggled, and Jake hiccuped a laugh and remembered that he was in an expensive fancy house. His flesh rose: "Aha!" he said, and stepped into the tub.

Saffron soaped him, raising a thick froth on his furry chest; she kneaded his shoulders, and her exhalations were warm and spicy. She spilled oils into the bath, and Jake drowsed in the soft, swelling mingle of odors, his dauber breaking the surface like a periscope. Saffron oiled it; he sang like a sick hog and plucked at her gown with a wet hand; she let the gown fall, stood smiling and waited for his compliments. He babbled sweet talk at her, sweet and low, slid his oily hand between her legs and tugged her into the bath. They splashed and slid like otters in the buttery water. Jake would not, or could not, wait. "Sit," he whispered, "sit, take it, take it." She sat above him showing her teeth, her creamy breasts bouncing; she took him into her and he cried out at the sudden warmth, seized her hips in his horny hands and rammed his way to heaven in a hurry, blowing spume like a whale, his whole body arching and exploding, fingers and toes and all. In time he let go and sank back, drowning happily. "So big!" she said. "You devil!" He had heard the words a thousand times before; he knew he had not pleased her, but her turn would come, for love or money.

Later he slept, on the k'ang; later he woke, at peace. First thing he saw was old Jim's behind, waving in the gloom; Jim was horsing Red and humming and his behind was not much different from a woman's, smooth and hairless and glimmering olive; he and she might have been one woman, breasts hanging, glistening and swaying, two heads, four legs, a strange beast rocking and cooing. Jim's hum rose and grew urgent; he flung back his head and yipped, and Jake looked away in simple decency and pillowed his face on Saffron's flower.

At dinner the girls served them. Jake ate like an orphan. The tea was aromatic and the girls sprinkled a powder into it for "a renewal of vigor." No need. The rest of that night their shadows danced on the walls. Saffron and Jake loved like serpents, braided a dozen different ways, pulsing and shifting, bobbing and tumbling; or like savages in some primitive carnival, a wild whirl of hot, wet flesh. Jim and Jake did not change partners. There was no need. They were all one body, moiling and plunging, one tribe, as if each of them was, and was within, and was beside, around, beneath, all the others at once. For one crazy moment Jake thought that he *was* Saffron, and had breasts. This scared him, and he laid off and drank wine.

In the morning they ate rice and salt pork, with green tea, and left tips. The teapot sat on a small brazier, and was kept hot by three burning coal balls. Jake raised the pot, set his letter to Mei-li on the coal balls, and laughed ruefully as it curled and charred.

14/   The sun lay sparkling on the sprawled caravanserai, the great Head of Packages, on men and camels, mules and donkeys and horses and ponies. The sky was blue and gold and the clamor was deafening, ceaseless, whoops and gabble, neighs, heehaws, the chants and complaints of men working.

For half a mile the flat plain boiled and rippled, the beasts agitated and restless, the men sorting, stacking and loading. Most were stripped to the waist; some repaired leather while others toted sacks, and many were shaving the heads of many others, and the sunlight glinted off razors.

Committees roved the field, brokers, bankers, merchants, self-important owners, men of the great trading houses, some harassed and gesturing, some gowned and majestic, one at least a genuine geezer, a couple of hundred years old and haughty, with a cobweb of white whisker, a boy to carry the parasol, and a caged yellow bird in his papery left hand: he passed near Jake, saw him, flickered in surprise and dismissed him as a mirage. Honey-carts circulated like bees among blossoms; maybe camel dung was special. A fat brown man in a loincloth pared a donkey's hoof with a short knife.

Soon long strings of camels would fade off the far reaches of the plain, creeping westward over thousands of miles and thousands of years. And other strings would meet them, crawling eastward, and fill the plain again, ebb and flow, forever, men dead and born, camels thrown away, horses lame, mules dead of thirst, but always more, always the ebb and flow, and far away the sunny plain would end and the frozen mountain passes begin, and the camels with bloody pads and pack sores, and white cranes flying and red bears in the hills. Jake was the only white man there, Jim said.

When they inspected the arsenal, Ch'ing said, "I do not like firearms. Businessmen dislike trouble."

"Trouble is also opportunity."

"It is also camels thrown away, and goods lost on the desert."

"Let me clean these. Nobody takes care of them."

"The desert," Ch'ing said. "Grease in the bore and then sand."

"Not only the bore. The inner works."

"Clean them," Ch'ing said, and sighed. "For luck."

While he worked, camel-pullers edged his way to stare. One was a hard, flat-faced man with a gold earring, stony eyes and a killer's mouth. He was rude: "Who are you, foreigner?"

"Ta-tze," Jake said, "master of arms for Ch'ing's caravan of the House of Wu in Tientsin. Who are you?"

"Why are you doing that?"

"Because these sons of mislaid eggs do not, and these weapons, neither cleaned nor repaired since ancient times and last used to bugger elephants, require the attention of a master."

"Such talk," the Chinese said, and they were friends for a moment. Jake never saw him again.

"In the old days," Ch'ing intoned, "we knew where they were."

"In the Ordos," Jim said. "The Elder Brother bandits."

"You were not born," Ch'ing said with disgust.

"They were nothing," Chu-chu said. "West of the Black Gobi were the worst. Killers of women and children."

"Foreigners attract them," Ch'ing said with a sour glance for Jake. "How it is, I do not know, but they always hear of foreigners. They ride hundreds of miles to snatch such freaks, and they hope for ransom."

They sat around the low fire, a dozen of them, some smoking crude pipes, some cigarettes. Head of Pot sat on a low stool, six inches off the ground; that was his privilege. They had eaten rice and a sheep, and when Jake left a string of meat on a bone he was reprimanded: the sheep had given his all for them and Jake had insulted his spirit. It was a trader's belief and not a camel-puller's, but the men of the caravan respected it. In a heap the bones gleamed yellow.

Above the plain, stars glinted silver in a black sky. Cigarettes glowed; belches rang. The small intestine was coated with fat, and was a delicacy; so was a tiny bit behind each ear. Jake had managed a cheek, but these more exotic cuts required experience and courage.

"And the villains of Yunbeize," one said.

"And those of the Sairon Nor." Nor was Mongol for a lake.

"Many, many," Ch'ing said. "Before my time there was the False Lama, and the renegade priest of Bogdo Ola. Now there are thousands, and of no courage. Deserters. Soldiers still in uniform. Japanese who will never go home. It is a world full of riffraff and foreigners."

"What do they do for arms?" Jake imagined the empty fetches of desert, no towns, no water; how could bandits live?

"They buy. They steal."

"And still you go."

"And will when they are gone," Ch'ing said.

The men approved.

"All will be well," Ch'ing said. "This Tartar tells me he brings good luck." They all nodded Jake's way and said hao. "Listen, Tartar," Ch'ing went on, "are those Brownings clean?"

"Yes. One is no good. A broken sear. It would empty itself at a touch."

Ch'ing grinned. "Like Chin Tan-te."

"Three pa of camels defile your mother," Jim said swiftly. "Those who can no longer get it up should refrain from criticism."

"Can it be repaired?" Ch'ing asked.

"Yes. I'll take a piece from the Sten and cut it to size."

"Too much talk of guns," Head of Pot said, old and skinny. Maybe when camel-pullers lost their youth and strength they bucked for Head of Pot. "And what about food?"

The men jeered and made gagging sounds.

"Why is that a problem?" Jake asked.

"Because the flocks are scattered and the nomads too. Because the bandits and soldiers take everything. There is neither honor nor stability and all under heaven is fucked up. In the old days," and Ch'ing's eyes gazed sadly off toward the old days, "we bought many sheep, or traded for them."

"When you throw away a camel . . ." Jake began.

"Shut up," Jim said.

Ch'ing sighed again. What they call a man of cares. "Well, he is new. And he says he brings good luck. And it is my fault in the first place for even wasting talk on a big-nose. So we must teach him. Listen." He raised a hand to Jake, palm out like a traffic cop. "Camel-pullers do not eat the meat of camels, little brother. Nor buy and sell the hides. Remember that."

"I'll remember."

"Camel-pulling is not a low trade, but a nation," Chu-chu said.

"All right, thanks," Jake said. "I have a lot to learn."

"Thank us later," Ch'ing said. "Thank us after a thousand miles of desert. Thank us after bandits. Thank us after poisoned grass. Thank us after the flies that drink blood. Thank us after a winter journey through Dead Mongol Pass."

A murmur rose again in the firelight, and men looked up at the cold stars. "Winter," one said. "Dead Mongol Pass. There we throw away men also."

15/   They rode out at dawn after the customary slop, and pointed northwest in a cool yellow glow, Jake aboard a camel. Ch'ing's principals had dumped some shoddy in Pao-t'ou, also wire and insulators, all at a handsome profit, so Ch'ing was less surly, fat with praise, and invited Jake to load light and be a guest. Jim and Jake contrived a lumpy hollow in the cargo and Jake clambered up and sprawled between the humps. Jim prodded Bad Smell to his feet and Jake damn near fell off in four different directions at once. He hung on and settled in, and the sky rocked.

They covered some twelve miles by early noon, and dismounted to let the camels lie down and snuffle up a ration of dried peas from nose bags.

They began to live by wells: three days to this one and seven days to that one. At the Well of the God that Injures Horses three old stone basins lay baking in the sun like altars. The water was sweet. At each well every man topped off his canteens and skins. Ch'ing would trot by to see that Jake had done right; then he would glower some and ride off.

Small businessmen popped up like prairie dogs. A leathery trader on a donkey, or two dried-up old-timers with a broken-down camel. They came shambling out of the west with a little cargo of pelts and a lump of pure jade, or a big bale of mountain wool, and a few strings of jerky like a fringe on the saddle. One wore a tall hat like an ice-cream cone. They bowed to Ch'ing and cried their wares, then watched deadpan as the rich caravan sailed past.

Jake was riding rear guard, this famous gunner with his rifle and his pistol, and clips and bandoleers woven into his cargo; he would turn to watch these traders disappear to the east, and they did disappear, shrinking to a forlorn dot and then nothing, as if they had evaporated in the dazzle. Hundreds of miles, alone on the rocky desert, with a load worth maybe a hundred dollars.

They were in a village called Shandanmiao when Jake met Major K'uang for the first time. Shandan was Mongol for a small stream, and miao was Chinese for a temple. That was the old name. On Jake's new map it was Santemiao, all Chinesed and with a new meaning, the three something temple, maybe virtues. An abandoned monastery, some traders and some nomads, some summer yurts and cloth tents, a teahouse, a famous horse doctor, a blind Taoist priest kept alive by the traders for luck, and many donkeys. Some women and a small rabble of scruffy, snotty children.

Jake was no richer yet and somewhat gritty. Sun and flies and the stink of camels. He was also raising a crop of crabs, and they itched like hell. There were women here, and he itched that way too.

The nomads were bastard Mongols, "mixed seeds" according to Jim, and no threat, some of them hardly wandering any more but spending much of the year here, the men herding their flocks out to distant pastures for a couple of months at a time and then herding them back.

The yurts were round, made of sheepskin and felt and patched with cloth, topped by low conical roofs with a smoke hole in the middle. The tents were cotton, some of it woven and designed and some of it just patchwork.

The women were not shy, and wore funny little hats with pieces of stone and metal worked into them; also long gowns over cotton trousers. Some of the gowns had high collars, also with ornaments worked in. The children did not wear much of anything.

Jake had been nervous when they first marched into Shandanmiao. He thought it might be women so near, and him not knowing if they flopped for nickels and dimes or if their men would stick you for looking. That was at dusk; next morning he understood. It was the straight lines. He watched the sun strike the village, and the light and shadow made straight lines. There were paths worn into the sand and rock, streets and alleys almost. It did not seem right. Citified. Jake resented it. He had become a man of horizons.

After breakfast he asked Jim if they could buy a woman.

"Indeed," Jim said. "The men are mostly away. These people don't care much anyway. In the old days they offered visitors a spare wife for the night."

So they bought a couple of women and burrowed into a small yurt at the edge of the village and it was like having your hat blocked. Like a shack outside a mining town. Jake supposed she was comely by local standards.

Then they went back to their camels and Hsü-to saw the cloud of dust.

Hsü-to rose up on his hind legs, made some thoughtful noises, shaded his eyes with a dark hand and called out, "Hungry ghosts!"

"What's a hungry ghost?" Jake asked Jim.

"An unexpected visitor." Jim squinted out at the rocky flats. The air shimmered. "Camels," he said.

"About a dozen," Hsü-to said.

The land was empty. Jake peered again and it was still empty. "Where? Help the blind. Pity the aged."

Jim laid a priestly hand on Jake's head and said to the others, "I told him many times, I did indeed. Over and over I warned him. Self-abuse, I said, leads—"

"What a dirty boy you are!" Chu-chu said, and to Jake, "Now you can see. That cloud of dust to the left of the red hill."

"Hill," Jake said. They had played no tricks on him yet, these were men and not boys, but maybe the time had come. In boot camp Jake had been sent for water grenades, rubber ramrods and other such items. "Red hill, is it. If this is a joke, it's a bad one. If it's true, you're blowing the cow."

Insulted, Chu-chu said, "Camel-pullers never brag."

Jake would not lie. Even ten minutes later he would not lie: "I see nothing."

"It comes of reading," Chu-chu said. "Slowly the small hole in the center of the eye is filled in."

"They're at a walk," Jim said. "They'll be here in two hours."

"Soldiers," Hsü-to said. "Two scouts riding before, out wide."

"You joke," Jake said.

"Bandits approach at night," Hsü-to explained, "so as not to be shot to death. And caravans are longer."

"Maybe it's just some travelers from the next town."

Hsü-to said, "There is no next town."

Jake went to his pack and came back with binoculars.

Jim cried, "Ha! A four-eyed person!" and they laughed fit to bust, Chu-chu booming and Hsü-to shrieking.

"What's funny?" Jake asked sourly.

Chu-chu caught his breath and whacked Jake on the shoulder. "It means a pregnant woman."

With warm interest Jim asked, "Who is the father?"

"I ignore this," Jake said. "The rude nattering of ruttish rams." He focused the glasses.

He saw a low red hill where none had been before, and a light plume of dust.

"Soldiers coming," Jake said softly to Ch'ing. The sun was high and merciless. There was no shade out of doors and there was no indoors without an invitation.

"The patrol, no doubt," Ch'ing said. "You too are a soldier, I think."

"I think so, too. Will you find out quickly if this patrol hears gossip of the east? By wireless, or aircraft, since we left."

Ch'ing squinted. "Indeed," he said, in shrewd good spirits. "If they take you off my hands, the goods are mine."

"You're a cold-blooded one," Jake said.

"A realist," Ch'ing said. "What could they have learned from Peking?"

"These are Kao's goods. If the manner of his dying was scandalous, the goods may not be left to either of us."

"Bugger," Ch'ing said. "You think well for an outlander. Wait by your camels. Hide your pink face until I come."

"Shall I hide altogether?"

"No. If this is who I think it is, he is a tough egg. Major K'uang. He hates foreigners, bandits and Communists in that order. Some foxy townsman would kowtow and tell him of you, and the rest of the day would be snakes and scorpions. Conduct yourself normally and in silence, like a good middle soldier."

Middle soldier was a Chinese way to say sergeant. Ch'ing was clever and Jake decided to follow orders. Major K'uang hated foreigners, did he. God damn. Race prejudice from a Chinaman!

As the patrol drew near, the population of Shandanmiao vanished. Jake had never seen Nationalist troops in action but had heard many stories, too many, all shameful. Of divisions that disappeared overnight, flanks left exposed because everybody lit out for home, payrolls embezzled by oily generals, brisk trade with the Japanese, rank bought and sold, villages looted and burned, enlisted men beaten and executed on some officer's whim.

When the troops rode in Jake vanished, too, huddled among camels and stacks of goods.

He peered out at the riders, and the two scouts out before. They were all lean, dirty and tired, and looked like fighters. Their shirts were crusty with dust and sweat. Three were bandaged. They wore crossed bandoleers and clip boxes, and their rifles rode in leather scabbards. They seemed to be one officer and thirteen men, but there were no signs of rank and they were dressed alike, alike hot and alike grim, faces shadowed under the bills of their fatigue caps.

Beside him Jim said, "These are rough buggers. These kill with both hands."

Jake believed him but was unimpressed. "Those are handsome camels."

The camels were of a rich reddish color, with dark rings around the eyes and a haughty flare to the nostrils.

"Tushegun camels," Jim muttered. "The best."

Jake said, "When I have my own string, they will be Tushegun camels."

*   *   *

Ch'ing was smiling when he strolled up with the leader, so Jake jacked himself upright. Ch'ing was carrying his camel whip like a swagger stick. "Major K'uang," he said airily, "this is our Tartar."

The Major was a large, handsome man with thick brows, big brown eyes and beautiful teeth. For a tick Jake was disgusted: a movie-star soldier.

But the brown eyes were cool and hard as the two men shook hands. "An unusual Tartar," the Major said.

"Major K'uang has been patrolling in the west for eight weeks," Ch'ing said.

"With success, I hope," Jake said.

"I lost four men," K'uang said, "and have three wounded. But we killed some dozens."

"Communists?"

"There are no Communists out here. No. Bandits."

"Then we owe you thanks," Jake said. "How far east does your beat run?"

"To Pao-t'ou," K'uang said. "All within the Wall could float to sea and I would not know it."

"Or care?"

The Major snorted. "This is most unusual. A foreigner so far west."

"All that is common was once unusual," Jake said. He noticed with annoyance that he was slumped, and half bowing, as if he did not want this man to feel shorter than himself, or to think badly of him. He straightened.

"Master Ch'ing tells me you are a military man."

"I am. I am also a merchant."

"Are you on active duty?"

"To an extent," Jake told him. "Let us say, detached."

"Ah. And perhaps sightseeing?"

"Surely sightseeing."

"And what is—or was—your exalted rank?"

"But a lowly sergeant."

"In time you will rise higher," the Major said. "You speak well. Do you speak English as well?"

"No." The Major was not fat. A good light-heavy, no waste motion, cool. He would not need to repeat orders, or to verify that they had been executed.

"I believe protocol requires that you call me sir," the Major murmured.

Jake said, "Yes, sir."

"You fought the Japanese?"

"Several times, sir." This was familiar ground, password and countersign. Jake stood easier. "I have few scars but they were painful at the time."

"I too. You will forgive my curiosity. It is my business to know."

"How not," Jake said courteously.

"Your superiors will reward your skills. I can tell."

"The last few I spoke to," Jake said, "seemed to respect me."

The Major nodded absently. He was scanning the caravan. "The House of Wu," he observed. "Your own goods?"

"Right here, sir." Jake pointed.

"I wish these kegs were beer," the Major said lightly. "U-S-N-C-B. You see, I too speak languages. Government supplies?"

Jake said, "Much of my freight was supplied by the military authorities. Those are nails."

"And the rest?"

"Cloth, wire, a few bricks of tea, cigarettes, cameras and so on. My papers and goods are yours to inspect."

"Papers?"

"My card of identity, with a true photograph."

"Please."

Jake stepped to his pack and fished out the card.

The Major looked from Jake to the photo. "What service is this?"

"The United States Marines."

"Those I know," said the Major. "Those I have heard of. Men of great resource. Still," and he smiled a thin smile, "we shall inspect your goods. But after the noonday meal. Come along."

The elder invited them into the large yurt. Ch'ing threw the camel whip in before him, and once inside, ignored it. He and the Major went to sit by the cooking fire in the center of the yurt, between the tent poles fore and aft. Warm, but doubtless the places of honor.

Jake edged around to the left among wicker buckets and skins of water. Across the yurt from him were stacks of wooden bowls and metal pots.

The old man sat with Ch'ing and the Major. Nobody paid Jake any mind so he shuffled around between the old man and the after tent pole, headed for a patch of empty floor where he could sit still and learn something.

The old man screeched at him.

"Fool!" Ch'ing said. "Never step between the fire and the rear tent pole."

"And how was I to know that?"

"Too late now," Jim said, with a great dirty grin.

The old man jabbered in Mongol; Ch'ing translated. The Major sat bored.

Jake gathered that he had contaminated the yurt and let in the spirit of clap or some such. He tried to look sorry and humble, like a stupid foreigner.

The Major spoke sharply. More quietly he said to Jake, "These are silly people. They would like to extinguish this fire and build a new one; to throw away this tea and brew a new pot."

"It is my fault," Jake said. "Can I make up for it?"

"They are primitive and superstitious," the Major said wearily.

The old man had tottered to the front door with a cup of tea in his hand. He flung the liquid to the sands.

"He is appeasing the demons that prowl empty spaces," the Major said.

"The guardians of the yurt," Ch'ing added.

"All is well now," the Major said.

Ch'ing spoke to the old man, who poured another cup of tea and brought it to Jake. He smelled like a bale of hides.

Jake bowed his thanks. The old man spat and turned away.

Jim said quietly, "Ch'ing told him that you were a foreigner so the bad luck would fall upon you. The demons will pursue you."

"Thanks," Jake scoffed. "Not much of a sin. One wrong step like that."

Jim cackled softly. "The longest journey begins with one wrong step."

Jake cursed him.

The Major had spread a map. "Now. Here we are, here is Shandan-miao. How do you propose to proceed?"

"We thought the northerly road," Ch'ing said, "but will first hear you."

"Northerly is best," the Major said. "The present concentration of bandits is in Kansu. They fear the true desert. Most are scum. There is the Mountain Weasel, who is better organized, but he is never far from Yü-men."

Jake could not absorb all of this, so sat quietly and sipped tea. K'uang's men lounged in corners of the yurt, and one at the door, and one outside, and it seemed to Jake that they were not at rest but standing guard, as if the caravan were under a kind of house arrest or temporary detention. He was suddenly uneasy about his goods. That was foolish, with all these soldiers around.

Though these soldiers were some bunch. They looked more like outlaws. Scarred and surly. They moved like big cats, and their eyes were never still.

Ch'ing was asking about the northern road.

"I cannot tell you much of value. I last took that road six months ago. One of my men froze to death. A few bandits may come down from Outer Mongolia, from the hills near Noyon. The Tiger's Assistant is out there somewhere. He vacations in Lanchow twice a year, you know. But I hear he plans to head west for good after this season."

Jake spoke: "Who?"

"The Tiger's Assistant. A Manchurian, and a bad one."

"A crazy name for a bandit."

Ch'ing said gravely, "He was killed by a tiger years ago."

"Well now," the Major said.

"His full name is the Tiger's Assistant Demon," Ch'ing said stubbornly, "and he was killed by a tiger."

"Hu Ch'iao Kuei," Jake repeated.

"The legend is," said the Major in some amusement, "that one killed by a tiger comes back in spirit form to assist him, and also acquires some of his qualities."

"It is no legend," Ch'ing said darkly. "I am a businessman and hard of head. I spoke to one who knew. Hu Ch'iao Kuei was killed by a tiger and his men saw him dead. Years ago, before the true war but when the Japanese held Manchuria. He raided against the Japanese. When his men returned for the body, it was not there. Later he was seen raiding all alone, and bullets did not slow him."

The Major shrugged. "As you wish. At any rate he is raiding now, with half a dozen men. Along the Hsinkiang border, last I heard. That reminds me: Kanfanfu no longer exists. But you will not pass that way."

"No longer exists?"

"I burned it. They sheltered bandits. This is rotten tea."

After a silence Ch'ing asked, "Where did you lose your men?"

"In the mountains near Yung-chang. One I shot because he ran. We were tracking a band from Ch'ing-hai, led by a Kashmiri. They were short of ponies and instead of dispersing they doubled up. Fools. We caught up with them and wiped them out."

Jake recognized the tone. He had heard other majors talk of other battles, and count heads. "Well, what now?" he asked. "Will you be allowed to rest?"

"Rest!" The Major almost spat. "There is no rest. Now I go to refit in Pao-t'ou, and take a bath, and then back across the Black Gobi."

"You should have more troops."

K'uang shrugged. "I should be a lieutenant, with such a small command, but we have too many majors. There is no serious work for majors these days. We have almost as many majors as bandits."

"Bandits," Ch'ing said. "It is the work of a lifetime."

"It will never end," the Major brooded. "But then," and he smiled briefly, "I like to kill bandits." The smile vanished. "There are not a hundred good soldiers in this country!" he burst out. "They are not *allowed* to be good!" He calmed himself. "Well, my men are good. And the American Marines are good," he said to Jake. "I have heard that."

Jake was embarrassed for him and spoke sympathetically: "We have bad ones too. Sometimes I used to think I had to win the war all by myself."

"Yes, yes!" K'uang cried. "I too." He sighed. "Well. We beat them, did we not."

"Did we not," Jake said.

One of K'uang's men came in and saluted; K'uang waved a lazy acknowledgment. The man spoke, quick and low.

"Ah, really?" K'uang asked, and his eyes flickered to Jake and away. Jake tightened. "With your conspicuous coloring," K'uang said to Jake, "you do well to act open and innocent, like an honest man."

"I am indeed an honest man," Jake said.

"And these goods, they are honest too?" The Major's ears were without lobes; in the dim light of the yurt his eyes were opaque, expressionless.

"They are honest goods, and they are all I have in this world," Jake said. "Sir."

"How I would like to believe you!" the Major said, and rose gracefully. He was handsome and lithe, and his smile was not a true smile. "Come. Let me show you a wonderful thing."

K'uang's killers stood like sentries in the sunlight. Like a firing squad momentarily unemployed. K'uang marched to Sweetwater and Bad Smell.

Jake saw his goods laid out on tarps. Cameras, compasses, cigarettes: like a bazaar, a street market. "It is as I said," he told K'uang.

"Ah yes," K'uang said. "And the kegs."

Jake saw the broken seals. The camel-pullers stood glowering. K'uang's soldiers looked on casually, but their rifles were cradled close. "Well then, the kegs," Jake said. "Nails. I hope they can be resealed."

K'uang said, "Nails," and stepped to the kegs. He tossed Jake a nail, and took another himself.

Jake examined it. "A nail," he said, and tossed it back. "Construction nails for scaffolding and such. Hence the double head. When the frame is no longer needed, the nails can be pulled easily and the whole dismantled."

"A nail indeed," K'uang said. "Now come look." He slipped the two nails into his shirt pocket and ordered Jake forward with a sharp gesture.

Nested neatly in each of the kegs were small, rectangular green-and-white cardboard boxes, many such, buried among the nails.

"Bugger!" Jake said. "Whatever it is, I knew nothing of it." He looked to Ch'ing for help. Ch'ing spat.

"You knew nothing," K'uang said.

"They were sealed!" Jake insisted. "With iron bands! With the seal of my own navy! Defile him! He told me never to trust a seal in China!"

"Who?"

Jake stood fuming and sullen in the noonday sun, and after a while he said, "Old Kao. Kao Hu-tsuan. My partner in Peking." He met the Major's eye then and said, still angry, flushed, knowing this was trouble and knowing he deserved trouble but not this trouble, "All right, Major. What are they? I really do not know."

And K'uang said to himself, This one is telling the truth. No question, he is telling the truth. A golden ox. The body of a warrior and the brains of a carp. He is telling the truth because his eyes say so, and the flush of his skin, and because he is not smart enough to lie successfully. His ears would turn blue, or his teeth drop out.

They are as bad as the Russians, or the English in their short pants. Look at him! He should be slaughtered and butchered. He would make fine steaks as the foreigners cut them.

Still, he fought. He has few scars but they were painful at the time. I should shoot him.

"I should shoot you," K'uang said.

"No," Jake said firmly. "I did not know of this and I have done no wrong. I don't even know what they are."

"They are penicillin," K'uang said.

"I thought at least diamonds," Jake said.

He is telling me the truth, K'uang said to himself. There is something wrong here, it stinks like shit to the smallest nose, but he is telling the truth. Ah, defile him! I have better work to do. And the caravan master, this old, crafty camel-puller: he glanced at Ch'ing.

"I know nothing of this," Ch'ing protested. "Major, you know me. You know the House of Wu. I curse myself for carrying a foreigner. Other than that I have done no wrong."

"A shame that we must carry foreigners."

"One must live," Ch'ing muttered. "He paid."

"Ah yes. A necessary evil."

Ch'ing muttered, "He is not truly of the caravan, nor of the House of Wu."

K'uang relented: "Be easy, Master Ch'ing." He turned back to Jake.

"It is in powder form," K'uang said, "and the vials in those boxes are full. It is, I think, worth its weight in gold."

Jake stood mute, with the sun bashing down on the back of his neck. He tilted the coolie hat. "I knew nothing of this."

"And if you had?"

Jake weighed that. If I had. "I cannot tell. I might have walked the crooked way."

K'uang nodded. He issued orders. His men stacked the small boxes. They spread tarps and emptied the kegs. Nails trickled, gushed, splashed, lay in pools. Soldiers picked through them and found nothing. "Corporal Shih," K'uang ordered, "have the kegs refilled."

Corporal Shih was a big one, tiny eyes and a great flat nose: the eyes photographed Jake.

"I am confiscating these boxes," K'uang told Jake.

I hope you get a good price for it, Jake said, but not aloud. God damn old Kao! Like a son to him, was I!

"I think I will not shoot you," K'uang went on playfully. "I will punish you by making you listen to advice."

"I will listen," Jake said.

"I advise you not to travel alone," K'uang said. "Henceforth and west of here, your nation and rank will mean nothing. Maintain an honest appearance. Do not adjust your hat under a plum tree."

"What does that mean?" Relief was chasing the anger out of him, and the small fear. This major would let him off. Damn Kao!

"Do not be furtive."

"I have nothing to be furtive about."

The Major sighed. "This is such an awkward moment for you to say that."

The two measured each other. The soldiers and camel-pullers watched and waited. Somewhere in the village children screamed, piping voices cursed.

"Whatever you are up to," K'uang said, "I believe you will fail. But I need wish you no evil. You will find plenty of evil without my help." He tossed a salute in Jake's direction.

Jake returned the salute snappily. "See you again. Sir."

"I doubt it," said Major K'uang, and strode off after a last hard look at all of them.

Ch'ing hopped and danced in a cockerel's fury. "Either," he screeched, "you are deficient in virtue or you are a sheep with four horns. Whichever, I will plaster the seven apertures of your empty head with camel turd."

"Stop this ranting," Jake told him. "I did nothing wrong."

"You should have *told* me!" Ch'ing cried. "We all buy-sell a little! It is the way! But we do not lie to the caravan master!"

Jake turned to Jim and showed palm helplessly. Hsü-to and Chu-chu were intent on Jake's goods, and the repacking.

"Then I will tell you for the last time," Jake said. "I did not know. I will not speak of this again. Perhaps I will not speak at all again because I am not accustomed to conversation with rubes, thieves, swine, one-horned rams and those who carry their brains in a small bag between the legs."

"Now I believe him," Hsü-to said.

"He was lucky," Chu-chu said. "K'uang also believed him."

"I am afraid to travel on," Ch'ing said in despair.

"Do not be more of a dunce than necessary," Jake said. "This is the end of the bad luck, and we have scraped through it with no harm done."

"No harm!" Ch'ing exploded, but calmed down immediately. "Why, that is true. So then, to work." He clapped hands.

"Everybody is working but you," Chu-chu said, and Ch'ing marched off in a huff.

16/   A few days west and it was honest-to-god desert sand, thick and drifting, an endless shifting dazzle of white sunlight. They pushed hard, forced marches, on the trail well before dawn with a long midday rest and supper by starlight.

They followed the northern track. Jim said it crossed more desert but fewer miles. Most of the Gobi, he said, was rock and gravel, a lot of it black, some of it flat as a lake for hundreds of miles. But there were also bad stretches of sand, patches of dune ten days across, and the air boiling and blistering.

With luck they would make this crossing in seven days, and fetch up at Dengin Hudag near an unreliable lake. "Sometimes it is not there at all," Ch'ing said gloomily. "In my grandfather's time it was ten miles west of now."

A week after that—with luck, always with luck—they would round the northern shores of Gashun Nor and Sogo Nor, two lakes only a few miles from the Outer Mongolian border. Jake traced the route on his map more than once. This part of the map was almost blank. Then another three or four weeks and they would reach the Turkestan border. Hsinkiang. After the Black Gobi and some mountains.

Meanwhile Jake was thirsty, and Jim was out of jokes and songs. Sand sifted into every damn thing: their eyes and their pants, their boots and their food, their weapons and their canteens. At night they stacked their pack saddles and hung their gear high; even so it was sandy by dawn. They sat about the fire in a breezeless cool night, and still the fine sand floated down unseen. Jim and Chu-chu played dominoes, and taught Jake how. "No such frivolity in the old days," Chu-chu said. "Only dice and cards." He owned a deck of cards, soft cardboard, two inches wide and four inches long, with dragons and leopards and camels for suits.

"I'm tired of mutton fat," Jake said. "Any chance of beef? Or game?"

"Beef!" Another foreign joke. "But game, yes. When we pass the sands. At the Five Ugly Foals are wild asses. And many ducks and geese on the lakes. Many edible birds. Cranes, and herons."

A couple of days later they crossed a faint track coming in from the north. Ch'ing had dismounted and was studying it. He swung an arm north. "Yunbeize," he said, "where the bandits lived in the old days. Hard men and without mercy."

"Anybody been along lately?"

"Hard to tell. With no wind tracks last forever. Hsü-to has gone to look for droppings. He went north this morning."

The track ran north forever. Mongol armies had used it centuries before. So much space. Jake was uneasy. So many thousands of miles. The line of camels was a comfort, and the camel-pullers were good company, tough.

"Let's move," Ch'ing said. "He'll catch up. He's riding Snowball."

And Hsü-to caught up; trotted into camp that night singing and cheerful. Not a sign of anything for three hours out.

"Then the luck has changed," Ch'ing said. "Give the Tartar a nice fat yellow piece of the small gut."

The luck had changed. The lake near Dengin Hudag was not too low and the water was sweet enough. When they had watered the camels and topped off, Jake went a little way aside and dropped his pants and scrubbed at the villainous crabs with one of his precious bars of soap. He had been scrubbing with sand, but that was abrasive, and caked if you were sweaty. He rinsed off. Then he had a better idea, and shouted to Ch'ing.

"Now what?" Ch'ing called back. "Sharks?"

"Will it offend any demons if I swim?"

"If you *what?*"

"If I take a bath."

He heard Ch'ing's mutter, and then mirth. "It will not offend the spirits," Ch'ing called, "and it will certainly not offend the rest of us." They laughed.

"Don't let it shrink," Jim yelled.

"Bugger all," Jake shouted, and plunged in, and enjoyed a good wallow. He was not sure that you could drown lice, but he gave it a good try. He could always pick up more tomorrow.

At supper they were a happy crew. Fresh water did that. They drank gallons of tea, and Ch'ing told funny stories about the Japanese, who always took half the goods but never seemed to suspect that the caravans also carried intelligence. How if you cursed the Chinese government properly the Japanese thought you were reliable. "I have spent my whole life cursing the government. What is lower than a tax collector?"

Later they lay back and smoked, and counted the stars. On the desert starlight was amazing. Even without a moon you could almost read. "You see," Jim said. "That's north."

"I know that. Up from the dipper."

"Yes. You people call it a dipper, too?"

"Yes."

"And there is the dragon," Jim said, "and the ox, and the emperor and his concubines." Jake barely looked. Peace was upon him. In the starlight, in the silence, he settled into the sand, and was a boulder in the desert. The night was cool but a fire now would corrupt his night vision and erase the stars. He dozed. They all dozed. Hsü-to woke them with a huge, racking yawn like a bull's bellow, and Ch'ing said, "Think if it had been the other end," and they all laughed and turned in. All but the sentries.

The first thieves came that night, with the camel-pullers sleeping like dead men, the sentries too. The camels stirred and whispered in mysterious humped rows, and the men lay sprawled and snoring.

One prowled near Jake, who judged later that the poor bugger must have taken a good sharp look at this white-haired monster with a nose like a goose's; it surprised a curse out of him, and the curse woke Jake. Jake's hand did not dart immediately to the .45; Jake did not seize him immediately by the throat. Jake hardly knew where he was. He saw a strange face. Then he saw a hand, and a knife in the hand, and he remembered Kao hanging, and Kao's goods, and he was awake. He was a new man in town, and this was a stranger of doubtful intentions.

So Jake's hand swept under the pack and came up with the .45, and Jake said the proper thing, which being translated was, "Do not move." The man understood. Then Jake hollered, "Thief! Thief!" and little mounds and humps of men stirred and shook. Footsteps pattered, running steps, and a shot sounded, and many fierce cries of "Turtle egg!" and "What now?"

There were three of them, and it turned out that they had come from the west on white donkeys and were armed with long knives. "And where before that?" Chu-chu was indignant. "To cross a whole desert with a donkey and a knife?"

"They're Torgut Mongols," Ch'ing said.

The caravan men stood in a loose circle at the center of the bivouac. Chu-chu and a little camel-puller from the first lien, a skinny fellow who looked more like a scholar, were covering three strangers and two donkeys. One of the strangers was Jake's contribution. Another had landed hard when Ch'ing shot his donkey out from under him, and Hsü-to, who was by then aboard a young cow, raced out and rounded him up. The third was plenty confused when everything went wrong, and sooner than make a bad mistake he stood where he was.

They all looked about nineteen. They were emaciated and might have been brothers. In rags. Dull of eye, and snotty.

"This is what happened," Ch'ing said. "They were cut loose from a caravan for thievery. That was a mistake. They hung about near the lakes because there is no other place. They lived for a little by stealing. Maybe they killed for the donkeys. Maybe there are bodies beneath the sand."

Head of Pot had built up a fire, and now it flamed forth, and the men seemed to twist and wriggle in the dancing light. The three thieves stood motionless, heads bowed.

"Desert rats," Jim said to Jake. "Not even rats. Little mice. Instead of stampeding the caravan and cutting out some real loot, they sneak up at night and settle for a brick of tea and a shirt."

The camel-pullers were annoyed. Sullenly they yawned and spat. One called for tea. Half asleep, Jake reckoned idly, as a man will count balls on a pool table or cows in a field. "Bugger," he said suddenly.

Ch'ing roared, "Now what? Are you never quiet?"

"The whole family is here," Jake said. "A couple more thieves could run off with a whole pa. How do you know there were only these three?" Chu-chu was already moving out, toward the tail, and the skinny scholar headed for the point on the double. "You two." Any two. Jake just stabbed the air. "Patrol. Together. A circle. I'll be along. Don't shoot me. Hsü-to: do you think there's anything out there?"

"One dead donkey."

"I'll be back," Jake said. Old Jake. Standing at the center of the universe, the god damn middle of the Gobi, in a pair of green underpants. He ran to his bedding and dressed. Aside from being half frozen, he faced trouble better with pants on. One of life's great truths. He slipped into cloth shoes, and loped off to check the perimeter about fifty yards out. He could see for miles, and every rock and shadow was a man or a donkey. He found wet blood and followed it, but not far; he gave up and turned back. Poor dumb beast, gut-shot and out there dying forever. One of the guards Jake had detailed almost blew his head off. Jake thundered through about thirty seconds of high-style cursing. "Excuse me," the guard said. Excuse me. Jake was warming up in all ways and beginning to enjoy this. Another great yarn for his grandchildren. He trotted back to the fire. "Well," he said to Ch'ing. "They have not overpowered you. Or taken your guns away."

Ch'ing spat.

"Nothing out there," Jake said, "except a couple of rotten shots."

"Shut up," Ch'ing said.

"Did they fire at your order?"

Ch'ing said kindly, "If I wanted you dead, I'd kill you. And nothing at all would be said about it."

Every camel-puller there, including Jim, looked hard at Jake.

"You're the boss," he said mildly.

Ch'ing turned back to the prisoners. They were kneeling now, heads bowed, submissive. Finished.

"What now?" Jake whispered to Jim.

Jim shrugged.

"They never even got anything," Jake said. "We're winning by one donkey." He sucked in a lungful of crisp night air. For a desolate, barren desert the Gobi was full of traffic and surprises. He moved closer to the fire and inspected the prisoners. "They're younger brothers," he said, meaning boys.

"Be happy they aren't Elder Brothers," Ch'ing snarled, meaning the band of outlaws. "We shoot them anyway."

"You shoot bungling children?"

"Bugger your mother," Ch'ing said without humor. The firelight painted his face orange and yellow in flat planes like slabs of wood, and his dark eyes shone like jewels, and behind him the desert slept. A small tug of fear stopped Jake's breath. For no reason at all, just the night, and the distance, the solitude.

"Changing the rules again," Ch'ing said. "We don't seem to do anything the way you want."

"I beg pardon. Forget it. I never spoke."

"No no," Ch'ing said, "no no, please. Distinguished visitor. You prefer to carry them along? Eating our food and drinking our water? No. Crop their ears and turn them loose? To wander and die of thirst, or to prey on other caravans? No. Send them up to Noyon under guard? Four days there and four days back. Give them to the police, or the army? All right. Where are the police? Where is the army? All right. What then?"

"It seems too much."

"We await suggestions. Lop their hands?"

The three men looked up then, and firelight flickered across their round faces. They were without expression, but one of them said, "No."

"You see," Ch'ing said.

The thieves were barefoot. Their lank hair flopped.

"All right," Ch'ing said to his men. "Back to bed." They fidgeted. "You," he said to Jake, "take them out some yards and shoot them."

The camel-pullers chuckled, and waited.

"Why me?"

"Master of the Armory," Ch'ing said reasonably, "and also a man of the three prime virtues: benevolence, fellow-feeling and humanitarian charity. Surely you will do for a man what you would do for a camel?"

Jake was silent, but soon nodded.

The men melted off into the lines of sleepy camels. Ch'ing and Jake stood together before the three thieves. Jim stood by Jake. Ch'ing smiled a light, wise, mocking smile.

"Stand up," Jake said. Ch'ing said it in Mongol. The men rose.

"This way," Jake said, and showed them; they moved. That, Jake did not understand. They were not bound and there were three of them and Jake had been holding his breath as they rose and turned. But they did not try to flee, and only marched across the sands, shuffling and stumbling. They did not even whimper. Ch'ing and Jim followed.

By the donkey's dried blood Jake told the thieves to kneel, and they knelt. Jake fought down a surge of excitement.

"The caravans have always passed this way," Ch'ing said suddenly. "Before there were countries the caravans passed this way." All about them lay the flat black fetches of a barren land; the horizon was the end of the world.

"No armies," Jake said. "No police. I understand."

"Nothing," Ch'ing said. "Only the rule of the lord of all under heaven."

"The lord of all under heaven."

"Old man God," Ch'ing said. "Remember that. When there is trouble we must do things his way." He spoke softly.

Ch'ing shot the first thief in the back of the head. The boy fell forward and settled on his knees and face, ass in the air, like a Mohammedan praying. Jake had forgotten what a small, flat snap the Nambu made.

Quickly Jake shot the second man, who rolled over and came to rest against the third. With his Lee-Enfield Jim shot the third.

"I have responsibilities," Ch'ing said as they walked back.

"I want one of the donkeys," Jake said.

"Oho," Ch'ing said, "this man is learning."

"I'll take the other," Jim said.

"No," Ch'ing said. "No need for two in the same lien. Ta-tze can have one, but to Gurchen only."

"Fair enough."

"Do you know," Ch'ing said, "I believe that we can be friends now."

17/ In a private room at the Southwestern Barracks in Pao-t'ou, Major K'uang Kuo-hua of the Nationalist Chinese Army, a tank commander long ago detached to desert patrol, was enjoying his first hot bath in seven weeks. The tub was of galvanized iron, with a small hardwood seat under water; both water and soap were scented, and his orderly, an eager orphan of fourteen, stood by with tea and towels. After the sere and crusty desert, the Major was pleased by the erotic swirl of the warm and faintly oily water.

"Qomul is full of garbage," the Major said, "and so is Pao-t'ou, crates and canvas, wrappers and worn tools and liquor bottles, and all with foreign script on it, Russian and American and Japanese. And our women speak gross words in those languages, and have learned to perform delicate acts in a gross manner. Have you seen Soochow? No: you are fourteen only. Well, in Soochow there are still establishments of quality where the women are clean, and lightly painted and powdered, and wear the ancient gowns, and mix hot spices, and play the old instruments. It is all disappearing, though. I pity you. You will never know China. I am the son of a provincial magistrate and a concubine, and there is pride even in that. There are no longer concubines, only whores.

"A towel. And sharpen my razor."

Shaving, dripping lather into the chipped basin, gazing into the small cracked mirror, the Major recited to himself, as always when shaving, the verses, mottoes and principles drummed into him for ten years in a stone-and-mortar schoolhouse in Wu-tso near the great lake of Sung-hua in the heart of Manchuria. They stood, fifteen or twenty boys of many ages, and recited in unison. "Fu-fu tzu-tzu." When the father is a father and the son is a son. When the prince is a prince and the minister is a minister. Then will justice and benevolence prevail. The Master said: The superior man dislikes the idea that his name will vanish after death.

"All those," the Major said to his orderly in the cracked mirror, "are to be laundered." He rinsed the razor, dried it carefully, folded it away, and washed his face. "A fresh, starched uniform," he said, pleased. "Underwear. Socks. What is that?"

The orderly bowed, and handed him two nails. "From the shirt pocket, sir."

They were those double-headed nails. Resentment boiled through K'uang, sour and hot. The foreign ox with his foreign ways. The arrogance of him. And yet K'uang was sure this ox had not, really not, known about the penicillin. A false note in that whole day, somewhere, but it was not the penicillin.

He juggled the nails. I stand here in a towel, hating one barbarian. How foolish!

A nail in either hand, he began a double toss to the wastebasket, but checked it.

He hefted them, one in each hand.

They were of clearly different weights.

He went to his small desk, sat, switched on the small electric lamp. "Orderly," he said, "my knife."

The boy scurried. He served efficiently and in near silence, but his heart hummed and his ears burned: he was serving Major K'uang, and the name alone left men short of breath. The campaign ribbons, battle ribbons, decorations and commendations. The legends of battles won and lost, in Manchuria, in Burma; of insubordinates shot; of his grace in the company of generals and their ladies; and how he had blown a train near Ch'ang-sha, and killed a thousand Japanese.

K'uang took the knife with a grunt, and shaved a curl of iron from the shank of the lighter nail. Dull iron, and more dull iron.

He shaved a curl of iron from the shank of the other, and gold gleamed out at him.

He closed his fist on the nail and looked about him: his orderly stood near the door, at attention.

The Major pictured the foreigner, a large man and strong, weathered skin and bleached hair. He tried to remember just what Jake had said and done.

He grimaced. "Defile him! He did that well!"

Four kegs! Say half the nails were gold, dipped in iron; say a hundred pounds in all. At least.

They would be halfway to Gurchen by now but they were a large caravan, slow-traveling and with much opportunity for delay, camels down, pullers sick, sandstorms. He might overtake them. Meanwhile on the wireless he would hail Peking about that Kao—that was it, Kao Hu-tsuan—and he would hail Captain Nien in Qomul.

He could order Captain Nien to meet the caravan.

Ah, no.

He considered this for some moments, and decided uneasily to avoid burdening Nien with too many facts. He would ask Nien to detain the caravan, and to impound the foreigner's goods. All of them.

And to impound the foreigner too. It should be no unpleasant task to apprehend and impound a foreigner. They bumbled through China like elephants, consuming, trampling, crushing, tusking.

18/   Jake was leathery and black like all of them, and except for the blond hair as much a coolie as anybody. His pee was bright yellow, damn near orange, because they drank so little. It was late summer now, and pretty soon the tamarisks would bloom, and they came to wells or gullies that should have run but were dry. And still the nights were cold, and they warmed themselves under saddle blankets and sheepskins. In the morning the sky was a clear gray, then pale yellow, then gold, then suddenly blue; at night the blue enriched to purple and then black, and the stars popped out like flares.

Sogo Nor was a roundish lake about five miles across in a two-day sandy depression. When they edged the north shore Jim called down a blessing on so much water, and Jake strained his eyes for ducks or geese, or partridge along the shore.

But Sogo Nor was brackish. They pushed west against the afternoon sun, and came to their oasis that night, a place called Erhlitzeho near the shores of Gashun Nor. By now the place-names were not reliable. Jake liked that: he was a long way from anyplace. He was in places that might not exist! Damn! Erhlitzeho could have meant several things in Chinese, or it could have been the Chinese twist of something Mongol like Öridzagol. Jim said, "Two Regions River." Erhlitzeho had no mayor or even citizens, but it lay by sweet water. They off-loaded, watered the camels, and set up for a few days of rest, prayer and light housekeeping.

More luck: a light cloud of dust moved in from the west next day, about midmorning, and every man took up a weapon while Hsü-to bounded onto Ch'ing's pony and cantered out to reconnoiter. He came prancing and sashaying back and let out a whoop. Jim said, "Ha. Fresh meat." Ch'ing reclaimed the pony and went forward with Head of Pot.

By now Jake could see the strangers, half a dozen Mongols and a herd of sheep. "Also cattle," Jim said, and soon Jake saw them, ten or fifteen head of scrubby horned cattle among about a hundred and fifty sheep.

"Cows," Jim said, but Jake was inspecting the cowboys. They wore skin hats shaped like Robin Hood's, and leather vests over no shirts, and ragged pants and cloth boots. They carried rifles and rode little brown ponies.

Two of them cantered out to talk with Ch'ing, and the others kept the stock milling slowly. Ch'ing talked with his hands and offered cigarettes and ushered them closer, and the camel-pullers gathered around.

Then they started to talk, and Jake was lost: Mongol, and bastard Chinese, and God knew what-all. The two Mongols sat, rifles butt-down between their legs, barrel leaning back against the left shoulder. They were cheerful but there was an irreducible wariness. Jim translated in a swift mutter. "They've been grazing the river here. It's drying up. They'll sell us a sheep or two."

Head of Pot was detailing the bargain he wanted. The Mongols listened without emotion. Ch'ing said the caravan was without money but heavy with goods.

The Mongols scoffed at that. They had no need of fancy silks or newfangled foreign inventions. They were grazing this side of the border to keep their feet out of such garbage. Milk in tins when they had sheep and cows! Russian nonsense, like eyeglasses for hunting when any Mongol could see as far as the moon and the stars! They were thirty miles from Outer Mongolia with a defile-it regular army and a defile-it telegraph and a defile-it police force. There was no place a man could go these days without running into eunuchs with badges and seals and stamps, who lived on foot. Men of no bones.

For the sheep they would accept silver. Or gold.

Ch'ing blew the mustache. The caravan was walking up. When it rode down there would be silver.

"They'd love a Browning," Jake told Jim, "with fifty rounds."

"Bugger yes," Jim said. "Four sheep at least." He sidled to Ch'ing and whispered. The morning light was harsh, a yellow-white glare, and on the desert four Mongol horsemen stood guard over their flocks as if they had been there since Genghis Khan. Ch'ing palavered roundabout. He let the Mongols know that these camel-pullers were a rough bunch, armed to the teeth and hell on bandits, and so good at pulling camels that they did not fear to throw away a pistol to men of good bones. Ch'ing himself had a Mongol wife in Gurchen. Men who traveled the desert were brothers.

The Mongols asked to see the pistol and ammunition. Ch'ing obliged. One of the Mongols tipped his rifle to the other, slipped the clip out of the pistol, popped a couple of cartridges into it and rammed it home, snapped one into the chamber, ejected it, ditto the other, pulled the dry trigger, opened the breech, took a quick peek up the barrel and grunted to his buddy, who had caught both cartridges on the fly. This was one newfangled foreign invention they knew a little something about.

Their rifles were nothing Jake had ever seen. They weighed about twenty pounds and looked like they burned coal.

"Six sheep," Ch'ing said. "A man works half a year for such a weapon."

The Mongolian rube said, "Horse apples. A man steals these from your drunken soldiers."

"Without ammunition," Ch'ing said complacently, "and the stolen ones are rusty, or the parts are broken."

"And this one? How do we know?"

"Fire it. Look at the gleam. Feel the good oil."

"And panic the sheep and cattle," the Mongol said, "and your camels." Though not their ponies, he explained, which were first-class Bar Köl ponies and well trained.

"Then my Tartar will vouch for it." Ch'ing jerked his head at Jake. The Mongols contemplated Jake.

"He is a master of weaponry," Ch'ing said.

They shrugged again. "Another Russian."

"Tell them it is good," Ch'ing said.

Jake eyed him, cool, and put out a hand for the pistol.

"Tell them it is good," Ch'ing said.

Jake stepped forward and took up the pistol. Quickly, like a magician performing, he stripped it and reassembled it. "Master Ch'ing does not lie," he said. "The pistol is like new."

Ch'ing managed a thin smile. "Bar Köl ponies," he said chattily. "You have wandered far with your flocks."

Oh yes. Ten years ago they had been west of Ming-shui, in Turkestan. Two years ago here, last year there. The water flowed one year and was sand the next. It was necessary to wander. Bandits were not a problem. They took only a sheep or two.

"Ah yes, sheep," Ch'ing said. "Three sheep will be acceptable."

"That seems right," the Mongol said.

"Sheep and not lambs. Fat and not lean."

The Mongols mounted up and trotted off. Shortly they rode back, herding a couple of dozen animals. The sheep looked more like goats to Jake, and he realized after a moment that they had been recently shorn. The Mongol said, "These are the best."

Ch'ing said, "They can hardly walk. They're starving."

"There are none so fat this side of Qomul."

"I see one or two that look edible."

The Mongol cut one out. "My personal favorite."

"How long has he been sick? Colic or worms?"

"Like a pet, believe me," the Mongol said.

"Poisoned grass," Ch'ing said sympathetically.

"A healthy wether, and all meat. No air in him."

Meanwhile the other candidates were baaing and milling and dropping many little pellets of dung. The second Mongol stood half smiling. The camel-pullers too were enjoying themselves, and Chu-chu sat by like a man at the opera, waiting for the moment to shout Hao, hao.

In a quarter of an hour Ch'ing and Head of Pot had the three they wanted, and Jake had enjoyed an interesting performance, his Oriental friends displaying local custom and picturesque tradition. From now on it would perhaps be Jake's tradition, too.

Courteously, his hands spread wide, the Mongol asked a question. Head of Pot bowed, and gestured that he should proceed.

The man of good bones yanked a sheep off its feet and onto its side; a knife flashed once in the brilliant sunlight, and there was a long slit in the sheep's belly; the man darted a hand inside, twisted and yanked, and held the sheep's heart high.

Chu-chu said, "Hao, hao."

The sheep fluttered like a leaf and died.

"That is a rare way to slaughter," Jake said to Jim.

"The Mongol way. Because so many of them are Buddhists and must not shed blood."

The world was full of wonders. Nomad shepherds who must not shed blood! Buddhists who live on meat!

19/   K'uang felt powerful, irresistible, in the wireless shack; it was the center of a vast web, the forces of order, of justice, of retribution, working with the speed of light to trap and devour the forces of evil. Qomul at his fingertips, and now Peking. One could speak to generals, to governors, without suffering the haughty glance, without disgust at their obesities and slothful ways.

The corporal completed the ritual of identification and introduction. K'uang took the microphone, and spoke to Peking. Of all but the nails.

"Yes. Penicillin."

Peking spoke.

"No," K'uang said. "The foreigner's identification was genuine, and he knew nothing of the medicine." His own voice surprised him: a tremor of guilt, the voice of deceit. "What concerns me now is his employer. Kao Hu-tsuan, a merchant. A shady merchant, I have no doubt. You must have a file on him."

The air crackled: four hundred miles away, in Peking, a colonel exploded. Kao Hu-tsuan was known, all right.

"The bastard is dead," Peking snarled. "A black marketeer of the worst stripe, with a particular thirst for gold. The secret police took him in, finally."

"Ah," K'uang said, and held his breath, prickling: what had the merchant confessed? "And what did he tell them?"

"Nothing," Peking said. "He never broke. Yüüü! They tried everything. He must have been a mess when he finally died. They hung out the corpse as a warning to other scum. All over Peking his gold lies hidden. And who knows what else. You must find that foreigner. Alive. You should not have let him go."

"He is with the caravan of the House of Wu," K'uang said, "and I have already warned Captain Nien in Qomul."

"Then go get him," Peking said. "If there is any question about your orders, have them call me here." And after a pause, "Is this Major K'uang of the train at Ch'ang-sha?"

"The same," K'uang said dryly.

A chuckle, floating four hundred miles. "A thousand Japanese dead, I heard."

"One exaggerates," K'uang said coldly.

"Find that foreigner," Peking said. "And bring him in alive."

20/   Three weeks later, weary, bored and snapping curses, they hove to at a well called Ming-shui, or Clearwater, in a range called the Ma-tsun Shan, or Horseshoe Hills. Jake tried to explain to Jim why they might as well be in New Mexico if places were going to have such names.

They hauled water. Water was not the problem Jake had imagined; there were wells and only a few went dry. The problem was feed. They had crossed the Black Gobi on a well-used track, and for days had seen no grass. Once across and into the hills they had seen grass, but it was a burnt, brownish blush on the hillsides. The camels were tired, and here at Ming-shui men and beasts would rest again.

But three of the camels were kept off water for a day. They moaned and bellowed while the rest tanked up. Chu-chu marched here and there importantly, like a judge at a state fair. He was the hoof man, and the first day he did some resoling. The pads of a camel's hoof were softer than Jake had suspected, and sometimes cracked, or split around a wee piece of grit that could work in and lame the animal.

Chu-chu had his assistants hold a camel down while he roped the neck and a foreleg. He presented the taut ropes to other assistants with a starchy sort of undertaker's gloom. Then he looped a line around the hind hoof he wanted and a couple more assistants stretched the leg out behind.

Jake waited for bones to crack.

The camel belched. Chu-chu worked fast: he cleaned the crack with a boomerang-shaped needle, slapped a camel-hide pad across it, and used camel-hair twine to sew it to the tough edges of the hoof. Then he stepped back soberly, like a surgeon, and the others waited anxiously like relatives in the anteroom. "Good," he said. "Next."

Jake hunkered and observed. All around him camels lay nosing at feed bags. Men shaved, repaired gear and told dirty stories. The sky was cloudless and the wind hot; a few had improvised half-tents. Head of Pot and Second Head bustled. Second Head was chopping white vegetables on his portable block, and Jake hoped for a banquet.

When Chu-chu had resoled four camels, he ordered a check on nose pegs. In this part of the world a bit was rare. These folks slit the calf's nose and shoved a wooden peg through, in a hide washer. They attached twine or rawhide to both ends of the peg, and if the calf acted up, a good yank put him in his place. Though often camels seemed indifferent to pain. And the Chinese to the camels' pain.

Jake did not know yet why three camels were being kept off water, but refrained from foolish questions. He bathed instead. Now and then a camel-puller sidled over to observe this exotic extravagance. Hsü-to squatted near the well clucking and rolling his eyes. "Yin," he said, meaning the female principle. "Water is full of yin. It will drain your strength."

"It will enfeeble my army of lice."

Hsü-to was emphatic. "Lice are born of water. A man is clean when he leaves Pao-t'ou. He stops at this well and that well. Aha! He has lice."

Next day Chu-chu worked on the three dry camels. Cold water, Jim explained, raised or dilated blisters. These three had been dried and rested for a day and now were ridden here and there to incite a good flow of blood. Then they were held in place as for resoling, and Chu-chu lanced their blisters.

Not exactly. He did not lance the blister itself. He drove a blade into the pad from the side. He was not opening the blister but relieving the pressure by bleeding the whole hoof.

This unfriendly treatment irritated the camels and they stomped angrily. Soon there were spurts and pools of blood to mark their dance. Chu-chu liked that. The demons were draining away. "They will be well," he said. "Water them now."

Next morning they were well. The men loaded up before sunrise and moved out, to take advantage of the cool hours. They had passed through a deep cut just after sunup when the world ended. Half a dozen bandits on swift ponies burst out of ambush and stampeded the caravan.

Jake was aboard his donkey, nodding along half asleep like a raggedy-ass Mongol trader with a mangy boar hide and a horned hat. Bad Smell poked along beside him, and behind her Sweetwater, and last in line Whore-of-the-Mountain shuffled with her long bell, ting-tung-tingtung, and the bandits exploded out of nowhere: war whoops, hoofbeats, shots, the camels blatting in panic.

The donkey shot forward, and Jake pitched backward and landed hard on the nape of his neck. Ponies thundered past. A shot deafened him. His donkey dropped. For a frozen instant he lived a nightmare, shrinking from an inhumanly scarred face, cruel and ugly: a huge man, prodigious, and that shattered face! He saw the eyes widen and heard the man shout "Keep this one" as he swept by, and then many swept by, like an army, and the dust was thick.

Jake heard shots, many shots, and the cries of men fighting. He heard hoofbeats and yip-yips. He was dizzy, and struggled to sit.

Master of the Armory.

He spat dirt and winced at the pain. He felt for the .45 but was much too late. A young man with buckteeth, sitting a pony on a tight rein, flashed a killer's smirk at him and said, "Do not move. At all." The advice was not necessary. He had a rifle trained on Jake's bellybutton.

Also Jake was paralyzed, and his gut ached. He wanted to vomit. He shivered.

After a time—maybe a minute, but it seemed like a year—the shooting and shouting died. The sun warmed Jake's back. He squeezed out a thought: these were smart guys, attacking from the east at sunrise.

He heard hoofbeats again and saw three horsemen approach over a rise, with two laden camels and a riderless horse. His guard never even looked around.

The three men rode to Jake and glowered, and he was staring again at the huge man of the scarred face. When the huge man said, "They killed Bayan. We killed a few of them," Jake's bowels shifted.

"Bayan," Buckteeth said. "Bugger."

"Kill him and let's go," another said.

"Easy does it," the scarred man said. He was big as a monument. He said something in a language Jake did not know, and the others laughed. Jake hung on. He could hardly breathe, but he would not soil himself or beg.

"That yellow hair," another one said, a tiny little brown fellow with a sharp nose like a mouse.

Ugly said, "That's gold."

Buckteeth slung his rifle.

Jake saw that it was a Garand. With tremendous, painful effort he understood that he had been captured by bandits in western Mongolia and that they were about to kill him, castrate him, throw him away on the desert, or blind him and sell him for a slave.

Buckteeth said doubtfully, "Ransom?"

Ugly nodded. He dismounted, and stepped to Jake. His boots crunched on the stony sand. At Jake's side he squatted. Jake forced himself to meet the man's eye. The scars were long furrows and ridges from hairline to chin, and the scar tissue was not burnt black by the sun, so the face was striped like the desert with yellow ridges and black gullies.

Ugly drew the .45 from Jake's holster. He liked the look of it and nodded. With a forefinger like a banana he poked Jake's belly. "Ransom," he said.

The fourth man was a handsome young buck. "There is no way," he said. "Take him to Russia? Look for his mommy and daddy?"

Ugly said, "True. But there is often something to be made out of foreigners. Once we had a railroad car full of them in Manchuria. We traded them for horses, guns and safe-conduct."

"Not this one," Mouse said. "This one is not useful. Not even a woman. Shoot him now."

"He might do for a woman," Buckteeth said. "Better than nothing."

"Strip him," Ugly said.

Buckteeth came alongside Ugly and removed Jake's shirt.

"A little bag," Ugly said. "Holy beads, no doubt."

Buckteeth ripped the bag loose. Jake had seen it coming and ducked his head, wriggling, so the wire only burned his neck and did not shear his head off.

Buckteeth squirted a stream of gold into the palm of Ugly's hand. "Now we're in business," he said, buy-sell he called it, like old Kao.

Ugly jingled the coins and poured them from hand to hand. "Six of the handsome little buggers."

"Seven," Jake muttered, massaging his neck. The wire had scraped, and raised a drop of blood.

"It speaks," Ugly said.

Buckteeth bashed Jake where he sat. Broke my jaw, Jake thought hazily, and tasted blood.

"Ah shit," he said in English. He was suddenly sore as hell; man about to die, he has a right to be annoyed. He hunched away from Buckteeth and snarled, "Bugger your mother and your father and all ancestors to the original generation of maggots. You are a defiler of dead dogs, you suck horse cock, and you could not hit a camel in the ass with that rifle if he was shitting on you."

Ugly's eyes widened. "This is no Russian," he announced. "This is a scholar. Hit him again, Momo."

Buckteeth slapped Jake backhand. Buckteeth looked like about a hundred and twenty pounds and he damn near killed Jake with the one blow. Jake's eyeballs rattled and his brains scrambled and whistled. The horizon tilted and blurred.

"Son of a Mongol turtle," Jake wheezed.

"I'm Japanese," he said, and whammed Jake again.

"Son of a Japanese turtle," Jake sobbed.

Momo spat a great gob on him.

"Take his pants off," Ugly said. "They hide things in the plum garden."

"Jewels," Handsome said, and laughed merrily. Jake tore off his shoes and shucked his pants, squirming where he sat. "Nothing hidden," he said.

"Green underwear," Ugly marveled. "Maybe he has a green pizzle. Or a blue ass like the African monkeys."

The pain was ebbing and Jake could see a bit. He was also beginning to think. A painful process at the best of times but he was under considerable stress here and had no choice. He was thinking that he would have to tell these people something really interesting. He would also have to be very lucky. Those scars. There was a chance.

"Take it off," Ugly said.

Jake took it off.

"A well-favored creature," Mouse said, "but no Russian. He must be a Turk."

"No," Ugly said. "I know what he is. I think I even know *who* he is."

Who? "An American," Jake said quickly, the fog thinning and his path clear, "wanted for murder and theft. I am traveling west to find a tiger's assistant and go to work for him. I have killed many men, most of them Japanese," that with a satisfying defile-yourself glare at Momo, "and am accounted the best rifle shot in America."

That shut them up. They froze like wax dummies, mouths open. Jake's blood was running again and he believed he had a chance; he forced himself to look rough and surly.

"Bugger my mother-in-law," Ugly said in holy tones. "Do you know anything else? Besides killing? Do you know horses?"

"Some. Camels, a little. Guns, a lot. Yours is a Lee-Enfield, short model, and that box magazine holds ten cartridges if it still works. Mouse there has a Kar Ninety-eight and God knows where he stole it but he can't have much ammunition for it. Dung-head here"—that was Buckteeth, old Momo—"has a pistol in his belt that I think is worth a pound of gold. Only a few such were ever made."

"I took it from a Chinese general," Momo said. "A pound of gold?"

"Too much chitchat," Ugly said. "So you can shoot."

"If this son of a whore's towel hasn't put my eye out."

"And what man have you killed, that you must run?"

"My partner. He cheated me."

Ugly's brows rose. "Old Kao? I doubt that."

Jake went popeyed. His heart hammered. Holy Jesus Christ. Holy Jesus Christ, what is this.

Ugly spoke what sounded like Mongol. Handsome wheeled his pony and cantered west.

Jake sat there with no clothes on. He was half blind and all scared now, and felt smooth and hairless between the legs, nothing there at all.

The sun behaved as usual, warm and friendly and enjoying the morning.

They heard hoofbeats and saw Handsome off to the north, riding east. Ugly sniggered. His lank black hair covered his ears. If any. "We allow you one shot," he said. "If you point the rifle the wrong way we will gouge out your eyes and skin you."

"Skin him first," Mouse said, "so he can watch."

"What did you mean—" Jake tried.

"Why hatch this dwarf at all?" Mouse complained. "We have his goods."

"Shut up," Ugly said, "or I will slit you from gizzard to gullet. I have taken a liking to this boy."

"What is this?" Jake croaked. "What's—"

"Will you shoot, or will you not?" Ugly asked.

"I will shoot," Jake said quickly. He pointed to Momo. "That rifle."

Ugly nodded. Momo unholstered his Luger, his American Eagle parabellum worth a thousand dollars. He sighted humorously along the barrel at Jake's crotch, which was momentarily without a tenant anyway. Then he tossed his M-1 to Jake.

Jake checked the safety; it was on. He slipped the clip in and out, and half drew the bolt. In as hard a voice as he could manage he asked, "What is Handsome doing?"

"Setting a target," Ugly said.

"Bugger," Jake said. "To make me shoot into the sun. Bring him back. Send him west."

"A regular general," Ugly said.

"A sergeant," Jake said, "which is much better." Kao, the man had said!

Ugly called out once, a steady high-pitched note, and in a few seconds Handsome appeared on a rise. Ugly spoke to him; Handsome dashed off to the west. He circled around some high ground and came out on the road, where the caravan had fled.

Jake's throat was tight, but he pried open the butt plate, and when he found the scrap of paper he thanked God. All scared boots in love with their corporal and learning how to shoot—Jake too, in his time —marked down the windage and elevation, so many clicks of the rear sight this way and that, on a scrap of paper and rolled it up and stuffed it inside the plate, where there was a little storage space for the ramrod and patches and such. Jake filled up on a couple of deep breaths and his blood flowed in a more standard manner. He had the shakes, though, and the paper fluttered.

He blinked slowly several times, and his vision cleared. His eye watered; he blinked it clear again. Lacking pockets, he took the scrap of paper in his teeth. He flipped the butt plate shut and checked the sling. It was worn but serviceable.

Handsome had set his target in the middle of the track, a little bundle or a sack of small goods. Ugly waited patiently and was amused. Momo showed all ninety-nine teeth, squinted along the barrel of his Luger and made a mocking pop with his tongue.

Jake slung the rifle as he had a thousand times and rolled himself prone as he had a thousand times. A thousand times and they were all practice for this time. He lay flat on the sandy rock. And him without a thing to wear.

"Good luck," Ugly said cheerfully.

"Bugger," Jake said, for the sake of pride and appearances.

Handsome had remounted and circled back behind the hill.

What Jake did then was, he offered a short prayer. There was doubtless some ancient Chinese bow-and-arrow grace to be said at such times. Lord of all under heaven. The camel-pullers had a friendly name for God, Lao Tien-yeh, old man God. So he shut his eyes and said, Old man God, I have sinned but forget that now. There is no man that sinneth not. I have made an effort from time to time and hope you will extend a little credit temporarily.

He made himself comfortable, or at least stable, and pulled in a few deep breaths to soothe the system. His right eye burned but the vision was clear. He adjusted the sling, good and tight, snapped the safety off, spat out the scrap of paper, read carefully, and set the rear sight. About three hundred yards. Estimating the distance, and verifying that there was no wind, he grew calm. A man doing the work he was trained for. A little shaky before the bell but once in the ring okay.

He sighted for the center of the bundle. His hands trembled; he waited. He clenched and unclenched his fists, and shut his eyes for a bit. The bandits were quiet. When he was ready he sighted again. He drew in another breath, let it half out, and lay like a rock. The front sight held steady. He squeezed off the shot.

He heard the crack but never felt the recoil. He rolled over and slipped his arm out of the sling, and lay on his back with the rifle heavy on his chest and the barrel cool along his cheek. He heard Handsome's hoofbeats, also his shouts, but could not make out what he was saying. The sky was huge, blue and neutral; the sun burned at his belly. He shivered, and went on shivering. He could not stop shivering.

When Handsome rode in, Jake sat up and tossed the rifle to Momo. He bowed his head. He had done all a man could do. If they blew his brains out now, it would not be his fault. And anyway, he thought, a last joke, anyway, if they kill me I will die without wetting my pants. He heard them jabbering but did not dare look up.

Then a hand wedged the target between his legs, and they all made rowdy laughter.

It was Jim's head, and Jake had made him a third eye, in the middle.

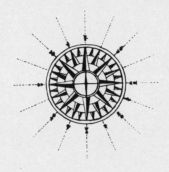

III / TURKESTAN

21/   Ugly was a huge brute with a fat, striped face, and his cotton shirt bulged: neck, biceps, belly, breasts shadowing like a woman's. He blocked Jake's horizon. Yet he was not fat; he was massive.

His eyes were not cruel and not kind. Jake was merchandise, and Ugly appraised him.

Jake was sucking in long breaths, and releasing airy grunts. Muscles leapt and quivered. His belly fluttered. He was sweating freely. He twisted to thank heaven, and the sun was a needle in the eye.

"On your feet, American."

Jake rose warily to a crouch, and then stood. His knees wobbled like the rubber man's in a sideshow; there was no stilling them.

The bandits laughed. "It will pass," Ugly said, and to Momo, "Give him his clothes."

"He's so pretty," Momo pouted.

Jake scurried to the clothes and dressed quickly. The difference it made: a man again. He knotted the sash and slipped into his shoes. He knew that he ought to be counting horses and camels, spotting weapons and making shrewd plans for a heroic escape. His eyes teared. He was not weeping but his eyes were tearing noticeably. His heart boomed.

"A big one," Handsome said.

"Taller than I am," Ugly said.

"A buggering giraffe," Momo said.

Jake could summon up no bright remarks so kept his gob shut. Kao. This striped animal had spoken Kao's name.

"Tie his hands," Ugly ordered, and Momo obeyed.

Jake cried out.

"Momo," Ugly reprimanded.

Momo slacked off.

"My hat," Jake mumbled. He ducked; the flat of Momo's hand fanned him. "And tell this Japanese dog to lay off me," he howled.

"Why should I tell him that?"

The question could not be answered. There was no reason whatever why Momo should not beat him to death.

"What about a fair fight?" Jake said. It sounded silly.

"But we try not to fight," Ugly humored him. He went on as if to a child: "You see, we are bandits and not soldiers."

It seemed very simple. Jake made painful efforts to understand this simple way of life. For some seconds he stood frowning. "Then there is no way," he said at last.

"There is no way."

"They will beat me when they want."

"They will beat you when they want."

"It does not seem manly," Jake said.

Momo slugged him on the shoulder; Jake staggered sideways. His arm died. "Tomorrow," Momo said. "Much buggering." He drew a knife and thumbed its tip.

"Now what is this about your hat?" Ugly asked.

"The sun kills all alike," Jake said, not looking up; humble; meeting no one's eye.

"Fetch it," Ugly told Mouse.

Mouse clapped it hard onto Jake's blond head, saying, "Long life and prosperity."

"Now," Ugly said, "where are the uniquely precious goods?"

"The two geldings are mine," Jake said. "All I own is on them."

Handsome slugged his other arm and send him hopping toward

Momo. The Japanese shoved him happily toward Mouse. Sun and sky spun. Mouse bulled him back to Handsome. They were not shouting and laughing like children in a playground; they were grim and sardonic like men who knew little amusement. Jake might have kicked out but thought better of it. He shut his eyes and hunched. The roof of his mouth tasted of vomit. Handsome set both hands on Jake's chest and pushed. Someone had knelt behind Jake, the kids' trick, and Jake went down hard, backward, crunching to earth on his bound arms. The breath whooshed out of him, and the sky rocked.

He opened his eyes to see Ugly standing over him, upside down, looming. "You must answer the question," Ugly said, "more accurately."

"You tell me about Kao," Jake wheezed, "and I'll tell you about the goods."

"You will tell us about the goods," Ugly said pleasantly, "or we will remove the appendages of the right side of your body, namely the ear, the eye, the hand, the plum and the foot. Then, because we are not barbarians and fair is fair, we will release you." Ugly shrugged. "We will then comb through your goods at leisure. I asked merely in good will. And to see if you returned our good will."

Handsome said, "Kill him now. What is this game?"

"I told you," Mouse said. "He is insignificant."

Ugly sighed. "And you were right." Upside down he drew a pistol; upside down he sighted.

Jake panicked, strangled, and could not speak; and then in a rush he said, "Major K'uang has it, Major K'uang has it, Major K'uang has it," and he was still saying it, again and again, when Ugly holstered the pistol. Momo said, "Listen to that," and Ugly said, "Stop your babbling, American, and tell us about it"; and Jake stopped his babbling, and lay like one dead thanking old man God. For his mercy endureth forever.

"It was worth a fortune," Ugly said in deep melancholy. They sat in a circle, all but Handsome who stood with a handful of reins while the ponies fidgeted and the camels lay snobbish and indifferent. Jake sat wrinkled and gray beneath the coolie hat. "It was worth two years of this riding and raiding for all of us. May the gods wither that bastard of a major."

"You know him," Jake said nervously.

"We know him."

"There was nothing I could do."

"Nothing. He would gut you like a fish. A man of no morals."

"Unlike us," Jake said, and for one second, a flash of the eyes, he and Ugly were comfortable together.

Ugly clapped hands. "To work." He sprang up. "You come along. We'll go through this garbage. Ho! What now?" His head back, he scanned the sky.

"A breeze," Momo said.

Jake felt it too. Far to the south he saw a single ice-cream cloud. "I'm thirsty," he said. Momo raised a hand but did not strike.

"Maybe tomorrow," Ugly said. "Momo, keep an eye on him. Listen, American. You have a name?"

"Ta-tze," Jake said.

"Tartar?" Ugly mocked him. "Then you can ride a pony till he drops, and drink his blood for food, and spit babies on a sword."

"It's only a nickname," Jake said.

"On your feet."

"My hands," Jake said. "I can't get away, I can't fight you all."

"Not with your hands tied, you can't."

"It's not necessary," Jake said.

"It is necessary," Ugly said. "You are too good a shot."

They watched Jake struggle to his feet. "I can't even piss," he said angrily.

"Store it up," Ugly said. "We use it to clean wounds. Now, what are these goods?"

Jake ran down the list. His mouth was dry. The hat was tilted; he righted it with a shoulder. His stomach was still knotted but he had earned a day, maybe several days. Later he would kill them all: a promise. The resolve eased him.

"Cameras," Ugly said, disgusted. "What is this big one?"

"Aerial photography."

"And where is the airplane?"

The bandits guffawed and swatted thigh. Jake had not seen an airplane the whole time. Only the couple of burned-out hulls.

"The cigarettes will do," Ugly said. "The wire is merely silly. These kegs, these accursed kegs: what else is in them?"

"Nails," Jake said. "Double-headed nails for construction."

"Let us check that."

"K'uang checked it."

Ugly nodded. "Of course. And we keep the tea. Coil those ropes. What are these boxes?"

"Tool kits."

Ugly spat. "For repairing ponies."

Jake shrugged. An eddy of sand rose spinning, and sprayed in the breeze.

"Dump it all," Ugly said, and the other three ripped into the goods.

"Aha!" Momo said. "A touch of home! A Model Ninety-nine. And in good shape. And ammunition."

"Binoculars." Ugly adjusted a pair and glassed the horizon. "We keep these. And those are compasses. Keep them also."

Handsome staved in the four kegs; nails spilled. He sifted through them; dumped them; a mound of nails rose. "Nothing but nails." He spat; he gathered handfuls of nails; they rained down, and another mound grew.

"Check all four kegs," Ugly said.

Mouse was tossing cameras to the dunes. "These goods are worth money," Jake said.

"Not to us," Ugly said. "We are not merchants. We are gentlemen and archers and travel light. We keep gold. Silver. Precious gems."

"Thousands of buggering nails," Handsome said. "Tens of thousands."

Jake saw his world thrown away on the desert. The breeze stirred; already a film of reddish sand had bronzed the nails. Soon they would be four tawny mounds marking the grave of Jake's hopes, just four more humps in the desert.

When the goods were scattered or packed, Ugly said, "Hao-k'an. One camel."

Hao-k'an. It meant good-looking. Handsome drew a long-bladed knife and cut Sweetwater's throat. While she bled he gutted and skinned her. Bad Smell chewed her cud and observed calmly. "The liver is good," Momo announced.

"My camel," Jake said sadly.

"We'll wrap you in the hide if you want," Ugly said.

Jake shut up.

Handsome hacked at the quarters. He was smeared with blood.

"No flies, anyway," he said. "I wonder how long before they would come."

"And maggots," Ugly said. "Take the shoulders too. Wrap it all in that brocade."

"Do not rush me," Hao-k'an said.

"No meat on the ribs," Momo said. "They drove them hard."

"No grass," Jake said. "Dried peas." In spite of himself he was absorbing this. Thus it is done, and so, leaving a head and many ribs and a pile of guts, a tail and a bloody hide.

When Sweetwater was butchered and wrapped, Hao-k'an stripped. He rolled in a patch of sand. Mouse went to him and rubbed him down; then Mouse and Momo polished him with a long sheet of cloth. He came away clean, abraded red in patches. He stepped to his pony and guzzled a long swig of water from a canvas-covered canteen. British army, Jake thought. His throat was like sandpaper. "You don't even stand guard," he said. "Suppose they came back shooting?"

"Never," Ugly said. "They cut their losses, always. It is the way. And we will not hit them again. The House of Wu has paid its toll for this trip."

They lashed the wrapped meat to their ponies.

"If we left him," Momo suggested, "we could cut up the other one and load the meat on Bayan's pony."

Jake panted in the noonday heat; they all stood in a yellow glare. The remains of Sweetwater seemed to simmer. Ponies shifted, edgy.

"I think not," Ugly said.

"What's he good for?"

"Bugger," Mouse said, and they laughed.

Ugly said slowly, "An instinct tells me to keep him."

"Ransom?"

"Ransom," Ugly said. "Hostage. Reward. He says he has stolen and killed."

"Mostly Japanese," Momo said, and smiled sweetly. "Tomorrow," he promised.

"He may be unusual," Mouse said. "He wears green underpants."

"All Americans wear green underpants," Hao-k'an said positively. "That is a fact."

Ugly stood pensive.

"I told you the truth," Jake said finally, "and that was a good shot." He tried to speak proudly and without pleading. Better a dead sergeant than a live beggar, he had always thought.

"It was indeed a good shot," Ugly said. "But I have other reasons. I have other plans. I have decided. Tie him to the pony." He beamed upon Jake; the ridges of his face stretched and bent. "You owe your life to my old friend Tu."

"Who?" Jake asked.

Ugly made big teeth: "He is also your old friend."

They ran a rope from one ankle to another beneath the pony's belly, and another from Jake's left ankle to his left wrist, a short one so that he rode doubled over, his right hand tight on the reins. Ugly and Momo rode before, and Mouse and Handsome behind. As they left the swale among the dunes Jake had time to turn his head once; he saw the bloody heap of Sweetwater, and the pile of guts, lightly sanded over by the gentle breeze; his goods too, lightly sanded over for all eternity; here lies Jake's new life.

And he saw Bad Smell watching after them, stripped of his burdens, only the nose peg to mark him as tame, and the reins lying useless. Then the riders crossed a low ridge and Jake lay forward, aching and thirsting, only the coolie hat between his sad, hard, empty head and the merciless sun; and he never saw Bad Smell again, and that night he ate a slice of Sweetwater's off-quarter, and was allowed one small cup of his own tea.

22/   "They eat with forks," Hao-k'an told the others some days later, "and they eat raw onion for breakfast. That is a fact."

Jake thought that he should talk with these four, that when they conceded him human they would ease up on him. But when he spoke they walloped him. "I too have killed," Hao-k'an said, puffing out his chest. "Many many. And a myriad of women have loved me."

The bandits rode in a diamond around Jake and he was learning what he could about their equipment:

The slung rifles and the bandoleers.

The knives longer than his hunting knife, longer even than bowie knives, and the blades curved slightly.

The khaki pants and cotton shirts stolen from some army.

The hats—Ugly's and Momo's campaign hats, Hao-k'an's cotton brimless, like a convict's hat, and Mouse's wide-brimmed felt, floppy now like some society woman's at a tea party.

The saddles, saddlebags, saddlecloths.

The felt boots, one layer, summer boots.

The old, tough leather—girths and stirrup-leathers and hackamores. The stirrups were of iron and well-wrought, and Jake was studying all this not only to learn but also to stay sane, when they rounded a bend in the road and Ugly said, "Ah."

Jake sat straight as he could and held his breath. He was approaching a village. It was four houses and a well, and beyond it he thought he could make out a true meadow.

He heard a sheep bleat. His throat was woolly dry, but his mouth watered.

Ugly urged his pony to a trot; the others too, smacking Jake's on the rump. Jake thought they were attacking.

The villagers—a dozen of them, including children—were shapeless and sullen. Jake thought they had a right to be. Their village was barren and hot, their houses were dug out of the dense yellow earth and roofed over with whatever came to hand: adobe, withes, several hides.

Ugly dismounted. "We need food and water. We mean no harm, and will pay."

"Pay." An elder's dull eye lightened in greed. "Women too you need perhaps."

"And why not," Ugly said.

"Ai-ya!" Hao-k'an said. "How many have you?"

The men were baked and scoured: hard, dry, skinny. The women were shapeless in cotton shifts—stringy women and unwashed, one pimpled and an old one toothless, with a plume of hair; they were hungry. They were all hungry. The elder said, "The army took everything."

"Not everything," Ugly said. "I see grass, and I see sheep."

"They are all we have. We have no grain and no oil for the lamps. We have no tea and nothing to smoke." The villagers shifted and muttered.

Ugly said, "We have tea."

The elder said, "We have water."

The others dismounted. Momo freed Jake, who slid off the pony but hung around his neck, stretching and wincing.

"Take the horses to grass," Ugly ordered. "Off-load, and tether them. When they have cooled down, water them."

Mouse prodded Jake. Together they gathered up the reins, and shuffled toward the sparse meadow. "We want a sheep," Ugly was saying. "Are you rich in water, or poor?"

Jake could not hear the answer. "Why do you buy here and not take?" he asked Mouse.

Mouse said, "Silence. Work."

At the edge of the meadow they off-loaded. The sun was low; short grass gleamed yellow-green, and the hills lay pink. Jake sniffed the air: it was dry, and bore a hint of dung and a hint of hay. He rolled his shoulders, and made circles with his head, to ease his neck muscles.

He tied the long split reins, each end to another pony's. Finally the five were tied in a circle, heads in, with enough slack to walk and graze. "I need water," he said to Mouse.

"After the ponies," Mouse said. "You talk too much altogether."

Beer, Jake recollected. About four cold beers now, on an empty belly in a dry body. A good buzz, that would be.

Mouse's nose was almost aquiline. Mixed blood. His accent was western, a man of borders.

Momo. Someday we will take Momo in our two hands and break him. And that Hao-k'an.

Jake lay flat on the grass, and dozed. Old Tu and old Kao chased each other through his mind. He felt his back mellow, and heard himself snore.

At Ugly's call he started, and jumped. Then he was ashamed and angry, and said to himself, God damn slave.

He untied one knot, to open the circle and make a line, and with himself at one end and Mouse at the other the ponies clopped and whickered toward the well.

"We are rich in water," Ugly called. He motioned Jake to work.

It was an old-fashioned hide bucket with an old-fashioned windlass, and braided rawhide for rope. The trough surprised Jake: an oil drum sliced in two the long way, and the halves laid end to end. Jake cranked and poured, and cranked and poured. He saw no markings on the drum.

The elder spoke in a border tongue, and laughed. Ugly answered in the same tongue.

Jake worked half asleep. He saw a palace with fountains, and marble pools, and tables heaped with succulent fruits, and women who were all melons and peach fuzz. Low in his swollen throat he hummed as he drew water, hummed and groaned, hummed and groaned in a chant, in a rhythmic chant, and then it was not so bad, with the vision of flesh and fruit, and the chant to work by, and his eyes half shut; and tonight they would give him food, and let him drink.

And they did: he stuffed himself with mutton, and drank countless cups of tea, and then they led him to the ponies and tied his hands behind his back, and tied one foot to the circle of reins. When they had returned to the women, he hopped up with great effort; the horses grazed, and brought him crashing down. He stood again; but what then? He could not mount. Suppose he could: how ride five ponies strung together in a circle? He could loose the reins, with his teeth. No: he tried, and was dragged on his face.

He lay on his side in the dark. And if he cut one free, and mounted, and cantered down the road? To what? They would check; he would have an hour's start at most; they would track him, and take him, and chop off his right hand.

So he slept. He slept on his belly, and the five ponies dragged him gently here and there all through the night; but he slept. In the late watches he thought he heard a flute.

"A shame you could not join us," Ugly said cheerfully next morning. They were pushing south with full bellies, well-watered ponies, skins and canteens topped off. Ugly had made ceremonious farewells, presenting two coins to the elder; Jake recognized the old Mexican dollars. Two bucks Mex. "With these people anything goes after dark."

Jake was glum. Half the day long his saddle moved like a woman, and Ugly was not making life easier with this talk.

"Old man God knows what I put it into last night," Hao-k'an said happily. "In winter these people bring sheep in."

"What people are they?" Jake spoke without thinking, and quickly hunched away from Momo; but Momo was weary and full.

"Qazaq blood, some Mongol and Chinese," Ugly said. "Since the rovings and transferrals of the war there has been much mixing. It was kind of you to watch over the ponies."

Jake cursed softly. Ugly laughed. Jake said, "Why do you rob caravans but pay villages?"

"The walls of a caravan are not in repair," Ugly said.

"You're afraid of a place with walls?"

"Afraid!" Their eyes met again. Ugly's were full of scorn. "No. I mean that the caravan passes but the village bides."

"What does that mean?"

"We need villages," Ugly said. "We need places to rest, places to water, places full of poor people who welcome us, who sell us their souls for a copper because we are wiser than the government and more honest than the police and safer than the army. Besides, they have nothing worth stealing. Furthermore, they will say nothing. If K'uang knew they had sheltered us he would wipe them out.

"So if we come this way again we will have no need to skulk. We are like fish, and the people are the ocean." He roared laughter suddenly, and rubbed his pony's neck affectionately; the pony caracoled, and neighed.

"What joke is that?"

"You would not understand," Ugly said. He repeated it to the others; they all laughed.

Without warning, Momo bashed Jake. "Tomorrow," Momo promised. And again he thumbed the tip of his sudden knife.

"Save that for K'uang," Ugly said.

Mouse groaned. "K'uang."

"He'll be along in a hurry," Ugly said, "unless this big-nose is lying. Though by now he may be dead, or suffering dysentery."

"Ah yes," Mouse said happily. "Or cataracts."

"Or a severe paralysis of the virile member," Hao-k'an offered.

"Or all of those," Ugly said solemnly, "and he would still come after us."

"These glasses are unusually fine," Momo said. "As good as the Japanese. We could set up shop."

"Shop!" Ugly snorted. "We sell off what we have, and we move."

"I would like to lay a bit by for my old age," Momo said.

Ugly said, "I think we will all manage to avoid old age."

23/   Ch'ing's heart was broken, and he raged at Chu-chu and Hsü-to each night. "The boy was a son to me," he cried. "I killed him. I took money from that cursed foreigner."

"We all killed him," Chu-chu lamented. "We did not keep a narrow heart and a wide eye."

The caravan was in Ha-mi, safe now; Qomul in the western tongue, a city, a true city, over ten myriads of people, a hundred thousand and more. Chu-chu's heart was eased by the sight of mosques. Also the city's pleasures beckoned after so long on the trail, but the pleasure was thinned without Chin Tan-te's moon-face, and his laughter and japes.

The men patronized public baths, restaurants and other places of amusement, some of them in flowery lanes. Ch'ing stayed with the caravan, and brooded. Time was money, yet he must wait for Major K'uang, who had ordered Captain Nien, by wireless, to detain the caravan of the House of Wu.

Ch'ing had not long to wait. K'uang had sped out of Pao-t'ou, promoting every man in his patrol, in lieu of furlough. Corporal Shih, who in any honest army would be an officer, was now a sergeant, with a corporal to help him, and the rest upper privates. K'uang drove them hard; they saddled early and rested late, and trotted in the cool hours, and clopped into Ha-mi only three days after the caravan.

"And how do you know that the foreigner is dead?" K'uang asked Master Ch'ing.

"Yüüü," Ch'ing said. "What else?"

"Ransom. Possibly collusion. The Tiger's Assistant—if it is truly he—is a notoriously sensitive man, and above all sensitive to silver and gold. I want to know precisely where they struck."

"Precisely is difficult. It was west of Ming-shui, an hour or so west, descending toward the middle plain, in the bed of the dry stream there, and we had passed through a cut." He hissed gloomily. "It is all cuts there, in the bed of the stream, and high banks and plenty of places for villains to hide."

"Yes, I know," K'uang said. "But Ming-shui is a place to begin."

"And from there?"

"Toward the Jade Gate Gap. We'll find them. A whisper here, a shout there. We'll find them."

"The foreigner paid me one hundred dollars U.S.," Ch'ing said. "The House of Wu offers that much for information or apprehension." It was an apology to K'uang, and a hope for the future; Ch'ing was greasing the mouth of the idol with fat.

"It was surely two hundred," K'uang said.

Ch'ing was silent.

"You will advance it to me," K'uang said softly. "I need it to keep my men going. There is nothing left to commandeer. My requisitions are rejected: the government believes that only Red bandits are bandits. The country drowns in foreigners and foreign weapons, but the generals sell them to the Communists against the day of defeat and bargaining. No one hears a K'uang. There are no supplies for a K'uang."

After a moment Ch'ing said, "I agree with all that. Thus has it always been."

"Not always," K'uang said dreamily.

"But I fear that you will follow other scents; or that you will be reassigned."

"Ah no," K'uang said, "and you may believe me: this I will do if nothing else ever. After all," and his tone grew dry and delicate, "the security of these great roads is my responsibility. What befalls you on these ancient paths of trade is to some extent in my hands."

"That too is true," Ch'ing said sourly. "And there was always something slanting about that foreigner. Very well, very well, two hundred it is, and I expect a full accounting."

"You will of course be given that," K'uang said smoothly, though both men knew that the matter would never come up again. "And henceforth, if an unworthy military man may presume to advise the greatest of caravan masters, henceforth be wary of passengers, and of merchants like Kao. You knew they were crooked."

"One does not ask," Ch'ing said.

"And consequently one's goods are stolen and one's friends killed."

"That had nothing to do with Kao, or with the foreigner."

"We do not know that," K'uang said. "Can K'uang scrub the country clean when Ch'ing trades in filth?"

"I will not again," Ch'ing said fiercely. "No more foreigners! Not the slightest foreigner ever! Not even a Korean! Not even a Cantonese!"

24/   **O**ne evening the bandits came to a river, a narrow yellow river in a broad brown bed, and they turned west. Jake had been theirs for a week only; it seemed months. He was afraid most of the time, not of beatings or death but of slavery, with chains and whips. He had been trained to disregard fear, so he wore it well, as others wore secret scars or false teeth. But he could not rid himself of it.

He drifted into reveries of throat-cutting; or picked them off one by one at three hundred yards as they fled across the dunes. He garroted Momo. No, strangled him. Bare hands. His hands closed on Momo's neck, grappled, crushed: bones cracked. Momo's eyes jutted. They jutted like . . . like breasts, and that was another reverie. Through the hot stench of ponies he tasted Mei-li; his throat closed, and his heart was sore.

Across the river he saw ancient watchtowers, and the ruins of a wall. The muscles of his back griped. He saw a tower every few miles for some days, and the low mounds of old wall. Doubtless interesting to the traveler of scientific bent, but some other time. Often Jake's head ached. He did his work, spoke little and was often smacked, but nobody seemed homicidal. One night Ugly offered him a cigarette. Jake had much to ask but held his tongue. He nodded thanks. The smoke seared. Momo said, "Tomorrow," and jiggled his brows. Far to the south, beyond the dun foothills, Jake saw majestic mountains.

The Jade Gate Gap connected Kansu and Hsinkiang. Jake liked it another way: China and Turkestan. Outside the pass a huddle of shacks and yurts had grown—since the war, Ugly said—to a village, occupied mainly by merchants, outlaws, whores and deserters from various armies. It was uncertain sanctuary: once inside, a bandit was fairly safe, though K'uang and Nien came prying from time to time and occasionally left a detachment to harry and annoy.

The men who watched Jake ride past might have been anything; they wore the baggy clothes and summer boots of the shepherd, the bandit, the horse doctor, the small trader.

They snickered at Jake, and called him Russian. Ugly rode scornfully, and stared hard. Watchers looked one look and away: the scars, and the stony eyes. Momo, Hao-k'an and Mouse ignored the spectators but rode tense and alert.

Even bound and doubled over, Jake felt the difference: his bunch were bandits, who knew no home and laid it on the line each day. But these observers in doorways were grifters, they were bartenders and discount brokers, and they were brave behind your back; he felt like a better man than any of them. Trussed and pinioned, chafed and galled, his back cramped and twitching, he was better than these street rats, and would rather be Jake. It was a crazy feeling and he could not analyze it.

He wondered if there was another white man here, and decided that he hoped not.

They jogged past shuttered shacks, and the shutters opened, and women peered out. Some of the shacks were roofed with canvas, tarps lashed tight through grommets. Some with sheets of metal: the war had not passed this way, but its trash had—materials, weapons, deserters, stolen trucks and jeeps. A familiar smell rose to Jake's nostrils: fires, dung, cooking oil and a ball of yen for sweetening: the smell of a city.

He wondered suddenly if he could be discounted, if Ugly could sell him now for half what a slaver could make on him later. The thought chilled him. He had never believed any of this, that he was a prisoner in the middle of nowhere and no better than a donkey. He did not want these bandits to leave him. He believed it all now. He knew just where he was, it was the Yü-men Kuan on his map, and it was not a place to be nameless and homeless and friendless.

He wished that Momo would make teeth, and whack him.

The village was a warren, and reeked. Ugly seemed to know his way. They fetched up at a wineshop with a large courtyard and stables, and Ugly kept them in the saddle while he palavered with the landlord. Casually, not seeming deliberate, the bandits eased their ponies rump to rump, and turned one pair of eyes to each of the four winds. Ugly palavered in Chinese, some tones reversed in the west, the song rising where it should fall, but Jake could follow: Ugly wanted the ponies seen to, and he was rapping out orders like an old cavalry sergeant.

There was plenty of water, Jake heard, and a little feed, mainly reeds and dried grasses, also dried peas. Gold? The gentleman would pay in gold? Then the feed was his. Also a stableboy of the first talent. There were no rooms in the wineshop, only rude benches and tables, but a square of sleeping floor could be reserved for five; or they could sleep in the stables with their ponies. There was mutton. There were women. There was no rice. There were other travelers, a group from Ch'ing-hai, some Tibetans with them; also some gentlemen from Kashgar hoping to slip eastward.

The stableboy was trotted out, and proved to be five-days-in-the-week-up-here. He goggled and giggled. His head was shaved and shiny. Ugly showed displeasure. He would hire another also, and if anything befell the ponies, the jolly landlord would find his teeth trickling into his large intestine from both ends.

The landlord stiffened, and Jake admired him for it. "No need to talk like that," the man said. "One cannot run a wineshop here without help, and I have plenty, and they are rough ones. No one fools with me. Your ponies are safe, Hu Ch'iao Kuei."

Ugly's eyes widened; he sniffed. "So you know me."

"Who does not?" The landlord bowed. "The Tiger's Assistant has no need to show claws and snarl. Men do his bidding with pleasure. But I too am known; I too stand straight."

"That is true," Ugly said. "I see it. You are not a slanting man. What is your honored name?"

"My unworthy name is Ying," the landlord said.

"Then tell this boy to love these horses, Ying, and to help us off-load, and in half an hour we want mutton in sauces, with ginger; also much tea, steamed dough and jugs of wine. Not small cruets but jugs."

Hao-k'an hummed, "Women."

"The yellow wine is very expensive," Ying said. "Kumiss is cheaper."

"Yellow wine," Ugly said firmly. "Oh, and this one, this one is a prisoner. We tie him to a post. Now, where does one commit nuisance around here?"

25/   By dark, Jake was an old toothless dog. He was allowed to do a human thing or two like empty his bladder; he swallowed mutton and steamed dough, and drank tea. Then he was tied to a post at the inner end of the tavern. Potboys passed him bearing platters, and soon enough he was hungry again. His hands were tied behind him, and the rope was looped about the post; with care he could slide his way down and sit on the floor, and by bracing hard and edging upward he could stand again. The post was a couple of feet across, one huge rough-cut log.

The wineshop was made of wood, mud, stone and odds and ends. Part of a Quonset hut. One wall had formerly been a log raft, or half a roof. On each table a small oil lamp flickered. Jake sat in deep shadow and was left alone for some time. The ceiling was a patchwork, what he could see of it: planks, sheets of metal, canvas.

His four friends had claimed two tables and benches, and stacked their gear against the wall. In the dim light, sullen and heavy, Jake was not sure who or what he was, not sure if he was thinking the word wall, or the word bulkhead as he had been trained to call it, or the Chinese for wall, or if it was only that there was a picture of a wall in his slow mind. He was confused by now, and afraid that he had been dulled by captivity. Sometime soon there would come a moment when he must not be slow of wit. A moment of opportunity or a moment of danger. That reminded him of something or someone, but he could not remember what or who.

He sat like a tame chimp and watched the travelers. Ying had called them gentlemen: a courtesy title. These were thieves and murderers. Some Tibetans, those round fellows with the brimless hats? And some from Kashgar. Jake heard languages. Laughter rose and fell, men cheered and coughed, belches rang. "Huo chi!" That was Ugly, calling a waiter. Mouse was sucking at a long wooden pipe. Jake envied him; opium would help now. Momo sat sneering faintly, as if he wanted to assassinate everybody in the room. Hao-k'an was lost in memory and mutton.

When these men had food, they ate for weeks to come. It was no doubt the same when they had women. Jake observed them stupidly. They ate. They ate. They drank. They rested and smoked and called the waiter again. Hao-k'an left and returned. They sprawled and made animated talk. Ugly sliced a Kansu melon with two quick strokes of his long knife; he took up a quarter of it and sucked the sweet juices. The air grew hazier.

Jake raised his head at the sound of music, and from the rear of the wineshop, passing close by him, a stocky girl in a light cotton side-slit gown emerged, carrying a mandolin. She pattered stage center, where Jake could look her squarely in the behind, and bowed like a school-girl. The customers roared welcome. Hao, hao. Hao-k'an stood up and semaphored, leering and screeching. The girl plinked; her voice quavered.

Silence fell, except for the girl's whine. Men halted in mid-chew, or cut short a swig. She sang a sad song, a song of borders and partings; groans of approval urged her on. The Tibetans swung their heads in unison, keeping time; the men of Kashgar, dark and leathery, with sharper noses, pounded softly on their table with flat hands.

The music died, floated off on a last ripple of breath; after a beat of dead silence, a lusty roar rose. Coins flew. Shouts also: requests, Jake supposed, and some calling for a dance.

A second girl skipped from the kitchen, stood beside the first, and bowed. The racket doubled.

Through the thin cotton, against the dim light behind them, Jake saw legs, the inner curve of a thigh. He did not want to be seen staring, so he lowered his head; yet he ogled from the shadows, and the hankering rose in him like a bloat.

Now one sang and both danced. They danced slowly, gravely, and little by little showed flesh: a leg rising through the side-slit, a sleeve falling back. The light was smoky and mysterious; the music soft, caressing.

The men were silent again, intent, breathless, still. Mouse was in another world, and smiled benevolently. Ugly's face showed sorrow, ancient grief.

Jake's mouth fell open as he watched. Brutish, he squinted out of the darkness at the waving legs, the rolling buttocks, at the muddy yellow lamplight oozing through the secret places. Heat rose between his legs. Unknowing and uncaring, he drooled: a strand of spittle fell from his mouth and oscillated, like a spider's first thread. From his chest, deep down, he croaked with each breath. His head sank lower, but his eyes glittered and stung.

One of the Tibetans, drunk, tried to follow the women out during the rowdy uproar after the show. Laughing and shrieking, making their way over the tables and benches like tumblers, his companions came clowning after him—to go with him, or to hold him back, who could tell? But the Tibetan found more fun on the way, and stopped suddenly; he spread his arms to hold his friends off, and spoke swiftly in a language Jake had never heard.

They goggled down at him, and behind them the noise and jollity died.

Jake tried to wipe his mouth on his shoulder. He blinked rapidly and made ferocious faces, waking himself. He drew in his legs and hitched his way up the post, tugging the looped rope higher with each hitch.

The Tibetan called out, and one of his men turned back to fetch a lamp. The Tibetan took it and thrust it suddenly at Jake, who stood impassive. The Tibetan laughed, and looked him over.

Jake shot a glance at Ugly, who was watching with mild interest. Momo was doing what he did best; even in the low, drunken light of the wineshop, his teeth shone. Hao-k'an seemed indifferent but Jake saw him swivel into a more attentive position, and nudge the dozing Mouse.

The Tibetan was not a big man, nor clean: he was rancid, and Jake thought of yak butter. Maybe these people smeared the body with it. This one wore a small pointed beard but was otherwise clean-shaven. In the lamplight Jake saw a bridge of blackheads over the man's cheeks and nose.

The Tibetan handed the lamp to one of his friends, and drew a short knife. Jake's mouth dried.

He saw Ugly speak, and Momo move. The Japanese slipped away from the table and strolled toward Jake. It seemed right. Jake almost shook in gratitude. Momo would dump this drunken son of a bitch on his ass.

Meanwhile the Tibetan was clacking a fat tongue against bad teeth and waving the knife. Suddenly he slit Jake's shirt front.

"Ah for Christ's sake," Jake panted.

The Tibetan showed surprise, and spoke. His companions laughed. They were small men and in their round hats they looked like bell-hops. Jake was drunk or crazy, or scared foolish: knives and bellhops and he had spoken English. Whatever happened he hoped it would be fast. Momo was coming to him. No. Behind him. He felt the tug at his wrists, another, and his hands were free. Momo grinned at the Tibetans and went back to his bench.

"Bugger your mother," Jake snarled after him.

The whole room watched Jake. The lean men from Kashgar sat back like experts; one munched a scallion, Jake saw, and poured kumiss from a jug. Kumiss was fermented mare's milk, and it did not seem now that Jake would ever sample it. His mind raced, his eyes saw everybody and everything.

With a second swift stroke the Tibetan slit the shirt crosswise. He exclaimed at the hairy chest, pointing and gibbering, laughing and strutting. Jake flexed his fists and rolled his shoulders. There was no place to go but he must move fast. Behind the Tibetan stood more Tibetans. Behind Jake was the kitchen, or the living quarters, or the cribs, but he would never make it. He glared at Ugly. This was not right. There was a breach of trust here. Cowardice from men who had not seemed cowards.

Jake had begun to sweat. He concentrated on the knife. The tip of it moved like a point of light. He knew there was a blade behind it, and behind the blade a hand, and a man, and behind the man more men, but the tip of the blade was all that mattered. It floated in a halo.

It struck at him like a snake, and cut a line of fire down his chest. The Tibetans shouted happily. Jake felt; his hand came away bloody. The pain vanished. He made teeth at the Tibetan.

But the Tibetan had turned away, and was laughing and crowing to his mates, over his shoulder. He began to turn back, bubbling giggles like a loony, his arm up for a backhand slash across Jake's nipples.

Jake saw Ugly move, and a streaking shaft of silver split the smoke between them. Jake felt the breeze at his right ear as he flinched away from the thudding smack. His hand was up and clutching even as he flinched. The Tibetan's blade caught lamplight, and started down; the Tibetan had not really looked at Jake, not really turned, and was still chuckling. Jake grasped the haft of Ugly's long knife, wrenched it free, lunged and slashed all in one motion.

He felt the blade split flesh, and sink in; felt it strike backbone, and quiver.

The Tibetan's grin faded. His eyes grew round and serious. He was puzzled. He seemed to be saying, This is not proper.

Jake's heart swelled. He drew a huge breath, embraced the Tibetan, and ripped upward.

He had spent twelve years of his life qualifying for that moment, and the surge of exhilaration dizzied him. Pure joy, flooding through him like liquor or yen. These others would kill him now, but there had been that moment.

The knife was free. Jake was almost smiling. The Tibetans closed cautiously. Jake waved the wet blade at them and called, "Aha! Aha!" He was sopping but blessed, swelling with an insane rapture, Jacob Alvin Dodds, God's fool, a long way from home and maybe only a short way to go now but he would not go alone. Then he saw Ugly and Momo moving, and hope struck him like lightning: maybe he would not have to go at all.

Momo fired as the Tibetans moved in. He sent a bellhop's hat spinning, and stopped the show.

No one moved then but Ugly, who padded up behind the Tibetans and spoke.

Ying the landlord came from the rooms behind Jake and said, "What is this disturbance?"

"Merely a quarrel," Ugly said. "These travelers will tell you it is true."

One of the Tibetans spoke. The landlord jabbered back. Ugly joined in. Their voices rose. Jake crouched, his lips stretched tight.

At a loud slam from the other end of the room they fell silent, and Ugly sidled, to keep an eye on the Tibetans but deal with this interruption. Jake saw that Hao-k'an and Mouse had the room covered. Their faces were innocent and attentive, like little boys at a puppet show.

One of the Kashgaris was on his feet. "We watched it all," he announced in Chinese, and then in the border tongue. "It was ill done by the Tibetan and well done by the Russian." He spoke with an air of great ceremony, and translated sentence by sentence. "And that is the end of it. And now we want to drink and see the women. And this arguing is incorrect and not just. And it works a hardship on travelers of good bones who dislike unseemly noise and commotion. And that is what I have to say, landlord, and we expect action." His companions thumped the table and congratulated him. He accepted their compliments like a politician, graciously, but it was no surprise to him that he was an orator and logician of historical importance.

Jake's knees wobbled. He was dizzy and wanted to throw his arms around Ugly.

Ugly spoke. He used his hands and spoke gently and persuasively. The landlord nodded, frowning at the Tibetans. Grudgingly, the Tibetans agreed to something. Then they protested again. Ugly shrugged and made an offer. Good enough, they seemed to say, good enough; and after a moment they dragged their dead friend back to their table.

"No more," the landlord said.

"It was not of our doing," Ugly said. He scowled at Jake. "Should have shot you first thing. Give me my knife." He stood, burly, and glowered at Jake. After a time he said, "It was indeed well done. Come and drink."

On Jake's chest the sweat ran mingling with blood; his hair and the shreds of his shirt were matted pink. "More kumiss," he said. Horse-teat wine, the Chinese called it.

"You forget yourself," Ugly said.

"You won't kill me tonight." Jake said. He sat between a drunken Hao-k'an and a drifting Mouse. Ugly and Momo sat angled at either end of the table, and no man's back was to a stranger.

Ugly poured with a grudging flourish.

Jake said, "Dry cup," and raised his drink. It sloshed and spattered.

He was still trembling like the aspen in autumn.

"A hero," Momo said. "A giant. A duke."

Jake tightened his grip on the cup and stared hard at its chattering brim. "It is not the same," he said in a rasping whisper, "as with the rifle, or the bayonet." Waves of fire and ice raced through him, and his vision blurred. Beyond the brim of his cup, across the room, the shadowy figures of Tibetans and Kashgaris gobbled and gabbled. Jake's shakes subsided. "That's better. It was because you tied me so tight."

Momo said, "It was having the oysters tickled by the point of a knife."

"It was the imminence," Ugly said absently.

"The what?"

"The soon-to-be of it. Death, his or yours."

"His," Jake said fervently.

"It is a moment of rare clarity. But afterward the humors and sinews go spongy and limp."

"Why did you bother?" Jake asked.

"You are my property," Ugly said.

"And if they had killed me?"

"We would have killed them. That, or slink out of town." Ugly spoke inattentively, heeding Jake little; his eyes roved the shadowed room constantly, and Momo's too. Like savages in a dusky forest. Now Ugly turned to examine Jake, not hostile nor friendly nor even interested, just looking.

Jake gazed back, and for some seconds they read each other; Jake felt older, wiser and stronger. "Look at them," Ugly said softly. "All these revelers, men of great strength and good cheer, in clothes of many cuts and hues. Smell the spices in the air, and the hot wine, and the perfume of women that still hangs. Feel the cup in your hand, and the bench against your hams. Remember the sun and the taste of fresh water, and the feel of a rifle's well-oiled stock. Then suppose you were that Tibetan, and all was cold and dark, and the hand of old man God lay heavy on your nose and mouth and eyes and ears. Tell me, American, do you think of such matters?"

"No," Jake said. It was the first time in months that he had spoken a simple truth, that he had not tried to be someone else, a camel-puller or a foreigner or a swaggerer. "I think of escaping."

Ugly nodded. "A good man makes plans. Only the slave does not dream. Well," and his scars creased, "would you prefer hot wine now? At my expense."

"Bugger," Jake said. "With my gold."

"You mistake. For some days now it has been my gold. No, Momo. We will not raise our hand against him tonight. Wine or kumiss?"

"Hot wine, then."

"Waiter." Ugly clapped. "A cruet of yellow wine for this warrior."

"Why were those Tibetans blowing the mustache?"

"They wanted reparations." Ugly's eyes roved again. A lizard scuttled across the ceiling and vanished into the dark. Ugly gestured after it. "You saw?"

Jake nodded. "A salamander."

"Never let one piss on you."

Jake drained his cup of kumiss. "What happens?"

"His spirit enters you. You cringe and scuttle."

"Hu-hu," Jake said. "Like the tiger's spirit."

"Be careful," Ugly said.

"You really are that one, aren't you? The one they talk about."

"Be careful," Ugly said. "We will not beat you here in front of all these strangers, but tomorrow Momo will scramble your brains."

Jake was still for a while. He remembered his questions about old Kao and old Tu, but he refrained. "What did you tell the Tibetans?"

"It was their man's doing," Ugly said. "That was agreed. But because this is not your country, we pay for their wine tonight."

"Not his country, either," Jake said.

"At least his eyes are the right shape. Here is your wine. And will you look at the waiter!"

The waiter wore a long slit gown and an ornate headdress, and was heavily painted, face white, lips bright red, black brows arched like tents. She might have been any age, and there was no telling what she looked like really.

Jake reddened. This might be a man, or a boy.

The waiter bowed, and placed the cruet on the table.

"Come here," Ugly said, and the creature pattered to his end of the table. Ugly stroked its face. It knelt. Ugly laid a heavy hand on its sleek head. Their eyes spoke.

Jake drank his cruet of wine and then another, and was permitted to sleep under a bench, against the wall. In the first faint light of dawn he was awakened by rhythmic nudges, and slowly he made out the huge bulk of Ugly's back; and then, looming at him over Ugly's shoulder, the waiter's milk-white face, and the smudged red lips, and the gleeful brows; and Jake could not have said if it was man or woman, laughing or weeping, alive or dead.

26/ It was a contemptible village of no name; K'uang sat his haughty camel and condemned the elder with one heavy-lidded glance. A barren village of sickly peasants, Qazaq mongrels! In winter they huddled together, half underground, and copulated with their livestock.

While they stood before him, lousy and ragged, he looked beyond them at their hovels of yellow earth. He recognized their trough: oil drums. A foreign trough. If not for the war they would drink from stagnant wells. An oil drum was a fortune to them, a new way of life.

These, my people! He hawked up a weighty gob, and spat. Sometimes he had visions of a new China, its population halved and all of them clean-limbed, bright-eyed, willing workers, patriots.

"The bandits who came this way," he said. "Describe them."

The villagers hung their heads and did not speak. A woman not yet past her youth was going bald: her hair struggled in tufts.

"Describe the bandits," K'uang ordered, louder.

The elder moaned. "No bandits. No strangers these many months."

K'uang drew his pistol. "Describe them."

"By the lord of all under heaven. No bandits." He was wrinkled, white-haired, dull of eye.

K'uang shot him dead, through the heart.

Even Sergeant Shih, who knew this major well, blinked.

The old man sagged like a sack of leeks, and sprawled.

"Who now speaks?"

No one moved. A small child wailed.

"Four," a woman's voice said. "With a servant, a foreign devil, yellow-haired. We only want to live."

"Ah," K'uang said. "And their goods?" He felt sudden excitement, but kept it from his face.

After a silence the woman said, "Arms, and saddlebags, and packs. Short of feed, they were, and without water."

"And they watered here."

"They watered here."

"Kegs," K'uang said. "Do you know what a keg is? A small barrel. Four of them."

"No kegs," the woman said. "By the lord of all under heaven."

"You lie," K'uang said.

"What is there to lie about?" The woman looked him in the eye. "In such kegs what would they carry? There were no kegs."

The woman was telling the truth. It made no sense. But he could not question further before his men, could not betray what he knew. Any one of them would desert, even kill him, for one of those kegs. Even Sergeant Shih. Even stiff, obedient Sergeant Shih. These are my men! These are the sons of Han!

Suppose he were to say it? Suppose he said, In those kegs is a lifetime of money. They would shoot him in the back, and squabble then, and shoot each other in the back until only one was left, and that one, a brute, would wonder then where he should go and what he should do. Kegs, he would say. Now where does one look for kegs? And he would wander the desert asking about kegs.

"So you fed them, and gave them water."

"There was no other way," the woman said. "We only want to live."

K'uang jerked his head at Sergeant Shih, who sidled his camel closer.

"Guard the men and the children apart," K'uang said. "The

women are yours. Butcher a sheep. We will sleep here."

He spurred his camel to the trough, and let him drink.

What fool would cache the kegs in these hills? It made no sense. Perhaps they had sorted the nails, kept only the gold, and transferred them to saddlebags.

Foreigners and their wily ways! Their schemes! This one he would track. This one he would close with. This one would talk: the words would pour forth like rain.

Struggling with Sergeant Shih, the woman cried again, "We only want to live!"

27/   The stableboy's name was Hui-te, which probably meant Bright Virtue. He spoke understandable Chinese. Jake asked him where he hailed from, and the boy pointed to a stall.

"Before that," Jake said. "When you were a small boy."

Hui-te glanced at the sun and carefully pointed west. Jake nodded. West was least likely. Salt marshes and desert. Mirages and bleached bones. Bright Virtue's nose ran copiously.

He was slow-witted but enjoyed Jake. The chain was a fine joke.

They were silent for some time, only the boy humming tunelessly as he did his chores. Jake helped him. Nine or ten feet of chain gave him a dog's range. He could sit in the sun, and that was a comfort; to be a slave in winter would be death. He could pace, or enter the stable and chat with the ponies, or use the straw and chips for a latrine.

The ponies fattened quickly, and were sleek in a matter of days. Jake was chained to a hitching ring set in the wooden wall. The chain was light but strong, and ended in a snug necklace. He was not in pain.

One day he cleaned weapons: again a tarp, patches, ramrod, the bowl of kerosene. It was not kerosene; it was a resinous liquid, cousin to turpentine. Momo showed a knife and opened his mouth to speak.

"I know," Jake said. "Tomorrow."

"Today," Momo promised, "if you foul those weapons." He squatted in the shade, smiling at Jake like a venomous toad; his hand snaked inside his shirt, and Jake tensed, but Momo drew forth a flute, only a wooden flute, and played dreamily. Jake enjoyed the Oriental melodies; the music sneaked into his soul, or his blood, and he felt his eyes slant, and worked patiently, and thought of flood and famine, and knew that all things were written.

It was a peculiar peace: a new world, the sun comfortable, ponies shifting and blowing, Jake's hands were sure and busy.

The stables lined two sides of the courtyard, bandits on the west, Tibetans and Kashgaris on the east until they set out for China proper. One of the bandits stood—or sprawled—guard. The Tibetans lurked, and Mouse would ignore them, or Momo and Hao-k'an smile with the glittering delight of devoted murderers. The Kashgaris ignored squabblers: they were easygoing men who chattered and chaffed, and walked spitting, as Hui-te said; only fearful men walked with dry mouths.

Jake ignored his guard as a rule, the more so if it was Momo. He had expected small freedoms if not acceptance, after killing, and now he was leashed and guarded.

"We wait for the new moon," Momo said.

The ponies were three bays and two browns. "What do you call this?" Jake asked the boy.

"The hoof." Bright Virtue's goofy grin vanished, and he was grave. "And this?"

"Ma-lieh." The mane. His answers were quick and solemn. It might be that he knew only ponies, but it might also be that he knew them well. So Jake learned the parts of a horse in Chinese: coronet, pastern, fetlock, cannon, knee. Girth and saddlecloth. And a phrase for potato that he had never heard, and almost did not believe: ma-ling-shu, the horse-bell tuber.

The bandits slept in the courtyard, a sentry awake always. Ugly transacted mysterious business here and there; the goods diminished. Flies buzzed; a low hum hung over the town; Jake heard shots one noontime; skinny sparrow-like birds pecked at the feed.

Hui-te taught Jake that ma-shih and ma-fen were equally correct for horse manure. Jake's hair was crawling down over his ears, and on his nape, for the first time in his life. He thought of having his head shaved but decided against it: they would nick him, or otherwise play games, and in the end he would look craven and villainous. If they allowed it, he would rid himself of his three-week beard. Bright Virtue said that Ili horses were not the same as Ili ponies: Ili horses were large and awkward and lacked endurance. They were not seen much here. They lived in the west, where men rode stallions. The men of China did not like the fuss and danger of stallions, and mares were not dignified. Geldings were best.

One afternoon, late, Ugly strode into the courtyard and Jake knew that matters were taking a turn; Ugly was moving briskly, and Hao-k'an and Mouse were all but marching. "Saddle up," Ugly ordered. "Empty yourselves." He paused before Jake. "Clip this chain off him."

"It was never necessary," Jake said. "Or the guard. What have you done," and he kept his voice level and hard, "sold me?"

Ugly slapped him angrily. "We do not sell. We ransom. And the chain was necessary and so was the guard. The Tibetans would have minced you."

"You mean I owe you thanks."

"You owe me nothing," Ugly said. "I have it all. And now you shut up and listen, and if there is one more word from you Momo will split your tongue." To all of them he said, "K'uang is west of Ansi and the Tibetans have taken that road east. They will tell him fine stories. The noise is that K'uang will level this place. God help us if they summon an airplane. I hear many things: the Communists are predominating in the east and taking cities in Manchuria. The Nationalist money is worthless. Ying guesses that the country has about a year left. These buggering bannermen like K'uang will be out for blood and looking for great victories so as not to be transferred east, and so as to keep their jobs whoever wins. If the Communists win we're finished anyway, so we're moving out now.

"We ride out tonight. We take stores, and all the water we can carry, skins and extra skins and more skins and four canteens to a man."

Hao-k'an spat. "Trouble coming."

"Not if you do what I tell you," Ugly said.

"You tell us nothing," Hao-k'an said.

With an edge to his voice Ugly said, "I tell you what you need to know."

"Then where are we going?" Hao-k'an tried to puff himself up, and only looked foolish.

"You want to stay here?" Ugly asked. "You see how generous I am. You are free to stay here."

Hao-k'an muttered.

"Speak up or shut up," Ugly said.

Hao-k'an shut up.

"We carry feed. There will be little grazing. The hardware is sold but every man take a compass and binoculars. Now hop to it."

He turned back to Jake. "Now you listen. You will ride in the middle but you will not be tied. If you make trouble you will be killed immediately. It is that simple."

"Where we going?"

Ugly's hand rose, but he checked the blow. "Bugger!" he said. "I should kill you now. I should have let the Tibetan kill you for a fair price. Now shut your orifices and make ready."

"It is not the new moon yet," Jake said. His chest tightened and his blood zinged, but he felt less a slave. Also this movement, this change, was exciting.

"Old man God wither your eyes," Ugly bellowed. "What do you know about that?"

Jake raised both hands, peace, peace, and risked a brief smile. Ugly spat and stormed off. "Hui-te," Jake said. "The bay with the notched ear. Make him ready."

Hui-te ducked and bowed and scampered to a stall. The others were working fast; Jake saw saddlebags flung, heard the ponies whinny; he went to the well and let down the bucket. When Hao-k'an and Mouse brought skins and canteens he was filling the trough. Mouse nodded and said, "Mmm," which was doubtless a compliment.

"I want a compass too, and glasses, and my own pack," Jake said. Mouse relayed the message. Ugly shouted yes, and after a moment went on, roaring, "Why is that boy working for him? Bugger-all twice over, has no one here any sense?" Hui-te scurried out of the stall like a scared goose, and Jake laughed softly. There was much to be said for having nothing to lose. "You saddle up, pig's turd," Ugly shouted. "A tight cinch and snug hitches all around, you hear? And remember this, somebody will have an eye on you always. Always! Small heart, you. Very small heart!" That was the Chinese way of saying, Be careful. Jake nodded. He would be careful.

He went to his pony, found his pack and his canteens, took two more canteens from a heap and went to the well to top them off. "Four skins of water each," Ugly told him. "They ride two before and two behind. Lash them so, necks together, and lash the tails below like a cinch. Snug and not bouncing. Bugger, they cost money but it will be worth it. Feed in the saddlebags. And in your pack if there's room."

"A lot of weight," Jake said.

"These are Qara Shahr ponies," Ugly said. "Tough little bastards from the Heavenly Range."

"The T'ien Shan," Jake said. "I know. With those long ears up front like that, and the Torguts raise them."

"Oho," Ugly said. "So you know something. Yes. And those good heavy necks and shoulders," he went on fondly. "They will take the weight. Bugger!" he said suddenly. "Horse talk later. Be quick, man. In minutes we ride."

But there had been a new look in his eye, and one that Jake liked. He went to work like a free man. He bore no evil intent for the moment and worked cheerfully. He would be happy to leave the Yü-men Kuan behind, wherever they were headed. He paused to go to a corner of the stable and wet the straw. For this hour he was in no danger; life was better and not worse. He almost whistled. Momo chucked him a compass. It was an expensive United States navy compass, mounted in oil, with sighting vanes that snapped up or lay flat. He rammed it into his pack, and hung cased binoculars around his neck. What else was in his pack? He groped: cloth shoes. Goggles. Flashlight. Other stuff. No time now to check. His map.

K'uang! Well, he would be glad to see K'uang if it came to that. Could he slow them up? Maybe. Small heart, small heart. And where was Ugly taking them? North was impossible, more desert. South, maybe, to Ch'ing-hai and the mountains. Not east because every man's hand would be against them, and every man's mouth too, saw them here, saw them there, and K'uang twisting to follow. And not west because west was murderous salt marshes and impassable desert, Lop Nor, the Takla Makan.

Who could tell, with Ugly? I owe him a little, my life maybe. But it should never have been his to save. I owe him nothing. Quits.

Bugger him. He owes me two camels, laden.

Jake was suddenly furious.

Just as suddenly he stopped being furious, and realized that he had been thinking in Chinese. God damn, he thought. There was no way to say God damn in Chinese. He would remember that. Keep ahold of the mother tongue, and when he thought he might be going Asiatic he would say God damn, and it would break the spell.

Jake used a long stirrup. No help for it, legs like his. He rechecked every line and strap. Set. It would be a pleasure to ride free, unbound, back straight. He ought to tip the stableboy, hey? He mounted. The others were almost ready.

"Hui-te," he called. The boy came shambling out, eyes wide, full of the men's and ponies' excitement. "I will tell you a secret," Jake said. "A story that you can tell, and a most unusual thing."

Hui-te's eyes loomed like fried eggs.

Jake bent lower, and whispered.

"Ah no," Ugly called, and strode to them. He pushed Jake back up, and shoved the boy away. "What did he tell you?"

Hui-te gibbered.

"What did he tell you?" Ugly took the boy by the throat.

The boy screeched and said, "He said he is your father."

Ugly released the boy and slumped. For a long moment he stared at the ground; he looked up wearily, shook his head, pointed the bone at Jake and said, "Tomorrow."

28/ At the great western terminus in Gurchen, Ch'ing supervised the sorting and stacking of his tons of goods. The men sweated and shouted; the vast field of camels, like the field in Pao-t'ou, swarmed with camel-pullers, traders, owners, clerks. Ch'ing shuttled between his camels and his office, a small bare room in a low stone building.

In late afternoon, when he had begun to think of relaxing, of riding into town to see his wife and children, Ch'ing received a visitor: a small, neat gentleman in a gray gown and a wide-brimmed straw hat. An elderly gentleman, of fine features and obvious style. Ch'ing did not know him.

Mastering his weariness, Ch'ing said, "Sir," and bowed tentatively.

The gentleman returned his bow. "Have I the honor to address Master Ch'ing?"

"I am that unworthy one," Ch'ing said. "May I know your estimable name?"

The gentleman flapped a fan, dismissing the thought. "Of no importance. I know how busy you must be, and will relieve you of some minor burdens: I bear written instructions and receipts for the goods consigned to you by Kao Hu-tsuan of Peking. I am to receive them of a foreigner."

"Hsüüüü," Ch'ing said. He shifted his gaze to the field of camels, and thought back to the desert. "I think we should sit down."

"Ah." The bland face altered; the old eyes blinked swiftly, twice. The two men sat at a wooden table. "A cup of wine," Ch'ing suggested.

"With pleasure."

Ch'ing poured; they sipped. "You must prepare yourself," Ch'ing said, "for bad news."

"Ah."

Ch'ing tried to read this gentleman, but the elder's eyes were opaque. "Very bad news," Ch'ing said.

"Please. Continue. I am prepared."

"Well then," Ch'ing said. "Kao's goods were indeed in the care of a foreigner. A roughneck. Outside Ming-shui the caravan was attacked by scurvy bandits. The foreigner and his camels—my camels! leased!—were taken. Also I lost one of my best men and had another wounded."

The gentleman blinked, and sipped at his wine.

Aha, Ch'ing almost said aloud. The old one sustains a shock. His hand trembles. "The foreigner is doubtless dead. The goods are gone."

"All the goods?"

"All the goods."

"So," the other said. With a white kerchief hemmed in yellow, he dabbed at his brow. "And these bandits?"

"The Tiger's Assistant and his sheep-defilers. Gone." Ch'ing waved. "Lost. Vanished into the desert."

"Ah," the other breathed, as if in pain.

Another crook, Ch'ing thought savagely. Another of these buy-sell gangsters. Well, now he will take a loss. Now I have some news for him. "I am sorry to tell you also," he went on smoothly and sympathetically, "that Kao Hu-tsuan is no longer among us."

"No longer . . ."

"He was hanged the day we left Peking. You have not heard?"

The fan was still; the eyes glazed. The gentleman spoke with obvious difficulty: "I have not heard. I correspond—corresponded—with none in Peking but Kao. Ah, the lord of all under heaven is a cruel master!"

"He is," Ch'ing said sullenly.

The other quaffed his wine and extended the cup. Such rudeness! But the man was under strain.

"So that is why I have not heard from him," the gentleman said. "I confess, I was worried."

"And with reason," Ch'ing said. "If I were you I would not chatter about that connection."

"Connection?" The fine, smooth hands showed palm. "I am merely a businessman. I never had the pleasure of meeting Kao."

"Nor will you in this life," Ch'ing said.

"How violent are the alterations of fate," the gentleman murmured. "You are quite sure that none of Kao's goods were overlooked? That none made their way, by inadvertence, into your own general cargo?"

Ch'ing exulted, suddenly and fiercely. "They did not. And if they had, you would be in no position to squawk, would you?" Then he relented: "No. I give you the word of the House of Wu. The goods are gone. The contraband, by the way, was not taken by the bandits. It was taken by the army after a somewhat more than routine search in Shandanmiao."

The fan flapped; the eyes blinked. "Contraband? Shandanmiao?"

"The foreign medicines," Ch'ing said.

"Foreign medicines." The gentleman seemed numb.

"You may of course apply to Major K'uang, or Captain Nien, in Qomul, to verify my account."

"Captain Nien. Major K'uang. No. Of all this I am ignorant." The old man was somewhere between stammering and stupefied.

"Crooked courses! Evil communications!" Ch'ing released his anger.

"Nothing was salvaged?"

"Nothing. There is more here than I know, and now I do not *want* to know! I have been swindled! My eyes befogged!"

"The construction materials, wires and nails and such?"

"Nothing. Diddled! And I lost a good man, and two camels!"

"Then I must not intrude upon your grief." The gentleman drew a deep breath, tossed off his second cup of wine, and smacked his lips in melancholy. He rose, and bowed.

Ch'ing nodded dourly, and waved him off. The gentleman fanned himself, bowed again and scurried away, flimsy and aged.

"Diddled!" Ch'ing said again, and poured wine. He raised his cup in toast: "Defile all liars, thieves, fat men and foreigners! Diddled!"

29/ West.

Jake's bay danced, insolent; Jake twisted the notched ear, and the pony settled down.

But west!

He tried to remember the magnetic variation hereabouts: doubtless small, east a few degrees. Ugly knew the road. And for Jake there was no dodging, no flight; he had to take his chances with these highwaymen.

They rode through a valley maybe twenty miles across, while the last light pricked out the low peaks of pink hills. Ugly called no halt, not for hours, while the dark fell and the moon rose, the waning quarter, sailing along like a small boat: Jake imagined a helmsman, and the hills towered like giant waves.

The night was cold, and Jake was hungry. His pony neither wheezed nor complained in any manner, but trotted on happily, a frisk of the head from time to time. Jake shivered, but his freedom warmed him. The north star was on his right hand and a fraction behind. He saw a paved road to the south, and when the vision had percolated through his frozen brain and shocked him awake, he peered again. It was a narrow river, silver and calm in the moonlight. The Su-lo. West! Who would have believed that!

Hours passed. He heard only the slap and creak of leather, and the clop-clop of many hoofs; he dozed in the saddle.

Ugly led them south to the river. Men and horses rested and drank. "I thought it would be dry here," he said, "but it looks good for some miles more. This is luck. You will not touch the skins or canteens until I say so."

Nobody argued.

"You see," Ugly told them, "it is two hundred and fifty miles to fresh water. Or so I believe. I have not come this way before. Mouse has, and he says it is about that distance, but you know Mouse. And even when we arrive the wells may be dry. So we are in the hands of the gods, and will give them all the help we can."

In midmorning they halted, boiling. Jake was sweating, and thanking those same gods for an insignificant item like his coolie hat. Ugly led them to what remained of the river, a sluggish brown creek. Without shade they sprawled, and lapped up muddy water. The ponies grazed on tufts of reed until Mouse broke out nose bags and dried peas; then the ponies seemed to say, Aha!, snorting as they champed.

Ugly's rucked face fattened like a full moon; he was merry. "A new life. If we live."

"If not, I will return in spirit and give you boils," Momo said.

"We eat," Hao-k'an said.

They built a small fire of tamarisk boughs and heated a desert stew, tea and flour and dried mutton. "A long time since rice," Jake said.

Nobody moved to punish him for speaking. They lay on the moist sand of the riverbank, cooler than desert sand. They were tired and peaceable. They slept. There were no flies.

Before dark the river vanished. A creek, a brook, a rill, a patch of mud. Then sand. "Speed is important," Ugly reminded them. "Not so fast as to tire the ponies, but a good steady clip. To reach water quickly is everything. Five days exhausted beats seven days weary."

"And if the wells are dry?"

"Ah. If the wells are dry."

They made speed. These ponies were something; Jake admired them, spanking along on a handful of dried peas and forty winks, but without water they would dry up and die as a man would, only quicker. He settled into his pony's rhythm and slept most of the second night, covered twenty or thirty miles dozing in the saddle.

Ugly woke him once. "To the north are salt marshes. If you are lost and find yourself riding on a sharp crust of salty earth, you are too far north. Also your pony will cripple himself, and the crust will slash his legs." He and Jake rode side by side for a time. The bandits took the point in a regular rotation, no word or signal needed, each man doing his three or four hours. "North of the marshes is a true salt desert, where nothing grows. It was once a great sea. Mouse has crossed it on a camel. It is malevolent and thronged with imps."

Jake shivered, not at the words but at the desert night. He called on his inner fires, and remembered sweat shirts, and rich, oily woolen sweaters, and the sheepskin jackets of his youth.

"Along its shores are the White Dragon Mounds." Ugly described them: mesas, they were. "Dunes to the south, marshes to the north. This is a very old track. The old Mongols used it, but they came with plenty of supply wagons."

Jake wondered if Ugly was cheering himself up with this chitchat. The moon sailed high, and south of them the dunes were a heaving sea. "Cold," Jake said. He remembered a chubby, docile girl, his first, half a lifetime ago; but those fires were well banked for now, and the image faded fast. He dozed; Ugly fell silent; the ponies trotted on.

Dawn again, and Momo's arm sweeping toward the southeast, and Ugly saying, "I saw. Not good."

Jake saw a faint pink-gray blush oozing up ahead of the sun.

"Early in the year," Mouse said.

Jake said, "What does it mean?"

Nobody answered; he did not exist. Hao-k'an scowled.

They were scruffier now, and Jake took comfort in that. Ugly's silky black whiskers grew in tracks between ridges of scar. Hao-k'an sweated plenty. Momo remained small and tidy, but his eyes were duller and his teeth asleep. Mouse had contracted, and tiny lines of weariness aged his sharp face. Jake himself was doubtless no beauty. His beard itched; he stank in his own nostrils. He remembered the luxury of a toothbrush; he would give a lot to brush his teeth.

At the daily halt, the sun riding up toward noon, they tumbled off like survivors. The ponies whickered and complained; one coughed.

"To work," Hao-k'an told Jake. The sky was clear now, and Jake wondered what the morning's omen had meant. He and Mouse broke out nose bags and leather buckets. "Check those buckets each time," Hao-k'an said. "No leaks, not one drop. No man knows where this Tiger's Assistant leads us. Maybe India."

"Persia," Mouse said, "where my ancestors lived."

Jake licked his lips and panted. The ponies whinnied and shifted; one screamed like a man in pain. They sucked noisily at the water, and wanted more.

"No more now," Ugly said. "A five-second swallow for each man."

Not enough, Jake thought. "Not enough," Hao-k'an grumbled.

"Another when we mount up," Ugly said calmly. "Rest now."

Jake wondered if he should drape his pony's head with a skivvy shirt, or cut ear holes as in the post cards of Italian donkeys. He decided this was not a time for imagination and initiative. If he kept his mouth shut, and his head screwed on, he would survive this. A reaction, maybe, to the parched and blinding emptiness all about him. He was too tired and thirsty for fantasies of revenge, but they stirred lazily in the back of his mind.

He lay back against his pack and accepted food, jerky only, no fire; no tamarisks and no poplars. He smelled hot leather, and the ponies, and himself. The bandits were too tired to abuse him. For small blessings large thanks.

He slept.

At sunset a breeze rose from the south; Jake inhaled it like cold beer and was about to say something jolly when Ugly muttered, "Maybe trouble. Mouse?"

"Hard to say. Early in the year."

"Well, keep moving," Ugly said. "If it comes at night we tether the ponies and hole up."

"No holes," Hao-k'an said gloomily. "It is well known."

"Stay together anyway," Ugly said. "It will come off the mountains," he went on thoughtfully. "A chance of moisture?"

"None," Mouse said.

"Defile it," Ugly muttered.

The breeze lapped at them, fitfully, all night. The wasting moon rose, only a crescent; even so the desert glowed like a sheet of ice. Jake ached and was less hopeful. They could not do this forever. They were more than halfway, he figured, but halfway to what? And what were they afraid of? More heat, from the south, or sandstorms.

Before moonrise the stars had lain like a bright mist, a great dome of silver dust, more stars than any man had ever seen; and now the crescent stood sharp, hard-edged. A full moon here would be like daylight. The emptiness was scary: not a bird, not a bush, not a desert mouse.

Not an airplane, either. Thank God for that at least. A bad way to go, gunned down from the air, gut-shot and helpless and cooking slowly.

At dawn the breeze was stronger and the sky to the east was rosy. Ugly cursed. In about the fourth hour of light, swirls of sand whipped off the shiny desert. Ugly cursed again and said, "Be ready. Goggles now." In the goggles they rode like monsters, inhuman; and the ponies grew restive; and the wind whined, and the sand whipped.

Ugly quit. "Now," he called out, and led them off the track into a swale, hardly a swale, a dip, no banks or walls to protect them, but still a dip. Jake saw it filling slowly with blown sand, burying them, and hoped that Ugly knew his business. They tethered the ponies, but not in the usual circle. "Let them put their backsides to it," Ugly said. "Tie this end to the foreigner."

"I can't hold back five ponies," Jake said.

"They will not travel," Ugly said. "It is no time for traveling." He hissed. "And if they do, they will travel slower with you to drag. Let them drink now, and quickly," he told Hao-k'an. "And then ourselves, and then we huddle and rely upon the gods." He turned again to Jake. "There will be confusion. And you will have more than one opportunity for suicide. If you release the ponies, or if you attack one of us. I hope such madness is not in your mind."

"It is not," Jake said. "I am a prisoner and not a lunatic."

Ugly flinched from a driving gust. The wind sighed and sang. The other three were tending to the ponies. Ugly and Jake stood close, goggles gazing into goggles. "When the caravans came this way," Ugly said, "a man would hear women singing, and bells tinkling, and he would be unsure of vision and would follow the allurements, and be lost. Sometimes a whole caravan. I suppose this is what they heard."

"I suppose," Jake said.

They were just two travelers, hatted and goggled and not much human about them, just two riffraff, two of the world's scum, on a bleak, indifferent desert.

"You were right," Ugly said. "In a bad spot sergeants are best."

Jake did not know what he meant, and did not ask.

They contrived a low wall of packs and saddles and goods; it was not much use, and they sat with the wind driving sand at their backs. Around Jake's ankle a rein was tied snug; beside him a pony snuffled and tugged. The men had drunk, and were chewing sandy jerky. Otherwise, there was nothing to be said or done. Like the ponies they huddled, and waited, while the wind shouted and the sand stung. The ponies remained visible; Jake was surprised that the world was not blotted out. The yellow world. The five goggled men sat like gods from another planet. Jake dreamed that this sandstorm was everywhere. Peking disappeared under sand; and Tokyo; places Jake had never seen, like New York and Paris and Moscow; places Jake knew too well, like Guantánamo and Saipan. In the end only these five men would survive. There would be no caravans to plunder or towns to sack. There would be no women. There would be an endless lonely trek. Jake would slay them one by one, and then the world would be his.

The ponies tugged; Jake grasped the rein and hauled. "No foolishness," Momo muttered. The ponies strained and leapt, and dragged Jake sideways. One neighed, a shrill scream; others answered. Momo and Hao-k'an joined Jake and reeled in; the ponies, shadowy now, stamped but quieted. Sand flew thicker. The yellow faded to a swirling brown. The men huddled, and bowed their heads.

"It could be worse," Ugly said.

"It will be," Hao-k'an growled.

"I have experienced worse," Ugly said. "I think we are far enough west here. Mouse says that between us and the mountains to the south is mostly gravel."

"Then it will blow gravel," Hao-k'an said. "And pebbles and then stones, and the mountains themselves."

"It will blow itself out," Ugly said firmly.

"I wish—"

"Shut up," Ugly said. "You begin to distress me."

Sand whipped at Jake; a pony screamed. Jake's eyes were safe and sheltered, yet he felt them grow gritty; it was all in his mind, but fat grains of sand lodged beneath the lids, and his vision dimmed. He was parched. He felt his body drain and dry, and his skin turn papery. He felt sand in his joints, in his mouth. He wanted to sleep. Exhaustion shook him suddenly and left him limp. He was not weak, only tired. He was paying for his sins. God mocked. A lonely Baptist, paying for his sins in the desert. Like that John. He remembered Sunday School, and the smell of hot pine planking when the wind came off the desert, and he saw his father, a face from the dim past, a lined old man, yellow-toothed and hot-eyed. I was not in safety, neither had I rest, neither was I quiet; yet trouble came. Yea. Indeed. And how. By the blast of God they perish, and by the breath of His nostrils are they consumed. Odd what a man remembered. But he would not pray. Better a dead shitbird than a live beggar.

He laughed aloud.

"Tell us the joke," Hao-k'an said.

"The weapons will be fouled," Jake said, "and I just cleaned them."

Ugly said dryly, "A sense of humor is invaluable."

The storm blew out slowly, diminished, and they were croaking their relief when Ugly said sharply, "Look at Weep-and-Snivel."

One of the ponies stood there on three legs.

The men were up like a shot, and left Jake sitting. It was some seconds before he understood that he was in trouble.

"The knee," Hao-k'an said. "Wrenched and badly torn."

The four men turned to pity Jake, and at first he thought they were blaming him, and then he saw what they would have to do, and his marrow froze.

30/ Ugly's shot exploded across the plain. Weep-and-Snivel pitched sideways and died with a thud. Jake died some, too.

Hao-k'an was lashing the saddle, leathers and irons to his own pony. He asked Ugly, "Horse meat?"

"I'm tired," Ugly said. "I want a bowl of boiled rice and some of those little shrimp from the southern ocean. No. No meat."

Jake sat on the ground, in the shade of his hat, and waited. Ugly met his eye but the other three were very busy. Momo frowned and muttered about luck.

Ugly came to squat beside Jake. "This canteen will last you three days, maybe more. I would leave you another but the important thing is the ponies. Without the ponies we are all dead, and we are stretching them even now."

Jake had nothing to say.

"You must continue big west small south. You will not have much moon so small heart to the trail. Rest in the heat of the day. Here also is jerky: chewed slowly it is satisfying and will keep you alive. Do you want fresh horse meat?"

Jake said, "No. Only the thirst matters. Will you leave me a weapon?"

"No," Ugly said, "because there is still a chance. Suppose in a day or two I come back with two ponies. You are too good a shot."

"Hsüüü, I would never do that. I give you my word."

"You have no word," Ugly said.

"A knife, then. Leave it on the trail as you ride."

"Yes. That, good. But," and he gestured sternly, a jab of the forefinger, "you will not take your own life with it."

"Bugger no," Jake said. "I have enough trouble without that."

"I would not be the cause of such a monstrous act," Ugly said. "Now listen, we are headed for a sometimes inhabited place called Abdal, near Miran, and also near the Cha-han-sai, a stream sometimes, though I am bound to say unreliable. If that is dry, we go on to a small oasis called Charklikh, unfortunately a day's ride past Abdal. At least. If we find water, we rest the ponies and one of us returns with a mount for you. If we find no water, we have no choice: we go on."

"Find water," Jake said.

"There are nomads in the area, some shepherds and unbelievably fishermen called Lopliks. They are not warlike."

"Ready," Momo called.

"In a little," Ugly called back. To Jake he said, "Do not follow women's voices, or the sound of musical instruments. Remember the Tibetan, cold and dark, and do not give up. Above all, keep your direction. If we come back it would be foolish to miss you. Keep the trail."

"Keep the trail," Jake said.

"This is the will of old man God," Ugly said, "and not my doing."

"I know that," Jake said. "I am somewhat depressed all the same."

"Yüüü, it chills the blood," Ugly said. "If it is not now it is later, and nothing can alter fate. Though we seldom know what fate promises. If you want, I can shoot you now."

"That is a kindness indeed," Jake said, "but I am unworthy."

"Remember, then. Big west small south. You have the compass. Water. I'll drop the knife up ahead. No hard feelings."

"Bugger yourself," Jake snarled.

"No need for harsh talk," Ugly rebuked him. "We do not want to throw you away. And we will find you again if we can."

"When a horse grows horns."

Ugly shrugged. "Old man God be with you."

"We move out," Hao-k'an called.

"Yes!" Ugly rolled up into the saddle. Hao-k'an, Momo and Mouse sat their horses facing Jake. No one spoke or gestured, they only stared at him; finally Jake pointed and said, "Tomorrow," and they liked his spirit, and they wheeled and trotted off.

Ugly lingered. "Well. You have fallen upon a bad time. Be a sergeant." He looked into the past: "I was a sergeant once myself." For a moment he sat straighter; his chin rose a fraction and his chest swelled. "All things can be done, man. Be strong."

Jake tipped the hat back and squinted up. "Listen: who is old Tu?"

Ugly's great grin creased his scars again. "Yes. I will tell you that. His full name is Tu Hsia-k'u, and he is a foreigner like you and a sergeant like you, and by a happy accident I had a word from him only weeks ago. Otherwise, you would probably be dead."

"Defile him," Jake whispered.

"You owe him much," Ugly said. "See you again." He trotted off.

"I god damn well hope so," Jake said in English, and then in a rage that purified the blood and bile, "Dushok!"

He saw Ugly pause, toss a knife to earth, and go on.

Jake rose and followed, like a beggar or a holy man.

In an hour they were gone from his sight. The sun was westering and in his eyes. The heat diminished, as if the sandstorm had fanned the desert cooler. Jake was thirsty. He knew some of his thirst was thirst, and some the expectation of thirst. He should be resting now, but he was walking off the insult, the bad luck, one million years of people, with glaciers and earthquakes and volcanoes, and continents drowned and oceans drying up, all leading to this moment, Jake Dodds, the boy genius of the horse marines, finally getting a little privacy. It was all his. Thousands of square miles. An emperor!

Dushok! That flag-waving gung-ho son of a bitch! So he knew Ugly, or knew of him, from before the war probably, from those educational trips through the countryside, and had got word to him—god damn! He did that to another white man!

*   *   *

By nightfall he had reviewed his sins. He had not drunk. He knew the dangers. You took one swallow so the parching thirst would not be painful; not to tank up, just to wet the pipes, and soon you took another, and another, and then you were out of water. No. The way to do it was to let it hurt. Let it hurt all day and rest often. Chew jerky to rouse the saliva. Take a swallow of water before sleeping. Be strong.

He was not scared. The soon-to-be of it was not upon him; time and the desert stretched before him, and he could nurse one full canteen for days.

The waning crescent would not rise for a while, but the clustered stars sailed in incandescent clouds, and the tracks were clear before him. Once in an hour he verified his course: west-southwest a half south. The Heavenly River flowed above: Chinese for the Milky Way. It was almost worth being here, lost and alone, to see that stream of white diamonds. He had traveled here and there, and stayed out late many nights, but never had the gods bribed him with this dazzle: as if they were showing off, or easing him toward heaven.

That first night's march was almost a pleasure. He was lean and tough, the air was cool, his cloth shoes were snug and light, he bore no burdens.

The solitude was new and invigorating. There were no hollows, no ridges, not even trees; no strayed asses or lurking foxes, no hidden nomads or desert lions. Only Jake. And before him the tracks of unshod ponies. He could see miles by starlight, half a continent, and there was no motion, no life, no sound.

He marched. He thanked the gods for thirty-mile forced marches, for previous iron-handed sergeants ("Do it, Dodds, just do it, you're not a soldier, you're a fucking Marine"), for knee bends and push-ups, for waterless maneuvers, even for the weeks without a woman so that whatever force and virtue there might be in his own jism, in his own yang, he had not thrown them away on yin, and they were all his to spend now.

Just before dawn his calves tightened. He lay face down, and made his legs relax; he sat up and massaged his thighs; he lay back and slept.

In midmorning the heat woke him: he rolled away from the relentless sun and gagged on what felt like a mouthful of flannel. He stretched and rose, momentarily dizzy, uncapped the canteen, and warned himself to swallow three times only.

He looked about him. To the south he saw mountains, snow-capped mountains. The scorched desert lay before him, barren and endless. He felt for his knife and compass. The pony tracks lay sharp, branded into the trail.

His timing was not good. He had slept in the cooler forenoon and would walk now in scalding air. He gathered spittle and swallowed.

Slow now. Easy does it. You got better than a Chinaman's chance.

In the true heat of noon, stifling and searing, he rested again. He dreamed constantly of his canteen, of the snow-capped mountains; but he had expected such dreaming and was armed against it. He closed his eyes and tilted the hat forward, but sleep would not come. A wet towel, like a turban: he would give gold for that. Later, he decided, he would think about China, and his career in business, and whether and where he had gone wrong.

Baking, he stumbled through the late afternoon, and at sunset—he forced himself to wait until the seething orange ball had vanished—he offered himself three swallows more, long swallows but only three.

He would not fall of thirst for another couple of days, but exhaustion might stop him. What he had accomplished? Thirty miles? Forty?

He rested. He watched the light fail, watched the dark gather, counted the first stars.

Lopliks. Where were the Lopliks? Fishing. Fishing! Orion sank low. Autumn coming. Dawn soon. He walked slowly, and more than once found himself zigging or zagging; he tried to concentrate on the tracks, but his mind wandered, and then his steps.

K'uang. If K'uang refused to quit, and came riding out of the sunrise! On his Tushegun camels! Would K'uang take him in, shoot him down, or pass him by?

Or a plane. A plane would buzz him, drop a can of water, drop food. How long? Since Peking. Since Peking he had seen not one plane aloft.

He staggered. He frowned, surly.

Four beggars executed. What the hell. Supposed to be five hundred million of these damn people. Where the hell is everybody?

Lopliks.

Do not think of fruit, water, or snow.

Dawn swelled, cloudless. He paused, and with great care took a compass reading. He snapped the compass shut and returned it to its case.

No use. I need water.

Not yet.

He concentrated: this was the second dawn. Ugly might have—and then again Ugly might not have.

Shuffle along, old bones. No birds even. No lizards or ants or any god damn thing.

Well, all right, I should not have.

Why not? These tax collectors and politicians and generals sending gold to foreign banks, sending furniture and antiques and dogs and cats, for Chrissake. Wearing cuffs and neckties, for Chrissake. Drinking foreign drinks and stashing away the dollars, for Chrissake. And they hang Kao.

Well, just get me out of this and—no. No, by God, none of that. No rice-Christian or any other kind, and we will not make the promises that men make and then break as soon as they have beer and a broad.

The mountains loomed, distant.

The pony tracks ran on.

He twisted to search for K'uang: nothing.

He counted a thousand steps, his mind empty.

Lopliks. God send me a Loplik.

He slept through the heat of the day, and most of the afternoon; he rose, and drank, and shuffled on.

Not a cloud, not a sound. No bells tinkling, no women's voices. Only sand and bare rock.

He shuffled through sunset, through dusk, through starlight. Had he seen the moon last night? He could not remember. New moon, maybe.

His stomach was knotted hard now, and his legs hot with twinges, real pain. God help me. A damned lonely way to go. Is there any other way? Always lonely. Lie in bed, children and grandchildren all around, you still go off alone. All those weepers left alive: is that supposed to be a consolation? Nobody going to cry for me.

"Jake Dodds is not much," he started to say aloud; a raucous croak startled him. Hell with it, he whispered, and took three swallows. Ah, aah. He remembered his thirst that long-ago morning in jail, and Kao there with tea.

He walked on. "Jake Dodds is not much," he said, "but he is all we have to work with, and we will not have him whimper and grovel. If he gets out of this, old man God, he does not plan to build a church. He plans to sin plenty. He plans to stuff himself with savory meats and strong drink, and then stuff his lady friend with something else entirely. Hell," and he laughed, "I need a fight. That's all I'm good for anyway."

You fight this desert. You fight those cramps. You fight that canteen.

When do the mirages begin? And the buzzards? Hell, no buzzards around here. No *nothin.* Won't even decompose. Somebody find me in five years, still handsome.

Another night passed, or maybe two, and he slept, or maybe not; his first mirage was not a pyramid or a pond but a shimmering pile of rock. By now he was thinking crazy in two languages, and making occasional speeches. His step was unsteady and his wake crooked, but two things there were that changed not: west-southwest a half south, and three swallows. He took his three swallows even when the canteen was empty; the motion encouraged him, and afterward he said, "Aaaah." Dimly he knew he was about to die, but his anger, or plain rudeness, overrode his regrets.

K'uang had not followed. No aircraft appeared. The Lopliks were elsewhere. In his lucid moments Jake thought he had trekked sixty miles. He would have liked to head south for the snowy mountains, but he had his orders. Ugly had charged him straitly. That was English, that was from the Good Book. Old man God really harpooning him this time: He disappointeth the devices of the crafty. And how.

In the end he gave out at sunset. He decided to sleep all night and see if he could make a few miles more in the early morning. He experienced no deep thoughts or visions. He did not repent. He sat for a while watching the sun go down. He looked one last look for Lopliks, caravans, cavalry, aircraft, the Red Cross or the Shore Patrol. Dreamily he fell sideways. He tried to smile. He slept well.

*   *   *

He dreamed that Ugly woke him: Ugly's scarred mask floated above him, blotting out the spangled sky. "A sip of water," Ugly said. "Only a sip. There. Bugger! This is a man. Another sip."

Jake's stomach heaved; he thrashed, and reached for his .45. "Easy, easy," Ugly said.

"West-southwest a half south," Jake said in English.

"Easy, easy."

In Chinese Jake said, "The color of the Buddha's hair is ultramarine."

"Hsüüüü," Ugly said. "All will be well. There was water at Abdal."

"Abdal."

"Yes. And now I have saved your life," Ugly complained, "and am henceforth responsible for you."

31/ Two days later Jake slid off his pony on the banks of the Cha-han-sai, a slow brown brook that a man could step across. "It has been broader, but we make no complaint," Ugly said.

"Good news," Hao-k'an greeted them. "We have a pony for the foreigner, and an ounce or more of gold dust, and some medicinal herbs."

"Then you have killed a trader," Ugly said, and stretched; after long rides his back sometimes ached.

"Ha!" Hao-k'an said. "Have we killed a trader. A young one, seeking Lopliks, and he put up a fight. We kept his donkey also. Welcome, Big-nose."

"There was mountain wool also," Momo said as they moved to the small heap of goods, "and a mile or two of sheep's intestines."

Jake drank, and drank again. Mouse stood by him, brow wrinkled, thoughts struggling, and after a bit said, "Nnnng."

Jake waited.

Mouse gathered words: "It is a great thing that we have done. To cross that desert on ponies, without a supply train. I have not heard of it before. In winter, yes. In winter it can be done by the carrying of much ice."

Jake said, "If it is truly a great thing, urge that bastard to set me free."

Mouse laughed at this outlandish notion. "But you are *goods.*"

"Forget it," Jake said. "What is there to eat?"

Major K'uang halted the column and waved acknowledgment to Pan and Ch'ao, his scouts. Sergeant Shih rode to his side, and together they glassed. "A fallen pony," K'uang said. Some of the story he knew, being a soldier in the desert. Two miles back the tracks vanished: hence, a small sandstorm. Up ahead, what seemed to be carrion: hence, a victim. One or more. A bitter pleasure warmed his heart.

He turned to survey the column: his dozen on camels, and the four supply camels, and the ancient camel-puller picking his nose, squinting fiercely against the late afternoon sun.

"Forward," K'uang called. Accursed slow camels! Those bandits were men; grudgingly he admired them, and fleetingly he wondered why it was always the adversary who was tough, disciplined and inspired. Bad bones, these, but tough. The American too.

How correct and how just if the gold had slowed them to their death! He fingered the nails through the cloth of his shirt. "Shih. I'm going on ahead. Follow at a walk." He kicked his camel to a trot.

Pan and Ch'ao stood grim. K'uang dismounted, and the three men contemplated the dead pony.

Pan said, "Plenty of tracks now, Major."

"Yes." They walked a few steps. "Four ponies. Followed by a man on foot."

"The man walking, and the ponies trotting."

"Yes." K'uang glanced ahead. "I wonder how far he got."

"It was the foreigner, was it not?"

"Of course. A tough one but not that tough. I would have enjoyed taking him, but this will do."

"A shame we cannot take the reward."

"A dead foreign thug is its own reward," K'uang said, and Pan and Ch'ao, startled, saw him smile faintly. A smile! They would tell the others about this. The smile vanished. "Too bad," K'uang said. "That left more water for the others. Well, let us ride on and gather up the corpse. I wonder if there is fear on its face."

By late October the bandits had traveled five hundred miles west and attacked one large eastbound caravan, which drove them off; one truck of the provincial army, which they ambushed and found full of steer hides and sheepskins; and two provincial post offices, which yielded a total of about forty dollars U.S. The villages were dry and dilapidated: a well and a few fields, and no money.

"Some bandits," Jake said.

Ugly said, "Shut up."

"I must have been your biggest haul in ten years."

"Shut up."

"Why will you not give me a rifle and let me learn a trade?"

They were camped in the hills outside a middling village.

"Go on in," Jake said. "Maybe there is a teahouse you could loot, or a candy shop."

Ugly scowled, and nodded to Momo, who sent Jake sprawling. "Mouse and I will go in," Ugly said. "It is of a certain size and there may be soldiers. Be ready."

Perhaps this was a nervous village, and the two would be shot down. But that would leave Jake with Momo and Hao-k'an. Jake did not know what to hope for. Most days there was nothing to hope for. They rode forever, and never arrived. A kind of hell. The wicked flee when no man pursueth.

At sunset the two returned, Ugly with a dragon's grin and Mouse wide awake. "Mouse will report," Ugly shouted, skidding his mount to a halt and leaping off like a tumbler. The evening air was cold, and Jake shivered. November.

Mouse slid off his pony and stood clutching the reins. "The name of the town is Ying-ch'ang," he began, "and I have brought wine."

They cheered and scrabbled for canteen cups. Mouse tossed a jug to Hao-k'an. "This dog also drinks," Ugly said with a mad crow of laughter, and waved a large folded sheet of paper at Jake.

"There is a played-out gold mine to the north of the village," Mouse said. "On the stream, with an abandoned shack. There is a clothes shop for sheepskins and half-finished boots. There is a wineshop with women and a barber. There is also an official post office."

"Is there not!" Ugly said happily.

"In the village are two hundred souls, perhaps more. There are eight soldiers and no police. The soldiers are arrogant and oppressive and the villagers hate them."

"As usual," Ugly said cheerfully.

"There is also gossip," Mouse said. "The war in the east goes badly and the villagers fear that deserters and riffraff will spill into the province."

"Riffraff," Ugly chuckled.

Jake kept a wary eye on Ugly; the man was clearly not normal.

"All this we had from a corporal," Mouse finished.

"You old dogs," Hao-k'an said. "You talked to a soldier?"

"Indeed."

"Is there news of K'uang?"

"None."

"You talked to a soldier!" Hao-k'an marveled.

"And later a whore," Ugly said. "But all this is merely chitchat. What a day!" he cried suddenly, and raised his cup. "Gentlemen! Favorable disturbances of the middle air! News indeed!" He flapped his sheet of paper. "We drink to bandits everywhere."

They drank. Jake wondered what the hell now, but drank deep; it was the red wine of the western oases, and it warmed him.

Ugly stood like a speechifier and unfolded his paper. It was outsize. Jake saw print, Chinese, and decided it was news of the war, or some old friend of Ugly's.

"To begin at the beginning," Ugly declaimed, "and omitting perhaps an unfamiliar word or two, the news is as follows. No, another drink first."

Hao-k'an poured.

"Ah," said Ugly. "Yah. Now." He beamed fiercely at each of them, and read aloud. "Wanted. By the authorities of America for theft, assault and desertion. By the authorities of China for theft, for traffic in gold, for gross fraud upon the military, for low banditry and for the murder of one Kao, a merchant, and one Chin, a camel-puller. And therefore by the police and armed forces of all provinces and neighboring states. One foreigner calling himself Ta-tze. And here," he flapped the poster before Jake, "is a word in your script. What does it say?"

Jake was struck dumb, and showed palm. "Wait," he said. He swigged wine, and blinked, and drew a deep breath. The others cackled like old friends.

He peered at the print. Jakob Alwin Doods, he read. "It says," and he drew another deep breath, disturbances of the middle air indeed! "It says Jacob Alvin Dodds, which is my name in the English language."

"There!" Ugly smacked him on the shoulder. "To go on: of great height and strength. Yellow of hair and blue of eye. Last noted in Shandanmiao and Ming-shui. Speaks Mandarin as well as English. A reward is offered equal to ten ounces of gold for information of accuracy and importance, twenty ounces of gold for his identifiable head, and thirty ounces of gold for the living man. Reports may be received at, and so forth, attested and signed by, and so forth, and dated the twentieth day of August, and so forth." Ugly spread the poster before Jake and said, "So you told us the truth after all, you scoundrel."

Jake sat stunned. He was trying to pull his thoughts together, but they were scattered all over the desert like a herd of runaway ponies: Kao, Dushok, K'uang—the old man in the gold shop: was he also hanged? Well, by God, now I know who I am!

Ugly broke the spell: he stepped to Jake's pack, rummaged, and tossed a bundle to Jake. The holstered .45, and the belt. Then the sheathed knife. Jake scooped these goodies toward him and said, "Yüüü."

"On your feet," Ugly said. "We drink to this hero."

They rose, Jake slowly, his mind sputtering. This was an event of importance but also a kick in the belly. He drank with them, and his blood glowed. He tossed the cup to the ground, said, "God damn," took two steps and threw a bludgeoning roundhouse right at Momo.

He flew for some time. Looking down he saw stones, grains of earth, footprints, like mountains and rivers. He landed on his back; the breath rushed out of him, and the sky spun.

The others were laughing. Ugly came to help him up. "Never," Ugly said. "Not with Momo."

Jake stood panting.

"Listen to me. It is not the same now. We cannot afford that. Do you understand?"

"You'll turn me in," Jake said. "Thirty ounces of gold."

After a silence Ugly said, with great contempt, "You gelded dog. Is that how you think? You have the mind of a pickpocket."

Jake made a wrinkled brow. "What, then? Do you turn me loose?"

Ugly shook his head helplessly at the others. "This one is afflicted," he said. "Perhaps the stresses of travel." To Jake he said, "Listen, you dunce. You are a man of good bones and a rare shot. Your weakness of mind can be cured by instruction, and your courage is not in question. Also you have no choice. You will join us, and learn a trade."

"Join you," Jake said, but a voice inside him, deeper, booming, said, Of course! Of course! What else!

"But no more insults," Ugly warned.

The others waited, curious and cautious.

Jake picked up his gun belt and strapped it on. He drew the .45 and checked it: clip, safety. He replaced it and reached for his cup. "No more insults," he said.

"Then welcome," Ugly said.

The others murmured briefly.

"Now, about this town."

"Open eyes and a small heart," Hao-k'an said. "The whores sound good but this one here will be recognized."

"A burden," Ugly said sympathetically. "Finally we reach places where no one knows me, and we have to put up with this one who stands out like a goat's pizzle."

"It is a calm and busy town," Mouse said, "and I had a great sense of safety."

"We could leave him out here, and go in to eat and drink and visit the women."

"If the soldiers notice, we can pay like any traveler," Momo said.

"And pick up some sheepskins," Hao-k'an added.

"Yes," Ugly said. "We have silver and gold, and if we handle matters calmly . . ."

"You make me sick," Jake said. "You provoke green winds in my stomach and turn my blood to vinegar. Eight soldiers! What if they recognize me! A great sense of safety! What men are you? Will you live in holes like rats, and skulk?"

"As we said," Ugly sighed, "no more insults."

Mouse said, "There is something in his head."

"I can let it out," Momo said.

"No no, a speech," Ugly said. "A speech. From our famous hiker here."

"Hsüüüü," Jake breathed. "A collection of *minstrels* is what you are. Many a joke and all precautions and no cash in the bag."

"Instruct us," Ugly said.

"We have all we need to take the town," Jake said earnestly. "Me for bait. Villagers who hate the soldiers. Eight soldiers! Eight puppy dogs, probably. We lock them up in their own brig and live like men. Resupply plenty, maybe even fresh ponies. We leave town with a full belly and winter boots."

"And much enfeebled in the male parts," Hao-k'an said. Momo swore in Japanese and Mouse said, "We could be wiped out."

"You might as well be dead right now," Jake said. "You never fight, you only slaughter. You eat garbage and cover a rotting woman once a month. A coolie does better."

"Listen," Hao-k'an said eagerly, "it could be done."

"We would need," Jake began, but caught himself up. "No. I have some ideas, but this one is boss."

Ugly said, "How delicate. But I am unworthy. What are these famous ideas? I see the day coming," he said to the others, "when this one and I fight it out."

After sunset the following day, Jake and Momo trudged shivering into Ying-ch'ang, and a fine crowd turned out, including many donkeys and chickens. The citizens gathered at the roadside in threes and fours as the two bandits, gabbling in Japanese and apparently laboring under afflictions, proceeded.

The barracks, of dirty brick and un-Chinese, were rectangular, with no courtyard and no spirit wall, with glass windows and a wooden door that swung inward. Outside this building a soldier halted them. Behind Jake and Momo, townspeople gathered like jolly hogs at swill time.

"Bandits," Jake told the soldier, as another came around the corner of the building. "Defile them. They have taken our all. Where is the police station?"

The soldier unslung an M-1 and prodded Jake's middle. The piece was filthy.

"That is useless and inelegant," Jake said. "Please point it elsewhere. We are hungry and ruined and have a report to file. Who commands here?"

"I see no weapons," Second Soldier said. The other, the marksman, gave this brief thought, and slung his rifle. "It is unusual," he said. "It is not what I am accustomed to."

"We must take them to Lieutenant Meng," Second Soldier said.

"That is wisdom," Jake said.

"This way," Second Soldier said, and to First, "these are foreigners."

"Yüüü," Jake said admiringly.

A whisper rose behind them; a voice cried, "Hang them!" and the crowd laughed. Another yelled, "Hang the soldiers!"

First Soldier flung the door open; Second Soldier thumbed the bandits in.

Lieutenant Meng sat behind a heavy wooden table and dozed in the soft light of an oil lamp. Jake saw racked rifles, stacks of documents, posted notices, hackamores hung on pegs, shelves of bowls and cups, an iron stove. A kettle hissed gently.

Meng started, came awake, and drew his pistol as he hopped up. "Who is this?" he asked angrily. "Is there never a day's peace around here? Why was I not told?"

Jake said, "Bandits. We have suffered bandits."

"Cover them," Meng snapped. "Bandits, is it. Red bandits?"

"Plain bandits," Jake said.

"Oh well," and Meng waved a tired hand; he seemed unaware that it held a pistol. Then he paused, as if reflecting, and the shine of his eyes altered. Behind him a door opened; Jake glimpsed bunks. "Everybody in here," Meng called. "We have an occurrence."

"Good," Jake said. "We will tell the story once to all. Those evildoers can still be pursued and punished."

"Indeed," Meng said. Four of his men had filed into the room, two of them barefoot, yawning, scratching and tugging at their skivvies. Meng said, "What are your names and where are you from?"

"Bright Virtue," Jake said. "American and more recently from Ti-hua the capital."

"Ti-hua?" Meng mocked him. Jake bristled. It was as if the light had dimmed or the wind shifted.

"Oguro," Momo said. "From Yokohama and more recently from Ti-hua the capital."

"So," Meng said.

"This afternoon we were set upon by ruffians," Jake said.

"And offered indignities, and our gold stolen, and our documents and warm clothing," Momo said, and swiftly in Japanese, "only seven men."

"Are we all here?" Jake asked. "Because this is a fearful story."

The soldiers muttered about a man called Lin, who was "in the usual place." "Fetch him," Meng said. "Pull him off her. Pai and Liu —you go. Take weapons. Patrol the streets. Small heart, sharp eye. You, Wang, search these two."

"I would rather tell the story once to all," Jake said, offended.

"Just shut your mouth," Meng said. "You are under arrest. Bandits indeed."

Ugly, Mouse and Hao-k'an had circled to the north and paused at the disused gold dig. Their tethered ponies grazed on brown river grass. The donkey stood stupidly.

"There is too much unknown here," Hao-k'an said, "and it is too long in one place. I like to hit and run."

"It was you who dribbled at the name of woman," Ugly said. "This is a good scheme. Risky, but it is as he said: are we men or eunuchs?" A foreigner shaming me, he thought sadly. Bandits! We are petty hoodlums. Dushok would grieve to see me so. Well, one day, at some other end of the earth, he would have a story for Dushok. One day when they were rich and secure.

But at which end of the earth? The world narrowed each day. A man rode a thousand miles for freedom and opportunity. Harbored lice and went hungry. In the west were plantations and orchards. Should he amass gold, and buy an orchard and live in a house with two wives, and soften slowly until death dissolved him?

He scratched his crotch. A whorehouse with a barber. No barber would shave him. The complexity of that face. A bath. And I will have a woman scrub at these crabs. These lesser dragons of the hairy forest.

"Time," Mouse said.

Jake's wallet lay on the table before Meng. "No papers," Meng said. "No money."

"I have a paper, in that wallet," Jake said, "but the money is stolen, and also our safe-conduct." He was sweating pleasantly and his pulse had stuttered into its old race. He was in trouble. It flushed out the glands, cleared the complexion, and took a man's mind off woman troubles.

"Your health card," Meng said. "All foreigners carry health cards. Inoculations?"

"Stolen," Jake said. Muscles twitched.

"But not your wallet. Interesting." Meng opened Jake's wallet and extracted the I.D. "Here is a picture of a man with hair like frost and no beard. And the rest is in a foreign script."

"English," Jake said.

"Aha! Yet you claim to be American. You see," he told his men, "every least thing must be questioned. We had better chain them now." His hand fell to a stack of documents. "Keep them covered, while I find a little surprise here. A rewarding surprise." He smiled at Jake. "Bandits indeed."

"Only five," Mouse said. "Two in their underwear, two with rifles ready. The crowd still loitering, so I slipped among them. Some have lanterns."

"Bugger," Ugly said.

"Defile them," Hao-k'an said. "Where are the other three?"

"In the whorehouse," Mouse said. "Two were sent to fetch the third."

"Then we move in," Ugly said. "You two observe the whorehouse. You must find those three and kill them quickly. Also quietly. At the proper time I must do the rest."

"Alone?"

"Ha. This is man's work, is it not? Besides, the new boy is right: one man who knows what is about to happen is worth four who do not."

"Fool!" Jake said. "While the bandits escape!"

"I do not think any bandits are escaping," Meng said. He leaned affably across the table, and slapped Jake with the pistol. Jake staggered sideways, and tasted blood. "It will be three days only," Meng said. "The courier truck will come from Khotan and take you there. I could kill you now, but you will bring more alive."

Jake felt of his jaw, and squinted in pain.

In Japanese, Momo said, "A full belly and winter boots. A famous idea. Dogs defile you."

"All is well," Jake said. "Only I cannot think. This lizard hit me."

"You will not speak foreign languages," Meng ordered.

"Courtesy to travelers," Jake tried. "I cannot understand your barbarous behavior. My companion has been abused by brigands."

The door exploded open: Ugly filled the doorway, grinning his monstrous grin and waving two pistols. Jake lunged for the table. Trying to look both ways at once, Meng snapped off a blind shot; Jake drove ahead, toppling the table on him hard. Bones cracked. There was scuffling behind him but he had no time for it. He trusted his men as he often had before, and trusted his luck too. He vaulted the table and came down in a crouch beside Meng, who was thrashing; he grappled Meng's gun hand to the floor, and closed his own right hand on Meng's throat while Meng emptied the pistol aimlessly. Meng arched, popeyed, and in time died. Jake grabbed the pistol and turned, crouching behind the table.

"Come out, come out," Ugly chirped. "You took forever back there."

Jake poked his head over the table. Momo stood calmly with two rifles while Ugly's pistols covered the four frightened soldiers. "These are employees," Ugly said, "and mean no harm."

It would be easy now.

Two quick shots.

And the others, when they walked in.

Jake prickled and sweated. If Meng had emptied the pistol. Or if he had left one cartridge but not two. A Browning. Jake could not recall how many times Meng had fired. He stood up and shoved the pistol into his waistband. "A small arsenal here."

"And ponies. We will leave town like a private army."

"And be tracked," Jake said. "Shot from the sky. Chased to the mountains to freeze." He inspected the prisoners. One began to speak; Jake slapped him hard.

"A case of grenades," Momo said.

"Momo," Ugly said softly, "chain these vermin to the wall before the new boy kills them."

*   *   *

There were three women in the wineshop, toothy at the unseasonal rush. The barber fawned; his razors were of the first quality, and he possessed a tincture of crushed petals for the hair. "You will allow me to borrow the razor," Jake told him. "You will bring me hot water and soap, and I will take a sniff of your tincture."

The townspeople were amazed but not hostile. "Each is of a different country," they said. "And there are more in the hills. Best to be friendly."

The women were three of a kind: middling young, middling pretty, middling clean. Hao-k'an strutted. "And if they do not, I will club them with it!" Jake had wondered if he would mind taking turns, taking a woman after Ugly or Momo; he did not mind. The women marveled at this increase in trade, at these outlanders, but they were professional and direct, and not modest.

Jake found that good. The first time, in the small room, on the stone bed heaped with quilts, he urged her out of her gown and stared, savored, breasts, hip, silky love-hair; he slid his hand between her legs; she clamped her thighs on his forearm, and bent to lick at him; he could not wait then, but pushed her onto her back, raised her legs around him and drove in. He lay still for a moment, with the warm, sweet ache gathering in him like tears; then he said, "Ah God," and finished with a hot rush and a roar. Plenty of time later for invention and frills. The mouth of a strange woman is a deep pit; he that is abhorred of the Lord shall fall therein. With luck!

Plenty of time for a bath too. And the bandits ate spiced meats and millet, and drank red wine made of the grapes of Yarkand. Jake and Ugly sat together across a round wooden table. "Which one did you have?" Ugly asked.

"How can I tell?"

"By the different gowns."

"Then what difference does it make?"

Ugly laughed. "Women." There was a new look in his eye.

Later Ugly said, "I had two sisters who were drowned at birth. There was no food for them, or room, or time."

"Yüüü," Jake said, grimacing.

"They still do that, here and there."

"I heard," Jake said. "Or sell them young."

"To houses like this. Well. A million die every day."

"Is that opium?" Jake gestured toward Mouse, across the room and dozing.

Ugly nodded. "You want?"

"Yes."

Ugly issued orders. The red wine was smooth and sweet on Jake's tongue. "I had a beer belly," Jake said. "No more."

"The healthy life of the horseman."

"Of the prisoner."

"Of the fornicator."

"Ah well," Jake said. "The ram and the ewe. Were you ever married?"

"With this face? As a boy I was very successful. Since the tiger I buy it."

Jake's pipe arrived, and Ugly waved him to a couch. "As a boy I was not so successful," Jake said, taking the pipe and rising, "so I buy it, too."

In the morning they ate well and filled two skins with wine. They trooped into the Rainbow Supplier of Garments, a little painted rainbow over the doorway, and allowed the wizened proprietor to outfit them, sheepskin head to foot, fleece-lined, hats with ear- and nose-flaps, roomy boots, half-stitched; they would finish the stitching themselves, to assure a comfortable fit; the awl and the waxed thread were a gift of the house. For the rest, Ugly paid. "We do not bother decent people," he said.

"You never paid the whores," Jake said.

"Nor did I deplete their stock. But I paid for the food and wine."

They returned then to the barracks and corral. "Momo," Ugly said, "check those prisoners. They will remember you," he told Jake, "and will give information."

"From that to killing me is a long step."

"True," Ugly said. "All the same, Momo, see to them. Now we choose ponies."

Hao-k'an was there with their own ponies and the donkey. For some time they examined teeth and felt of legs. In the end they kept two of their own and three of the army's. "These brands," Jake said.

"Hsüüü," Ugly said. "If anyone is close enough to see a brand, we are lost anyway. Leave the donkey, Hao-k'an. The donkey is vulgar."

They packed and mounted, and rode down Main Street in their soft, unstained sheepskins. They rode like paraders, festooned with bandoleers and grenades. The villagers cheered; the whores waved and stuck out their tongues. "Those soldiers may abuse these people," Jake said.

"What soldiers?" Momo asked with a fat, nasty laugh; and five bandits, tired but happy, with full bellies, expensive new wardrobes and possibly the clap, rode for the hills.

32/   Among the hills and villages south of Yarkand they plundered and killed, crossing and recrossing the Yarkand River. Close to the ancient city they saw roads, trucks, bodies of soldiery. They filled their little leather bags with pieces of gold and silver. They filled their wineskins when possible, and emptied them fast. "And in the end what do you do with the money?" Jake asked. "Where do you keep things?"

"There is no end," Ugly said. "It is a way of life. We are not bankers. We conquer each day as it comes."

Jake scoffed. There was nothing of the conqueror in five bandits killing a trader for twenty dollars' worth of silver, ten bricks of tea and a breasty jade goddess that Hao-k'an admired; or shooting his donkey; but it was the way of life. And at times his blood ran hot with the freedom of it. The pounding pleasure of a raid. The terrified faces of ordinary men and women, scattering. Their string of luck: no one shot until Jake himself took one along the ribs.

He rose in the stirrups sometimes and whooped like a redskin, bawling out his exultation as he bore down on a fleeing sentry or a terrified merchant. He knew that he was killing. It was not pride that he took, but pleasure. All about him men killed and stole: governors, bankers, officers, pimps. In this, all men were brothers. To the east, a civil war, and brother truly against brother. Jake was just another brother. That he enjoyed the life did not make it wrong. No: he loved the life. No colonels, clerks, college boys or Shore Patrol. No ambitions even. All such fell away.

There was only each day, and the surge of his blood; each day's bet against the gods, and he was a winner. He was a born winner.

Well, there were bad moments, too. One bad moment was a bullet along the ribs. Hit him like a truck and knocked him off the pony. He lit rolling and squeezed off a full clip before he passed out, and his last thought was, So, like this. In some village, nowhere.

In another village, nowhere, a fine moment turned bad: they drove off not soldiers but another pack of outlaws, killing three of eight, and Jake put on a show as the losers fled. He stood on a wall with his yellow hair flying, and sighted on the leader's ermine hat a full quarter of a mile off, and brought his man down. The cheering mob chaired him to the wineshop, Jake making big teeth and blessing them with two fingers. In front of the wineshop a small black dog, smooth-coated and rat-tailed, was already gnawing at a dead outlaw.

Jake grinned down at the outlaw, at the white popeyes in the bony face, and a trick of death tugged at the corpse's lips: he grinned back, a crooked grin, one side of his face contracting in glee. Suddenly the dog too looked up at Jake, and the dog too grinned.

Jake scowled, hopped off the sedan chair, shoved angrily through the mob, and went to his pony, where he fiddled with the stirrups and would not speak, not even to Ugly.

Well, no honey without stings, and even the bad moments were a man's bad moments. A man, he told himself savagely, a man! As if somewhere inside him was a woman and he was afraid to let her out. His butt grew tough in the saddle. His sheepskins broke in well, and lay snug on him. Cold winds pounded at them from the southeast, and banks of clouds formed and dissolved; in the hills he sniffed at winter, and loaded brushwood for fires.

The Rainbow Supplier of Garments beat his breast. "They never paid. They took the best I had. They looted. They beat me." The crowd muttered.

"Is that so," K'uang said coldly.

"Nor did they pay us," First Whore said. "They threatened and raped and performed unnatural acts." The crowd oohed.

"What acts could possibly be unnatural to you?" K'uang asked.

"The village was wailing in terror," said the Mayor.

"All two hundred?"

K'uang's men were loading the eight corpses onto a cart; a pair of horses sagged in the noonday glare.

"We have no weapons," the Mayor said. "We are forbidden weapons. Only the soldiers had weapons, and the soldiers did not protect us."

"That much is true," K'uang said. "Of course, you assisted the soldiers."

"To the utmost," said the Mayor.

"And we were cold to the brigands," Second Whore said, "to diminish their manhood."

"No wonder they did not pay you," K'uang murmured. "Well, I fear I must burn the village."

The villagers wailed; the Mayor dropped to his knees and struck his head upon the ground. Only the children giggled.

Rainbow Supplier risked an angry tone: "The others could not protect us and you will punish us now for their weakness. Unjust! Unjust!"

"The soldiers too did not pay," First Whore said. "Never!"

"Or for food," said the Mayor from the dust of the road.

"Who saw them ride out?"

In the cautious silence cartwheels creaked. K'uang spoke to Sergeant Shih. "We must execute a few."

"Well, I saw," First Whore said. "From the window."

"Ah." Playfully K'uang stroked her cheek with the tip of his swagger stick. "Dear lady. What were they carrying? Boxes, saddlebags, barrels?"

"Well, no boxes," she said. "And no barrels."

"Saddlebags large or small? Heavy or light?"

"That I cannot tell," she said.

"I saw too," the barber said. "Also from the window. The saddlebags were small. There were also skins, as for water or wine. They spoke," he confided, "of Yarkand."

"So," K'uang said, and to Sergeant Shih, "burn the village."

The Mayor crawled to K'uang's boots and set his face between them. "You will not," he pleaded.

K'uang kicked him away. "Stand up, you old fool. Why should I not?"

The Mayor scrambled up, hunched and bowing. "Spare us. Spare these children. Spare us."

"So you can be cowards again. Is that what you would teach your children?"

The crowd stood silent. A voice cried, "Then arm us."

First Whore said, "Can it be . . ." and lost heart.

K'uang said, "Continue, dear lady."

A look of stubborn courage settled on her round face. "Can it be that you punish us because you cannot punish the bandits? Because you cannot find them; and if you found them you could not catch them; and if you caught them you could not kill them."

The Mayor's eyes widened; he trembled. The barber hissed. The crowd froze.

"Dogs defile you all," K'uang said clearly. "This one should be your mayor." To the woman he said, "You spoke poetry, as in the ancient books. All right, then: when I have them I will bring their heads here, on poles, and we will stand the poles here on the main street."

"Good," she said.

"And *then*," K'uang said, "I will burn the village. For now, we will execute this jackal of a mayor."

"Take me instead," First Whore said. "The whole night. Free."

"Oh, that too," K'uang said, and turned away.

She blocked his path. "No. No. Are you no better than a bandit?"

He took her by the throat. "Never say that again." For many moments he read the whore's face, then flung her away. "Keep your mayor," he said, "and keep him from my sight. Later you will explain unnatural acts."

Mouse talked of Afghanistan, and Momo of Kashmir. Mouse said that India was now two countries. How, two countries? "Halved," he said. "One is called Pakistan."

"How do you know this?"

"I was told in Ying-ch'ang. Furthermore, the two countries are at war."

"Interesting," Ugly said. "Opportunities. But too late for this year. In the spring, perhaps. When the Communists come, we must find another home." He peered off toward the southern mountains. "Yü-üüü. Not in winter."

They crossed a ridge, and he halted them. "Look there."

They looked down on a valley, and a village, smoke rising from some twenty houses, and around the village row upon row of small trees.

"Orchards," Ugly said, "for tomorrow. For tonight, mutton and wine." He hunched, and blew a small cloud. "Yüüü," he said, "winter."

The wine warmed them and loosened tongues, and they spoke of ancient battles and of women. Jake told them about the grand skirmish at the Palace of the Night Chickens, and as he spoke he knew for sure that this was the life for him, the bad with the good, and they cried "Hu!" and "Ai-ya!" and "Hao!" They wondered then if it was the same with women of all countries; was the construction the same and was there hair between the legs? Was a kiss on the back of the neck forbidden and therefore effective? No: in Jake's country kissing the breasts was of more importance. "Ah, kissing the breasts!" they said. Momo's marriage had been arranged when he was nine; when he was twelve a housemaid—his father was a lawyer of eminence, with many servants—had taught him much. Jake had been fifteen, and they mocked him: a late starter.

"More than half my life ago," Jake said. "I remember it. The only American girl I remember well and with a favorable emotion. A spring night, with a moon, and she was a schoolmate, round and healthy and smelled like strawberries. Thrice we did it, and many jokes."

"The first time is not good," Hao-k'an said. "Experience is needed. That is a fact."

"Not true," Jake said. "It was indeed good," and for a moment he remembered the moonlight on her fat nipples, and the steaming tangle of her silky muff. And the endless kisses. He remembered hoping that nobody would ever hurt her. "Maybe the best. Hsüü. With the women of my country a man must be careful and scheming. Otherwise it is rape, and they holler and fuss. A man asks only to give joy, and then he has to be prissy and careful. It is all planning and priming, and by then the joy is gone. Methods and procedures, and mysterious fastenings, buttons, hooks and eyes, and not a one will help you, knots and elastics, and it is no life for a decent man. And afterward debates and litigation. But not that first one." He drank deep. In the firelight they all drank.

"Youth," Ugly said. "Nothing like youth. In my youth I too was prodigious."

"Even I," Mouse said.

Jake lay back beneath the blizzard of cold, white stars.

"It is the vigor and juices," Ugly said. "One is inexhaustible."

"One is indeed," Momo said.

"One is indeed," Jake said. "When I was nineteen I would fuck anything with hair on it, including the floor of a barbershop."

They cried "Hao!" and slapped thigh.

"One is handsome too," Ugly sighed. "Defile that tiger anyway."

The others were silent.

After a moment Jake said, "It was truly a tiger, then?"

"It was," Ugly said. "In the forests south of Chilingho, which is in Manchuria near the Russian border."

"A Siberian tiger."

"Yes. A huge old bugger. I can still smell him. I wake up sometimes. He was old and all bones, and his teeth were rotten. I was in the army at the time."

"You?"

"Indeed. Did you think I was born a bandit? And a handsome young fellow I was, and you know my rank. Better than a general, you said. The Japanese had swept in with that dog-defiler P'u-yi for a puppet, and our armies fell apart and deserted, and gave themselves to rape and banditry. After about four years of that I was headed for Russia with three of my men. This was in 1936 or so. The Russians are foreigners and I have no use for them, but they were better than the Japanese. At the midday meal that old tiger roared out of the woods, and my men were away like rabbits, defile them, and the old fellow sent me buttocks-over-crown with one swipe. But I was wearing furs, stolen furs, and the thickness of them saved me; on my belly his hind claws drew blood but he did not open. It looks like a bowl of noodles now.

"And then neither of us moved. We lay like lovers while he

breathed his stinking breath into my nostrils."

Ugly brooded. "The legend is true. He was old and tired, and he wanted me to kill him, and to take his virtue. His eyes told me that. I put the knife into him just behind the shoulder, and worked it. Blood poured from his mouth, and into mine. What gods there are were speaking to me, through him. I swallowed his blood, and spoke to him; he was happier then, and he died."

Ugly flipped open his shirt front, and a necklace of claws, like old ivory, caught the firelight.

"I bled badly. My nose and cheeks were minced, my belly too, and when I reached a village I was covered in blood and dripping, and the villagers screamed and ran. There was an old woman who did not run. A Manchu woman with bound feet, and a witch, one of the old people with secret ways. I was expecting you, she said. She stripped me, and cleaned me, and smoothed ointment on my wounds, and sent her grandson, a trapper, for the skin and claws. 'There is a foreigner in the village,' she said. 'I was expecting him too.' A crazy old woman. The foreigner was called Tu Hsia-k'u, and he was a great traveler, also a sergeant. I believe he had been sent to the north to gather intelligence.

"I told him that the tiger's spirit had passed into me, and he did not mock. I told him what I knew of the Japanese, and we sorrowed for China. While I healed I told this Dushok of my plans, that I would gather a band of men and harass the Japanese. Again he did not mock. Then I was healed. Laughing girls stopped laughing when they saw my face, and little children stared.

"We traveled together to Harbin. He told the police and the Japanese patrols that I was his servant, and they believed him because he was a big-nose and I was very unpleasant to look at. There we parted, but I got messages to him in Tsingtao.

"Then ten years passed, and he was in Tientsin again, and he sent word to all the evil elements among his old friends, and that word was brought to me in Lanchow a year ago, so we are friends again, and have corresponded. Though he says he is leaving."

"And he told you of me," Jake said, "and you came after me."

"Came after you, no. That was an accident. But his last letter reached me: to Lanchow, and then hand to hand and mouth to ear. There are doubtless some tens of men in China looking to kill you or bring you in. All your life you will look over your shoulder," Ugly said with a smack of satisfaction. "Dushok said you were a man of no bones, that you lied to your friends and would take from them. Even among our kind, no one will trust you. I feel a tendency to trust you but it is not a strong tendency."

"I have no other life now," Jake said. "I have learned a new trade."

Ugly said, "Ha! A fly on a horse's tail does not wear iron shoes."

They mocked Jake happily.

"Dushok wrote that old Kao was hanged," Ugly said. "I never knew old Kao but had heard of him."

"I too," Momo said. "Before I deserted, I was stationed in Peking. Kao was a rare old thief even then."

"There was a little dried-up man in a gold shop," Jake said sadly. "He ran a small foundry and times were bad. I hope he was not hanged."

"All the penicillin," Ugly said, also sadly. "And yet it was small change. He was a rich old dog. We should have waited and hit you the second time out, when you had his jewels and gold. Did you really plan to go back to Peking, and make a second trip?"

"If all went well. But all did not go well."

"You make a little here, you lose a little there," Ugly said.

Jake smiled. "He used to say that."

"All this talk of women and money." Ugly sighed heavily. "I think I will drink all night."

"Good," Hao-k'an said. "We will all drink all night. Any man who sleeps forfeits half an ounce of silver."

"Drink is a comfort to the lonely traveler," Ugly said.

"It is a friend to the soldier," Mouse said.

"Though it cannot dispel real sorrow," Ugly said.

"Yet sorrow is easier to bear when fuddled," Mouse said.

Ugly said, "An emperor of the Shang made a lake of wine, surrounded by trees on which were hung rare and spiced meats. He gave famous parties with debauchery of all kinds."

"Less history and more wine," Hao-k'an said.

So they lay beneath the glitter of ten thousand times ten thousand stars, and told stories melancholy and cheerful, and staggered off to sprinkle the bushes, and Momo fell in the fire, which was very funny, and by sunrise they were playing the chiu-ling, or winegames conducted by an elected leader, and were in the fierce grip of chiu-hsing, or elation caused by intoxicants, and later they saddled up and lashed tight and rode screaming down the mountain to sack the nameless little village, or at least steal some breakfast.

That morning K'uang was outside Yarkand, lecturing his troops. "Whatever happens, I want one of them alive. It is essential."

His men sat or sprawled in the stable yard. Only Sergeant Shih stood.

K'uang paced, to warm himself in the nippy morning air. "We ride to kill, but we offer mercy, and will parley. Is that clear?"

It was clear.

"Now: these ponies are your brothers. They are the best Qara Shahr ponies money can buy, or the army commandeer," and the men laughed, "and they must be cared for like mistresses; you must keep them well fed, and see that they drink often," and the men laughed again—indeed, the Major was in a rare good mood—"and you must brush their hair, and give them plenty of rest, and mount them gently." The men roared laughter in great gusts, and K'uang allowed himself a broad smile.

At night, visions of gold held him wakeful, and he wondered if he was, after all, just another Chinese bandit.

"Eeeeee-ho!" Ugly shouted.

"Eeeeee-ho!" Jake shouted, and the others screamed, "Yah-yah-yah-yah!" They pounded down the mountain and into a hollow, and the horizon blurred and vanished, and they rose up over a low ridge, galloped down a long hillside and were in among the fruit trees, the trees almost bare now and the regular rows of them flashing by Jake's eyes like ranks and files of men on parade.

Soon he could see the dragon, and he knew that this was a special day. It was a long dragon, red and blue and gold, with huge, wicked eyes and triangular fangs. It twisted and pranced down the main street as firecrackers pop-popped; it wagged a scaly tail; it was wearing blue cotton trousers and cloth shoes. Jake whooped laughter. A holiday. With a poor-boy parade, a couple of dozen people. He saw, or sensed, the mud-brick huts, hovels, chimneys, frail plumes of smoke, tots in the road, a goat and chickens.

A band played: the tinny, reedy sound of three or four village instruments. Then he heard Ugly shout, "A wedding! A wedding!" and saw the two sedan chairs side by side, two bumpkins bearing each like a stretcher; and he heard Hao-k'an gurgle a drunken laugh.

The procession halted as the bandits swept nearer, and the bandits split, some to the left and some to the right; the musicians fell silent and the people stared, paralyzed. Jake thought this was a great joke, a wedding day these people would never forget, and he was hawhawing when the bride flung open the curtains of her chair and leaned out, bewildered, fear on her lovely face.

Jake galloped on past but his heart stuttered and for a moment he was almost sober. The face had been perfect, dark eyes sparkling and the glossy hair shining beneath an embroidered headdress: a princess it was, or a throwback, close to what he had dreamed of, hoped for, a face not quite Mongol yet more than Mongol . . . Jake was not thinking well, and confused flashes crossed his mind: the woman's face, Asia, great migrations, Persians, Japanese, jewels . . .

A little like Mei-li. Jake roared aloud and wheeled for another look, but he was too late: Ugly had her, leaning down to pluck her out of her chair. She fought, she scratched, but she was swathed in yards of ceremonial raspberry-colored gown. The villagers cried out and ran in many directions. The bearers dropped her chair and fled. Other bearers dropped the groom's chair and fled; he was spilled onto the road, and Momo's pony trampled him, Momo yip-yip-yipping.

Ugly's left arm pinned the princess to his hip, head down. A watchman in blue cotton and a mandarin hat ran bowlegged toward them, ringing an iron bell and shouting, "You will not! You will not!" Jake thought that was the funniest yet. He laughed until the tears came, and he hiccuped.

Then he saw that he was alone among the villagers; the other four had cleared out. He kicked at his pony. He slipped in the saddle but righted himself. That was some woman! A beauty. A real beauty. Bandits' luck!

They rode for an hour without pursuit, Jake licking his furry lips in the cold air and squeezing the drunkenness out of his eyes. Ahead of him the woman lay still, on her belly across Ugly's pony's withers; Ugly squeezed her astern and laughed. Mouse called to Momo, and they giggled and passed the joke to Hao-k'an.

Jake had loved women for an hour, bought them, taken them in cars or on beaches, gloomily fighting their No! and their Oh, you bastard! but this was new, this was a kidnap and the hair of his flesh rose again: he wanted this woman. The excitement was painful.

They struck the Yarkand River and turned downstream, and soon Ugly halted them in a bowl of brush and reeds. They were half sober now, and panted, dismounting. "An interlude," Ugly announced. "Time out from banditry!" Jake and Hao-k'an tethered the ponies, and the four lesser bandits hunkered while Ugly led the woman forward like a ringmaster. She was wailing, and covered her face with both hands.

"What a ride," Momo said. "What a hunger I have."

Ugly tore the headdress from the woman. "A beauty," Mouse said. The raspberry gown was embroidered in gold and dark blue; Ugly ripped it away from her. Beneath it she wore a close-fitting shirt and loose trousers of the same stuff.

Jake's breath steamed.

The woman fought; Ugly took her under the arms, and Hao-k'an tugged her trousers off. Ugly's knife flashed; he slit the shirt and tore it away. She stood naked in the cold air, only a necklace and pair of red cloth shoes left to her. She covered her sex with both hands, and hunched; Ugly took her by the hair and tugged her head back.

"A beauty," Mouse said again.

The woman was weeping now, almost without sound, streams of tears.

Abruptly, Jake's heart closed to this.

"No fat on her," Hao-k'an said.

"Chinese women are never fat," Jake said, and could not keep contempt from his voice. "That is a fact."

They stared at him. His face was sullen, he knew, and he tried to lighten his expression. "Keep her warm, at least."

"A freezing virgin," Ugly said softly.

"How do you know that?"

"We can find out," Momo said.

"It was her wedding day," Jake said sadly.

Ugly laughed. "Then she was expecting something like this." He shrugged. "The ripe plum falls."

The woman's eyes were on Jake. He gazed at her body, he could not help that, the round young breasts, the cold, stiff nipples, the narrow hips and neat black bush; and then at her eyes. She pleaded. He looked away.

"Listen," he mumbled, "let her go. We have no time for this. They will pursue."

"Speak up, friend." Ugly let her go and took a step toward Jake. "Pursue? Not that bunch. Farmers."

"Yes," Jake said, "and we are gentlemen and archers, and do not bother decent people. So you said! So you said!"

"What is this?" Ugly asked. "You blow the mustache for a woman?"

"Pay no attention to him," Hao-k'an said, and pranced to the woman; he took her by the crotch and moaned: "Ah! Hsüüü!"

"Look at him," Jake said. "No archer, but a pig."

Hao-k'an dropped her and snarled, "Bugger yourself."

"Rape," Jake said. "Rape. I don't like rape. I like women. They are almost the only thing I do like. I like them as a man and not as a pig."

"Women are like locusts," Ugly said.

"Let her go."

"Too bad you are not a woman yourself," Ugly said. "That would be some big blonde."

"I gave you Ying-ch'ang," Jake said. He had no chance against the four of them; he was not afraid, but very tired. The flavor of lust was gone from his tongue, and he knew what had chased it. His mouth was full of shame, and it tasted like bad fish. And yet he ogled the woman, the forlorn breasts and frozen nipples, the chill golden skin.

"You gave us nothing," Ugly said. "You were a dead man; you are an outcast; and the laws of men are not for you. Or for us."

"Then you are no longer men."

Ugly stumped up and planted himself before Jake, plenty mad, neck drawn in and angry eyes blazing under a black frown. "But not yet eunuchs. You priest! They die every day, starving, twigs for bones and hands like birds' feet. Or beaten to death," his voice low and fast and bitter, so that Jake, looking into the dark eyes, knew that Ugly too had swallowed his share of the universal bellyache; knew that these others were nothing, beasts, but Ugly had once been steel and had suffered his own corrosion. "Some landlords seize peasants' daughters," Ugly went on tightly, reining in his own rage and shame, "at twelve years of age and teach them to suck the prick. The poor eat sand and grass and their bones dissolve. A woman of my village was relieved of a tumor and it proved to be a petrified baby and she died at the quack's hand. The rivers sweep them away and drowned children clog the narrows." Ugly was panting now. "Armies come and go and leave mounds of dead. We are all shit and nothing matters. Not even you. So take your baby face outside this camp for an hour and do not interfere with the pleasure of your betters."

"You don't want her," Jake said. "You don't really want her."

Ugly knocked him down. Jake blinked at the bright autumn sky and said, "She's freezing. She's half dead. You rape a corpse."

Ugly hawked up a gob and spat on him.

"Good luck and prosperity," Jake said. "Animals."

Ugly was suddenly cheerful. "Yes, yes, animals for the moment. Listen: go stand watch. Tomorrow we will be friends again. What is one woman? And you: you have never struck a woman? Never taken a woman who cried out and fought?"

Jake's bones burned.

"So," Ugly said. "You see?"

"A priest," Hao-k'an said merrily.

Jake plodded toward his pony. Behind him they fell silent. He could not look at the woman. What was a woman? They would gun him down and go back to their games.

The great white merchant of Central Asia. Dodds the tycoon. Selling a virgin for a day of life. He turned. "Listen," he shouted. "We're quits now. Quits."

Ugly waved happily. "Quits it is. You're one of us."

Mouse wrestled her down, and Ugly turned to her, clapping his hands; Hao-k'an was mouthing eager gibberish. Momo, hand on his holster, smiled faintly at Jake.

The next day she drank tea; she tried to eat a strip of jerky, but gagged and then vomited. The bandits kept her warm but now and then stripped her to stare, to comment or to abuse her. Jake kept to himself and would not look at her. At night, on watch, he had remembered Mei-li and others. Also he had fallen asleep, but no harm done: he awoke at dawn to the same rolling plain, the same empty hills and clear, remote sky.

He sat apart, and heard their scufflings and cries. He considered himself. Sheepskins, weapons, a map and a compass. Binoculars and bandoleers. Four grenades. Lice. That to show for thirty years of spit and polish, courage and cowardice, medals and mistakes. He wondered how many men he had killed, how many women he had violated. It was always a violation, was it not? He rubbed his scruffy beard. His feet stank; his body was filthy, layers of crud; his breath doubtless foul. The price of freedom.

From the ridge above the bowl, where he kept watch, he could see a long way north in daylight, over the falling hills and the sparse lines of poplars. To the south the hills rose to mountains. High in the mountains snow gleamed.

The evening stars spoke to him later. They were cold, distant and neutral, and made him sad: they said to him that we are born and we suffer and we die. He believed them.

"What do you do up there," Hao-k'an asked him, "rape your hand?"

"Dogs and worse," Jake said gloomily. "At least bitches can fight back."

He was one of them, so they considered this. "What would you have us do?"

"Too late now. Take her back, maybe."

"And be killed," Ugly said.

"Then there is no way," Jake said.

She might have been blind. She moved like a puppet, but without expression, not even the painted smile, frown or leer of the performing doll, and no sound; only the silent tears. No one beat her. Jake would have understood a beating and been angry, but not full of horror and other emotions, new and nameless.

Or if the men had relished her. If they had taken her with thunderations and bellows, if they had stood like bulls and impaled the goddess while lightning flashed and mountains split.

No. Hao-k'an with a dirty nose said "Ha!" and pulled her onto his lap and spilled himself like a baboon. "Ah, ah, ah," he said, "ah, ah, ah," and flung her away.

The empty eyes accused Jake, and the bruised mouth, the gown in tatters, the chilled blue flesh. He supposed they would shoot her when they tired of her. She did not look like Mei-li, not really; she had been more beautiful than Mei-li when they took her, but now Jake could not think of the two as the same sex or even species.

He did not know her name, and did not want to. By the fourth day he was numb. Ugly had gone mad, settling so long in one camp. They would be tracked and wiped out. Jake hardly cared. The woman was shivering by the fire. The others were playing the Chinese version of scissors-paper-rock and pounding each other lackadaisically.

The woman was looking at Jake with dull eyes. He met her gaze and looked away. She sat huddled in the ruins of her bridal suit. Her hair was filthy now, long and lank, trailing on the ground behind her where she sat like a broken doll. "Foreigner," she said softly. She had yellowed like a tooth.

Jake met her eye again but did not speak.

"Kill me," she asked.

It had been a beautiful face.

"Kill me, foreigner."

He had known she would ask.

"What am I?" she said through quick tears. "I am nothing. A bruised peach, a trampled pear."

The air was cold and clean, and the hills were cold and everlasting in the late light. The woman was small, a speck; so was Jake.

"Every moment is pain and shame," she said, "and I feel the madness coming, and I will scream and soil myself, and they will leave me here to die, or shoot me. Do it now," she urged him, softly as a lover, "do it now."

He looked at the men, sprawling and squatting. His elder brothers. So I have learned a trade. "I cannot," he said. "It is too late."

He gazed again at the woman, so as not to forget: already her eyes were hollow dead smudges; her lips were swollen, her cheeks discolored; blood stained her gown. Behind her eyes was a great void, an emptiness he had seen before behind the eyes of the poor, or the badly wounded, or prisoners.

Then for an instant the despair vanished from her face, and was replaced by a pure, lively, consuming contempt.

Jake's innards turned to ash and clinker.

The woman drooped, hugged herself, and seemed to grow smaller, like a great-grandmother abandoned by a primitive tribe. Momo and

Hao-k'an, laughing, stood up and drifted toward her. "Like a foreign wheelbarrow?" Hao-k'an could not believe it.

Jake rose as if offended by them, and passed behind the woman. He paused long enough to lay his left hand on her head in blessing and farewell.

His right hand drew the .45 and shot her dead.

They might have killed him before the echo died, pure reflex at the sight of this yellow-haired fool with his pistol out, in the middle of camp and this not a business day. They might have thrown knives, or rushed him. For the time it took to kill her, and to replace the automatic in its holster, Jake did not give a god damn.

All they did was stare. Even Ugly was shocked. They stared down at the heap of dead woman, and up at Jake's sullen eyes.

Then Hao-k'an said, "O nourished of a harlot!" and drove at his throat with both hands. Jake knocked the hands apart and drove a left and a right to Hao-k'an's face; Hao-k'an howled at the insult, windmilled in and took Jake about the middle like a wrestler. Jake kneed him in the chest, and bashed him hard on the back of the neck. Hao-k'an weakened and Jake kicked him off, fetching him a hard wallop on the ear as he went by. Hao-k'an's nose was bleeding and his breath came hard. He snuffed air into him and bored back in. Jake set himself, and Momo took Jake around the neck from behind.

"God damn you," Jake roared. He bent fast, slipping sideways to Momo, and brought his shoulder up into Momo's chin. He rammed Momo, trying to slip Hao-k'an's charge. Momo's hand was on the haft of his knife; Jake smothered the move, clenched hard on Momo's fist, and Momo shouted in pain.

Hao-k'an knocked Jake off balance and caught him with a hard backhand; Jake's lips popped, and he felt blood spurt. At the same moment the long scratch on his ribs, where somebody's bullet had given him a bad moment, flared into pain. The pain made him sharper. He righted himself, feinted a hook and started a kick. When he heard the shot he dropped all offensive plans and hit the deck rolling. He came up squeezing the .45, and Ugly stomped it to the ground.

Breathing hard, they glared. "You will not," Ugly said. " 'Frequent reproofs diminish friendship.' "

"This misbegotten egg," Hao-k'an began furiously.

"He had no right," Momo said.

"He owes me," Hao-k'an said.

"Time to move on," Jake said, his voice almost shaking as matters caught up with him. "You would have killed her tomorrow. And while you tickle yourselves, the enemy closes."

"He owes me," Hao-k'an said again.

"He owes me too," Ugly said, injured and melancholy. "He owes me his life and now he owes me a woman." With interest, curiosity and an odd nod of the head he met Jake's eye. "It was formerly all so simple," he complained.

"Pigs defile you all," Jake said, "I'm bleeding." There was a line of fire down his back. "You Japanese bastard. You ripped right through these sheepskins. Mouse! Take a look at this."

He was used to it now, the sudden truce. Among Marines, or between Marines and soldiers, fighting would go on for half an hour and end only with departures. But here the twig flared and died, and was soon cold. Hao-k'an would joke with him over wine.

"You killed a woman," Ugly said.

"Do not speak of it again," Jake said. "*You* killed her. I gave her rest."

"This is almost deep," Mouse said. "I must wash it in wine."

Jake squinted at Ugly. He refused to look at the woman but her face floated before him. "Bury her," he said.

"Do not joke," Ugly said. "You killed her; you bury her. You can do it tonight: I give you a double watch, the late watch and the dawn watch."

Hao-k'an laughed. "Thus he pays."

Jake sat down near the fire. He groaned aloud as Mouse bathed the wound.

Ugly said, "Yes, yes, the heart of man is heavy; his years are short but his days long. You are a strange animal, you are. A good deal of Kao in you, and something of Dushok, and a little of me. Well, cheer up and learn a trade. We have summered you, and now we shall winter you."

Jake's pony bore the body out of camp that night, and Jake kept watch a way downstream where the land was softer and less stony. He scraped out a shallow grave in the moonlight, and tried to think of the proper words, standing alone in the silvery dark, with a wind sighing up from the southeast and his pony whuffling. "He that smiteth a man, so that he die, shall be surely put to death," Jake said. It was not the sentiment he wanted but it had a bearing on this funeral. "Ashes to ashes," he said. "Dust to dust. From everlasting to everlasting." It was in the wrong language but it was the best he could do. After a sharp struggle with his gloom, a deep gloom and painful, he said, "I'm sorry, I'm sorry," and swept loose dirt over the body.

He swung aboard his pony then and rode to the top of a knoll. From there he could see a long way north, even in the light of a half-moon. Except for the steady rush of mountain wind, the night lay cold and still. Jake dismounted, hobbled his pony tight, checked his M-1 and .45, and made himself comfortable against his pack. The woman's face pleaded with him. Voices spoke within him. He invented an old Chinese proverb: three bandits are one man, two bandits are half a man, one bandit is no man at all.

He dozed, and started awake, heartsore, and stamped his feet and ran in place to keep himself warm. At dawn he saw a line of stunted poplars grow into the light and take form. He saw miles of hills and swales, pockets of deep shadow and the bright flow of hilltops where the first light struck. The poplars seemed to sway. He repeated his proverb. He did not see how he could buy his way back. He did not see what he could do now, ever, that would make him even half a man again.

Again the poplars swayed. He uncased his binoculars, scanned the horizon, watched the poplars shift.

They were advancing as well as swaying and they were not poplars.

His hands shook. He focused the glasses and saw a line of men on horseback. Two scouts rode before, out wide.

He waited in the swelling light. Below him by the Yarkand River the dead woman lay. What he did now would be his offering to her. It would make him, in his own eyes, even less than no man at all, but there was no easy or prideful way. Maybe there was no way at all.

In time he saw the slung rifles, and the discipline of the column. He could not distinguish faces or clothing, but he whispered, "K'uang!"

He freed his pony, settled his pack, weapons and gear, including two spare clips and a bandoleer, four grenades, a canteen of water and one of wine, and mounted up. He sat his pony on the knoll and kept watch to the north. He removed his sheepskin hat, and fluffed his blond hair. He waited. Soon the column halted, and two men dismounted. They raised binoculars, and glassed him; he raised his own, and glassed them. The two men mounted, and the column picked up speed.

Jake walked his pony down the knoll, nodded a last salute at the woman's grave, and lashed the pony into the freezing waters of the Yarkand River. It was swift and narrow here, and the pony was swept downstream, but he found footing on the far bank. Jake made a wide cast to the west and then veered south, toward the mountains, and kicked the pony into a trot. By true sunrise he would be lost in the folds of the foothills.

Some time later he heard much shooting, a distant, playful sound like firecrackers.

33/   He rode climbing, followed the river upstream, detouring at rapids and falls but returning always to the river because now it was all he had, his only landmark. In a few days he would not know for sure what country he was in. But others had come this way. There was the shadow of a trail, and he saw cairns and signs, stones heaped by the hand of man.

The rise of the land was quick, and his pony struggled. By the evening of the second day the pony was crashing through lacy ice at the edges of the stream, and slipping on patches of snow, and Jake was hungry. He was also talking to himself, aloud, because there was not much else to do. He could talk to his pony, and did, but it was not satisfactory, first because the pony had no name, then because he never answered, and then because Jake felt bad riding him up and up into this freezing waste of rock and snow, pretty soon not even trees to nibble on. "Can't even tell you where we're headed, old boy. India, maybe. Right now I would like to see one of those wild asses. Never saw a wild ass the whole time, much less ate one. Best eating west of Peking, somebody said. Hell, maybe they're all gone. Extinct. Like us. We got to find you a name . . ."

The hunger kept him alert: to signs of game, but there were none; to signs of K'uang, but there were none; and to the weather, and there was plenty of that. Squads of thin gray clouds marched up from the southeast, and the wind was bittersweet, a cold wind running down off the mountains, but with eddies and layers of warmth, like a lake where your feet would be warm and your belly cold. Jake blessed all sheep: he was sheepskin from top to toe, including gloves.

A couple of days, and no more forage for his pony. A couple of days more, and no more jerky for himself. By then he would have crossed a rich caravan headed for Kashmir. The last of the season. They would be herding a few live animals for meat, and there would be bags of flour, and delicate tea from the high mountains. No: they brought tea *in,* around here. Jade, then, and gold dust and mountain furs. Maybe fruit, packed tight and the nippy air keeping it fresh.

Or he would find a customs hut, well stocked, abandoned for the winter.

"I guess I better call you Skinny," he said to the pony one evening, "or Ribs. You beginning to look like Job's turkey." He checked his heading often. For three days, or four, it was hard to keep count, he rode southwest, climbing always; then southeast, the wind in his face. The river was important. Men lived along rivers. He figured he had ridden a hundred miles or more on this sheep's intestine of a trail, and about two miles straight up. Maybe three. There was a difference in the breathing. Old Ribs labored and wheezed.

Jake was famished. For a day or two the hunger was like an iron hand squeezing his stomach. He did his best not to dream of steaks, pea soup and bowls of spaghetti. Finally he gave himself free rein, and ordered visions from an endless menu. He ate snow, and could salivate forever. He ate it slowly, a finger's worth at a time, not wanting to freeze an empty belly.

He imagined an iron vat full of Head of Pot's sheep stew, and the flavors and smells were a millionaire's delight. The remembrance dizzied him. After pondering, he decided the dizziness was real, of his body and not of his mind.

At night he bashed through the surface ice and watered Ribs. All day long he uprooted the rare stunted shrubs, and at dusk he found a hollow, or sheltered under an overhang, and built a small fire.

He decided he was fooling himself, and was really on his way to nowhere, and would fall asleep in a drift someday when he had eaten old Ribs and run out of matches. He was doing one thing only, pushing on, and was otherwise empty and not worth small change. So he was oddly cheerful. "Hell, this is a trail," he said. "A trail goes to a *place.*" Later he said, "Hell, I'll walk to India if I have to. Wherever that is." He felt light-headed, wide-eyed and stupid, better off not understanding. A village idiot. Also his side hurt, where he had been shot, and his back where he had been slashed.

On the sixth day, maybe, a gloomy day, cold and overcast, he slopped water into a boot. He had kept Ribs hugging the northwest slope of a ridge, mostly out of the wind, and slid him down to the river for rest and refreshment, and the ice gave way.

"Hell," he said, and led Ribs to a sheltered niche. Ribs was a bay, a tough little pony once nice to look at. He was also food. These days Jake saw dull mutiny in his eyes. "You just stand guard," Jake said. Breathing in great gulps, he sat down, took off his jacket, removed the boot, drained the water and dried his foot on the jacket's fleece.

"Now how we going to dry this boot?" he asked the pony. He left his foot wrapped in the jacket and leaned back, bone-tired and puffing white plumes. "Don't know what to do. Might be we ought to go back down this hill and take our chances. You stand still a minute."

He hopped to the pony and unlashed his pack. Ribs whickered softly, and for a few seconds Jake stood rubbing him behind the ears: a pearly gray sky and a skinny frozen pony and one tired sojer, rifle and grenades and bandoleer lying on the ground useless, pistol at his belt, inedible, spare clip, full, in his pocket, and a heavy pack dangling from one hand, and his breath steaming, and the pony's, too, and in the whole frozen world nothing else moved.

Jake hopped back to shelter, collapsed, tugged his jacket on and groped in his pack. "Now lookee there," he said, pulling out a cloth shoe. "That's a genuine Peking shoe." The shoe fit snug enough but the sole was too wide, too stiff, to slip into the boot. Jake whittled away at it, and trimmed it down to a ragged sock. He rummaged for a green skivvy shirt. "Horse marines always there when you need them." He made a legging of the skivvy shirt. He jammed it all—foot, sock, legging—into the boot. "Hell," he said, stomping, "that's pretty good." He stood panting. He went to pat Ribs, and Ribs sidled.

"Easy now," Jake said. He stepped forward to reach for the reins but Ribs backed off.

Jake stood still and talked sweet. "Let's just make it through to-night. Tomorrow we got sunshine coming, a warm spell. That's a promise."

Ribs whinnied, and backed onto the ice. It cracked beneath his hoofs; he lunged, and scrabbled to firmer ice. Between Jake and Ribs a line of water frothed. Ribs turned and trotted off.

"Now don't do that," Jake said. "You got no other friend in the world, you hear?"

Ribs ignored him, cried out like a man in pain, stumbled and showed teeth.

Jake gathered his gear and followed. He tested the ice, and detoured upstream where it seemed firmer. Cautiously he edged across. Once he was away from the ridge, the wind curled down on him, dank and shrewd.

Ribs was well ahead of him. Jake left the ice and struggled up a snowy bank. His pack weighed a ton, and the air was no nourishment; he pumped it into his lungs frantically and it was never enough. He topped the bank in time to see Ribs fall.

Jake tried to hurry. He dropped his pack and sprinted, but his feet were leaden and the snow was icy. He slipped and plunged. Ribs slid slowly. The reins were trailing up toward Jake and there was a chance; Jake drove himself forward. The slope was steep; Ribs gathered speed. Jake lunged, flung a hand toward the trailing rein. He missed it by a man's length.

Ribs screamed, sliding down the slope; his legs thrashed. Jake lay prone, gulping air, and watched the pony go. It was a long slope, a quarter-mile anyway, with a drop at the bottom: Ribs slid down, faster and faster, and hit the edge and just disappeared. Fell out of the world into a ravine or a valley.

Jake sat up. All about him he saw snow-capped mountains. "There goes a lot of meat," he said. "There goes a month's worth of groceries."

He unhooked the left-hand canteen and shook it; the last of the wine gurgled. Clumsily he screwed the cap off. He lay back and poured the wine into his throat. He sat up then and threw the canteen down the slope. It clattered, bounced and slid.

Jake's ribs and back hurt. He thought he might be bleeding.

Later the wind died, and Jake thanked God. "For small favors. You really giving me hell in all other respects." The wind picked up immediately.

He understood that he was about to die. Not within minutes, but soon enough. Hours, maybe. He was trudging uphill in late afternoon, toting all his gear like a miser on Judgment Day. The gray sky was thicker and lower.

Not supposed to have much snow here, he reassured himself. Not much rain in this part of the world, therefore not much snow. What does fall, sticks awhile.

He was blinking in the wind, and reeling.

Considering death, he found himself not scared. Annoyed, yes. A pain in the ass, to say the least. "But a little deep sleep never hurt the weary wayfarer. God damn. How oft is the candle of the wicked put out." With the weather closing in he would have to choose: ridge or valley. The wind blew the snow thinner on ridges, but it also froze the bones. In a valley he could hope for shelter, but maybe drifts too. Either way he would starve.

The wind decided him: it was blowing a half-gale and knifing right through to his sweetbreads.

He turned, heaving for breath, turned to look back down the long, hard road he had come, as if he might be able to see all the way back to the foothills, even to the plain, all the way to green Yarkand where the river ran wide, slow and friendly, and the orchards drank in sunlight.

"That's a long, long way," he said, and then he said, "Holy Jesus Christ and hsüüü!" because about a mile behind him a man on horseback was crossing a rise, and some yards from him another, and then a line of them, Jake counted a dozen, looming one by one out of the white hills, picking their way, little bundles of man-horse like a file of warriors in a scroll painting.

It warmed a man, it did, to be that sought-after. They would shoot him on the spot, most likely. Unless he was worth more alive—those thirty ounces of gold. But money would not matter to K'uang.

They would have food, rations. They would bivouac and build a fire.

Fumbling, stiff-fingered, he hauled out the binoculars. He flopped prone in a hump of snow.

Traveling light and traveling tight: twelve men, twelve ponies. Sheepskins and furs, probably, and half asleep.

So: no mount for Jake. He would stumble along behind, bound. "Seems to me I *did* that," he mumbled. Sons of bitches might not even feed him.

Suppose you take out one or two. Look for K'uang, or number one, anyway, whoever that is, and put one through the fat part of him.

While Jake's mind worked strategy, his hands worked tactics: he set his gloves aside, unslung the rifle, checked the clip and safety, opened the bolt a fraction and let it spring shut.

And where does this get you? Farther up the mountain, without a paddle. So you slow them up. Terrific.

He was drunk with hunger and fatigue, and he built his thoughts laboriously.

But if you turn yourself in, they tie you up and abuse you some more. Cut off your trigger finger, or your nose or some damn thing. Or hang you. We had enough hangings this year.

Where's the consul when you need him?

He was warmer now. Warm with danger, but also because he was once more engaged in honest labor—namely, digging in and fighting foreign soldiers.

Half a mile down the mountain, the column pressed toward him.

"You old bastard," he said. "K'uang, you old soldier. Some happy day you and me going to fight on the same side."

With the glasses he confirmed: two scouts out front, a third some way behind, and then K'uang; K'uang himself and no other.

K'uang was dropping back, checking his column.

The light was diffuse, so Jake would not fret about optical distortion. He was firing downhill but not enough to matter. Three hundred yards was a comfortable range and his favorite. Not firing into the next county, but nobody pointing a bayonet at you, either.

He laughed, foolish, tipsy with the love of all this. He remembered the rifle range in boot camp, rapid fire . . . fahr! and the corporal saying later, "Five in the black, boy, can't ask for more."

Okay, gunny, and what you planning to do about this half-gale? Maybe thirty knots, sailor, what do you do about a thirty-knot cross wind? How many clicks?

Tell you what you do, boot, you pretend that man's moving sideways thirty miles an hour, and you lead him to windward, that's what you do, and never mind the clicks.

He understood suddenly that they were on his tracks, real tracks, Jake's footprints, and he hoped they were not the kind of trackers who could say, Seven minutes ago and a callus on the right heel.

No. They came on. From there Jake would be a rock in the snow. He sighted. The column snaked on. He flexed his fingers.

He was sighting to the right of the lead scout, and waiting the last few seconds, when a shot scared the bejesus out of him, and the lead scout stood up in his stirrups, tall and astonished, and pitched over backward.

Jake had not fired. For half a second he froze, and then the sergeant in him took over: he swung his front sight fast and took out the second scout.

A third shot echoed his own, and the trail was empty. Only the two ponies, racing downhill, dragging the two dead scouts. Not three seconds had passed.

Jake had fired only once. He hugged the snow. Danger all around him now, no telling who or where. He followed his aim up and down the trail, and along the ridges.

Until a giant snowflake blotted out the front sight.

He eased the rifle off his cheek. He saw a screen of snow; time to close up shop for the day. He rolled onto his back and stared up at the borning storm. From an opal sky huge flakes fell softly, endlessly; listening, he seemed to hear a gentle white hiss as they drifted down.

Closing him in, friendly and peaceable. Covering his tracks. This was a good time to push along, if he could see where he walked. To put some space between him and K'uang, and between him and whoever else that was. Somebody in these hills with a rifle. Somebody who shot at soldiers and not at Jake.

Maybe didn't know I was there. Came up a side trail, saw the soldiers. Well, he knows now.

Damn, that's good! Just one single other human being out there! And not a bad shot, either. Poor old K'uang. One at a time, gents. Plenty death to go around.

The storm drove him on; wind and snow lashed at his back. In the lee of banks and ridges the wind dropped, and the snow floated gently to him. He was edging his way down a valley, moving northwest, he supposed, though directions were no longer of any importance, like languages and table manners.

He wondered if that sniper had food. Some Tibetan, maybe. That abominable snowman, maybe, what they called a yeti, like a big red-headed bear stomping through the mountains hollering, Yankee go home. Maybe he would track Jake and break out the hot noodles. Or that little fatty yellow piece of sheep's gut would go fine about now. There was not much left to Jake. That wee little firefight had used up some of his glands, some last bits of sugar and moxie.

Also the light was fading. He was kicking through fluffs of snow, but the drifting was not serious. Easy did it, and a sure foot. His muscles strained and folded like cardboard, and ached. On will alone he had come five miles or more; he might be circling. The valley seemed to run as valleys do, a long straight path slightly downhill. In the lee of the south wall snow swirled but did not assault.

He sensed an overhang, and hugged the wall. The shelter was not a cave, only an indentation, but the sudden absence of wind and snow, and thicker silence, made him feel at home.

He slipped out of his pack and rifle, sat back and yawned. He ached all over. He had nothing to burn. A few matches, plenty of cartridges and therefore powder, and no wood. The case of his binoculars was some sort of fiber: he could slice it and try to nurse a blaze. The stock of his rifle was wooden, but a fighting man gave up his weapon last of all. A gentleman and archer. A bullshit merchant from the west. Get rich quick with Dodds. Five hundred million customers. Where were they all? Never mind that. Your own fault, gunny, nobody else's; not Dushok's, Kao's, Ugly's, K'uang's or God's.

He was on the verge of sorrow, of true remorse, of asking help, so he said, "Tough titty," in a hard voice. He released his second canteen, uncapped it and drank: the water was slush, bitter cold, and tasted of metal.

He checked his pack and pocket for scraps, a missed strip of jerky, a pumpkin seed. Nothing. This was not the first time his hands, seeking food, had found clips or grenades; he did not curse, or make bitter jokes.

He missed Ribs. He remembered stories of men who had gutted fresh-killed horses and crawled inside to keep from freezing. The old

Mongols drinking from a pony's vein, plastering it over with mud, swarming a thousand miles in a week.

He remembered the smash of that bullet along his side. He remembered the dead bandit grinning at him, and the grinning dog. He remembered the beautiful bride.

He looked, and saw the blinding darkness. He listened, and heard a snowflake fall.

He slept.

iv / NO MAN'S LAND

34/   J ake woke up in a small, cold, golden cave. He knew that he was alive because his bones ached, also his flank, also his back. He groaned: he was prepared for death, even sleep was a blessing, nature had worked a full night to build him a tomb, and now he was alive and it was all spoiled, with pain and exhaustion and struggle to come.

As the snow fell and drifted, the easterlies had swirled it higher each hour around Jake's little scoop in the hillside. He had slept in a frail, spun igloo. The golden light was sunlight on a skin of snow.

He heard a chant: frogs, or priests, or angels. He did not punch through to the surface. He was too weary for fighting or even for flight, and would rather fade away here in his cool hollow than go forth to war again.

"Eh-eh-eh," he heard. "Eh-eh-eh, eh-eh-eh." It was a sound he had known all his life but he could not place it, not just now. Gloomily he gave up. He wanted to doze again but his bladder pressed. More proof that he was alive. In heaven there was no pressing of bladders. In hell there would not be all this snow.

"Eh-eh-eh!" His igloo shattered, and he flinched back; his hand went to the butt of his pistol but lay there limp. Bright light dazzled him, and heaving dark drifts swarmed in on him, bleating and plunging. He blinked against the glitter, and his hand rose to ward off a fat sheep; his fingers sank into warm, oily, tangled fleece. "Eh-eh-eh!" They crowded in upon him; he clung, and hugged. The sheep were warm and cheering. They were meat and gave milk.

Beyond the sheep he saw endless miles of rolling white immensity, and a clear, shining, infinite blue sky, and the blinding golden glare of winter sunlight.

He also saw two men in sheepskins. They were tall and dark-skinned, and made the big teeth of surprise. Jake was too tired to do more than look. As far as he could see they were unarmed, but carried crooks.

He filled his lungs. The air was crisp and clean. The sheep moved on, dropping small pellets of dung. Jake raised a hand in peace. He was too weak to stand. He thought he might be light-headed and hallucinating. His breath steamed pleasantly.

The shepherds approached, showing curiosity but not fear. Jake made no move toward his weapons. He placed his palms together in greeting. The shepherds did the same, and kicked through the trampled snow toward him.

They squatted to see him close up. Jake smiled feebly. One shepherd spoke; Jake understood nothing. The other unslung a small skin and offered Jake liquid; Jake opened his mouth to the squirt. It tasted like buttery tea, sweet and thick. He felt it trickle into him, and smiled again.

His hands flapped weakly at his rifle and pack. The shepherds understood: these were all he owned. They pulled off his boots, and for one sad moment he thought they would loot him and leave him.

No. They examined his feet and chattered, and one rubbed the flesh. Their noses were longer and sharper than the Chinese noses Jake was used to.

One of them spoke urgently and plunged off after the sheep. The other mimed orders at Jake: wrap your feet, put on your boots. Jake did that, panting and straining. The shepherd nodded, and patted him on the head.

Jake indicated the rifle and pack. The shepherd told him to carry them, and Jake shook his head, miming collapse. The other spoke and laughed, then picked up the load and waited.

Delicately Jake worked his way to a standing position. He could see long dark valleys in the distance, patched sparsely with snow.

He felt like an old man, but a raffish zing buzzed through him. He was not panting fiercely with the joy of life; all the same, his heart still beat. There seemed no way to kill him off, and he wanted to thank somebody.

The shepherd pointed after the receding sheep, and urged Jake along. The sheep were winding slowly down a narrow valley, not much of a valley, more like a sunken trail, drifted now, but its banks hemmed men in and kept them safe and sheltered. Beyond the sheep, farther down, there was less snow. In spring the gully would be a stream, and the snow would melt and run off to join some river flowing north, and the river would make an oasis a hundred miles across like the Yarkand oasis. All that from the snow that Jake had thought his shroud.

He labored for breath. So high up. He wobbled forward after his new friend. His boots crunched the snow; he lurched, and caught up with the shepherd in a drunken burst of uncontrollable strides. "Bless 'em all," he sang. The shepherd peered back, startled, and grinned a great grin; his eyeteeth were missing, symmetrical gaps. "Bless the long and the short and . . ." Singing was tremendous work. The altitude. So near to heaven. The cold. How could angels sing? Jake squinted, and saved his breath. He marched in silence and felt queer. The snow-covered trail seemed to rise to meet him.

The days without food, or the cold, or the singing, or the thin air, or all of those: the white world spun slowly, and then faster, snow and sky merging in one brilliant blue-white sheen, and Jake crumpled in his tracks, out before he hit the snow.

35/   H e woke again one day smiling vacantly, like a not very bright little boy who wanted to make a friendly impression. A man in a sheepskin hat with upcurling eaves was bending over him. Jake was sweating under a thick pile of blankets; he was sluggish and drowsy, as if lamed and gelded by peace; he was safe.

His vision cleared. He was lying in a yurt, or a tepee, or something between, spacious and warm, above him a slit for smoke and a line of blue sky. Daylight filtered yellow through the hide walls. Half a dozen men sat about a small fire, eating and drinking. Their murmur was the murmur of gossip, of work and money and politics.

Jake's doctor spoke, in a language Jake did not recognize, and the men set down their bowls and padded to him. Jake was naked and warm, and wanted soup. But first other needs: he sat up, placed a grateful hand over his heart, and said, "Pss-pss."

The Doctor understood, and helped him to his feet, and led him to a large iron kettle half full of urine. Jake bowed thanks and prepared to contribute. The others consulted gravely, and he supposed they were discussing his circumcision, or his grenade scars. Then he found that he could not perform this simplest and most automatic of functions. He waited foolishly. After half a minute the Doctor, or the Chief, anyway the wearer of curly-brimmed hats, spoke decisively, clapped twice, and led the others out of the tent. Immediately Jake flowed.

He stood by the fire afterward and sniffed at a vat of soup, and wondered what customs he was violating, what defilement he was committing and what demons he was offending. "Tum and det me," he called. "I am froo." The men crowded back into the tent. They examined the vat of urine, as if expecting color changes, or foreign fish.

Jake meanwhile slipped back under his heap of blankets. They were not sheepskins but true blankets of rough and oily wool. He was in a remote but luxurious mountain hotel, with snuggly blankets, central heating, indoor privy and—he saw now—room service. A boy seven or eight was bringing him a bowl of soup.

Jake sat up and offered his cheeriest thanks. He was not tired now, only weak, as if he had been sick for a long time, feverish. He sniffed the soup; his mouth watered in a rush. He sipped. "Aaah," he said. "Mmmm." The others approved. It was a mutton soup, with strings of gamy hot meat and chunks of some small tuber. Lotus root. Who could tell. He felt his flesh seize upon the nourishment, felt his blood take it in.

These men were darker, yes, and their noses sharper. He saw a pair of dark hazel eyes. Light woolen tunics, sheepskin trousers, sheepskin shoes like moccasins.

They jabbered softly as he sipped and slurped. He listened. He knew nothing of this language. Or almost nothing. At moments he seemed to remember it dimly, as if it had been spoken by a fat uncle when Jake was in the cradle. But he was happy not to speak, or understand. He was God Almighty tired of wrapping his tongue around other people's noises.

They took the bowl from him, and brought his pants, shirt and boots. These had been boiled, or somehow laundered; they felt soft, clean, luxurious. He saw his rifle, and a bandoleer and the pistol belt, lying across his pack near the wall. Grenades, he remembered. Grenades and children, a bad combination. He stood up, and once again they inspected this foreign body, covered with curly golden hair like a gilt carving of some totem, half man, half bear.

The flap rose and fell, and two women slipped into the tent. They wore trousers under tunics, and conical fleecy hats. They were young, but shapeless in the winter clothes; their dark eyes smiled; they were pretty. They stared at his body and murmured.

It did not matter to Jake that he was naked. He was clean too; someone had bathed him. He sniffed the skin of his arm: bathed and oiled. He rubbed at his beard; these men were clean-shaven. He bobbed a short bow to the women. They spoke a few joking words to the men, who laughed. Jake felt at home, warm and well-fed.

Yah, he said to himself. Easy now. These folks probably do a human sacrifice once a year. And guess who.

The women handed garments to the Doctor, who passed them to Jake. They were of rich, soft wool: one was like a sweater, the other —for God's sake, long johns! Balbriggans! With feet! A dirty yellow in color but soft and not scratchy.

He grinned at the women, and dressed.

36/   In the frosty air goats and sheep came into heat, and bucks and rams were encouraged with songs and shouts. The Doctor —his name was Zang-aw, but Jake always thought of him as the Doctor—undertook Jake's education. "Gyag," he said, pointing. Jake said, "Yak." The Doctor nodded and said, "Gyag." These animals were huge but gentle, almost six feet at the shoulder, mostly black and a few black-and-white; they were about halfway between a bison and a hairy cow, except for the long bushy tail. The calves—Jake thought of them as calves—were skittish.

Jake kept looking over his shoulder, but no man pursued him. Maybe after enough trouble a man was absolved. The passes and hills lay peaceful. He practiced sign language. The Doctor introduced him to two shepherds, calling him Jay-kha, and Jake recognized his rescuers; he flattened his palms together, bowed and made thank-you music. They grinned and patted him. Jake waved northeast and asked, somehow, if they would show him the trail. They laughed, and their snowflake-fingers fluttered: no, they would not show him the trail.

The passes were closed.

The sheep were black and gray and curly-haired. The goats' hair was long and fine; half-grown kids cavorted. Jake was allowed to carry skin buckets of milk. Yak's milk, goat's milk, sheep's milk. On racks of wood and bone, scraped hides stretched, drying; the vats of urine were tanners' vats. In the corners of tents bales of wool stood heaped; men and women spun, on simple wheels, and wove, on simple looms.

On the fourth night the entire tribe gathered in the Doctor's tent. Jake hoped it was not the whole tribe, that there were watchmen, outriders, shepherds sleeping among the flocks; he could not shake the lingering fear of pursuit and invasion.

Supper was over, roast yak and a kind of wheatcake or bread, and that buttery tea, salty, greasy, hot and tasty. They were ogling Jake and discussing his fine points. Jake understood not one word, but he was sure they were being witty: "Look at the size of that beak," and such. As they chattered, they patted one another on the head, shoulders, arms, cheeks.

Then jugs appeared, and women poured from them into earthenware bowls; the children too drank. The Doctor proposed a toast. They all sipped. It was beer. A third cousin to beer. Jake belched. The tent was warm. Jackets had come off and were heaped in a corner, and the nomads—Jake too—sat in their undershirts, like at the boilermakers' picnic.

Jake was having a fine time but wondered about the evening's purpose.

After a round of drinks, the flap opened and a man entered briskly, a medium-sized man much like the others but with a few differences. He wore a blue skullcap embroidered in gold, and when he had removed his jacket and flung it on the pile Jake saw that he wore a necklace of turquoise and silver strung on rawhide.

A woman had entered beside him, a tall, strong-featured woman who seemed to stand apart, as if even in a crowd a certain space and privacy must be hers. Her hair was braided into dozens of plaits, and each plait was bound by a bit of colored thread. Her face was broad and friendly, and her dark eyes glistened in the firelight. She too discarded her jacket, and Jake saw that she was a good big-boned woman with big round breasts. He thought he might have known that from her face.

Jake was impressed by the knife at the man's belt. It was the first long knife he had seen here, almost a sword, curved, in a leather scabbard decorated with brass coins and seashells. Seashells!

A long knife that could be reserved for strangers. Jake stepped to his pack. The tent fell silent. He dumped his worldly goods to the floor. He found what he wanted: his .45.

He squatted there for some seconds, and finally decided he was the biggest god damn fool east of Suez. He shoved the .45 back into the pack. These were decent people, and he would not molest decent people, and if he was to be the star of some sacrificial performance —well, they had plucked him from a snowdrift and granted him a few days more of life. Easy enough to live like a wolf; he wondered if he was man enough to die like a lamb.

He returned to his place and breathed easy. He did not believe that people in their undershirts, who patted one another all over, who fed him meat and beer and then belched with him, would take his life.

The man in the blue skullcap cleared his throat, tipped up a bowl of beer, gargled and launched an oration. The tribe encouraged him with cries and grunts. His eyes flashed at Jake; more than once he pointed. Jake made an effort to look agreeable and trustworthy.

When the speaker drew the long knife, flourished it, and spoke with boisterous emphasis, Jake coiled some; but the man restored his blade to its sheath, delivered one more vehement phrase, and sat down to a swell of applause.

After that they all congratulated Jake, clapping, patting him, bowing; they brought him another bowl of beer.

He did not know what had happened, but he accepted their tributes, their friendship and their liquor, and beamed like a trained bear until the party broke up. "Good night," he said as they left. He could not help himself. "Good night. Good night."

The fire burned low, and there was a great sound of pissing, and men and women went to their blankets, in couples and threes and alone, and then all was night, and silence.

37/ Jake unloaded the rifle but not the pistol. He left the pistol in his pack, with the grenades and ammunition, and spent some minutes discussing these engines with the Doctor, laying down an absolute prohibition, nobody was to touch, man, woman or especially child. The Doctor reassured him. The pack was set between Jake's bedding and the wall, and covered with a goatskin.

The day was fresh and sunny, only a few tiny clouds scooting westward like a squad of fluffy owls. Children smiled shyly as Jake passed; women grinned openly. He smiled back but minded his manners; local custom was still a mystery, and there would be no escape here from an angry husband.

Jake climbed a hillside, sat upon the ground, and took stock. Close as he could count, these people numbered about sixty, half of them female and a quarter of them children. A rich tribe and a happy one. Doubtless they sold off wool, or bartered for supplies: those knives, and the jewelry, and the sacks of barley.

This valley was their winter pasture, cut off by the high snows from everything, everyplace and everybody.

They were a peaceful people and somewhat Buddhist: by the Doctor's bedding stood a portrait, in many colors on a wooden board, of the Buddha or one of his followers, and in the four corners of the painting were a chicken, a cow, a yak and a sheep. The Buddha, or a similar reverend, was holding a flower, maybe a lotus.

The valley was three miles long and a mile wide, and a narrow, icy stream trickled through it. This was home until the spring thaw.

Well then, he told himself, I will do honest labor and be one of them.

Family life was odd here: uneven, you might say. It seemed to Jake that there were men who bedded down with two women and women who bedded down with two men. He was not sure. A new boy would not shuffle around gawking. Ten large tents for sixty people, supplies and ceremonies. So more than one family in a tent, if family was the right name for it.

The women used rouge: blushes of crimson on the forehead and cheeks. They wore conical hats trimmed in lambskin, and were beautiful; even the old women, who looked like gods' wives. The men were beautiful, too, and Jake wondered if he was going soft in the head. Or really dead. Was this some other place? Or maybe he was just learning about folks.

He remembered tales of people who lived a long time, mountain people in many countries who worked hard and breathed the high, thin air, and wrinkled slowly; whose blood ran fresh and clean, whose legs were springy at a hundred. He wondered if the Doctor here was five hundred years old or so.

He wondered if there were wolves in these mountains, or leopards. He asked if men could cross the snows.

The Doctor enjoyed the joke. Flutter, flutter: snow. In the dirt, with his knife and fingers, he made a relief map: the valley, the mountains, the passes. He snowed. Snow filled the passes.

"I hope so," Jake said. "I sure to God hope so," and he squinted northeast and told himself not to worry. But he also told himself to keep his yellow hair covered, and not to stray.

He supposed he was still in China. But he had wandered much, and several days were missing from his memory. This might be India, or Pakistan, even Afghanistan. Or Tibet. Or the Congo, for Chrissake, what difference does it make?

There are no wolves or leopards, he decided, or these people would bear arms. He had fallen among people who did not need, or did not care, to carry weapons. Only the short knife that men and women alike wore in a skin sheath at the belt.

At sunset the tribe gathered. All of them, it seemed. They gathered before the tent where hides were stored and tanned. The stench was rich.

In the fading light, the man in the blue skullcap and the big-boned womanly woman led four young rams through the sorrowing crowd. Or wethers; Jake could not tell. The people raised their hands high, and a brassy tinkle sounded. Beside Jake the Doctor too made music: Jake saw tiny finger-cymbals. A low lament arose.

Blue Hat led the sheep to a stout wooden frame. One by one he dumped them on their sides and tied their hind legs with rawhide. Still the clash and wail filled the twilight.

Blue Hat lifted the bound sheep while the woman knotted rawhide over a bar. When all four sheep hung dangling, their backs to the tribe and their ears twitching as they bleated, the lament grew louder, the clash of cymbals quickened, and the nomads shuffled in place, a sad dance of death. Quickly Blue Hat drew the long, curved knife and cut four throats; quickly women darted forward with bowls to catch the blood. The Doctor called, Well done.

The brassy jingle ceased, and the wail.

The sheep died, and hung still. They bled out while the tribe mourned. Four men set to cleaning and skinning.

The Doctor stared up at the evening star, and Jake thought he was asking pardon. Jake remembered the camel-pullers, who would not leave a shred of meat because the sheep had given his all; and the nomads who must not shed blood, the Buddhists who lived on meat; and something of the nomads' sadness swept over him: that we eat what we love, destroy what gives us life, betray the helpless. Everything eats everything else, and the strongest is man, and he dies, and feeds the weakest.

By now it was dark, and fires pricked out the night. The Doctor urged Jake to the main tent, and the people were laughing again. The Doctor jabbered happily, and Jake almost understood: there was to be another assembly and another fine meal. Good. This mountain air sharpened a man's appetite.

*   *   *

Slices of meat rose in stacks. From an iron pot the smell of liver floated. A shepherd was unsealing earthen jugs. In the general chat and chuckle there was much patting. Reassurance, or approval, or just affection. On the shoulders, the head, the belly, the fanny. They patted the children, and the children patted back.

In time everybody was seated with a bowl of meat and a bowl of beer and one or more barley cakes. Outside, a wind had risen, but the fire blazed and warded off winter demons. The Doctor spoke and a small cheer went up.

One of the shepherds stood. Hastily he swallowed meat and barley cake, washing it down with long gulps of beer. Faces shone greasy in the firelight. This was one of Jake's two shepherds. He spoke, and the others were still, and the wind sang softly in the small silence. The shepherd swigged again, and began.

He told the story of the yellow-haired stranger in his cave of snow. Faces bloomed at Jake. Jake drank and listened. He heard only sounds, not words, but he understood. A blizzard, and the sheep not yet down. The two men herding them close, into a small bowl, and settling them for the night, sleeping among them for warmth. And the end of the storm, and the sun rising. And the sheep breaking through a thin wall of snow, and there lay the stranger.

The shepherd bowed at the ovation, and sat down; he made hungry sounds, and sent his bowl to be refilled. It was an intermission. Everybody's bowls were refilled, and reed baskets of barley cakes made the rounds.

Jake was a great celebrity tonight and enjoying the party. He waved to his fans, and smacked his lips over the yak and beer. The tent was full of hilarity and fondness. It was warm, too, and some of the men and some of the women were doing without their undershirts. Seeing women's breasts Jake felt pleasure and not lust; but lust too.

The second rescuer rose. He cleared his throat, delivered a short prologue, and took up the tale.

They came close to the stranger, who was close to death and harmless. They examined his feet, and rubbed them. The man was not frozen, not close to death after all, only weak and tired. Too tired to carry his own burdens. They had talked him to his feet and started him down the mountain. He sang. "Beh-seh-*ma,* beh-seh-*ma.*" Jake guffawed and applauded. The tribe made gleeful cackle.

And now something Jake had not known: they had lashed him across the backs of three sheep, and the sheep had carried him down the valley.

A cheer for the sheep.

Jake hoped none of the three had just been slaughtered.

A round of beer. The shepherd sat, and conversation grew general. Jake felt that he ought to turn to somebody and make small talk about the price of wool. Men and women patted one another. The children were busy collecting bowls. Some of them were preparing pipes, and Jake was surprised to find tobacco here.

The woman beside him touched his arm, and he turned to look down at her: she was offering him a softball and a small knife. He took both, and sniffed. It was not a softball but a cheese. He thanked her with a bob of the head, cut a chunk of cheese and passed along the ball and knife. He stuffed cheese into his mouth and then, on impulse, patted the woman's shoulder. "Ah ah," she said, and patted his leg. Mellow, he patted her breast, and then pulled away, uncertain. The others paid no mind, and the woman patted his leg again. He tugged his undershirt off and sat beaming foolishly.

Soon the pipes were lit, and passed around. The small children did not smoke. The pipes were long, of wood but with stone bowls, and were decorated with small blue stones and narrow brass circlets. Jake took a deep drag. It seared. Desperately he tried not to cough. This was not tobacco. He pointed to the bowl and looked the question. The woman beside him said, "Charas."

That meant nothing to him. It was not opium. There was a pipe for every two or three people; they smoked, passed the pipe, smiled hazily. A sweet languor dulled Jake. He tried to warn himself, but against what? They were all smoking. They would not harm him. They had celebrated him tonight.

He plied the jug, and sent it on.

The Doctor rose and called for silence. Blue Hat also rose, and his woman.

The Doctor spoke. He seemed to wait for an answer, or an objection, and none came. He applauded. He pointed at Jake, and waved a command: Come over here.

Jake bumbled to his feet, blinking. This was maybe an initiation, or he was to be given a new name. Well, thank God he was already circumcised.

Carefully, as the room ebbed and flowed, he made his way among the seated people. He stood before the Doctor. He nodded to Blue Hat and the woman. Firelight flickered, reflected in her dark eyes.

Blue Hat's hand went to his belt. Jake did not flinch; he no longer believed in trouble. These were people who patted, and who did not enjoy slaughtering sheep, goats or yaks. Firelight glowed and faded, glowed and faded, like daybreak and nightfall.

Blue Hat removed the belt, and the long knife in its long scabbard, and handed them to the Doctor. He removed the necklace of silver and turquoise, and handed that to the Doctor. Then he removed the blue skullcap and set it on Jake's head.

A low roar of pleasure greeted the act. Jake touched one hand to the hat. Speech seemed called for: "I hope the previous occupant was not lousy," he declared, to another chorus of approval.

The Doctor spoke, and hung the necklace on him. He offered Jake the belt and the knife.

Jake understood that this was a solemn moment. Unfortunately, he was full of roast yak, barley cakes, beer and something called charas. He accepted the belt and the knife. He raised one hand for silence. The Doctor clapped twice.

"Now hear this," Jake said. "I'm glad to be aboard. I run a taut ship but you'll find that I'm a *fair* man. Keep your weapons clean and no grab-assing on the chow line. The smoking lamp is lit."

The shouts and applause were music. All these people seemed so happy. Nothing like a little charas after dinner. They were clapping and hollering so loud he hardly noticed that the Doctor was giving him Blue Hat's woman.

But then he did notice, and he prickled hot and cold. Her dark eyes and full lips smiled up at him, and streaks of red make-up gleamed in the firelight.

At first the world spun and shimmered, and he lay like a hog, clutching at her, fetching her breasts tightly against him and breathing slow, beery gusts. She clutched his buttocks, and moaned in turn; in the dark he could not recall her face. He embraced the hot bulk of her, rolled on his back tugging her with him, and stroked her flanks. His little corporal seemed a man apart, soft and polite, drugged and drowsy, until he surged up to suck at her heavy breasts. She exhaled a hoarse whine and jolted toward him, pressing his head tighter against her; her nipples swelled, came alive. His little corporal was a big sergeant then, and the pangs of desire were a murderous affliction, an infinite grief, sweat starting on him and the sweet, unending ache like a fever.

He rolled them over and hung above her. He eased her legs higher until her calves pressed on his shoulders, and he slipped into her sweetly, found his motion then, his pace, slow strokes, and a joy built up in his heart, his belly, his loins, a great pressure of joy; he thrust faster and she bucked to meet him; he slowed, and moved in a tender circle. Her hands drew his head down; he kissed her, and licked her face, and she too licked, their tongues met, caressed, dueled; lips sucked lips. She purred; he blubbed at her like an animal. Her purr throbbed, and she drove at him, and he felt the heat building in her; her pussy clenched on his old dog, her breath pounded.

She whimpered then, and whined again, a long thin keening whine that broke to a sob; and all the pain and sorrow and loneliness, the hankering and love welled in him, and tears too, and he cried, "Aaaaah," and came in a scalding rush, and came, and came, and came; and lay panting then into her mouth, and she into his, and they lay guggling and mewing softly, like animals; and like animals they slept.

38/ His duties, and the woman's, were these:

To slaughter, so that no other in the tribe would have to kill.

To herd the goats, milk the does, lance any abscesses.

To gather dung. Yak dung was like cow pies. Goat and sheep dung fell in clusters of small pellets. Jake passed some of his days with a large, floppy bag slung across him like a paperboy's bag. The children too gathered dung, and bore it to Jake.

To dump the dung at the wetter end of the pile, and to take shovelfuls from the drier end. These shovelfuls were pitched into wooden forms. Jake and the woman tamped them down, and tamped again, and set heavy stones, trimmed to the size of the form, to compress the dung further. There were one hundred and eight wooden forms, and each day eight of them yielded bricks of fuel.

To be faithful, one to the other.

The woman's name was Tha-shi. She instructed Jay-kha. To slaughter he must wear the hat, and use only the long knife. He must wear the necklace at all times. He was not to touch her from sunrise to sunset, but at night nothing was forbidden.

*　　　　*　　　　*

The goats' milk was slightly chalky but not unpleasant. Jake hung hide buckets of it on a yoke and carried them to the tent of the woman Lakh-nuban, in charge of the manufacture of cheeses. Jay-kha naturally thought of her as the Big Cheese. Lakh-nuban's man was called Amila, a round, jolly man, a sheep doctor and good cook.

The pleasure of milking amazed Jake. Here again, Tha-shi instructed him. He squatted beside the doe and stroked the full udder, smoothing off loose hairs. He set the hide bucket beneath the doe and took a full, warm teat in each hand; firmly and quickly he squeezed the milk down and out, alternating, squeezing and not pulling; it shot into the bucket and frothed.

Tha-shi was custodian of the dung shovels. She took care of them as a butcher would his knives or a carpenter his tools; in sparsely timbered country dung was life itself, warmth. The shovels were of metal, with wooden hafts, the metal shaped from a sheet of iron— bought, no doubt, from a caravan, like the knife blades, like all metal. The knives were bone-handled, except the slaughterer's. This was wooden-handled, and the blade was of shaped steel, sandwiched into the handle by crude rivets and circlets of brass, like the circlets on the charas pipes. Jake wore the slaughterer's knife all day. He gave his own to the former Blue Hat.

Only the yak dung stank. Sheep and goat dung was almost clean. Jake learned to stoop and scoop quickly, popping a yak pie into his bag, or using his left hand to crowd fifty sheep pellets onto the shovel. He reckoned two hundred pounds on a good day, and never too much: fires burned in nine tents always.

Tha-shi loved his body. He had not before known a woman like this, who fucked not for money or in duty or curiosity, but because she loved fucking, as she loved the buttery tea, or a good lean goat chop, or beer and charas, who loved it as she loved sunshine, or milking, because it was a natural and necessary part of her life, and life was good. Jake was at first shocked by the direct good cheer she brought to bedtime. "Aaah!" she breathed, wrapped her arms about him, rubbed her face in the hair of his chest, fondled the cock as she fondled a lamb. "Mm-mm-mm," she hummed, peaceful and unhurried. She cultivated his body like a gardener. Here again she instructed him.

Jake was Blue Hat now, dealer in death, collector of pellets and pies. Blue Hat and Tha-shi, being special, lived in a small tent set apart, and Jake was grateful. In the larger tents there was, he knew, no embarrassment or modesty. A man loved his wife or wives, grunting, exclaiming, giggling; or two men loved their one wife, and there were humorous arguments over priority. In time Jake could have liked that, but for now he enjoyed the privacy.

He learned from Tha-shi. Learned to please her by holding back, or to come with a rush—anywhere, anyhow—without apology and without shame. She loved to make him come. She loved to come. "Ah, good! Ah, good!" Each come was a triumph, an offering to the gods and a reason for living. Slowly Jake learned not to think, not to plan, not to fret: only to do what his body asked, to do it tenderly and do it often—and to say a little something now and then. To whisper or hum or sing out. "Ah ah ah ah," he sang down the scale, or "Ee-ee." Or in English, and she understood; in the firelight she grinned and licked at him as he said, "Oh yes, oh yes my fat girl. Oh yes I love your breasts and belly." Tits, he said once, but not again: goats had teats.

Mong-chen and Khu-lat, his two rescuers, pampered him. He was their mascot, their poor deformed baby, plucked from the blizzard. Mong-chen showed him an abscess, and taught him to lance it with the red-hot tip of a knife. Khu-lat taught him to trim an overgrown hoof. They explained that in spring certain yak calves went blind in the second month; it was the will of heaven, and those were eaten.

Jake was grateful and made magic for them: he brought out his binoculars and patiently, by doing, not saying, instructed them. The shepherds were astonished and almost fearful. They conferred with the others, men and women. The Doctor meditated this miracle for some days and Jake, impressed by the power of novelty, regretted his brashness. He had altered the life of the tribe.

The Doctor ruled: this demonic necklace would be hung in the main tent, and used morning and evening to locate stragglers, search for omens or yetis and confirm the absence of malevolent influences. It was forbidden to the children.

Jake himself used the glasses at dawn, noon and sunset, to scan the northeast approaches.

He was now the owner of a whetstone, a dense, grainy stone, and a jug of oil, rendered animal fat he supposed, and each night after milking, whether or not he had slaughtered that day, he was expected to perform a ritual sharpening of the long, curved knife, and to film the blade lightly with oil before he tucked it away.

He cleaned and oiled his weapons also.

Tha-shi gossiped, and he was proud. One night he sat her up on him, and lay still while she impaled herself, riding, wiggling, laughing aloud. "Oh boy," he said. "Oh boy oh boy oh boy."

"O boi," she said, "o boi o boi o boi," and some nights later, passing a tent, he heard the hoarse groans of love and a woman's answer: "O boi o boi."

Jake the bringer of fire: forever and ever in this tribe that would be the o boi position. He was proud; his cup ran over.

When Tha-shi was in flux she slept alone and untouched. Jake understood, and spent those four or five nights in purification; it seemed right. He worked at it, remembering sin, lies, pain inflicted and lives taken. He asked the mountains for forgiveness. Or the stars. Or the windy demons that prowled the star-strewn winter sky. All these were old man God; and they were a better God than he had ever known; and in time they forgave him.

Tha-shi relished food as she did love, as she did all the day's doings and rhythms. She smacked her lips fatly over barley cake and yak butter. With the joy of an artist she chopped a yak calf's fourth stomach into small pieces, and covered them with brine in an iron pot; this had to do with the making of cheese, and after some weeks the liquid was poured off and presented to Lakh-nuban. Tha-shi hummed while she worked a sheepskin. Tha-shi spun yarn, or sat at a simple loom, and her whole body entered the work. She smoked charas also with the whole body, sucking in tremendous breaths of it, rolling her shoulders, rocking on her hips, grinning, squeezing her own breasts with the joy of it all.

One sunny, freezing day Tha-shi and Jake watched a hawk sail over the valley; her eyes shone, and she raised her arms to the bird, and Jake saw for the first time how beautiful a hawk could be, the sailing and soaring, the oneness with air and light.

After each slaughter women bore off the buckets of blood. The butchers, men and women, set aside tough meats: cheeks, neck, flanks and shanks. The cooks, men and women, sliced and chopped the meat into iron kettles, and added water, and handfuls of herbs including wild onion, and careful measures of barley, and then the blood. They stirred, hummed and chanted. They cleaned and scalded sheep's intestine, and stuffed it with the muddy red hash, knotting off every six inches or so.

They were making blood sausage.

The links were slipped into boiling water and left to simmer for half an hour. They were stacked and stored. Some nights they were split the long way and fried on metal sheets. On those nights beer was always served.

Tha-shi was not a great beauty, and Jake thought she might be as old as forty. Some of the younger women were great beauties, with delicate features and flashing eyes, but Jake was not tempted. Tha-shi was well-fleshed, not fat but altogether a woman, with buttocks that he could grasp and knead gently, with a long, thick bush of love-hair to tickle his nose, with fat, broadly nippled breasts to lay his face between; and because she was older, and yes, well-used, the moist bog between her legs was a rich and abundant swell of eager flesh, sometimes gathering him in and holding on, other times lunging and insistent. Within her, he drowned in her heat, sinking feverishly, blindly, to the earth's molten center.

To the children he was an object of curiosity. Shy but not afraid, they stared into his strange blue eyes, or stroked his alien yellow hair; they patted him, and sometimes hugged his legs. He felt inadequate, with no tricks to show them; he could not create shadow-figures, or make a coin disappear. He could walk on his hands, and they clapped and squealed, as if it was a piece of happy logic that this stranger, so much unlike real men, should walk upside down.

He liked these children. Children were hardly human, but he enjoyed this dozen or so, with their snapping eyes and ready laughter. He missed something in them. What it was, he learned one morning when Lakh-nuban called them to her. They came scampering and tumbling, shrill and eager, and when they saw what she offered they flung themselves at her.

She shooed them off, and one, larger and insistent, his voice cracking as he shouted, elbowed. He jolted a little one, who sprawled, landed with a thump, and split the skin over his cheekbone. Blood flowed. That was what Jake had missed, childish brawls, rough-and-tumble, and he was glad to see it, until he also saw that no one was moving.

Lakh-nuban's finger-cymbals whispered. The older boy wilted.

Jake went quickly to the younger boy and helped him up; the little one was flattered and excited by that, and quit his yawping. Jake examined the cut. In another world, a stitch or two. He called to Tha-shi, who nodded. He patted the boy, kissed his brow, and pushed him toward Tha-shi.

He went to the older boy then. He knew that he might be transgressing now, but what the hell, it was only a little grab-assing on the chow line, and he did not like this righteous and namby-pamby kind of punishment. He was almost angry. He did not like this sorrowful holiness, and for the first time he doubted these people. If there was not room here for the rumpus and scramble of children—it made no sense.

He patted the boy, and hugged him, and the little face cleared like the valley after a snow flurry, when the flocks rippled like cat's-paws and light and shadow sprang forth. Jake stood beside the boy and faced—almost defied—the others.

Lakh-nuban spoke, and they all laughed and resumed motion. The little boy leapt to the bigger one, and patted him, and was patted, and the children crowded around Lakh-nuban, who was breaking a long rod into small chunks, and passing them out. Jake lined up with the others, and more laughter rose. Lakh-nuban embraced him warmly, pressing her belly to his, and handed him his portion. Jake popped it into his mouth, and chewed.

It was dried sap. Spruce gum, maybe. The children champed at it with cries of delight.

Tha-shi led her patient to the tent.

*   *   *

Waking in the night, mind sleepy but senses fresh, Jake savored the richly mingling smells of blood, love, dung and smoke. Tha-shi too smelled rich, and so, no doubt, did Jake. He remembered showering every day. Public baths in Peking. The extinguish-aches parlor, and Kao across from him, sweating and plotting. He remembered Hao-k'an, bloody from butchering Sweetwater, cleaning himself in sand.

He hardly noticed the odors, and when he did, he relished them. Tha-shi washed each month, when the flux ebbed. Jake had not bathed, or been bathed, since his arrival here. But smells were part of him now: the smells of sweat, of gutted beasts, of a woman's parts. He felt like a healthy animal, nose to the ground, sniffing in news of the world, of life and death.

The blankets too smelled faintly, the oily aroma of fleecy wool. Jake was warm and full-bellied—putting on a pound or two. Alive. Full of juices.

He rolled over to lay his head between Tha-shi's breasts. She whispered. His arm lay between her legs; she squeezed gently, and suckled him. Soon she murmured with more passion, and soon he cupped her mound; she drew up her knees, and he melted into her like butter on hot bread. In the warmth and firelight, the fumes and scents of a nomad's winter, he spent himself hugely, and she was pleased, and they slept entwined.

So the winter passed. Nights were long. Jake rose in the dark. One evening, a banquet, surprises: roast yak, round after round of beer, and the cakes were not barley cakes but of another grain, buckwheat Jake thought, and there was saffron to sprinkle on the meat, and spruce gum for all, and later plenty of charas and singing. A clear, cold night. Jake decided this was the solstice. "Merry Christmas," he said. "Merry Christmas. Happy New Year. Kung hsi fa ts'ai," which was the Chinese New Year's wish, joyful reverences and make a fortune, and then "Buen año." They dragged deep on the charas and answered, "Hwaw boom." Jake said, "Hwaw boom."

Meat, tea and beer. Jake was hard. His major and minor passages were clear, and his solids and fluids harmonious. His skin glowed, he could stand great cold, he wore long wavy blond hair and a long wavy blond beard. He felt that he would never again be sick, never again grow the smallest pimple. He was not sure that he could stay forever, but he postponed those considerations. The thaw came; the stream babbled and swashed, rising. A current of motion, of change to come, rippled through the tribe. Jake sniffed the wind, and saw that his cows, ewes and does were heavy with increase.

One night Tha-shi brought them charas and a pipe, and after a long time of love-making and smoking Jake saw the Tsou Yü, the righteous beast, a white tiger with black spots, which did not kill living things and appeared only when the state was ruled in sincerity and benevolence. He woke at dawn in love with them all. He would learn their ways, and give himself a new name.

39/   The first time Jake saw company coming, four round figures far down the valley, to the southwest, the breath left his body. He padded to his tent. He sat out of sight, peering down the valley. His hand was steady, but swallowing was less easy.

"From another valley, lower down," Tha-shi said placidly. "They come to see the yellow hair."

"How do they know?"

"They know."

The four shepherds were old friends. There was much whooping, some happy applause, many cheerful women. Jake was pleased that these were not enemies but wondered what news they brought. His first sight of them had been a moment he would not forget, a puzzling spasm of fear, rage, sadness, exhilaration.

He joined Tha-shi before the tent. A good big woman. He stood beside her, and she smiled up at him. A good big happy woman. She patted him firmly and said, "Ah."

"After sundown," he scolded. "Do not be-goat me before sundown." The language came awkwardly and slowly; he spoke many words and phrases but without grace or music.

"You big yak," she said, still grinning, her eyes glistening with affection.

The Doctor came to them, leading a crowd. "Blue Hat," he said, "these are friends," and he recited the four names, which Jake did not catch. They crowded closer, shy and amazed; Jake bowed, and patted their shoulders. They gobbled approval and whacked him lightly.

"I saw one of these once," one of them said. "Over by Mintaka, it was, in a caravan from Rawalpindi. He had glass eyes."

"Tell of the boxes," another said.

"Well," the first one said, "it is cold out here and we have come a long way. Some tea," and half an hour later, when they were all jammed into the main tent, drinking buttered tea, the four newcomers close to the fire, he went on: "This fellow had a box for everything. He looked at us through a black box that click-clicked. He had leather boxes for cartridges and a round box with a hat in it. A straight box containing paper and paints. A metal box for money. A small paper box for magic round seeds that he swallowed with water. The pony master told us all this. But the queerest of all—"

"Yes, tell them that," his friends urged.

"—was a box of flowers, grass and leaves. You know how it is by Mintaka. You can travel for a week and not see a tree. But this fellow saw more than the field mouse. Aha! he would say, and jump off his pony to pull up a drop-of-blood."

"That is a flower," Tha-shi whispered to Jake.

"Or the bone-grass that even yaks will not eat. He placed such harvests within folds of paper, and on the folds he marked such and such a day, and such and such a place."

"In his own country he was a great lord," another said.

"Where was that?"

"Well, to the northwest somewhere. Then he would celebrate his discovery by drinking from a spirit-vessel. At his belt he carried a water-vessel and a spirit-vessel. And he had yellow hair like that." Squinting up suddenly, the visitor asked Jake, "You know him, perhaps?"

"I do not know him," Jake said. "In those countries are many with yellow hair. Women with yellow hair who paint the lips red but not the forehead."

"The lips!"

"And," Jake salted the talk, "the women sleep with only one man; and many women, if the man dies, they never again sleep with a man."

"I believe that," a visitor said. "I believe all things now, since I saw the house that flies and shits fire. A strange and dirty people— though," and he bowed toward Jake, "not this one, I am sure. The collector of grass, according to the tale, used to wipe his hind parts with fine paper, in the morning, and then leave the paper on the trail."

After a moment of speculation and mild embarrassment, the Doctor said, "Not this one."

"No. My greetings to the Blue Hat," and they all drank tea while Jake enjoyed belonging.

At night, after a good meal of mutton, the visitors came to the point: "There is a yeti."

"Oh gods," the Doctor said.

"He was seen in the Valley of Pools. A huge creature. It was snowing, but according to reports he was seven or eight feet high and covered in reddish fur."

A yeti! An abominable snowman! My God, if you could capture him and take him out . . .

Jake winced in shame, a painful, burning pang of pure self-disgust. You could take Tha-shi out, too, and maybe sell her to a zoo, you silly bastard.

"He killed a sheep," the man was saying, "and left a heap of offal. He was then reported on Long Tongue of Ice, still a way off but a bit nearer."

"So far west," the Doctor mused. "Never have I heard this. Over by Karakoram in my father's time, and east of there, and high up where the great river is born that flows to the southern seas."

"These are evil times," the visitor said. "Demons prosper, and gods weep."

"You have come far with this news," the Doctor said.

"And also to see the Blue Hat," the visitor said with a smile for Jake. "Ah! Good! Charas! You are a noble people."

"It is the meanest sort of charcoal," the Doctor said politely.

"It goes well after cheese," the visitor said. "The shepherd who saw the yeti on Long Tongue of Ice was an old man and dim of eye. He said the yeti had the face of a man, but striped."

Jake set down his bowl. His hand was still steady, but the breath left his body again.

"Well then," Jake said later, "if there is a yeti we must open our eyes. We must go to the far corners of our valley each day, and look."

The Doctor approved. "I believe that where there is one yeti, there is another. It is not natural that a yeti would have no father and no mother and no wife of his own."

"But if he is old and angry," Jake said, not knowing the word for rogue, "like the bull yak that quarrels and is cast out, he may be alone."

"What is," the Doctor said, "is meant to be."

40/ K'uang lay back on a reed-matted stone couch; the pallet crackled and whispered. He was sometimes weary, and bound here and there by tight, twitching bands of muscle. On certain nights his eyes would not close. On those nights he dreamed of ancient China, of a land green and wooded, checkered by plowed field and lush pasture, crisscrossed by placid canals. A land of small towns, of stone-and-mud buildings, of healthy bullocks. A land of smoking chimneys and roast pork, with the barbarians outside the Great Wall, and the westerners only a rumor.

A land of magistrates and princes, where soldiers carried strong-bows and wore golden tunics, and hats with horns.

"Ah defile it!" K'uang exploded.

"My dear fellow," said Colonel Liao, "it is nothing personal. We simply have no light aircraft. We have a P-40 that won't fly. We have a DC-3 that will, but we can't go poking through the hills in a DC-3, can we now? Besides, if those fellows are where you left them, they're above three thousand meters. Can't go flitting about like a dragonfly at three thousand meters, can we now?"

"It seems so little to ask."

"So is a bowl of rice, but in time of famine . . ." Liao shrugged. "Forgive me, but you seem so persistent. These men may be dead. They may be in Pakistan. Of course, if they *are* up there," and he glanced at a huge wall map, "they're in that chain of valleys. But it sounds insane to me."

"I must be sure," K'uang said. "It is . . . special. I have suffered. They have killed my men."

"Well, but this is no time for a private war. In the east we have all the war we can handle."

"The east," K'uang said scornfully. "Politicians and intellectuals. 'So many pecks and hampers,' as the Master said, filling themselves from the public store."

"A cigarette," Liao offered. "A glass of red wine."

"Yes, thank you," K'uang said, and slumped in his chair. "Then there will be no aircraft for me."

"I'm sorry," Liao said.

"Is it worth it, what I do?"

Liao thought it over, sipped at his wine, and murmured, "The Master said, 'What the superior man seeks is in himself. What the mean man seeks is in others.' "

They absorbed the ancient sentiment in silence.

"What do you seek?" Liao asked gently.

K'uang drew ferociously on the cigarette; smoke poured from his nostrils; he made no answer.

41/   Jake knew all about the facts of life, but spring astounded him. The air remained cold, but the wind died. Mong-chen and Khu-lat explained: this was the moon of the waking bear. At the end of the moon of the waking bear, the grasses would stir, and soon afterward the tribe and all its flocks would make a long journey to spring and summer pastures.

Meanwhile calves, kids and lambs were dropping like rain, and that was mainly what astounded Jake. The Doctor kept a tally, carving lines into wooden tablets. The shepherds kept close watch; a troublesome birth was a crisis. Yak cows stood bowlegged and straining. In time the calf appeared, in a slimy sac, and slid to earth. The cow moaned, and turned to lick the sac from the calf's face. The calf quivered and twitched, and inhaled; the cow licked it clean. A baby yak. The calf struggled to rise, and in minutes was on its feet, punching for the teat. Then the calf collapsed, resting, and the cow strained again, and a soggy mess of afterbirth plopped to the ground. The cow sniffed at it and then, steadily and uncomplaining, ate it, munching and whuffling. The cows' milk was at first creamy and yellow, then white. The calves seemed all head, and their hoofs were soft and cheesy.

So with the lambs, which came mainly as twins; so with the kids, also twins mainly but with a few singles and triplets. Once in the morning they found a doe kid nursing and a buck lying dead, smothered in its sac: a first birth, Mong-chen explained, and the mother had become confused, neglecting the buck, which came first, because busy with the doe, which came too quickly afterward. The dead buck was cleaned, skinned and eaten that night.

The first milk was most important, Khu-lat said. In it were the virtues.

Among sheep and goats, the twins and triplets could be of both sexes and would grow up strong. But among the yaks, twins were rarer, and must be of the same sex. If one was a bull and one a cow, the little cow would be deficient, and not a proper female: the male principle would override the female principle in the womb, and the little cow would be born queer, sterile and of demonic spirit.

Jake too kept watch, with Tha-shi, and one night a doe strained, and cried in pain. By the light of a torch Tha-shi showed Jake: the head was presented, but beneath the chin only one hoof had appeared. The other leg was bent at an evil angle, and must be found and straightened. Jake held the doe's head, and spoke words of comfort. Tha-shi slid a hand into the womb, and groped. She found the shoulder, and followed it down. Gently she tugged at the leg. She found the hoof, and brought it into place beside the other. She called Jake to look, and he came around in time to see the tiny head, and the tiny hoofs beneath it like weird whiskers; and the kid popped out like a cork from its bottle, and within a minute was on its feet, dripping slime and bleating. A twin followed, cleanly, and they left the doe to lick the kids and chew up the afterbirth.

Soon the sunny plain was dotted with young. They leapt and butted. They flung themselves to one side and then to the other; they ran, faked left, faked right, leapt high, turned one way or the other in midair, and lit running. The kids were spotted and striped. Tha-shi said the stripes and spots would fade as they grew. The mothers nuzzled and licked, and stood with resigned expressions as the kids braced themselves, tails wagging, and rammed for the teat.

The kids must be watched for a day or two. If they did not pass proper droppings, they must be dosed.

Jake was exhilarated, but not by the miracle of life: he was impressed by the richness of it all. Something for nothing. Dozens, hundreds, of baby yaks, sheep and goats. He thought he must be a rancher at heart.

But he was not. He was the executioner, the bringer of death and denier of life, and he was kept busy with new duties: the best bull calves, rams and bucks were marked, and the others were castrated before their third week, and Jake was the castrator. He was not made happy by that, but he understood. Carefully and sadly he slashed the scrotum; Tha-shi applied hot gum from a pot. The testicles were stewed, and eaten at a series of solemn banquets, with the Doctor making short speeches and the tribe chanting to the music of finger-cymbals.

The baby livestock, and the stewed testicles, led him to wonder why Tha-shi did not increase. He might be seedless, or she. Maybe she was a barren woman, and they connected barrenness with death, and that was why she was Blue Hat's woman. Well, she was his woman now, and he blessed her.

Later the wind rose again, and the oily-coated flocks huddled against spring drizzles. After each rain, when the sun emerged and the valley blushed greener, Jake marveled at the bleating, mooing, cavorting throng of beasts, and at the geese that whooshed overhead in long skeins; at the ravens that patrolled in pairs, and the hawks that soared; at small flights of pigeons that dipped and fled; even at the colonies of homely, stocky, short-tailed birds that came to stay and lived on dung.

On the hills that hemmed the valley, shrubs and flowers bloomed; Jake recognized a kind of crocus. Sometimes when he stood looking out, big himself with so much life, time seemed to halt, and the beasts and birds froze, a hoof raised, a head cocked, wings spread, a kid at the top of its leap, the patches of blossom still, the wind holding its breath.

And every year this came about. For these people every spring was this spring, and the old were not displeased to die, because next spring they would return as kids or pigeons or crocuses. Jake seemed always to be smiling. He wondered again if Tha-shi might bear children.

*　　　*　　　*

Riding up the mountain after a long season of busy-work, Major K'uang should have felt younger and more vigorous. But he felt older, and sour. Drier, and bitter. Like a once-ripe fruit fallen in a deserted courtyard, waiting only for ants. His country had not long to live. All winter he had done a politician's work, or a policeman's. His men had chafed, and he was forced into bribery: long leaves, extra rations, even seizing gold from petty bureaucrats to lavish upon his squad.

Even dickering with a brothel for the residential rate. Pimp K'uang!

And he was weary from the long, hopeless fight for an aircraft, and the impossibility of explaining truly.

He was also angry that grass-bandits—not even big-city gangsters! —had outsmarted him.

He was angry that three men had been taken dead, and that two had fled like foxes.

He was angry at his own lack of faith, his own despair and disillusion. He had found himself wishing that the Communists would win, once for all, so that he could join them and do a soldier's proper work; they would surely have to fight the foreigners, *some* foreigners, which could be looked forward to.

His dreams of gold humiliated him.

So he was curt to Sergeant Shih, who one day said, "Desert formation is perhaps not appropriate to foothills and mountains."

"Do as I say," K'uang growled. "We track not an army but two hopeless men. Shall we travel like bears, and be picked off one by one, or like wolves, in the strength and safety of the pack?"

Another day Shih said, "The camels plod in line; the mountain sheep show horns in all directions."

"They will be fleeing, you fool," K'uang said. "When we see how they flee, there will be time for deployment. If," he added gloomily, "they are not dead, or in Kashmir."

"It seems much effort," Shih said, "for two hares that may have fled the meadow."

"There is much at stake," K'uang said.

Up and up they rode. The weather improved each day. The Qara Shahr ponies were tireless. Now third in line, now fifth, K'uang searched the hills. Preceded by his scouts, he pursued his victims and his fate.

*   *   *

Jake had no notion what month this was, by the old reckoning. It was the moon of late lambs, and the days were longer than the nights; the wind was unreliable but gentle, shifting sometimes to the north and west. Along the edge of the valley, the stream was in roaring spate.

One morning he was squatting in his undershirt by the bricks of fuel. He was still in sheepskins, but it would not be long now. He was listening to the herds and the stream and the soft sigh of the spring breeze. The taste of tea was strong in his mouth. He saw three kids dash, halt, leap high, reverse and toss their heads, and he laughed aloud at the sheer life of it.

He began tipping bricks from the wooden forms. Tha-shi had been giggly last night, and he was still dreamy with it. The tribe was preparing its move to summer pasture, and he wondered what the journey would be like, how they would assemble their burdens, strike their tents, load the yaks; which direction they would take. Carts would help; no, wheels could not go where they traveled.

He was sweating lightly and finishing his chore when a change in the air halted him. He squatted, frowned, and listened.

Still the stream rushed, the beasts baaed; the sun was friendly.

But he heard no human voice, no child's cry.

He looked up, and saw his people standing very still. They were staring off to the northeast.

Khu-lat and Mong-chen were stumbling down the valley, down the slope Jake had first descended, from the Unmelting Bridge of Snow and the Bowl of Grass-in-Hanks. They came on like stretcher-bearers, trying to trot in rhythm, their burden swaying; they paused to hitch it up, and cried to the others. Khu-lat carried the yeti's feet, and Mong-chen the shoulders; Mong-chen bore a slung rifle.

Long before he could see the tattered sheepskins, or the bandoleer, Jake knew their burden, and prayed that it be dead.

Khu-lat and Mong-chen laid the body before Jake. The head lolled. Jake knelt and swiftly removed the gun belt and the knife. He handed them to Tha-shi, saying, "Put these with my own."

"It is no yeti," she said.

"It is no yeti," he said, gazing down at the drawn, scarred face. "It is a man, and he is cold, hungry and more than half dead."

"Then we will warm him and feed him," she said, "and give him life. Look how his face is striped."

For a long moment Jake did not speak, but then his bones seemed to straighten, and his heart to open. "Yes, that is what we must do," he said. He turned to the Doctor, whose face was grim. "In our tent. I want him with me until he is well."

"So it will be," the Doctor said.

42/ Ugly was so filthy that Jake had to cut the underclothes off him. The torn and stained sheepskins were supple, and the winter boots slid off whispering, but what Ugly wore beneath was a patched and scabby second skin, grown into his flesh, the wrinkles and seams of his armpits, groin and backside accepting this graft of cloth, sweat, dirt and blood. What passed for socks was a soggy mass of raw wool.

Yet the necklace of tiger claws gleamed like ivory. Tha-shi caught her breath, and turned wide wondering eyes to Jake.

"It is his spirit," Jake said. "Leave it on him."

He cut through the second skin; he and Tha-shi washed the body with hot water and the paste of fat and ashes that the nomads used for soap. Rolls of dirt formed, gathered, and stripped away. Ugly's feet emerged in time, patches of bright, smooth skin shining out as the crud dissolved.

Tha-shi rubbed oil into the scars and said, "How he must have been hurt, this one." Jake was seeing some of these scars for the first time, and agreed with her; he scowled at the webs and grids, the slashes and punctures, old ones that were only fine wrinkles and others that were white welts. "A tiger did some of this," he said.

Again Tha-shi's eyes widened. "A tiger. Here we have no tigers. Only the leopard, and the bobtailed-cat-with-tufted-ears." The motion of her hand ceased on Ugly's belly, and she looked up: "Can you tell that by the scars, or did you know this one?"

"I knew this one."

"A friend," she said, marveling.

"I knew him."

He could not be sure what ailed Ugly. Simple exhaustion, plus hunger and exposure? No frostbite. Heartbeat quick and light, but regular. The man did not seem feverish. Tha-shi laid blankets on him, and Jake remembered his own resurrection.

"One of us must be with him when he wakes," he said. "If it is you, you must call me at the first sign."

But it was Jake. In the morning watch, just before dawn, Ugly stirred and muttered. Jake braced himself: the man might come out of his sleep with a lunatic's fierce lunge. Ugly's eyes opened, and gleamed in the firelight. His head turned; he stared at Jake. "Am I alive?" he whispered. "Or are we both dead?"

"We both live," Jake said. Chinese was old and comfortable in his mouth, like a mother tongue. "This is indeed a hungry ghost!"

"Not yet a ghost," Ugly said, "though you did your best."

"As you once told me, only a slave does not dream of escape."

"But you have not escaped." Ugly's voice grew stronger. "The tiger has tracked the Tartar."

"Be easy," Jake said.

"Yes," Ugly said. "If you wished me harm I would have slept on." He rested. "Still, I will tell you, because we fought together." He rested. "I came to kill you, and I mean to do it."

"But not for a day or two," Jake said.

"In fairness," Ugly said, "I recommend that you kill me now."

Jake sat unmoving, and waited for advice from his innards. Soon he said, "I will not."

"Dunce!" Ugly said, and clucked like a man of sorrows.

"If these mountains could not kill you," Jake said, "how should I presume?"

Ugly said, "What is this place?"

"It is the winter pasture," Jake said. "Nomads of the mountains. This is my tent and my fire. These are a peaceable people and you may be easy."

"Is there food?"

"Plenty."

"Plenty! Yüü. I did not eat every day. I lived in caves. I froze my plums off. Well, no." His hands moved, and he looked interested. "I see that you have stripped me. And such blankets!"

"There is soup," Jake said, "if you can sit up."

"I can try. What kind of soup?"

"Yak soup."

"Yak! Never in my life have I eaten yak." Groaning and huffing, Ugly struggled to one elbow. "Like a baby," he said.

"Like a lamb in the first hour," Jake said.

Ugly fell back. "A moment."

Jake went to the fire, and spooned soup into a bowl. He sat beside Ugly.

"You killed them," Ugly said conversationally. "You killed Momo and Mouse and Hao-k'an."

"Do not talk of that now. Here. We raise the head, so, and I will feed you, so."

Ugly swallowed hot soup. "Bugger. I can feel it in my fingers and toes."

"In a week you will be the old Ugly."

"The old *what?*"

Jake smiled. "Well, so I always called you to myself. I never knew your real name."

"Nor will you now," Ugly snarled. "In a week I will be the old Tiger's Assistant and I will unseam you. Ugly!"

Later he said, "My body breathes in a new fashion."

"We scraped a year's supply of bird droppings off you," Jake said. "We laundered you, and oiled you."

"Not good," Ugly groaned. "The great catarrh will sour my blood, and flux and congestion will bleach my spleen."

"Foolishness," Jake told him. "In Peking I showered each morning, and was not sick a day."

"It is the big nose," Ugly said. "The elements of disease collect in the big nose, and are blown out into special kerchiefs. Speaking of big noses, my nether nose is engorged with piss. What is to be done about that?"

"Can you stand?"

"I can stand." Then, "You son of a syphilitic turtle!" He was like a man seeing devils, or watching a cobra dance: hatred flamed in his face; also fierce pleasure.

Jake forced a small smile. "While the Tiger's Assistant is a man of the best bones."

Ugly subsided. "I am a bandit by trade."

"And so was I."

"All the same," Ugly said, "I must kill you. For Momo and Mouse and Hao-k'an."

"Well then, you must," Jake said. "But first you must piss. Then put on some weight, and regain your skill of hand and eye. When the moment comes, I will give you a fight."

"You will not know when the moment comes," Ugly growled.

"Up now," Jake said.

Ugly flung the blankets back and rolled to his knees. In the firelight he hung for some seconds, sucking air. He placed one foot flat and rocked forward, then hung again, not able to rise and not willing to fall back.

Jake stepped toward him. Ugly glowered, as if about to spring and savage. Jake remembered the knife whacking into the post as the Tibetan turned. For many seconds he and Ugly stared, renewing various principles of heat and cold.

Jake extended an arm and braced himself; Ugly clamped a hand on it and strained upward. On his feet, he panted. Jake led him across the tent to the pot. "Who is that?" Ugly asked.

"My woman," Jake said. Her eyes gleamed; she watched without stirring.

Ugly snorted. So this foreign fool had a woman. They came where they were not wanted, and took everything. A virgin of fifteen years, no doubt, given to him with much bowing, with hisses and creamy words, of fifteen years with good fat hams and fresh lips.

Ai, this was a piss! In the performance of the rites, the virtuous man does not begrudge. The easing of his bladder was a blessing to body and mind. He broke wind also.

Better. In a day or two he would be himself, and he would stamp on this foreigner, and see what these people had to offer. It was perhaps time for a true holiday, as at country inns in the old days. To eat one's fill! And the gods grant me such a fire every night!

He was warm as he had not dared dream in his caves; warm and sleepy, invaded by friendly odors. A woman, was it. Well, he would see about that too.

By the third night Ugly had been presented to the Doctor and several of the men and women, but he was still in Jake's care and, as Jake put it, under house arrest. "Until a great powwow tomorrow."

"P'ao-wao? What is that?"

"A meeting," Jake explained, "where the tribe will decide whether to emasculate you, or only tie you between two stallions in rut."

"The funniness of foreigners is an eternal mystery. Where are my weapons? Or yours, for that matter?"

"In a safe place."

"Well, if these people are of evil intent, I want the pistol at least." Ugly nodded to Tha-shi, who was setting out bowls and platters. Tha-shi patted the top of his head; Ugly mocked Jake.

"It is the custom," Jake said mildly. "The women here pat children and those who are loony."

Ugly shook his head and spat into the fire. Jake howled; Ugly drew back in alarm. "Now you have offended the demons of the fire," Jake said despairingly. "We must purify the tent. Up, man, up! Take off your pants!"

Ugly rose, and his hand went to his belt. "Bugger!" he said then, and scowled. "Defile you!" He sat down. "Defile all foreigners! Defile all their missionaries, defile all their soldiers, defile all their women here and abroad! And may the fiery eight-pizzled dragon defile all jokesters of whatever nation, trade or nose!" Then he smiled sheepishly.

Jake was keeping score: every grin was a point for the home team.

Ugly tore into the roast yak, stuffing down barley cakes too; all day long he belched and nibbled. He swigged deeply of the tea; Tha-shi filled his cup. "They hit us like lightning," he said. "We were all dopey, fucked out and exhausted, but we came up shooting. I saw daylight and tried to streak through, hanging on the off side of a pony, but the buggers blasted the pony to pieces. So I rolled and came up shooting again, and knocked one of them out of the saddle and hung around his pony's neck and kicked hard. The pony flew, a real Qara Shahr. And the others must have kept them busy just long enough." He frowned. "One at least had a clear shot at me. I believe he froze. He was perhaps a rookie. It was dawn, and the buggers had all day to chase me. More than once I thought I was gone." Again he frowned. "It was . . . it was fishy. Well, a long day. The whole time I had clutched my rifle."

"Then you did not go back to help out."

"Help out!" Ugly stared. "Crazy man."

"So you left them," Jake said. "You do not even know that they are dead."

"Enough of that," Ugly said. "That is dangerous talk. There comes a time when each looks out for himself."

"Indeed." Jake spoke politely.

"Bugger yourself," Ugly said. "All right, then: I might have done the same. I say that to you. But scores must be settled."

"Scores must be settled. So you fled up the mountain."

"I did that. Tracking you. I kept cutting your sign."

"And it was you who fired at K'uang, just before the snowstorm."

"It was indeed. I never thought those fools would come so far. That was not bad, that crossfire. In that manner whole armies can be made to vanish."

"Beer?"

"Beer," Ugly conceded.

"It is barley beer," Jake said, and passed the jug.

"Yak is good," Ugly said. "Not as good as wild ass, but good."

"Tell me something," Jake said. "What is charas?"

"Charas? Hashish. You have that?"

"Plenty. It is to us what tobacco is to others."

"Us?"

Jake showed palm. "You see."

"What is the blue hat?"

Jake explained.

"Bugger," Ugly said. "Some merchant! Some bandit! A nomad, without gold or silver, wading in guts."

"Tell me another thing," Jake said. "Once you did not molest decent people. If I make no trouble, will you leave these people alone?"

"I make no bargains with traitors," Ugly said.

"They will feed you, and send you along to the next place."

"The next place! And where is that?"

"I am not sure," Jake said, bringing interest and friendship to his voice. "From here I think you can go south to Rawalpindi or Srinagar, and maybe west to Faizabad. They must meet a caravan from time to time, because they have barley, and sheets of metal."

"Kashmir," Ugly said. "A land of lakes, and dark women."

"So you survived," Jake said. "You must have been a good sergeant."

"The best." Ugly swilled beer. "Bugger! The best! I am thirty-nine years old and have been a soldier since nineteen twenty-seven, the last day of the third month, when I signed on with that weasel Chiang and marched north from Shanghai with him."

"But you are not a Shanghai man."

"No. Honan. I was a hand on the canal boats. Much travel."

"And much since."

"Much since." Ugly darkened. "This comradely gossip will do you no good." He snorted angrily and spat into the fire. "More beer."

Jake obliged.

Late that night, after plenty of jollification, Tha-shi left Jake and went to Ugly's bed. "He has no woman," she whispered to Jake. "Every man must have a woman."

On one elbow, Jake glowered into the fallen fire. The smoldering dung flared and hissed. Once more he waited for inner counsel. He tried to still all voices but the voices of these mountains and his own heart. He was rosy with the charas, and the voices seemed clear and simple.

"Yes then," he said, and patted her. "Rain sweet dew upon him." She bent to lick his lips, and slipped away. She was naked, and her buttocks gleamed in the low light; he smiled at them. They were old friends.

Ugly thrashed and exclaimed, protesting in Chinese, "He will kill me."

Tha-shi did not understand; she soothed him.

"Tartar," Ugly called, "is this one of your fool's tricks?"

"It is no trick," Jake said sleepily. "It is the way."

Ugly sneered: "If you think this will save your life . . ."

"For that I will kill you," Jake said. "For speaking thus and for even thinking thus. You are a loathsome pig and you wallow in the filth of your own diseased mind. May your fruit ripen and fall prematurely." More calmly he went on: "It is the way here, and a good way for men who do not fear the affections and humors. Be good to her, do you hear me? Be good to her or I will gut you before I slaughter you."

"Hsüüüü," Ugly said in wonder.

Soon Tha-shi giggled. Jake did not mind. He was hazily content. He liked this Jake better than the old one.

In the morning Ugly seemed bewildered, almost timid. After the meal he spoke: "Yü. What I said last night." He grimaced.

Jake left Ugly thinking, and went out to gather dung.

Late in the afternoon the tribe gathered, and Jake led Ugly forth. In new sheepskins and boots, with a new hat square on his head, Ugly looked almost dignified. He tried to swagger but soon gave it up.

Jake made his speech with pauses and gestures, like an old man recalling wars on a winter night. His voice rose and fell, now harsh and now soft. "This one and I have ridden together. We have crossed deserts together where horses could not survive, where the trails are marked by heaps of bones and the wells are full of tears."

The tribe murmured and clapped at some of his finer words. "To find me he fought the mountains all winter. He lived in caves. We thought he was the yeti. He killed sheep and he is sorry for that. But he has done a great thing: how many men have fought the mountains in winter and won? He was imprisoned by passes solid with snow, and he heard no man's voice for a season; and now the passes are clear, and alone he has made his way to his friend."

And he may yet kill me and all of you, but that is a chance we must take. All I can promise is that he will kill me first.

Surly yet alert, Ugly resisted his soul. These were fine flocks and a rich people, much to be taken here, and he tried to concentrate on his memory of Momo, Mouse and Hao-k'an, to keep his rage and greed alive. But like all gentlemen and archers he respected style, and these honest and handsome people had plenty of that.

The foreigner looked good. A funny blue hat, and the tip of a scabbard beneath the sheepskin jacket. The Tartar.

But a scheming and treacherous Tartar, he thought fiercely. No better than a Qazaq. A good man in a fight, but a thief and murderer after all.

He squinted sidewise at this traitor.

Jake went on about Ugly's size and strength, and his quickness of mind. The tribe was dividing: from the faces he guessed that there were many who would accept one stranger, that being the law of the mountains, but not two, that being an invasion or maybe a dilution of the blood or other nastiness.

And half of Jake's mind was elsewhere: he was not fool enough to believe that one winter with these people had made a saint of him. He was a fighting man by habit, and it might come down to that: him and Ugly. He suppressed a tiny ripple of excitement.

But only a ripple. The deep joy of fighting was gone. A man fought for his life, but he was no longer sure that a man who would kill was worth keeping alive.

His brain grappled, and slowed. These outlying trails of his mind were little trod.

The decision was never made, because Khu-lat came ambling merrily down the valley, herding some tens of sheep. With Jake's binoculars bouncing at his breast he seemed important and official. The Doctor sent two boys to take the sheep in charge, and waved Khu-lat to the council. "Where were you?"

"At the Bowl of Grass-in-Hanks, and beyond. Well. The stranger is a big one, and strong."

"The question is, what to do with him. He is friend to Blue Hat."

"There are more," Khu-lat said. "With these glass eyes I saw them. Also I am hungry. It is one of those days. The air is clear and cold, and whips a man's hunger."

Jake asked, "More?"

"Yes," Khu-lat told them. "I sat on the great knoll above the bowl

and I could see for three valleys. I saw nine men and eleven ponies."
To the Doctor he said, "It is like Mintaka. Men from all over the
world."

"Give me the glass eyes," Jake said. "In which wind and how far?"

Khu-lat extricated himself from the strap; Jake tossed the binoculars to Ugly. Khu-lat pointed with the whole arm: "This wind. With
the glass eyes they were small."

"How small?"

"Small as maggots. Smaller. Small as ants."

"Faces?"

"No faces. Nor heads."

"How many hills and valleys?"

"Two hills, two valleys." He clucked in awe. "You have many
friends."

The Doctor, old Zang-aw, was not as pleased.

"What is this gossip?" Ugly complained.

So Jake told him.

"It can be no other," Ugly said, back in Jake's tent. "He is insane.
His head is on backward."

"They tracked you. You brought evil."

"I came in search of evil," Ugly said. "I came to wipe it out."

"So did K'uang," Jake said bitterly. "One man's evil is another
man's religion."

"All very poetic. But what now?"

"Well, there is no choice. Not for me, anyway. Bugger all authorities!"

"No trouble," Ugly said. "These are only soldiers."

"Nine of them."

"Let us smite the tyrants. The age of archers is passing, but we will
leave a story or two."

Jake said, "Good." His blood quickened. "We will kill K'uang for
Momo, Mouse and Hao-k'an."

Ugly said, "We will kill K'uang for the pleasure, and because it is
a virtuous deed. Now, how do we accomplish this? Can we decoy
them onto that Unmelting Bridge of Snow, and blow it out? With a
nest of grenades?"

"Never. Too solid. We have only four grenades."

"We could tie down the releases with this yarn that they weave, and run a long strand to them and burn off the wool at the proper moment."

"Blockhead," Jake said. "The wool is oily and will not burn."

"We could roll it in gunpowder. Break open cartridges."

"And if it fails they are across the bridge and we have no grenades. You are too much the gentleman and archer and not enough the sergeant. One does not fight by luck but by brains and balls."

"Dogs defile you," Ugly said with his monstrous grin. "That is good talk to hear again."

"What we will do is this," Jake said. The two men squatted together in a corner of the tent; by the fire Tha-shi cooked. "We will use a herd of sheep as cover. Crawl among them or cling to their bellies."

"Fool," Ugly said. "We take out two or three and are then marooned among the muttons. Meantime it is raining sheepshit."

Jake said gravely, "That is why we will not use yaks."

Ugly's laugh boomed, hraw-hraw-hraw! "Dogs defile you twice more," he gurgled. "You are almost human."

"Ambush," Jake said, "and a cold night ahead. They will camp in the bowl, I think, hugging the walls and out of the wind."

"Then we sleep out tonight."

"Yes."

"Bugger. No woman and no charas."

"Afterward."

"Ah well, afterward . . ." Ugly began.

Jake was filling a clip; he snapped a cartridge in and peered up. "Afterward what?"

"Nothing. We have no ponies."

"We do this on foot."

Ugly made teeth: "And so cannot run from them."

"You can run if you want to," Jake said. "Listen one listen: since Dushok, I have been leaving scabs behind me all over Asia, and losing friends as fast as I make them. Well, not again. You run if you want to."

"I will not," Ugly said. "I have passed enough time in caves, eating the wind, and the bumpkins going bald at the sight of me. Besides, you could not do it alone."

Jake laughed. "These are only soldiers." He set the clip on a skin, removed the bolt, and ran a patch through the barrel. He understood now that a man did not keep his weapons in order for no reason. His palms were sweaty and a pleasurable prickling warmed the backs of his knees. "Your weapons in order?"

"All in order. The stock is cracked and I have not much ammunition, but it will do."

"Tomorrow you will have a prince's choice of weapons and ponies," Jake said, "unless you force me to kill you."

"When a horse grows horns," Ugly snarled. "I shed my milk teeth long since, and am not to be buggered twice by a pig's egg."

"Hsüüü, you sound healthy again," Jake said. "Now listen, and I will frame out a counsel."

"Defile his ancestors," Ugly complained, "this is no pig's egg, but a generalissimo."

The people clustered, silent and fearful. Jake and Ugly stood before them, dressed for war. "See to the flocks," Jake said to Zang-aw. "No one will harm you." It was an easy promise. If harm came to them, Jake would be beyond reproaching.

The Doctor asked, "What will you do?"

"We will do what must be done," Jake said.

The Doctor bowed his head and sighed. Jake went to Tha-shi. He stood before her and looked deep into the dark eyes. He touched his cheek to hers. They patted and stroked. "Tomorrow," Jake said. Tha-shi lowered her eyes and did not speak.

There was a ripping within Jake. That he must leave her. That he would kill. That he could still fizz at the prospect of a good fight, and would never be a good man. Unless dead; and if it came to that, this was the best way.

Again he caressed her, this strong round woman, no longer young, this warmest and best that he had ever known. He embraced her, and buried his nose among the one hundred and eight plaits of hair that he had counted many times.

"Bandits should not marry," Ugly said.

43/   They slipped northeast along the wall of the valley, keeping to the shadows. "Sentries," Ugly said.

Jake glassed the slopes. A westerly wind washed them. The sky glowed dusky blue.

"Bad weather would help."

"No chance."

"By morning?"

"No chance."

They walked in silence.

"The knoll is where he would put a sentry. Or even camp there, to keep the high ground."

"Then we wait lower down."

They walked in silence. The mountains and meadows shaded purple. "We rest now," Jake said. "We find them after dark. They are arrogant and will keep a fire alive for warmth."

"Not arrogant," Ugly said. "Foolish. They track phantoms."

"It will be easy," Jake said. "One man who knows what is about to happen is worth four who do not."

"We could move in during the middle watch, no? The fire will dim their night vision."

Jake propped his weapon against the rocky wall, and shifted the small bag of grenades to his lap. "But if we lose one or two at night, we become the hunted and they the hunters."

"Dawn, then."

"First we look one look."

"That being so," Ugly said, "I will sleep. Wake me without fail should lively events overtake us."

Jake smiled at him. "You show great trust."

"You need me. Two Tartars are better than one."

"And two tigers."

Starlight favored them, a vast spangle crowning the mountains; there was no moon. "It is time," Ugly said. "The Hunter and his Dog are well to the west, and the Chariot of God is on end."

"You call it that? I thought, the Dipper."

"Both."

They moved carefully now, skirting patches of crunchy snow. The glow of the campfire was faint; they saw it at the same moment, and stopped. "On the knoll," Jake whispered. "They will have a sentry there, and another on the Unmelting Bridge of Snow."

They edged forward, and up a small slope. "There. The bridge."

"And the sentry."

"I see him." Jake caught him in the binoculars, a huddled shape in starlight. "Half asleep."

"Then I must work west now."

"In a little. Rest awhile."

They sat. Ugly took the glasses, to place the man and the terrain. "We let the first two cross, and hit the others on the bridge. There will be two for sure?"

"Three times have I seen him on the march. Each time, two scouts out wide. You saw them."

"Yes." Ugly returned the glasses. "I have remembered something. A thing I must tell you."

"Now is the time," Jake said lightly. "Tomorrow I may not be listening."

"Or I talking," Ugly said. "Well, it is this, and I hope it will not spoil your day. The fact is that the price on my head is now fifty ounces of gold."

"Oh, you braggart!" Jake said. "To humiliate me now! Unless," he asked hopefully, "the price on my head has been raised?"

"It has not," Ugly said firmly. "Thirty ounces alive."

"It is the discrimination against foreigners," Jake explained. "The insulting Chinese prejudice." After a moment he went on: "Is it really such a life? You never tire of it?"

"Pride," Ugly said. "Yes, I tire of it, but it is my life, and pride keeps me going."

"Pride," Jake said. "Not all of it is to be proud of."

"There is that," Ugly conceded. "Possibly I did not enjoy that with the bride."

"Or I running out."

"This winter I wanted only to kill you and then quit."

"Time for that tomorrow," Jake said. "No foolishness tonight. The risk is too great."

Ugly was hurt. "What do you take me for?"

"Well, what are you?"

Ugly sighed heavily. "Yes. One is what one is, it seems."

"So it seems to me too," Jake said. "This rifle is my friend, and fits my hand like an old hammer."

"And you will yet drive a few nails with it," Ugly said. "Well," and he stood up, "time to go. Give me a couple of grenades."

"Yes. Take a wide swing down there and stick to cover. The ground rises to the west. Find a hollow. At first light the wind will doubtless draw from the west."

"Advice," Ugly said bitterly. "Instructions from a bull calf. I am unworthy."

"No need to blow the mustache," Jake said. "We may yet be friends."

"When the walnut whistles," Ugly said.

"Then bugger yourself," Jake said. "We have still one good fight to fight."

"Two," Ugly said. "See you tomorrow."

"If that is how it must be," Jake said, "see you tomorrow."

* * *

Dawn was a tricky time, the vision lagging behind the light, humps and hollows like horses and yaks. Jake lay snug enough, well hidden in the spring grass and with a good field of fire.

They would take out two each, quickly, in the center of the line; with luck one would be K'uang. The scouts would race back, and the other three would scatter. Long snap shots then, if necessary the ponies.

It was no use unless every man of them died. Maybe they would panic and mill, and he and Ugly could pot them like the old buffalo hunters.

Range about two hundred yards. I hope that slob is not straight across from me.

When it is finished he will lie waiting.

Jake heard voices.

A clear morning. Jake grinned: the sun was more in Ugly's eyes than his own.

Above them a flight of bar-headed geese whirred through the morning. A bird of good omen.

Jake worked his fingers. The air on his face was cold, but his body was already warm with the action to come.

He set the pistol on the grass before him, and the grenades.

The plan was good enough; now if they could execute. The arm is long, as the Chinese said; let us hope the sleeve is not short. It ought to be easy.

He thought of Tha-shi and his heart swelled. I suppose I am in love with her. You would not pin her photo on the wall; Dushok would laugh. No. He would not.

You fool. This is not a time to think of your within-woman.

The two scouts came at a walk, their ponies breathing smoke. Through the short grass Jake sighted. They passed on. Beyond them, the white ranges, glittering in the early light; a sharp, bright morning.

The line of seven followed. One of them was K'uang, but there was no knowing which; they rode slumped and huddled into their sheepskins, and K'uang was not one to wear the brass of rank or sport a flag.

The pack ponies trailed the last man, who would have to cut them loose. That would take fatal seconds.

It was too easy on the face of it, but Jake knew how much could go wrong, a missed shot, a dud. Of the line of seven, Two and Three were his, Four and Five were Ugly's. Those four should be easy. One, Six and Seven, and the two scouts, might require some fancy shooting.

Many months since my last shot. Like love anyway: each time the first time.

He started at a queer, windy, gasping sound.

He was panting.

He calmed himself, and drew down on Two. A few seconds now.

Major K'uang was barely awake, but already thinking how it was all gone now, all rotten and smashed. He liked to ride remembering firefights near Mukden in the early days, and skirmishing on the central plains without air cover, and the Japanese making great slaughter, so that even regular troops had to fight like guerrillas, in holes or behind walls.

If he missed these two, he would quit. He had months of leave due, and months of worthless money.

If he found them—ah. Negotiations. From here he could, if he chose, reach any of four countries.

His own thoughts sickened him. How fine, once! The train at Ch'ang-sha, and the enfilade, and then the hand-to-hand!

That he would never forget. That alone justified his life.

Jake fired. Two sagged. Three had hardly looked up when Jake fired again. Three sagged; his pony reared. Like an echo of his own shots, two more cracked; Four and Five sagged. Whowwhowwhowwhow, the blasts bounced among the hills. Ponies whirled, men cried out. The last man sawed frantically at his lead rope.

Jake glanced south. The scouts were pounding back, firing wildly, whow whow; they had swung low, off the saddle, on Ugly's side. "Fire," Jake said. "Fire, god damn you." One and Six swung toward him, galloping; Seven cut himself free and raced after them. "Fire!" Jake said. "Fire, you son of a bitching Chinaman!" Horror froze him. The soon-to-be of it. The now-to-be of it.

Ugly exulted and said, "A-ha-ha!" Four and Five were down, and the others showing tail. Now, he thought, we will let that scorpion's egg sweat for a bit.

He waited only a few seconds, but they were sweet and happy

seconds. "Sweat!" he said. "Sweat!" A great joy filled him, and his heart laughed.

They spotted Jake and veered, firing. By then he was alive again, and killed one, but the scouts were coming up on his left, and a bullet plucked at his sleeve.

He fired, and fired. It was all he could do. He tasted bile and fired.

One still came, and only one. The scouts were no longer shooting but there was no time to look, or even to reach for the pistol. This one too had swung low on his pony's neck, but he was not firing. He was ten yards off and still not firing when the pony dropped, cartwheeling. Jake saw K'uang flying at him, eyes wide, mouth twisted, shouting like a madman. Jake snapped off one shot, and K'uang fell out of the sky, immense, dead or alive, and hammered Jake's face into the frosty grass.

Ugly had finally roared up out of his grassy nest and dashed across the field. The scouts were down, two of his better shots, no one moved, the ponies screamed and bucked and tossed their dead weights. The one survivor was bearing down on Jake. Ugly fired quickly, on the run, and cursed: he missed the man but hit the pony. The pony tumbled. The soldier flew like a bird, still clutching the rifle, and slammed to the ground. Bugger, right on top of him, and Ugly sprinted. Defile that round-eyed spawn of a misbegotten frog! Defile it! A good man who deserved better than to be crushed to death by a flying soldier! Defile it, defile it, defile it!

He panted toward them.

Jake fought for air. He heard K'uang's breath rasping, haaarh, haaarh, and felt groping hands; Jake's rifle was somewhere, no use, and he could not see, but he flailed with one arm and drew the curved knife, tugged it free of the scabbard, free of the folds of his jacket, tugged it loose and slashed. K'uang rasped and whimpered, he was hurt, but his hands were clamped on Jake's throat from behind, and the knife slashed air.

Jake drew his knees up, heaved and bucked. He and K'uang went over on their backs, Jake on top now. Jake jabbed backward, driving the blade past his own ear; it struck bone, and K'uang slacked. Jake tore free and rolled over, and for one icy moment stared down at K'uang, at the bloody face and the twisted, working mouth. Jake had slashed his right eye out, but the left eye gleamed. "We share," K'uang gasped, "we share." Jake sighed, a great, rushing, weary sigh of sorrow and relief, and cut K'uang's throat.

Ugly came pelting across just then. Jake was too drained to do more than curse. "You treacherous jackal. You defiler of crones."

Ugly cackled cheerfully and said, "You make a little here, you lose a little there."

44/ Now this ghost is indeed hungry," Ugly said.

They were sitting beside K'uang's corpse, letting their blood calm and their breath ease.

"First we make sure," Jake said.

"Yes. That was a fight."

"It was more my fight than yours," Jake snarled.

Ugly's eyes flashed with the fun of it. "Not so pleasant, a whole squad coming at you and the sentry off duty."

Jake avoided the bright, accusing eyes.

"Nobody can shoot straight from a running pony," Ugly said. "Not even myself. They should have dismounted but had no time to think, and were afraid to also: they were far from home and the ponies were their round-trip ticket."

In Chinese that was a come-return fire-cart document, and Jake squeezed out a small smile.

"Well, let us make sure of them," Ugly said, "and round up the ponies and the loot."

"And the bodies," Jake said,

"As to that, nothing will help them now."

"This is a pasture," Jake said.

"Villain that I am!" Ugly slapped his brow. "Of course. You are a man of taste and elegance. I always said so."

One man still breathed; Ugly shot him in the head.

"I remember that one from Shandanmiao," Jake said.

"The death of old friends is the greatest sorrow."

They had to shoot two of the ponies and leave them in a ravine, K'uang's and one gut-shot. The pack ponies had vanished. Ugly asked, "What can we do with seven ponies? Such wealth."

"So many weapons," Jake said. "I suppose we should strip these men and sort the stuff."

"Luxury," Ugly said. "Yüüü," he said, and scowled, with something on his mind.

"Say it."

"Well," Ugly said, and looked squarely at him.

Jake met his eyes this time, and waited calmly.

"Well," Ugly said, "quits?"

Jake saw that he meant it, and did not answer for a moment, to lend himself dignity and pride. Then he nodded. "Quits."

Ugly clapped him on the shoulder, and turned away to busy himself with the fastenings of K'uang's sheepskin. He hunkered, his back to Jake, and muttered to himself as he worked.

Jake contemplated the broad back of him. There was no evil this man had not done, and very little good that he had, but by God the balls of him! Squatting, mumbling, offering Jake this shot. So as to be dead or sure, and either way to sleep easy ever after.

When Ugly rose and turned, Jake was sitting, back to him, gazing off at snowy peaks. Ugly nodded once, sharply. Now there was a man of good bones. Offering this moment. So as to be dead or sure, and either way to sleep easy ever after. Well, foreigners were perhaps not so different after all. They held life cheap, but who did not?

Jake stood up and said, "I must tell them."

Ugly looked within.

"I'll be along in a while and help you with this," Jake said.

For another moment Ugly looked within, and then he nodded. "The old horse hankers after his stall and his beans. Go, then."

Jake sweet-talked up to a sound pony, and stroked its neck. He mounted, and rode down the meadow, leaving his rifle and pistol, and the grenades.

When he reached the northern edge of the home pasture, he saw them all gathered; he picked out Tha-shi's face. He thought they had gathered to thank him and to praise him. But soon he saw that they stood in the clear light confused, like sunflowers on a cloudy day.

He rode to the Doctor and dismounted. "It is well," he said. "They are gone, and will not return."

No one spoke. Not the Doctor, not Tha-shi, not Khu-lat or Mong-chen; no child smiled up at him. Beyond them the pasture lay, early green, and the flocks grazed and whispered.

"It is well," he said. "I tell you it is well."

"It is not well," the Doctor said. "It is not the way. The snow leopard and the lamb do not share water."

Jake seemed to shrink and cool. He met the Doctor's flat, dark eyes and saw strength in the calm face, the thick straight brows, the small hawk's nose.

"But I rid you of—"

"No. You summoned it."

Jake looked for Tha-shi, and found her. They shared a long glance, level, heavy with all their days and nights.

"We do not curse you," the Doctor said. "But it cannot be."

Jake saw then that Mong-chen was wearing the blue hat, and his heart shriveled and cracked.

Tha-shi came to Jake and opened his jacket; he could not speak. He looked into her eyes and saw nothing. He touched her cheek; she felt nothing. She would not meet his eye, and seemed to be looking with no interest at his chin. She slipped the silver and turquoise necklace over his head, and carried it to Mong-chen.

The Doctor held forth both open hands.

His throat tight and his teeth hard together, Jake freed the scabbard from his belt and surrendered the curved knife.

The Doctor drew the blade; it was rich with muddy blood. Finger-cymbals clashed. The flat jingling went on for some time.

Jake stared off at the distant tents, at the stretched hides, the yaks, the sheep, the goats he loved, the valley in green bloom. Smoke curled, and he remembered warmth on winter nights, buttery tea, the gentle comfort of charas and the gentle love afterward.

He drank in Tha-shi's face, strong and sweet and a bit worn, the shining eyes doleful now, the full lips grim; never again would he count her one hundred and eight braids. This woman, who had taught him all he knew that mattered: to love, to look upon death with sorrow, to milk a goat.

In a moment she looked away, and stepped closer to Mong-chen, downcast and submissive.

Soon they moved away, all of them, turning from him and trudging down the slope. He was left alone. No one looked back.

"Ah no," he said, and stood like a man of marble, wanting to curse them aloud. You'd be dead without me, and your flocks too, and your tents burned and your women raped—no no no. Without Jake Dodds these nomads would live forever in peace and plenty.

"Tha-shi!" he called. "Tha-shi!"

They halted then, and Tha-shi turned, but none other; he saw the vague bloom of her face, and already her features had blurred.

"Tha-shi," he called, "may it always be spring with you!"

A moment more, and they were dispersed to their tents, Tha-shi and Mong-chen to Blue Hat's, and there was no human being in sight: only the long sloping valley, the inching herds, the tents and stretched hides and curling smoke.

They had left him his pack, and some smaller bundles. He squatted. They had left him slabs of yak meat and strips of dried mutton, and a white cheese and a sizable ball of charas with a small pipe, and some tens of barley cakes.

Now he wanted to curse himself, or God, to run howling from valley to valley—

He sucked at the cold, thin air. He had been awake all night. He had gone without breakfast, and fought on an empty stomach, and a man could not live through the day eating bitterness only.

He packed and mounted. Far down the valley kids leapt and dashed like silver fish.

Ugly was hunkered beside a heap of rifles, pistols and canteens. Jake saw a compass, a pile of silver coins, a skein of bandoleers.

"These two bays are the best ponies," Ugly said, gesturing with a fist. "The others we will lead and sell."

Jake dismounted, and said, "You knew."

Ugly nodded. "I knew."

"It is the way, I suppose."

"It is the way. You see," Ugly said kindly, "they have their way and we have our way. One is what one is."

"And cannot change?"

The sweep of Ugly's arm took in corpses, dead ponies, loot.

Jake persisted: "All my life?"

Ugly showed palm. "Who can say? We did a good thing today."

"I thought I was paying for my sins," Jake said sadly.

"Nothing can be paid for. What is done is done."

"Still," Jake said, "I am not what I was."

"That can only be an improvement," Ugly said.

"I feel lighter within, yet full of pain. And listen: no more making ghosts and widows."

Ugly did not speak.

"Defile it!" Jake cried. "This hurts! This is indeed pain!"

"She was a meritorious woman," Ugly admitted.

"There was a harmony," Jake said, "and I believe my heart is now a cracked bell."

"A bitter music in the blood," Ugly said. "That happens once or twice."

"I suppose time and diversion will mend me," Jake said.

"As to that," Ugly said, "I have a thing to show you." He opened his fist.

In his palm Jake saw a double-headed nail. "Hsüüüü."

"I found it in K'uang's shirt pocket."

"A souvenir," Jake said, "that he took from me in Shandanmiao."

"In Shandanmiao," Ugly said. "Well. Look one look." He tossed it to Jake.

Jake looked idly, and then sharply. Along the shank some of the iron had been peeled away, and beneath it the nail gleamed gold.

"Four kegs," Ugly said. "Two hundred pounds."

Stunned and breathless, Jake said softly, "Old Kao."

"That old bandit," Ugly said. "Do you know how much money that is?"

"If," Jake said, "they were all like this."

"If half were like this!"

Jake said, "It is no wonder that K'uang was persistent."

"I believe he told no one," Ugly said. "He thought we had them, or had cached them."

"As in a way we did," Jake murmured.

"Indeed," Ugly said, and they speculated in silence.

"Well," Ugly said, "first things first. I am still hungry. Shall we eat a pony?"

"They gave us food," Jake said, "and even charas."

So they ate yak's meat and cheese, and drank water from a canteen. They kept all the weapons because weapons were, after all, an item of trade. "Lash the corpses tight," this one said. "I pity the ponies," that one said. They sorted gear, and secured their packs for a long journey. They snugged their sheepskins and their hats. They mounted, and their feet found the stirrups. They reined in tight, and sat for some seconds preparing the soul.

They started down the mountain then, side by side; and watching them ride off, both on bays, no man could have said which was the one, and which the other.